THE ATHENIAN WIDOW

Out of the blue, a young Englishwoman offers a columnist on a leading London newspaper a bombshell of a scoop: a detailed account of her New York life as the part-time mistress of a rich, radical Presidential candidate, idol of the young, recently assassinated in a turbulent, triumphant campaign.

The impact of these detached and uninhibited confessions upon the editor and his team, and the fierce battle to publish and be damned—or to suppress—are the themes of Robert Harling's new novel of Fleet Street.

The action of *The Athenian Widow* moves from London to Carolina, from New York to County Kerry, and is ruggedly played out between the middle-aged editor, over-conscious of slowing down; his thrusting younger deputies; the touchy Washington correspondent; the beguiling young diarist and the Presidential candidate's imperiously rich widow now determinedly sequestered in the Deep South.

By the Same Author

*

The War

AMATEUR SAILOR

THE STEEP ATLANTICK STREAM

Novels

THE PAPER PALACE

THE DARK SAVIOUR

THE ENORMOUS SHADOW

THE ENDLESS COLONNADE

THE HOLLOW SUNDAY

Art, Architecture, etc.

THE DRAWINGS OF EDWARD BAWDEN

THE WOOD ENGRAVINGS OF
ERIC RAVILIOUS

HOME: A VICTORIAN VIGNETTE

THE LONDON MISCELLANY

HISTORIC HOUSES
Conversations in Stately Homes

MODERN FURNITURE
AND DECORATION

THE HOUSE & GARDEN
DICTIONARY OF DESIGN
AND DECORATION
(Editor)

THE ATHENIAN WIDOW

A NOVEL

Robert Harling

1974

CHATTO & WINDUS

LONDON

Published by
Chatto & Windus Ltd
40-42 William IV Street
London WC2N 4DF

★

Clarke, Irwin & Co Ltd
Toronto

ISBN 0 7011 1971 3

Printed in Great Britain by
T. & A. Constable Ltd
Edinburgh

PART I

–1–

Let no traveller from an antique land take this for an antique tale. The Athens of my story lies 32° 47N, 79° 57W, deep in Carolina, one of a dozen Athens in the United States, but, more to my point, the home of Melanie Stirling.

And the time was a year ago.

But, first, I have to go back almost two years. To Mason. Then to Ann Toynbee. And then to Melanie Stirling

–2–

After *New Sunday* had been taken over and killed off by its new owners, I had offers from a couple of rivals for a column along the lines of *Faces & Places*. Fleet Street flops are apt to cause more comment than flyaway successes.

Mason also rang to suggest lunch.

We met at Rules the following Monday.

He hadn't changed much in a year. Still the same thick-set, short-legged, grey-haired, grey-suited man of middle height, middle age and middle brow. Plus the same strong-boned jutting jaw. Plus a little extra girth. Plus a dewier dewlap. But that was all the change I saw.

After we'd been through the menu and chosen, he said, 'Why don't you come back?'

'You wouldn't give me enough space.'

'Or money, I daresay.'

That was less important, I said–and meant. I had come out of the *New Sunday* débâcle with a year's tax-free redundancy pay-off.

'At this stage I'm far more interested in how much space you'd give me than how much money.'

'Oddly enough, I might be able to meet that kind of greed,' he said, smiling. 'I've been asked to take over the Sunday.'

'You didn't agree!' I said, surprised.

'It was put to me in a lucrative way I couldn't easily refuse,' he said. Mildly defensively, I thought.

'I always thought you'd end your days still editing *the* great liberal daily.'

'So did I, but apparently not. The top brass say they want my kind of editing for the Sunday.'

'I see their point, but you seem to be doing well enough where you are.'

'That's what I thought, but Sunday sales are sagging, I gather.'

'And Mason's the appointed saviour?'

'So it seems. I'll need some new blood. Naturally I thought of you.'

'Very flattering. Not quite new though. Pseud-new.'

He laughed. 'Call it what you like, it seems to work. Anyway, you left us. I never wanted you to go.'

'But I went. And learned elsewhere.'

'That's another reason why I want you back. *New Sunday* changed some of my ideas. I liked a lot of what Spurway did. I'd like to have a bash at doing much the same kind of thing.'

'Most of what he did, he did because he was Spurway,' I said, gently, even if unkindly.

'And you think I'm no Spurway?'

'Aren't you doing quite well as Mason?'

He sniffed, by-passing an answer, saying instead: 'Anyway, would you consider coming back – if the terms are right?'

'I'll think about it. But why so keen on *Faces & Places* now? Last year you damned it.'

'I didn't damn it,' he protested strongly. 'I was sceptical. Like the rest of Fleet Street. Now I want to copy it.'

'There was nothing new about *Faces & Places*.' I said. 'An old-fashioned gossip column brought up to date, that's all. Artists, inventors and unknown boffins instead of starlets, tartlets and upper-crust bums. A veneer three-thou-of-an-inch deeper that's all.'

Mason laughed. 'Whatever it was, it worked and got talked about. The three thou made the difference. I want it – or something like it.'

'And if I came back I'd have a free hand?'

'Absolutely.'

'I'll think about it.'

'Don't you want to discuss terms? Your ideas of your own worth must have escalated since you left.'

'Not unduly, but let's talk terms.'

We talked terms and Mason talked sense. So that seemed all right.

By that time we were half-way through a shared Chateaubriand and a shared Monthelet. We nattered on for the remaining half-hour or so, turning over Fleet Street gossip; rumours of mergers, hints of skids under him, her, them, the rest. All good misanthropic stuff.

Then, quietly, somewhere amongst the tittle-tattle, I offered the view that somebody or other was over the hill, a worn-out husk and all that. Mason agreed, and then, after a pause threw in the over-casual query: Did I think he was showing his own age?

'I don't know your age. You've got the OK greying locks, the intriguing lines of maturity, the frown of responsibility. Is that what you mean?'

'That's not what I mean and you damn well know it.'

'How old are you, anyway? I've always assumed late forties or something equally fashionable.'

'I'm fifty-three, fifty-four next month.'

'Prime of an ill-spent life.'

'Kind words will get you nowhere. What's your real opinion?'

'I'm no good at this kind of quiz. Get your reassurance elsewhere. See a female psychiatrist.'

He grinned. 'You're not forty yet. It makes a big difference.'

'Look,' I said, 'I've just discussed coming back to work for you. Would I, if I thought you had one foot in the grave?'

'Maybe other people think I have. Perhaps I'm being kicked upstairs.'

'You've certainly got it bad. If they really thought that, you'd get paid off in the usual Fleet Street style. Relax. Start dyeing your hair or something.'

'Most of that's still there, thank God,' he said complacently, running his hand fondly over his thick iron-grey hair *en brosse*. 'But one gets a bit over-conscious of other things. Weight, for instance.'

'Lay off this claret, then, and that second hunk of bread if you're so scared of kilos, strokes and sudden death.'

'It's not so much the sudden death touch,' he said reflectively. 'It's the slow, decaying quality of the so-called living cells that nags. Reflexes, power of decision, self-confidence, self-doubt. All that jazz.'

'Out-of-date slang dates you more accurately than slower reflexes.'

He smiled. 'Nevertheless, those are the worries,' he added quietly. 'You'll come to them in time.'

'You've let this youth-cult stuff get you down.'

'It's easy for you to talk.'

'As far as swinging youth's concerned, I'm a burnt-out case. For their life-style, anyone over twenty-one is on his way to the wax-works.'

'I suppose so,' he said, musing, 'I find I'm a bit out of touch occasionally. I've got two boys, as you may remember. One at

Keele, the other at the Slade. And a seventeen-year-old daughter just leaving school. A trio like that can make a man feel pretty square sometimes.'

I laughed, 'You were born square. You got where you are by being square. You're the squarest star in the squarest outfit in so-called modern Britain: a would-be liberal newspaper.'

He laughed. 'Snide asides were always part of your stock-in-trade.'

'But it's true. You sit in that damned office, scribbling your leaders, trying to square the conscience of the collective liberal world. And now, because you suspect the whole thing's out of date, you begin to think you're on the way to the crypt.'

'I bloody don't,' he said sharply, stung at last.

'Well, there's one consolation. There's damn-all you can do about it. The wrinkles will come. The arteries will harden. The bell tolls.'

'Not just yet. I'm taking some necessary action. I've persuaded one or two young men to join me.'

'Young men such as?'

'Tom Vaughan for one,' he said quietly.

I felt him watching me for the effect. I disappointed him. 'Why not? He's a natural for the part you've got in mind. The professional voice of the professional youth movements.'

Mason grinned, but the grin had a kind of nailed-on-look about it. 'Why the sneer?'

'Because he's so obvious. The Etonian with the common touch. The editor-designate since Isis days. The voice of youth who's never out of Television Centre. An ego the size of St Paul's.'

'I need someone like that.'

'You don't need him. You've had him pushed on you.'

'What balls you do talk sometimes, Paul.' The words snapped out.

'It's been suggested, then. A good idea for the paper and all that.'

'I've done all the suggesting. He's what I need,' Mason repeated stubbornly. 'Apart from his television work he did a first-rate job at the *Western Mail*. And he had a good grounding in the facts of life on the *F.T.* I could do with a side-kick like that.'

'Isn't he a somewhat upper-crust side-kick for your bourgeois-Marxist viewpoint? Although I do notice a Welsh-mining-valley lilt creeping into his voice on the box these days.'

Mason laughed briefly. 'I always tend to forget your talent for denigration. Why are you so down on Vaughan?'

'Vaughan's *your* man. Let's hope he'll be the answer to your monkey-gland problem.'

Again Mason laughed. Again not very warmly.

'As I see it–despite your denials–you've had Vaughan wished on you by the Board,' I said quietly. 'You don't want him, but you think it politic to take him on. You want me back as an ally and some kind of counter-weight to Vaughan. That's the way I see it.'

'Why don't you put up a brass plate and move over to the Harley Street area? Mortimer, the poor man's psychiatrist. Reduced rates for Fleet Street consultations. Have a brandy.'

'Thanks. Where are you proposing to put my column if I do come back?'

'Page opposite the leader.'

'How much of the page?'

'The whole page,' he said, watching for reaction with a glint of triumph.

'You're kidding.'

'I'm prepared to put it in writing and guarantee the position for at least a year. It makes sense, anyway. I want to make it the most talked-about personality column in Britain. Can I do more?'

'I doubt it.'

He had certainly saved his winning stroke until the telling moment. 'Let me have your answer inside a week,' he said.

I knew the answer already. And so, I suspect, did he. No other offer could ever beat that as a temptation to a journalistic ego.

–3–

Leaving Mason, wandering through Middle Temple, down towards the Embankment, and a meditative walk, I thought about his problem.

We stare in the mirror a thousand times a year, give or take a score. We see few changes. Half a dozen times, perhaps, we see a line that must have come overnight, a slackness unnoticed a week ago. But we shrug the irritant away. A nuisance but no more. We'll take things in hand. Start limbering up. Take a sauna. Join a health club. Take up squash again. Sudden change and swift decay are not for us. Such frailties are for others, the oldies.

Mason, it seemed had decided that fate was pushing him the oldie's way.

–4–

One of the many advantages of living apart from one's wife is that between meetings one has time for reflection on points for future discussion.

I had two days to reflect on Mason's proposal before meeting Helen two nights later for dinner in my erstwhile home in Chelsea.

I usually dined her or dined with her on Wednesdays, the au pair's night off, occasionally on Fridays, invariably on Sundays.

'I think you'll go back,' she said after I'd reviewed the three offers over a drink.'

'Why?'

'You're not exactly non-adventurous, but you're not conventionally adventurous. Mason's offer is just about made-to-measure, especially as it's another Sunday newspaper. I suspect you got to like the weekly cycle. Less of a rat-race than the daily stint. You'll also be working with some of the people you know. And you'll get a chance to elaborate on what you were doing for Spurway.'

'You read me like a book.'

'Some of the pages are easier than others. The chapters get a bit blurred when a new woman's due to be written in.'

'Never had any–except you.'

'You've never been without one. Who is it now?'

'I lead the simple, single, celibate life, as you well know.'

'You couldn't if you tried. You're a congenital liar, stoat and hypocrite–and smooth as tooth-paste in all three roles.'

My daughter, Marion, now eleven, came in then. That cut short the genial abuse. She was a dead keen art student at the Lycée. Over supper she wanted to discuss Art Nouveau, not my best subject, but I stood up manfully if un-aesthetically to her third degree.

After that we had a three-handed game of Scrabble. Then we set about getting Marion to bed, a process apt to take something over an hour. Then we had a drink. Then another and another. Around midnight we went to bed.

'Did I tell you, you were right about my going back?' I asked Helen at breakfast.

'More or less.'

'How did you know?'

'As I said, I'm psychic about these job things. I draw an outsize blank about the rest of your life. I wish I didn't, but that's the way it is.'

In a way I was rather relieved about the blank, I decided later, walking back to my own flat in Swan Court on the other side of the King's Road. My current 'blank'–in Helen's word–was Victoria ('call me Vicky') Holt, a tall, leggy, blonde divorcée, working as PRO for a film-making group with cultural pretensions. I'd met her three or four months before at a press show for some terrible wildlife-on-Exmoor film her outfit had made. I'd even managed a paragraph about the place of the otter in the English way of life.

'Blank' was quite a good moniker for Vicky, I decided.

–5–

A fortnight later, in late January, more or less inevitably, I went back to the same outfit but a different paper from the one I'd left a year before. And the job seemed to be all Mason had promised.

I was grateful, I even tried to forget his preoccupation with his arteries, glands and reflexes. But how could I, after that lunch?

–6–

Basically, as Helen had said, I'm a non-adventurer. I like familiar faces and places. The Sunday set-up I joined was almost as familiar as the daily I'd left a year before.

I wanted to use the title *Faces & Places* for my new column. Mason tried, via our solicitors, but the new owners of the now-defunct *New Sunday* were bloody-minded. They'd dropped the feature but reckoned they had a copyright in the title. Bloody-minded on my own account, I rang Spurway, now reflourishing in his brave old television world.

He sent round a note that same morning, saying that (a) *Faces & Places* was my coinage; (b) as far as he'd been concerned all rights were vested in me; (c) the celebrated case of Mary Delaney versus Lord Kemsley and *The Sunday Times* had surely fixed a precedent for that kind of thing, and (d) as far as he could see I could go right ahead, especially as the feature had been ostentatiously discontinued in the now-absorbed *New Sunday*. There was thus no question of passing-off and/or infringement of copyright.

Armed with this letter, Mason waited until the Saturday morning before my first feature appeared and then sent round a note to the new owners–or rather incorporators–of *New Sunday*, informing them that he proposed to start publishing *Faces & Places* that weekend. No injunction followed. We went ahead.

So much for the title.

Spurway, as usual, had come out of the exchanges with his image as the generous-spirited damn-you-all bravo reburnished. After all, *Faces & Places* had been his very own phrase.

I telephoned my gratitude.

'These characters think they can buy anything with their bloody millions,' he blasted-off. 'Even one man's own three words. The hell with them! When are we lunching?'

'Soon, I hope. I'll need to keep an eye on the television world in this new version of your old column.'

'I'll keep you well-informed, buster. I also need to keep my Fleet Street contacts in working order, too. The propaganda potential of the box don't hold a candle to the olde-worlde corantos of Grub Street.'

'I'll bear it in mind.'

'I'll give you a couple of weeks to get into your stride. When we lunch I'll fill you in on television studio paranoia. Nothing down your alley compares with the show-biz depressives and mean-gutted technicians with whom I spend my days.'

'The Grub Street vocabulary's still in working order, I notice.'

'Why not? I'll probably have to talk my way back out of this non-vocabulous world one not-too-distant day,' he said, signing off.

–7–

Curiously, I found I didn't miss the colour printing of *New Sunday* in the new feature. An inner belief that I'm a black-and-white newspaper man at heart was confirmed. I enjoyed my sabbatical monotone miscellany and found no limitation in filling the page to the last pica.

Judging by the coverage the feature got on radio and television programmes devoted to the Press, some pundits, at least, were glad to see the feature revived.

Mason was delighted. By the end of April he gleefully announced that the circulation people were claiming that the paper was putting on sales again and that *Faces & Places* was getting its full share of comment and bringing in nostalgic readers of the killed-off *New Sunday*. God knows by what soothsaying methods they make these discoveries and double-check their findings, but who was I to protest?

I was still lost in wry astonishment that a man can write seriously and anonymously about the personalities and problems of industry for ten long years–as I had done–and not get a pennyworth of the bogus kudos he gets, within a month, from putting a by-line to a page of journalistic chitter-chat.

–8–

I gave Helen dinner at the Etoile a week after I'd started.

How did I like my return to the Sunday treadmill? she asked.

'I'm a creature of habit. I find a regular job more congenial than regular leisure.'

'As a non-wife with too much leisure I see your point. I'd be fair game for any lousy but regular Latin lover. Not even a regular husbandly evening homecoming to look forward to.'

'You haven't suffered from my tetchy homecomings for three years. It's better this way. And you know it.'

'I don't know it. I'd like to start again. A woman gets lonely.'

I changed the subject. I preferred my present substitute for freedom, however hazy its outlines, to the marriage I had known. I preferred being answerable to no woman, no timetable, no responsibilities of any consequence, preferring a patchwork relationship that worked–for me–to a marriage that hadn't worked–for either party.

In any case, I had other involvements. Vicky was currently claiming a good deal of my spare time. She liked, she said, her occasional sojourn in Swan Court. She liked bustling around and keeping things tidy. As I'd recently lost my more-than-willing daily, Molly, whose long-distance lorry-driving husband had been transferred to a haulage outfit in Coventry, I was glad to take what the pagan gods had offered in her stead.

Selfish? Without a doubt. Utterly, wolfishly, unforgivably. But it was a better basis than the one I'd promised to share with Helen for better or for worse a dozen years before. We have to work with what we've got.

Helen broke into these mildly morbid reflections asking whether I liked working with Mason again.

I said quite.

'You don't sound all that enthusiastic.'

'Spurway spoiled me for the Mason-type editor. I liked the way Spurway was here, there and everywhere, rarely in his room, always looking for trouble. Middle name Mercury. Mason scarcely ever leaves his room. Probably feels a lot safer there. He hates trouble.'

'He's an older man.'

'As he begins to point out. But it's not just age. He's always edited from his room. He feels more vulnerable out on the stone or in the newsroom. He'd far rather play the old liberal oracle in his book-lined room.'

And when does the young Welsh wizard arrive to help out the ageing oracle?'

'Next month.'

'Will he cut across your tracks?'

'He could, I suppose, but I've a fairly privileged position. Only Mason can shoot down my copy. I suppose Vaughan could at a pinch. Nominally, as an assistant editor, he'll be my superior.'

'Will you mind that?'

'It's never bothered me. Authority's usually in the label rather than the man.'

We talked on as we progressed through the meal to coffee and brandy. Secretly, I doubted whether our meal would have been as leisurely or talkative had we been the well-married partners we had supposedly been once upon a time.

We went back to Milner Street. I stayed the night.

An odd kind of set-up, no doubt, as I've said before, but at least it semi-worked, which is some kind of achievement in a less-than-semi-perfect world.

–9–

The Honourable Thomas Caradog Vaughan, only son of the thirteenth Viscount Merion of the County of Merionethshire, joined the paper in early March.

Mason called me into his corner room overlooking Fetter Lane and Fleet Street to introduce us.

I'd never met Vaughan, but recognised him immediately. Television personalities always resemble television images, a fact emphasized in Vaughan's case by his curiously black-and-white appearance. Even on colour programmes he looked black-and-white.

He was broad-shouldered, slightly above middle height with thick black hair, parted low on the left, above a face of extreme pallor. The features were clear-cut: bold nose below thick eyebrows, above a wide, well-shaped mouth, cleft chin. The eyes were clear, grey and unusually direct. He was well-dressed in a fashionably high-cut double-breasted blue-black suit, bold-patterned blue-and-white striped shirt and dark blue tie, mildly flared trousers, buckled black shoes. In an effectively, affectedly anachronistic manner, he looked, I thought, more like a nineteenth-century sailing master out of Portmadoc or Newport than a twentieth-century publicist out for himself. He was plainly a tough but elegant customer: a man to watch in all circumstances.

We exchanged a few pleasantries before Mason got down to business.

'As I see it, Paul,' he began, 'Tom will take over the leader-page as my winger and, if necessary, deputy. He'll carry the title of Assistant

Editor, Leader Page.' He smiled. 'That still gives us only two assistant editors–pretty low by current Fleet Street Standards–but we'll make out.'

Mason went on: 'As you're so essentially part of the centre spread, Paul, I thought you and Tom ought to get to know each other as soon as possible. As I see it, you obviously have complete freedom to write about anything or anybody you like, but if Tom spots something or somebody shaping up for a story, it's up to the pair of you to get together for discussion. We'll all meet at the usual eleven o'clock conference on Tuesdays, Thursdays and Fridays, of course, but things are apt to blow up all through the week as we know.'

Would Vaughan do any writing? I asked.

'He'll certainly be writing some of the leaders at some future date and he'll be responsible for headings and general make-up of the leader page–along with the layout people, of course.'

We talked about the centre spread for ten minutes or so, but we were discussing a theorem. New men bring new problems as well as solutions–sometimes.

I left in a convenient lull.

–10–

Mason's leader page was undoubtedly the most politically committed page in British journalism. He had made his considerable international reputation by that daily page. Now he was seeking to do the same sabbatically.

But a journalistic reputation is a complex and subtle affair. What goes for a daily is frequently a dead loss on Sundays. What reads well in a crowded train, can read less persuasively in a reflective armchair. Mason sensed that. He was plainly concerned with the problems of his transition and the maintenance of his reputation.

The new leader page Mason had evolved represented a considerable financial sacrifice on the part of the proprietors. No advertisements were now allowed on the page, and only one eight-inch double-column advertisement on the *Faces & Places* page, opposite. The arrangement left me with space for something over two thousand words plus picture. I had nothing to complain about.

The leader page was usually divided between three features, depending on Mason's Saturday view of the state of the world. On crisis-ridden week-ends he might scrap the three features and run one major article. In common with most other editors he thought more words meant more authority.

But why quibble? In his time, hadn't he been named Journalist of the Year, won the Swaffer Award, represented British Journalism at foreign press jamborees, given the Sandars Lectures at Cambridge, attended luncheon and garden parties at the Palace and God knows what all? Give a man his due.

Faces & Places usually comprised about half a dozen items of three hundred words apiece plus two or three snippets of fifty words or so. From time to time I gave particular prominence to a personality, a building, a cult, an invention in the news. But by the time I'd included a photograph, a pocket cartoon and/or a diagram, I was beginning to be pushed. No journalist ever has enough space.

—11—

With the facilities of hindsight I now see how skilfully Vaughan handled the rest of us in those early weeks.

Although Mason might seem as decisive and authoritative as he'd ever been, time was inevitably running out on him. A fifty-four-year-old editor of a paper with a desperate need for circulation has plainly got to keep running pretty hard. And others were on his heels.

Vaughan was at his smoothest in editorial conferences, usually a time for the display and interplay of personality, acumen, perspicuity, bloody-mindedness and all the other talents vouchsafed to men of goodwill, journalists and bishops included.

But Vaughan bided his time.

—12—

At these editorial conferences, half a dozen of us sat in a ragged crescent facing the editor at his desk. Likely stories were discussed, political issues analysed, possible leads dissected.

Steve Logan, features editor, was the most vocal performer. He was a tall, balding, dark-eyed, jowly Mancunian, in his late forties, convinced that he had come up the hard way. A brash and lively mind had taken him from Hulme Grammar School to a youthful captaincy as a wartime gunner in Burma, thence, post-war, to Wadham on an Open History Scholarship. He'd returned as local-boy-made-good to the *Manchester Evening News*. After ten years there he'd come to London.

In conference he was a bit of a bore. Because his own pages were usually sewn up fairly early in the week he was more relaxed than those of us with the main part of the week's work still ahead of us. At first sight he seemed overloaded with bonhomie but this geniality was deceptive. In argument he lashed out at anyone he thought antagonistic to his viewpoint. He was inordinately (and illogically, I thought) ambitious, professionally and socially. He occasionally talked of returning to the North, but that was undoubtedly the last move he or his Wimbledon-born-reared wife intended. He wanted to beat the metropolitan city-slickers at their own game. But his aggressiveness and basic insecurity were sometimes hard for the rest of us to take.

Gerry Markham, foreign editor, mid-forties acted as something of a foil to Logan. He was a tall, drooping, professorial-looking Wykehamist. Pale-grey watchful eyes blinked fretfully behind heavy horn-rimmed specs. After serving briefly in the FO following a National Service stint in Army Intelligence and a New College fellowship, he had joined the *Guardian* where he'd been a leader-writer. Mason had recruited his talents some two years previously. Rumour said he'd desperately wanted the editor's job in the recent shake-up, but he showed no outward animosity towards Mason, probably thinking his own day was still to come. He reserved most of his drier asides for Logan. In conference he made his contributions with great earnestness as if involved in a tutorial with dullards. He was also inclined to imply that he'd just received his information five minutes previously by scrambler from the Elysée Palace, the White House, the Kremlin or Bonn. He was rarely interrupted. Mason, with some justification, set considerable store by Markham's sources and reliability. My own view was that although he was a first-rate foreign editor, he'd reached his ceiling. Few men, however, know their professional limitations, least of all journalists. How could Markham know that he was as hopeless in his dealings with other men as are most Wykehamists? A curious fact, but consider Mosley, Cripps, Crossman and a score of others. Cleverer-than-thou gets inculcated too soon, perhaps, but Markham's hat, I suspected, was still in the ring for Mason's job.

Herbert Paxton, political editor, was a pipe-smoking, sandy-haired Midlander also in his late-forties. He'd spent his first twenty years in journalism on the *Birmingham Post* and still kept a week-end cottage in Warwickshire. He made few contributions to the conferences, but each was carefully considered, invincibly conventional, marginally constructive. He might have yearned for an editorship, but he was too set in his ways and job and knew it. In any case, the

Parliamentary Lobby for him was an addictive club and drug; and he was apt to seem somewhat lost outside its labyrinthine but cosy corridors with their perennial puzzles of personality and policy.

Dick Spicer, managing editor, was a tall, square-shouldered man in his early forties with straight fair hair which gave him an unusually boyish appearance as if he were No 3 in a Henley crew. He was an odd man out in Fleet Street: a one-time engineer from Keyham who had left the Navy to become yachting correspondent for a daily and then branched out. Although he had an outwardly and agreeably cynical view of the men and manners of the day, he was, at heart, a true-blue RN type, longing for leaders of worth and integrity to spring up overnight to restore Great Britain to her one-time greatness. His cynicism was a protective coating. True to his service training he was one of the least flappable men I've known.

As managing editor, Spicer's main weekly task was to get the paper away on time, to haze all contributors and to co-operate with the advertising people, tasks which he did supremely well. So well, in fact, that his worth was invariably taken for granted. If, against long odds, his name had been included in any short list for the editorship, everyone would have acknowledged his virtues but none would have recommended him. He was a natural second-in-command. Yet had he kept to words and the use of words he might have been a starter. *Moral*: If you want the top job in a technical outfit never do a technical job.

This group, with Mason at the centre and Vaughan and myself at the farthest peripheral edges, comprised the cabal of the paper. A hundred others helped to write, shape and print the sheet, but these men were the heart of the matter.

–13–

In these sometimes contentious meetings Vaughan held his own by near-silence. Although at least ten years younger than any of us, he seemed to have an intuitive feeling for the moment to voice an opinion. Then he spoke quietly, briefly, effectively. Usually he was a silent listener–as I was myself. Indeed, I normally had least to say, probably because I yearned to get back to my job.

Returning to our rooms, after one of the early meetings, Spicer said: 'When Tom Vaughan opens his mouth he usually talks a lot of sense. Have you noticed?'

'In the kingdom of the gabby the one-word man is king.'

'You're dead right. He skips the bull. It's quite a relief. He's certainly a change from those firework displays in aid of the Steve Logan benefit performances.'

I laughed.

'You seem to have reservations,' Spicer said.

'I didn't say so.'

'But you have,' Spicer went on, still probing.

'Not exactly. I'm intrigued by Vaughan's flexible technique, that's all. On the box he revels in free-for-alls, cuts his opponents down to size, interrupts the commentator, hogs the mike and the screen. Here he's like a young Daniel come to judgment.'

'Well, I like his contributions here. We could do with a few more Daniels around the place. Wonder what his ultimate ambition is.'

'Here or in the denser jungle outside?' I asked.

'Here, of course.'

'Editor, I suppose–like everybody else's.'

'He's at least five years too young. But as Mason'll probably be here for another five he may have timed it just right.'

'His timing's impeccable. I think he'd already impressed his Lordship upstairs long before he met the rest of us. And I suspect our young friend's lordly father also knows his Lordship upstairs, too.'

'Useful stuff,' Spicer said reflectively. 'Trust a Welshman or a Scotsman to get the English way of life lined up. If you're right–as I suspect you may well be–nobody else stands a chance.'

'Nobody,' I said.

–14–

But others had other ideas about Vaughan's future.

Steve Logan, carrying his plateful of comestibles, joined me in the canteen a week or so later. Half-way through his steak-and-kidney pie he moved the conversation round to Vaughan. How did I think the wonder-boy was making out?

'Quite well, I'd say.'

'What d'you think he's after?'

'The editorship, of course. The only job most journalists want–with one or two notable exceptions.'

'He'll have some stiff competition.'

'Present company excepted?'

'Not a chance. I'd be in there, brother, fighting for S. Logan. What chance would you give him?'

'Your ambition's showing a bit too much, Steve. It's been showing too much for the past two years. And Vaughan, I suspect, knows the top brass here on far more intimate terms than you'll ever know 'em. Week-ends, for instance. Boodle's, for instance. Frankly, I think Vaughan's their nominee.'

'You're probably right. And I don't know a single damn director. So you think I ought to watch that there ambition? Curb it and so on?'

'Don't ask me. It's no good hiding your light and all that. Far better go your own way. I'm no good as a fortune-teller. What beats me is that you or anyone else should want the job.'

'This isn't some very subtle double-crossing smoke-screen you're putting up? Sure you're not in the running? All men are enemies when it comes to this kind of contest.'

'Include me right out. I'm a scribbler not an admin-type manipulator.'

'I don't see an editor's job that way.'

'Every day it gets more and more that way.'

'In that case I'd be the best admin-type manipulator-type editor-type-editor you ever did see.'

He finished his pie. 'One needs to be a dago with a dagger and a couple of teenage nymphet daughters to throw into the balance in this kind of racket. Pity mine are both married.'

'Vaughan's not even married.'

'The bachelor bastard!' Logan said succinctly. 'Not even queer, I suppose?'

'Who knows? Who cares? Isn't it a uni-sex consenting world we live in these days.'

He got up. 'The coffee's no damn good here,' he said leaving. 'I'm off to my espresso joint in Holborn.'

With relief I went back to the *Midday Standard*.

–15–

My own relations with Vaughan were friendly enough and after a few wary weeks gradually became friendlier.

He had an easy manner, didn't throw his weight around, left me alone. On that basis we couldn't help but get along. Like most journalists, I'm primarily a worker-with than worker-against. One needs to be. On that basis alone, I thought Logan something of a goon.

As far as *Faces & Places* was concerned, Vaughan, reasonably enough, liked to know in advance what subjects I proposed to tackle so that he didn't double-up on the leader-page. Normally I was dealing with less momentous men and matters than those crowding his augustan galleys. From time to time he suggested names: a visiting soprano to Covent Garden of whom the music critic expected much; a photogenic young horsewoman from Galway coming over for the Badminton trials; an oddball inventor with a motor-car guaranteed to run on paraffin. And so on and on. Such suggestions are the life-blood of a personality column. I got them from all over.

–16–

Logan's underlying tension *vis-à-vis* Vaughan suddenly erupted at a Thursday editorial conference in early June.

Mason had suggested that Britain's case for the retention of Gibraltar should be examined by a panel of international jurists; that such a panel should be convened at the paper's invitation and expense and that we should try to share the expense and project with the BBC or one of the ITA outfits.

The scheme obviously had possibilities for international interest, but Markham and Logan were against the project from the word go. Perhaps they both detected the influence of Vaughan in the project.

Markham said: 'Who's to choose the jurists? If we're not careful we'll have a trio similar to those characters UNO sent to Aden. Men against Britain from the word go. We'll get one of these so-called dialogues with all the cards stacked against us. It's a dangerous game.'

Disputation broke out; pretty heatedly. Mason listened carefully. Vaughan stayed silent. Then Mason turned to him, asking his views. Vaughan put forward a reasonably persuasive case. We would show ourselves as internationalists rather than Little Englanders. We'd certainly recoup all our outgoings by world-wide syndication. The series might even put up sales.

Markham broke in again: 'Supposing our chosen jurists gave a unanimous decision against Britain's continued tenure of the Rock: Wouldn't we find ourselves in rather an onerous position for a newspaper?'

'Doesn't any worth-while newspaper risk that possibility every day?' Vaughan countered. 'Governments aren't always right.'

Markham nodded, but went on: 'All the same I'm against this. One hundred per cent. I think it's the kind of project that *Paris-Match* or *Stern* might undertake, but certainly not a reputable British newspaper. Any foreign jurist would have to vote against our continued tenure of the Rock. It's not logical in this day and age. But we're there.'

'You make a good case,' Mason admitted with, I thought, a touch of relief.

'For not rocking the Rock,' Vaughan added quietly.

As with more momentous explosions, the real blast came after everything seemed to have cooled down. Staring straight at Vaughan, Logan said, 'Some new-style internationalists can't stand old-fashioned patriots. Noticed?'

Logan's query was so pointed that Vaughan had to answer. He said simply, 'I think it's possible to be both. But we're no longer right just because we say we are and because we've got bigger and faster gunboats.'

Now Logan had an opponent on the personal terms he preferred. 'It's usually a lot easier to be a good internationalist on your terms–in print–than a patriot on my terms–say three years in Burma, two as a prisoner.'

Unfair, considering Vaughan's age, but Logan was no believer in Queensberry rules.

Vaughan said: 'I'm afraid I can't match your martial experiences. All I know is that there's frequently more than one–sometimes even more than a dozen sides–in a two-nation quarrel. Suez and Panama showed that.'

'Why not try telling the Arabs, Jews, Panamanians, Yanks and Russians how to be good boys for a change, then?'

'I've tried, from time to time, and will doubtless do so again.'

'Patriotism, for you, seems a dirty word.'

'Not at all. But I've often found chauvinism turns out to be.'

'You seem to specialize in fringe definitions.'

'I'm a persistent seeker after truth in all things,' Vaughan said, smiling.

'Or over-simplification.'

'It's possible–judged against more sophisticated standards than my own, of course.' Vaughan admitted, smiling, unperturbed and way ahead on points.

I wondered why Mason was allowing the punch-up to go on. He sat watching the two men as if hypnotized. Then, very quietly, he said: 'Let's leave it for a couple of days, shall we?'

The rest of us returned with noticeable reluctance to discuss the remaining features on the list. Anything was anti-climax after Logan-versus-Vaughan. The sudden flare-up had been too raw and personal on Logan's part to be dismissed as one of those flurries likely to attend any discussion of a newspaper's policy, plans and projects. If Mason, the would-be peacemaker, were to be removed, only Vaughan or Logan could remain. Not both. That was certain.

Leaving the meeting, Dick Spicer said, 'My God, Steve's certainly got it bad. That venom of his will give him a stroke one of these days.'

'It certainly won't give him the editorship.'

'I think you're right.'

–17–

Later that day I had to interview Lord Justice Scranton, a crusty old Law Lord who had, on the previous afternoon, made an out-of-reason, out-of-season attack in the Lords on the general moral laxity of Britain, with particular reference to homosexuality. I thought it worth an interview with the old boy. So did Vaughan. In a permissive age, articulate diehards are news.

I checked on the old boy's entry in *Who's Who*. He was in his early seventies, and, to my amusement, had been a member of my own college. He'd seen active service in the First World War, got a DSO and was, apparently, unmarried.

I rang Grant Lovell, head of our resident legal staff, to ask for any less formal data on the judge. 'I was never up to him myself,' Lovell said in his own version of the judicial manner. 'I gather he's a tough old numero with some out-of-fashion views, but you'll probably find he'll talk and talk. All these judges do, released from their pontifical official silences. Any evening at the Garrick proves that.'

I got to the judge's place in Eaton Square around half-past-six and was shown straight up into a very impressive library. He was a gnarled old bachelor in his early seventies, I judged, but agreeable, ready to talk and an amusing contrast to an interview I'd had the previous day with a self-confessed, drug-addicted, bi-sexual, teenage pop idol. Just the kind of citizen, in fact, the judge had been so thoroughly castigating in the Upper House.

He confirmed all that Lovell had said about judges' unbuttoned verbosity. The air was soon full of unquotable aphorisms. At one point he said Britain needed an oligarchic form of government. 'Authority is far too dispersed and diluted in any democracy.'

And later: 'Far better that any battle for power should be fought between an intelligent few than a rabble of morons.'

'Wouldn't your system make for great inequalities?'

'Our genes establish great inequalities at birth, Mr Mortimer. So-called maturity merely emphasizes them.'

'Not a very optimistic view of the world.'

'I do not have a very optimistic perch from which to view it.'

I rather liked him, especially his parting shot: 'Unless one is born Genghis Khan, or Napoleon, Mr Mortimer, one must accept the age one lives in. I therefore accept democracy. Not very willingly, perhaps, but there it is.'

Around half-past seven I left him in his high and comfortable library, with his books, his Regency furniture, his Courvoisier, his phobias and his loneliness. Somewhat to my surprise he suggested that we might dine one night during the following week and discuss these matters further. He would be grateful, he said, rather engagingly, for the opportunity of discussing the state of the world with a member of a younger generation not involved in the Law. Somewhat to his surprise, I suspect, I said I'd be delighted. In any case I doubted whether any invitation would follow.

Walking towards Sloane Square I wondered, as usual, how much, or rather how little of the interview I could print: it would certainly take some tricky writing and most of that would doubtless be legalized and bowdlerized by Lovell. Newspaper lawyers are a squeamish bunch. Meantime, I had other more superficial matters on my mind.

–18–

For one thing I was due to be dining my blonde PRO. I rang her from a call-box in Sloane Square and begged her to eat a biscuit and translate my dinner invitation into supper; half-past nine au Père de Nico. As usual she was agreeable. That was one of the maddening things about her, I thought, ringing off. She was always so damned understanding of the journalistic way of life.

I took a shower and then got down to the somewhat tricky task of depicting Lord Justice Scranton as I'd found him: a paradoxical old boy with a mind as lively as a precocious undergraduate's and views as antique as Caesar's. The portrait took a little more limning than I'd reckoned on. I quite enjoyed the task. I'd found him a curiously sympathetic anachronism.

–19–

Vicky Holt was beginning to be irksome, I decided, as I shaved around nine-fifteen.

I had no justification for such ungenerous thoughts. My piece on the judge had finally gone quite well. I had written something over six hundred words which would prove an entertaining exercise for reduction to three hundred.

Like most other people in the PRO game, Vicky was too respectful of what she called 'the real thing' that is, old-fashioned scribbling. Her journalistic career-by-proxy was loaded with references to 'the Street', 'stories', 'embargoes', 'deadlines', 'releases' and the rest. They made me squirm. Her over-ambitious, day-dreaming yearning to edit a woman's page on a pop daily made me sad. But not very.

Yet she had been a useful contact during a tricky interim period. After Molly, my perversatile daily had disappeared, I had found myself for a bleak week or so in demi-semi-celibate circumstances I hadn't known for years. Vicky had changed all that–within hours.

She was living apart from her husband, a motoring correspondent for one of the Sundays, and was only too delighted to have a fresh escort around the pubs and eating-places she loved.

She was tall, handsome and well-dressed in a sexy kind of way; blatantly so, to judge from the staring and nudging that went on in any bar we visited. She enjoyed the flutter she caused and, in a pridefully, self-consciously masculine kind of way, I suppose I did, too. But like so many tall blondes she wanted to be a small blonde. In desperate compensation, she had cultivated a little girl manner. Frequently I was in a mood to strangle her as she uttered one of her delicate *moues* at some mundane blasphemy or obscenity. Seated, I was apt to think of her as a fairly petite *objet d'artifice* and to find myself lulled into a mildly indulgent mood which never lasted for long. She was a girl to delight the shades of that old romantic, Sir Philip Gibbs. To her, Fleet Street really was The Street of Adventure.

Poor Vicky! It was none of her fault. She was only too anxious to please. Especially back at Swan Court. There the little girl role was swiftly exorcised by her congenital genius as a six-foot sensualist. Splendid, blissful, incomparable Vicky, I thought at those times. How can I ever let you go? Those magnificent breasts, bared and braced for action. Those exquisite thighs, so blissfully obliging. Those legs so orientally entwined about my nates. Where could I find their counterparts? I wondered, only too literally.

Yet somehow I knew that soon, regretfully and with infinitely nostalgic yearnings between the nocturnal hours of ten and two, I would have to let her go. But not just yet. At least, not before I could spot a possible successor.

Meanwhile, I went down by the lift, out into the King's Road and began to walk slowly towards Vicky and my supper.

—20—

Choosing her frugal supper—for she was unashamedly determined to retain her beautiful beautiful body–Vicky said, 'In a way I'm glad you had to finish your story. They had one of the press things on the telly tonight after the news. Your editor cropped up on it.'

'In person?'

'No, just his name along with most of the other big shots.'

'In aid of what?'

'How old should a Fleet Street editor be?'

I was suddenly very interested. 'And what was the general conclusion?'

'Generally it was decided it was a youngish man's game. Best for the under-fifties.'

'Who decided?'

'A couple of commentators.'

'Who were?'

'I forget their names. One we're always seeing with big specs, a pointed chin and terribly knowing manner. The other was new to me.'

'Very descriptive. Who did they mention?'

'It all started with a thing about *The Times* and the *Sunday Times* having editors in their forties. Then the *Express* and the *Mail*. Then they got on to the *Observer* with David Astor hitting sixty and the *FT* with Sir Gordon Newton older still. Then your chap somewhere in between. But they seemed to concentrate on him.'

'Tom Vaughan wasn't in the programme?'

'No. I know him. At least I'd recognise him. A real glamour boy. Anyway, he wouldn't dare: isn't he on your staff?'

I nodded as I topped up her glass with more Piesporter. She rattled on: 'He's sometimes in the programme but not tonight. I adore him. He doesn't care a rap for anybody. Is he fun to work with?'

'Subdued fun,' I said, groaning almost audibly. 'Continue your reportage.'

'Now you're taking the mick. I always know. You bury your chin in your chest, kind of resigned-looking.'

'Not at all,' I protested, looking up too sharply. 'I only see Vaughan at editorial meetings. These television firework characters are apt to be a lot quieter away from the cameras and the mikes. Not such glamour boys and whizz-kids.'

'I suppose so. Is your editor such an oldie, then?'

'I hadn't noticed it until he mentioned it a month or so ago.'

'How old do you think an editor ought to be?'

'The age he's best at.'

'Isn't that what's called begging the question?'

'All right, I'll beg another question: what age d'you think a blonde bombshell ought to be?'

'Ideally, twenty. But anything up to thirty'll do.

'Will you be as big and blonde a bombshell at fifty?'

'Now you're being squalid. I'm sorry I brought the subject up. Fifty's obscene.'

I gently pressed her beautiful knee beneath the table. 'Nonsense', I said reassuringly. 'You may be a silver-haired bombshell by then, but the magic will still be working.'

But my reassurance didn't work. 'You're turning the whole damn thing into a funeral,' she said, pouting.

'I'm sorry,' I said. 'And I'm digressing. What was the general conclusion, if any, about the antique editors?'

She was still pouting. 'Roughly I suppose what you said just now: the age he's best at.'

'Who's to decide?'

'The boss, as usual, I suppose.'

'D'you think my editor would have been flattered by the programme if he'd been watching?'

'Not much. Not very much at all, in fact.'

The waiter put down our plates.

'Are you still sulking?' I asked.

'I never sulk. I was hurt, but only momentarily.'

'Because I suggested that you'll hit fifty one day?'

'I shall be dead long before then. I'd rather kill myself.'

'Why?'

'I couldn't bear having all those wrinkles.'

'Some wrinkles are terrific. Mason's f'r'instance.'

'Who's Mason?'

'My aged editor. The one who got interred on the telly tonight.'

'Of course. That was his name. You must think me a nit.'

I denied that. Too tepidly perhaps, for she said, frowning: 'You're in a very peculiar mood tonight, Paul.'

'Diagnose it.'

'You seem so damn keen on silver hair and wrinkles . . .' she began.

'Fallen arches, cracked dentures, malignant tumours . . .' I continued.

'Oh, my God,' she groaned.
'But you started it,' I said.
Generally speaking, it wasn't our night.

–21–

Another of Vicky's intimidating characteristics was a talent for early rising after late and strenuous nights. She could prepare breakfast in utter silence before appearing by the bed like a mythological, all-providing warrior queen, enjoying a lull in the battle.

There she stood, holding a well-loaded tray, impeccably painted, powdered and coiffured.

How could she do it? I moaned.

Sheer abundant good health, was her reply and recipe.

The miracle was performed yet again the following morning.

I gulped my thanks as I took the first beneficent mouthful of orange juice and told her she was an angel; a false move as it happened. She had her answer pat. 'You ought to consider taking me in for keeps, then. Both our marriages are washed up. We could start again. You're the right age for me. I need an older man.'

'That telly programme last night's gone to your head. I'm still this side of forty, remember?'

'I'm still this side of twenty-two, remember?'

'Isn't that hitting a man below the belt at this time in the morning?' I asked plaintively, reaching for the coffee.

'Somebody's got to say it. It's all fairly obvious to me. We get on marvellously. Especially in there,' she said, stabbing at the bed with her Ryvita. 'I admire the kind of work you do. Even when you're being utterly bloody, as you were last night, I still like you. God knows why, but I do. Besides you fit in miraculously with my horoscope.'

My bladder was too near bursting-point for astrological assessments. 'Let's talk it over next time,' I begged.

'And when will that be?'

'Say next Monday.'

'What about the week-end?'

'I've a long piece to do on the Maritime Museum,' I said, taking a long chance, struggling up. 'And I've one or two family commitments. Let me ring you Monday morning.'

'I may ring you before.'

'Do that,' I said limply.

By the time I'd reappeared from the bathroom, she'd gone, but

Girl Friday to the last, she'd taken *The Times* in from the front door and put it by the tray on the bed.

Life is intolerably unjust I thought as I buttered another piece of toast and poured myself a second cup of coffee. Vicky deserved something a great deal better than my matutinal misanthropy.

—22—

I scanned *The Times* to see whether their TV writer had a piece on the Editors' programme. He had: an amusing send-up of the goggle-box buffs deciding the fate of Fleet Street. He hadn't mentioned Mason. I then rang Spurway at his home in Richmond. 'A bit early to start the day, isn't it?' he said. 'I'm scarcely airborne yet.'

'I need information. There was a telly programme about the Press last night . . .'

'Not ours,' he cut in, 'but I saw ten minutes of it. Then we had a dinner party. Or that, at least, is what my wife called it. I called it a bloody downright waste of good nosh and booze.'

'I'd like to know who master-minded the programme.'

'Wasn't it on the credits?'

'I didn't see it. I only heard about it.'

'What particular angle are you interested in?'

'Only in who set it up. The geezer behind the credits.'

'Shouldn't be too difficult. Your bloke Mason came in for a bit of clobbering by faint praise in the clips I saw. Tom Vaughan's often on that programme. He wasn't last night, I take it.'

'A sensitive and understandable absence, I gather, from what I heard was said.'

'Too true. OK. Will do. About time we lunched again.'

I agreed. We made a date for the following Tuesday.

Shaving, I wondered whether this little TV brouhaha would upset Mason.

—23—

It did. That Friday wasn't Mason's finest hour. He moved round the office with what seemed a paradoxical combination of heavy frown and would-be youthful step.

But, first thing, I was too busy going through the Scranton type-script to spare much time for Mason and his inner doubts. There were the quarto pages before me, beautifully, even exquisitely typed by my secretary, Pat Gow. Wide margins, double spacing and never a mistake. Sheer invitation to the sado-masochist in every writer. 'I'll go through this draft and then you'd better make a final copy and get ready to go down by taxi to his lordship at the Law Courts. He can check my facts, tell him, but the opinions are all mine and inviolate. Just tell him that if objections should arise. You can even memorize the phrase.'

'I know it by heart,' she said, disappearing, grateful for the chance of meeting the great man who'd been 'so sweet', she said, on the telephone.

Somewhat unenthusiastically, I went into the morning editorial conference.

Vaughan was currently education-minded. He thought we needed a leader on the Comprehensives. He had circulated a memo on the subject the previous day.

Mason apparently agreed. If we weren't careful, he said, opening the meeting, we might well be letting slip the lead we'd built up during recent months in the big Comprehensives controversy.

Needless to say, as fee-paying parents on a great Liberal and liberal paper, we were all for this great educational experiment, etc., etc.

Philippa Howe, our Education Correspondent, who'd been called in for the meeting was on the defensive. She was a dark, attractive, curvaceous blue-stocking in her mid-thirties, married to a lecturer at University College London, and one of the few women I've known whose attractions were enhanced rather than diminished by enormous black horn-rim specs. One couldn't help but speculate about those specs, so to speak. Did they stay on and so on and on? That morning they kept coming off and going back, such was her nervousness over Mason's criticism.

'I thought we'd been covering the subject pretty thoroughly,' Dick Spicer said in his most protective and conciliatory manner.

'We've had no leader-page reference to the subject for a month,' Mrs Howe piped up.

'Wasn't it rather up to you to make a case, Philippa, if you thought we were falling down on the space we've been allotting to the subject?' Mason asked, rebuking gently but firmly. 'I may not be either a young parent or a young editor, for that matter–as I gather the goggle-box seems to have made plain last night–but I am interested in the subject. I've even got three youngsters still being educated at so-called advanced levels.'

But none ever saw the inside of a Comprehensive, I wished somebody, including myself, might have the guts to mention.

'Nobody would have thought so, the way that Mr Bloody Bennett slanted his programme,' Logan boomed, too loyally, I thought.

'Thanks for the thought, Steve. I missed it myself, but heard about it, needless to say. One or two of you may remember that I sacked Bob Bennett as our television critic four years ago. Critics never forgive or forget. Sorry, Philippa, you were saying. . . .'

Well, he'd made his doleful point, so we went back to Comprehensives. The meeting drooled on. We escaped just before lunch. Philippa *would* now write a leader, reiterating the points she'd made in a leader two months earlier. Nobody put it as simply as that, but that was the gist of the debate.

Pat Gow was back with an unimpaired typescript. 'Judge Scranton sends his compliments and congratulates you on your capacity for total recall,' she said in pride-by-proxy.

'C'est la mode anglaise. Toujours la politesse avec la justice.'

'No kidding. I think he meant it.'

'Good for him.'

'He's also given me three possible dinner dates for you.'

'He's a lonely old bachelor. Why don't you go instead?'

'He's very sweet. And I'd go like a shot, but he specifically invited you.'

'All right, I'll check. No, you check. You know all my more respectable movements. Fix a date.'

She smiled benignly. 'One message: will you ring Mr Spurway? I'll get him.'

–24–

'As far as I can gather,' Spurway began, 'my spies–not always the most reliable of sources, but not bad third-raters–tell me the programme was devised and generally bashed through by Bob Bennett and Kit Martin. Apparently Bennett carries a bit of a sawn-off shot-gun for your Mason man. Sacked by him, I'm told. But one of my chaps–fairly high up–contends that Vaughan sowed the first poisonous seed at one of these lunching gabfests these TV characters live by. He says Bennett is Vaughan's secret hatchet man, so look out down there in Liberal Lane, buster. Did Mason see the programme by the way?'

'He says not, but I suspect he did. He couldn't have resisted it.'

'Well, I don't suppose we'll ever know, and it's not all that important except to Mason. The victim never forgets. See you next Tuesday.'

A minute later Vaughan rang. Could I dine with him the following Tuesday? Boodles. Eight o'clock.

Tuesday looked like being a fulsome day. I said 'Fine', and he could see my Lord Scranton piece in half an hour if so-minded.

This time he said 'Fine!'

–25–

Spurway still kept to the Savoy. He was enjoying himself, he confessed during the whirlwind monologue he called conversation.

He'd just completed a new ten-part series for the autumn: *The Meaning of Physical Beauty*.

'Sheer physical beauty, buster. It'll have the biggest audience any series has ever had. All the old queers in Britain will be glued to the box in the third in the series. That, believe it or not, is–I'll spell it out in 72-point caps–*An Analysis of Masculine Beauty*. It may sound like a Reith Lecture, but it's not, believe me. All we've done is to select a gallery of good-looking goons from history–engravings, paintings and so forth–starting with Adonis and coming up to date with Carnaby Street. We've added some of the better sequences from the archives on the beautiful men of the movies then pass on to the heart-throbs of the ballet world. We've even got a commentary by a young Old Vic boy who's a bit of an Adonis himself. Riveting. Not a fig leaf in sight.'

'Take a grip on yourself. What about womanly beauty?'

'We've not forgotten you, Mortimer. There's a fantastic programme on the beautiful chicks. More my line, too, I admit. Wait till you see the sequences from the Garbo classics. Even my rheumy old eyes almost wept when I saw her back in 'Tovarich'. I was a fifteen-year-old schoolboy in the Black Country again, longing for her, saving up my shekels to get to Hollywood and warm those long Scandinavian legs. But I kept to the local slag.'

'Trust Spurway to settle for bird and bush.'

'Why not? Garbo wouldn't wait!' he cried in mock-anguish.

'Who else?'

'Some of the most beautiful stars of the early screen, of course. Did you ever see a bird called Vilma Banky? God, she was ethereal. We come right bang up to date with Hepburn, Cardinale, Lisi, the lot. Not bad, eh?'

'All in the nude?'

'No, alas. But we've not forgotten the soft porn, buster. We leave that till last. An examination of our national attitude to nudity:

vaginal, genital, anal . . . that kind of thing. Must give Whitehouse and Longford a break. Fascinating.'

'What about childish beauty or is that too corny or porny for you?'

'A couple of programmes all to themselves. The beautiful demons, somebody's called 'em. And they're right. What's new with you?'

'Mine would sound like a Sunday School outing compared with yours, but, meantime, anything to add to the aged editors programme?'

He shook his head. 'Everybody forgets, except the victim, as I said. All dead duck. I never had much time for Mason, anyway. A pompous old bore. The worst kind of pious, dogmatic, bogus Liberal clot. I could never understand your fondness for the old fraud.'

'He's most of what you say, but he's also genuinely after a few major improvements around the place. And he believes in newspapers. Ultimately, he's for the old, the poor, the lost, the forgotten.'

'That lot!' Spurway scoffed, umoved. 'But he's still a third-rate bore and second-rate bully. And not much of a journalist, despite his professional medallions.'

'Perhaps you'd rather have Vaughan.'

'They're both pint-sized dictators dressed up as quart-sized radicals.'

I laughed. 'Spurway's instant character chart. You ought to market whatever gadget you use.'

'I use Spurway's all-seeing, horn-rimmed eyeballs,' he said, and, to prove the point, took out his specs to survey the menu for a suitable sweet-toothed finale for his meal. I skipped.

'How long's Vaughan been with you now?' he asked.

'About three months.'

'Give him another three months. He'll either have Mason's chair or be ready to move on. He's got to have some really big thing under his belt before thirty. He's the classic infant-prodigy type.'

'I don't think he'll get Mason's job.'

'Maybe not, but it's that or something equally sizeable. He's got to be the most brilliant under-thirty whizz-kid of his time. It's a self-inflicted wound that characters like Vaughan give themselves when they're about twenty and President of the Union.'

'And after that?'

'He'll consolidate whatever big job he lands, then look around for another he can run in double-harness–press and telly or telly and press. Then, around thirty-six, he'll start getting worried again. That's the next danger age. I know. I've been through it all.'

'Poor old Spurway,' I muttered. He grinned.

–26–

Six hours later, Vaughan was offering quite a contrast to Spurway's braggadocio. Sitting in Boodle's dining-room he seemed modest, considerate, a ready listener, a judicious contributor to any discussion that cropped up.

Inevitably we talked about the paper. Slowly I became aware that, in a subtle kind of way, he mildly denigrated every aspect we discussed. A recurrent phrase was '. . . but it could have been better' or '. . . it could have been differently presented, you'll admit, Paul.'

'You've said that four times,' I said at one point after he had damned with faint praise a previous Sunday's leader on racialism on which Mason and Paxton had laboured half Friday night.

'But it's true,' he protested. 'We're no more than half-hearted radicals. I wanted the whole of next Sunday's letter-page thrown open exclusively to the immigrants. Their point of view. Their writers. Their photographers. They've got 'em. The editor shot it down.'

'And what if we start losing readers with your ideas.'

'I don't think we would, but it's a chance we ought to take.'

He went on, steadily developing his theme throughout the meal, continuing over coffee. Sitting in the noble Adam Room cosseting a brandy, I considered the implacable profile. Despite the carefully phrased sentences and their casually deprecating theme, he was, I judged, as ruthless and ambitious as any commissar.

'Why don't you try your hand at a few leaders?' I asked.

'I made a promise to myself and to Mason when I joined the paper that I wouldn't try to do anybody else's job for six months. I've made suggestions, initiated innovations, but I've not attempted anybody's job for him. I propose to keep things that way.'

'Which job would you most fancy moving in on?'

'I'm happy where I am,' he said.

I didn't believe him.

–27–

As Spurway had prophesied, that TV programme left its mark on Mason.

During the following week, on Wednesday, I spent half an hour with him at his request. He beat about the bush for ten minutes or so, buttering up, saying how well the column was reading, how much he'd liked the Scranton piece. Then he added in a too-casual aside: 'But he was a bit long in the tooth, Paul, don't you think?'

'Maybe, but he had some very odd ideas. Odder ideas than I've had from any teen-age oddball in all my scribbling days. They made good copy.'

'That's true, but he's an ageing English eccentric. Perhaps we ought to look around and see what the younger generation is doing abroad?'

'I suppose they're swinging, too, in their own national idiom, but I doubt whether they'd made odder or better copy than Lord Scranton.'

But Mason wasn't to be deterred.

'Why not push off for a week or so, later this month, Paul, and file a series on what the younger generation in the rest of Europe's capitals are up to? See what they're doing. Find out whether Britain's young have had any impact on youngsters abroad. Fashions, attitudes, morals and so on.'

'Can't our people or stringers file their views?'

'I want somebody who knows the scene back here and can write about the comparisons he sees.'

'I suppose this is Vaughan's idea.'

'Fifty-fifty. His and mine,' he said. Somewhat sheepishly I thought.

'I think you're sacrificing your own judgment in favour of somebody else's. The best thing you could do would be to fire Vaughan and start again on your own know-how, hunches and beliefs. Currently you sound like someone on his way to the almshouse playing hopscotch with the kids en route.'

Mason laughed. 'As usual, you're overplaying your hand for the sake of what sounds like a good phrase. About a tenth of what you say has some substance, the rest is typical Mortimer hot air.'

'Not this time. Seriously: what about getting rid of Vaughan? He's doing you no good.'

'There I disagree. He's doing me a great deal of good. And the paper generally. Whatever you say, Paul, a man in his mid-fifties is apt to get out of touch unless he's got children, which, fortunately I have. He also needs to work with the young. I was in some danger on the last count. I was making the mistake too many politicians make, thinking young men are those ten years younger than myself. Tom's given me another pair of eyes.'

I let the subject drop.

'So you'll dateline my column from the continental capitals as, knapsacked, I wander hopefully o'er hill and vale?'

He nodded, smiling.

'Shouldn't you have sent your youngest and brightest star? What about Philippa? Or Vaughan himself?'

Mason smiled. 'Oddly enough, he thinks you're a better journalist than he'll ever be.'

'He specializes in king-size packets of soft soap. When shall I go?'

'What about a couple of weeks' time? I suggest you take in Paris, Berlin, Rome, Vienna, even Prague if you feel like it. Plus the northern capitals if you want to.'

Well, why not? I thought afterwards. Wasn't I as ready for a good all-round, free, swanning trip as the next man?

PART II

– 1 –

But I didn't go on my latter-day Cobbett's Tour of Swinging Europe.

That Friday morning, the third of May, during a mass political teach-in sponsored by the students of the Universities of California, Berkeley and San Francisco, Gregory van Beinum Stirling was assassinated.

Stirling, as a liberal-minded Democrat, seemed to be rescuing the party from the shambles left by Johnson, the death of Robert Kennedy and the troubles of Edward Kennedy. His long-term campaign for the year-off Presidential nomination seemed to be breathing new life into a party down on its uppers. As a man of thirty-nine he had time on his side. Plus money. Plus glamour. Plus a beautiful wife. Plus an organization. The Presidency seemed well within his grip.

As the rest of the world knows, being any kind of liberal-minded anything in the US is a dicey game to play. Yet Stirling, in common with most other saviour-type mavericks, seemed to think the Holy Man had a special interest in keeping him alive. He seemed to see himself as the prime necessity for the rehabilitation of the nation.

That kind of vision is best held by someone whose enemies are in front of him. Stirling, like Gandhi, the Kennedys and Luther King, never seemed able to learn the basic political truism that a man's major enemies are invariably behind him or at least hidden. Stirling was shot in the back five times – as you probably remember. But I'll go back to our side of the story.

– 2 –

By Friday evening a Sunday newspaper has, generally speaking, taken shape. Four or five news pages plus the leader page and possibly one feature page are all that's left to take the stories that pile in by the hour all through Saturday via Reuters, PA, UP, staff men, foreign correspondents, stringers and ever-hopeful free-lances. Hour by hour, space has to be allocated. Those remaining news pages are continuously reshaped as the worth of incoming stories is evaluated.

That job was generally shared between Mason, Vaughan, Spicer and the news editor, Bob Reid. I was scarcely ever involved, and was glad enough to leave them to it. I had enough on hand. My page was usually ready for final checking by six o'clock.

–3–

Around six o'clock that Friday I was in my room studying a final page proof of *Faces & Places*, the last I would see of it before publication–unless Mason wanted to remake the page on Saturday morning to take in a personality who'd suddenly hit the news.

Markham came in, holding a cable. He seemed pretty tense and asked whether I'd seen Spicer around. I hadn't.

'Greg Stirling's been shot. In Los Angeles,' he said.

'Killed?'

'Doesn't say. More follows.'

'That'll mean a lot of changes. I'd better hold on.'

'Probably a good idea. That's why I'm hunting Dick.'

'Have you told the editor?'

Markham nodded. 'He wants a meeting in ten minutes.'

'Have they caught any one?'

'No news yet.'

'Spicer came in. I've just heard the news, Gerry.'

Markham's secretary, Caroline Bruce, a tall, leggy young thing with dark hair, red lips and looking serious for once, came in. 'More on Stirling,' she said, handing over more cables. She couldn't resist her moment. 'He's dead.'

Markham recited as he read: 'STIRLING DEAD ARRIVAL HOSPITAL STOP STATE EMERGENCY DECLARED LOS ANGELES STOP NO ARRESTS YET STOP MESSAGE ENDS STOP MORE FOLLOWS STOP' He handed the cable back to Caroline. 'I'll see you in a minute.' She went.

'Well, I suppose he had it coming to him,' Markham said, as if musing. 'Curious, isn't it, the way there's always a bum somewhere in the States who'd rather rich boys stayed playboys or, better still, stayed dead.'

'You're jumping to conclusions, smearing a whole class,' I said. 'You don't know yet. Perhaps another rich guy shot him.'

'That's right. You're jumping to conclusions, Gerry,' Spicer said, taking my armchair. 'We don't know yet. Paul may be right. Perhaps another dedicated rich guy did the job, killing off traitors to his class. Or possibly a poverty-ridden, old-fashioned but active idealist who just didn't like rich guys. Maybe he had a point at that.'

'Could be,' Markham said, smiling obligingly. 'Anything could happen there. But I still think it'll be another case of another nut-case psycho-killer with no apparent motive.'

'From Puerto Rico or Louisiana I'll put a quid on it and I've no inside information,' Spicer said. 'Don't forget I spent six months there last year.'

'Can we ever forget?' I groaned. 'The poor man's Brogan.'

Spicer grinned, unperturbed.

'I'm more interested in the way these rich American liberals seem to have a built-in death-wish,' Markham said. 'There's a thesis to be written on the way they have to work off their consciences about their inherited millions.'

'Comes dangerously close to taking money far too seriously,' Spicer said.

Markham didn't smile; he was already too busy with his thesis.

'Well, we might as well start tearing up the whole bloody paper,' Spicer said. 'Let's go along and see what the editor's got in mind. You'd better come, too, Paul. You'll be in on it, that's for sure.'

Leaving the room, Spicer said: 'If I happened to be thirty-eight or thirty-nine or whatever he was; had fifty millions or whatever he had; had a glamour-puss wife or whatever she is; had three or four kids or whatever he had, I'd be damned if I'd dedicate myself to the welfare of that outsized land of morons and hoodlums, offspring of the dregs of Europe, Asia and Africa.'

'We're lucky,' Markham said, grinning. 'We only deal with the dregs of undersized, underworked Britain and her threadbare so-called Commonwealth.'

'Who continue to behave, I'm happy to say, in their predictably lazy and disgustingly reasonable manner', Spicer said. 'Not a single assassination this week, I'm told. Have you heard from Roth?'

'I've got a call in now. God knows when I'll get him. The lines must be absolutely clogged. I suppose he'll want an extra four thousand words.'

Bernie Roth, our man in Washington, was notoriously extravagant in his estimates of the worth of his prose. 'He can have two thousand all in,' Spicer said. 'Even as it is, with the mornings cleaning up the best of the story, we'll have to clear a couple of pages for Mister Bloody Stirling.'

'Mason will probably want more,' Markham said. 'Stirling was a great liberal, don't forget.'

We went across to the editor's room. Vaughan and Logan were already there with Bob Reid.

Mason began by saying he'd decided to clear most of *Faces & Places* for a long obit. I detected the influence of Vaughan and groaned aloud. Spicer backed me. 'The dailies will give it the full treatment tomorrow,' he claimed. '*The Times* will undoubtedly give him a full four-column send-off. And we're proposing to give three pages to a dead Yank who'll be deader still by Sunday morning. Isn't that overdoing things? Readers will be punch-drunk with Stirling. And we all know Bernie will file a book. He was a hundred per cent for Stirling. Let *Faces & Places* go as it is,' he pleaded. 'We'll need the relief and we also need to get a few pages away tonight, Stirling notwithstanding.'

'But this killing's almost as big as either of the Kennedys, every bit as big as Luther King's,' Markham said.

'Jack Kennedy was different. He was the President,' Spicer said. 'Robert Kennedy and Luther King got their come-uppance mid-week, anyway,' he added. 'They were footnotes by Sunday.'

'Even so, each of 'em had the best part of two pages,' Mason pointed out. 'I've just checked. And Stirling was every bit as big as Jack Kennedy was two years before *he* got the nomination. And this is a Friday, remember, just as Jack Kennedy's was. The Saturdays got scarcely everything then and they won't overmuch this time.'

'I'd give Stirling two pages and no more,' Spicer said stubbornly. 'You'll want a piece on the leader-page plus an editorial. He'll still be the lead on page one. World reaction and so on. If you still say you want more, I'll have to find space somewhere, somehow, of course, but that's the way I see things now.'

Mason turned to Markham, 'What are you asking Bernie for?'

'Up to two thousand words.'

'That's two-thirds of a page in itself. Fifty inches. Plus display and pictures. A page,' Spicer said.

'What about pictures?' Logan asked.

'On the way,' Spicer said. 'Here they are. Come in Neville.'

Dixon, the tall, broad-shouldered, no-nonsense picture editor, came in carrying three large folders. His noble Roman profile was set seriously for once, ousting the usual ready laughter which did much to counter continuous problems provoked by wayward agencies, missing cameramen, inflexible press dates, delayed trains, planes, despatch-riders and the rest of his world-wide picture service.

'These are the best. The Californian pictures are coming through now, on the wire.'

'They'll be no damn use to us,' Spicer said. 'The dailies will take their pick like the vultures they are.'

Dixon lugubriously agreed. He suffered the fate that attends all picture editors of Sunday newspapers: he was always being scooped by the dailies. The only pictures he could call his own were those of Saturday: weddings, The Boat Race, Trooping the Colour, the Cup Final, the Lord Mayor's Show and precious little else. He bore these tribulations bravely.

We went slowly through the pictures.

Greg Stirling had certainly been a highly photogenic subject. There was scarcely one poor picture amongst the hundreds we scanned. Deep-set eyes, strong nose and chin, and a certain intensity of expression that did nothing to hide his high and vast ambition.

'Well, he's better-looking than most of our bald-headed Tories and pot-bellied Socialists,' Spicer said, looking over Dixon's shoulders.

'I'm afraid you're right', Markham agreed dolefully. 'Politicians in any country–at least of the West–are apt to look like pierhead comics.'

'Any family shots?' Mason asked.

Dixon had plenty. The Stirlings *à deux* in their house in Carolina The Stirlings *à deux* on ski-ing holidays in Plymouth, New Hampshire. The Stirlings *en famille*, also in Carolina, with their three children, two boys, twelve and ten, and a girl of six. The Stirlings in and out of their clapboard house in Georgetown, Washington. And so on and on.

'They're certainly the beautiful people,' Spicer said at the end. 'As a family they weren't unduly shy of the camera, were they?'

'It goes with the job', Dixon said.

'Like Kennedy, he seemed to need a family image as well as the Man of Destiny touch,' Markham said.

'Well, he got his Man of Destiny pay-off,' Spicer added.

Markham took up another of the pictures. 'It's a bit ironic when one thinks of crusty old geezers like de Gaulle, Adenauer and Salazar dying in their beds at eighty and ninety, and this *Time* and *Newsweek* cover job getting his before forty.'

'He put in for it,' Spicer said, unmoved. 'Nobody asked him. Occupational hazard.'

Mason had other views. 'A great statesman in the making. A pity it always seems to have to happen this way over there.' He turned to Spicer. 'I think we really do need three pages, Dick. We don't want to underplay a story of this magnitude. The *Sunday Times* and the *Ob* will give it all they've got. I'm sorry, but that's the way things are shaping. I'm willing to let *Faces & Places* go more or less as it is, although I'd like Paul to lead with some little-known anecdote about Stirling if he can dig one out. We might get something out of Roth for that. I'll certainly want most of the leader page for Stirling.'

'Okay,' Spicer said simply, recognizing the facts of life.

Caroline came in. 'Mr Roth on the line from Washington, Mr Markham.'

Markham crossed to the telephone, asked the operator to transfer the call.

'Let's decide what we want from Bernie,' Mason said in the general hub-bub. 'Certainly a personal view. Bernie got pretty close to him in recent months. And I suppose we ought to have think-piece on where does the US go to from here? Bumping off all the men who try to lead 'em to bigger and better things.'

'They seem to breed a steady supply of these death-wish characters,' Spicer said. 'If a man will insist on setting himself up to be shot at, there's usually somebody around prepared to have a go.'

'You sound as if you think the States is just the HQ of the Mafia and damn all else,' Markham said.

'I hope it sounded like that. That's exactly what I do think and intended to imply.'

'I can't agree with you, Dick,' Mason said. 'It's a great country with a vast hope for the world.'

Spicer was unabashed. 'Facts are currently on my side,' he said equably.

'I'm not such a pessimist,' Mason said.

'Bernie on the line, David,' Markham said.

Mason crossed to the desk. The room went quiet.

'Hello Bernie. A bad day for the world. No, I'm glad you stayed put. Nothing to be gained by flying out there. And you'd be out of our time zone. Look, we're remaking the paper here and want to make our plans for an early start. Could you give us a hint of what you'll be filing?'

Roth was quite a talker, even at transatlantic rates. Mason listened. At last he said, 'Good. That more or less fits in with our plans. I quite agree. No, stay put. What we want, above all, is a really updated personal appraisal of the man. A few anecdotes would help. Paul could use material like that in *Faces & Places*. And we'll need a round-up of the US press reaction. Where's his wife – widow? No, I see that's difficult. Let it rest, then. Hold on. I'll pass you over to Gerry. He's making signs. OK. He'll take you in his own room.'

Markham left. Dixon took up his picture files under one arm, the half-dozen prints Mason had chosen in his other hand, and left with Logan. Spicer was already at Mason's high desk, flicking through the miniature make-up dummy to see which current stories were expendable.

I thought it time to go. 'How much will you want to change *Faces & Places*?' I asked Mason.

'A lot depends on Bernie. Reluctantly, I've come round to Dick's view – that we'll probably need your page more or less as it is, as light relief if you'll pardon the expression.' He smiled wearily.

Spicer looked up from his make-up problems: 'I think we'll hold pages six and seven open for our long-winded fond farewell to Stirling. Plus your own requiem, on the leader page. Plus a leader.'

Mason agreed as he invariably agreed with Spicer's technical decisions. He even smiled again, although he didn't approve of levity on momentous occasions. Men who made serious newspapers ought to act seriously. Shut away in his book-lined room, he probably saw us all as recorders of history, with himself as a kind of Warden of Our Souls, as Spicer had once said. The illusion began and ended in that room.

Meantime, he had a Livery Company dinner at the Guildhall, he said. What time would we be going?

'Probably around midnight,' Spicer said glumly, at the door.

'Not very late,' I said.

'I'll ring later,' Mason said. 'Thanks, Dick.'

He waved me to hold back. He stood by his tall make-up bench for a minute and then turned and sat down at the swivel-seat behind his desk.

'You're working too hard,' I said.

'I don't work half as hard as any of you. But then, you're ten years younger. Makes a difference.'

Fifteen years younger, I thought, but said: 'Why d'you go to all these glad-rag dinners? They must bore you to sleep, surely to God.'

'One makes the occasional useful contact,' he said, adding, as if reassuring himself. 'They're usually profitable in one way or another.'

'To you or the owners?'

'To me, basically. Keeps me in touch.'

'With what? With whom?'

'I know your views. That I only meet other fuddy-duddy Establishment figures. You may be right, but I don't think so. I'll try to ring later.'

'Depending on the number of courses and toasts, no doubt.'

'Probably,' he said. He got up to go. He looked sad, tired, overweight. 'It's about time we had another lunch, Paul.'

'Any time you say. Don't forget I'm off on my Cooks Tour next week.'

'I think we'd better postpone that for a week or so. What about next Thursday? This ghastly affair will have subsided a bit by then, although there's sure to be some kind of aftermath.'

'If I'm not going gallivanting round swinging Europe, I'd be delighted,' I said with some relief.

'We'll be able to see how America's taken it by then,' Mason said, still preoccupied.

'They'll be going through one of their great national self-flagellation sequences,' I said. 'The usual kind of thing: All of us must share the guilt for this terrible deed, but we're big enough to fight back. With suitable quotes from Lincoln and the Kennedys, of course.'

'I sometimes think I've got the sickest staff in London,' Mason said, smiling wearily. 'As well as the most pleasant and efficient, of course. God, I must go. I'm late already. Thursday, then. I suggest from now on we try to lunch on the third Thursday in every month. See how you're placed, Paul.'

I wondered how long the proposed arrangement would last. One month? Two? No more.

I moved to the door. He stood up.

'Whatever Dick says,' he said, too nonchalantly, 'I still think it might be a sound idea to write one or two unfamiliar items concerning Stirling into *Faces & Places*. Bernie always over-writes. See if you can extract one or two anecdotes from his stuff and build them into your page as the opening pars. Tell Dick we had a few words before I left and that's my view. I think it would be a pity if our main personality feature went to press without some reference to Stirling, don't you? Bernie knew him extremely well.'

'I'll tell Dick. I'll come back after supper and see if Bernie's filed anything I can use. Perhaps I'll call him.'

'Yes, do that. But don't overdo things, Paul. Dick has a point.'

I hung around for another hour or so and then wandered round to Chancery Lane to have supper at the Terrazza. After an escallop and half a bottle of hock I felt in better form for the night's work.

I got back around nine to find Spicer, Markham and Reid almost submerged by python coils of cable. They were cobbling the story as best they could out of the tens of thousands of words being filed by the newsmen of the battered but still wordy brave New World.

–4–

The assassination had come as a ghastly climax to a week of unprecedented triumph for Stirling. He seemed to have captured the student body of the West Coast as readily as he had sewn up the Ivy League colleges of the East and the mass-student-factories of the Middle West.

What had begun as a students' jamboree had turned into a political whirlwind. Not only students but hundreds of thousands of others had suddenly begun to see some of their yearning hopes and idealism reflected in all that Stirling promised. One pollster had estimated that Stirling had over seventy per cent of all United States students north of the Mason-Dixon line solidly behind him, and well over eighty per cent of those to the south. A formidable prospect for any rival.

Early days of course, and a lot could have happened to have diminished his popularity within the interim months before the Primaries, but few professional commentators had been prepared to nominate any rival to Stirling for the Democratic nomination. And who could the Republicans have put against him with any overwhelming hopes of success? Nobody, it seemed.

Against that euphoric background, Stirling had gone to the West Coast, had finished an hour's speech, followed by an hour's close questioning by students. He had then become the centre of an extraordinary demonstration. His car had been stopped so that he could be escorted from the campus by a hundred bands, groups, glee-clubs and the rest. The noise had been like Coney Island on Independence Day. Stirling, standing in an open car, plainly enjoying his triumph, had been shot five times, each shot in the back. The joyous caravanserai, passing through a complex of college buildings, had become a riot. The killer – or killers – seemed to have got clean away.

Those were the bare details. The parallels with the Kennedy assassinations were plain enough. The major difference–that Stirling was in overwhelmingly friendly territory–had made no difference. That he had been gunned down in front of the generation to whom he had begun to seem the leader they could trust, added to the horror of the day.

Hence the tens of thousands of words concerning one man's death.

–5–

Some time after ten o'clock, reading through yet another cable, Spicer said, without looking up, 'How many Yanks die every hour?

Hundreds must be. I bet two thousand unknown Americans, northerners and southerners, men and women, black and white, citizens, soldiers, sailors and pacifists have died meantime, in battle, on roads, at home. And not a word here to spare for any of 'em.'

'Isn't that what fame's all about?' Markham countered. 'I've just been talking to Bernie again. He's in tears.'

'He was always the emotional type,' Spicer said. 'He was full of world-suffering when I saw too much of him last year. What did he say between the tears?'

'The usual. Stirling had more to offer than Kennedy ever had. Less tied to brothers, friends, advisors, admirers, hangers-on. Tougher. More of a loner. More of an idealist.'

'He'll no doubt bring it all out in his piece,' Spicer said, gloomily.

'What about the widow?' I asked.

'She's been flown out there. She was at home in Carolina, it seems. Bernie says they were very close in an unusual kind of way.'

'Why unusual? Any close relationship is unusual – especially in marriage,' Spicer said.

Markham smiled. 'Apparently she never got over her bewilderment concerning his political convictions. Why he went in for all this barnstorming and wheeler-dealing in the Senate. When she married him, he wasn't even interested in politics. She's got even more money than Stirling ever had, Bernie says.'

'She sounds a very detached lady,' Spicer added. 'I'd like to meet a rich, beautiful, detached widow one of these days.'

'Doesn't a wife in that kind of set-up have to be pretty detached?' I asked. 'Anyone with Stirling's ambition and urge to power is finally only in love with himself.'

'I doubt whether Roth will echo your dyspeptic views,' Markham said, smiling. 'He's a hundred-per-cent Stirling man and fan.'

'So I've gathered.'

'Anyway, I'm calling it a day now, Dick,' Markham said wearily. 'The rest can wait till morning as far as I'm concerned. It's one o'clock. We'll have a hell of a day tomorrow.'

'OK by me, mister. I'll turn it in, too. See you at eight-thirty.'

–6–

The front pages of the dailies were, of course, smothered with the killing.

Grainy eight-column pictures by satellite of Stirling standing in his car, laughing gaily, a moment before death, were contrasted with pictures of the shambles a minute later. Meaningless pictures of Stirling being taken into a Los Angeles hospital. Stand-by pictures of Stirling at home with wife and family.

Dixon was already in when I got to the office around nine o'clock. 'I've been through all the overnight pictures. The mornings have had the best, needless to say. There's nothing exclusive and nothing new for us,' he said savagely. 'We'll have to work with leavings or what everybody else has got.'

He did, however, have an exclusive set on offer, taken by a young freelance who had been in New York the previous summer when Stirling had been speaking to an open-air political club meeting at the University of Columbia. Dixon had fixed an option on them until ten o'clock. Spicer, Markham and myself went through the pictures with Dixon. Their main virtue was to show Stirling in much the same kind of situation as that in which he'd met his death. The pictures were clear and sharp. Stirling's striking good looks and charm came out vividly.

'Who's selling?' Spicer asked.

'An LSE graduate. He was over there on a Harkness grant.'

'How much?'

'He wants a hundred.'

'Say snap. He'd have got treble for a set like this from the *Mirror* or the *People*.'

'He's a responsible citizen. He came here.'

'Good. We'll have to start making up the damn pages any minute. Where's Tim Forrest? These bloody layout people are never around when you need 'em.'

The day was as mad and frenetic as the Saturday following Kennedy's death, the day of the Churchill funeral, the Saturday of the Six-Day War. We worked as if possessed by demons, and, of course, enjoyed every minute of the teeming hours. Such days take their place among a newspaper's manifold toxic lures and legends.

–7–

Roth had plainly enjoyed writing his piece on Stirling. He said as much when I rang him to suggest extracting a couple of anecdotes from his piece for *Faces & Places*. 'Otherwise they might have been cut,' I said at the telling moment, 'which would be a pity.'

He readily agreed.

As his views of Stirling had some bearing on all that happened later, I quote his much-pruned piece as it was published.

Gregory van Beinum Stirling, known more widely as Greg Stirling, was another of those Americans who could not bear the thought that he was just plain stinking rich in a poverty-ridden world.

Stirling couldn't avoid being rich. His wealth came from both sides of his family: on one side, industrial building on a massive scale; on the other, New York real estate. And he married – for love – a woman far richer than himself.

His father was a Scot, a young and ambitious engineer from Inverness who came to the United States towards the end of the nineteenth century, began to specialize in designing roads and bridges, but soon began to see that the designer is always the loser whether the bridge stays up or falls down. If the bridge stays up he gets his fee, word gets around, he gets more commissions and more fees. But he never gets anywhere near what the builder gets.

So Stirling senior moved into contract work. By the time the United States entered the First World War he was one of the nation's largest builders of roads, bridges, harbours, factories and barracks. And because he was a first-rate admin man as well as an imaginative engineer he began to outstrip all rivals in this specialized cut-throat world.

At the age of forty-six he took time off to marry an eighteen-year-old New Yorker, one Clara van Beinum, whose people had been in New York since it was New Amsterdam, and had spent their years circumspectly and profitably – buying up odd pockets of land the way other people bought pieces of furniture.

Contrary to all the prophecies of the wiseacres, Stirling and his young bride were happy. She travelled with him as he moved around the country supervising his considerable industrial empire. Still travelling, she bore him three children: Gregory, Glen and Sophie at two-year intervals. Each also carried the van Beinum name.

Greg Stirling had a curious schooling. He was at a preparatory school in the United States until he was thirteen; he was then sent to Loretto, the famous Scottish public school until he was eighteen, commuting across the Atlantic between terms. He went first to Harvard, then moved on to MIT, the world-famous Massachusetts Institute of Technology, where he showed much of his father's skills as an engineer. He then joined a British contracting firm in India.

Something traumatic happened to Stirling in India, the result of a combination of mysticism and misery, he once said. Whatever the reason, he returned to the United States after a year – he was then twenty-three–explained to his father that he was going into politics, passed up any possibility of taking over direction of his father's vast enterprises in favour of his younger brother, Glen, also an engineer of outstanding talent and achievement, who continues to run the Stirling Construction Corporation of New York and Philadelphia.

The strangest thing about Greg Stirling's decision was that his father took it quite calmly. Stirling once told me, with filial pride, something about the interview. His father had said. 'Why not, if that's the way you feel? *Bridges* were my big thing as a young man, but if *people* are yours, go ahead. Working out an ideal is worth more than running a business, however big. You've got enough money to be your own man. Why not go to it?'

'And supposing Glen had made the same kind of decision?' I asked Stirling.

'I guess my father would have said the same thing. He said nobody owned anybody else's life. The business was his. He'd enjoyed building it up, but that didn't give him the right to make it a prison for future generations that hadn't asked for it. "Who wants a damn great business to be hung around his neck at birth?" he once said. All he asked was: Did I want the top job in whatever I wanted to do? It wasn't being top dog that was important, but it was the only place to get things done. When I told him I wanted a very top job indeed, he said OK.'

So, in 1954, Stirling began the long haul towards the Presidency. His father, who died in 1960, watched his son take his first tentative strides. His mother is still alive, 60 this year.

He was a good deal younger than the Kennedys and their coteries, and far more radical in his political thinking. He quickly began to make his voice heard, especially amongst the students. For the first five or six years of his political life – that is until the early sixties–he seemed to be ignoring anybody over twenty-one or two, and it was a deliberate policy. 'By the time I'm ready for the Big Time,' he said, 'they'll be in their thirties and on my side. But I shan't let up on their younger brothers and sisters. By then I ought to have the best part of two generations on my side. By their mid-thirties even the best of 'em will be getting away from my kind of thinking, but they may still have a nostalgic yearning for the dreams of their youth. I'll be the first politician any American in his twenties and thirties can put a name to – that'll take care of well over half the United States.'

He was well on his way – until last Friday.

One of Greg Stirling's greatest drawbacks was the way he looked the part he sought to play, a fact which inevitably aroused the antagonism and envy of rivals less fortunately endowed. He looked like a crusader, a hero, an idealist, a dreamer. He also spoke and acted like one, although, when he spoke, his grey eyes had more in common with a sailor's than a dreamers.

He was over six feet tall. With his dark skin, black hair, worn rather long for an ambitious politician, bold and resolute features he seemed more akin to the Iroquois or Cherokees than to his Scottish-Dutch forebears. His frowning gravity and fierce eloquence made him a formidable figure in debate or when angered. Yet, to his half-dozen close friends, he was a light-hearted companion, lively, unpredictable, considerate and quixotic.

Despite their wealth, his marriage to Melanie Louisa Gardner when he was twenty-one and she seventeen was a love-match in the American romantic tradition. Their devotion was complete. That his wife was also extremely rich inevitably added to the criticisms that politics, for him, was a rich man's game, that he was another grand master of the new-style paternalism. He acknowledged the criticisms, but rejected them. 'The poor always know the poor, the rich the rich. Up to the age of twenty-one – when I married – the only chicks I'd met were daughters of my parents' friends – rich folk,' he said. 'That's how I married my wife.' He aimed to change things, he said, mainly by making the poor less poor the rich a lot less rich.

His own considerable fortune was applied to several causes that interested him, notably to two New York clinics for the care of autistic and spastic children; to the Van Beinum Foundation for the study of poliomyelitis and a similar institution for the study of arthritis.

He had several unusual disadvantages to overcome in his political career; the built-in belief of the supremely confident man that people can be persuaded to sane action by sane arguments; a total unawareness of any kind of ill-health; an inclination towards arrogance when confronted, as he usually was, by intellects less clear-cut than his own. He also never understood poverty the way the poor do – by being broke.

Yet despite these disabilities – and another dozen or so could doubtless be added to the list – Greg Stirling seemed well on the way to carrying all before him. Certainly no Democratic nomination could have stood against him in 1972 primaries. To a personal magnetism comparable with that exercised so casually but effectively by John F. Kennedy he added a far more committed radicalism plus a ruthlessness in action which the Kennedys certainly never matched and which sometimes scared even his closest and most sympathetic friends.

Gregory van Beinum Stirling would have been forty next Thursday.

A good piece, I thought, reading through the uncorrected galley. Even well this side of idolatry, despite Roth's well-known hero-worship of Stirling.

Roth had also filed two other long pieces: a long analysis of the gap in radical America caused by Stirling's death and a bitter report on the proven ease whereby anyone can kill anybody else in that great country of the free-for-all.

–8–

'Bernie's turned in just what we needed,' Mason said, bringing a galley through into the newsroom. 'Have you read it?'

Spicer nodded. 'For once he doesn't read like Stirling's PRO.'

We were standing around Spicer, Reid and the chief sub, Guy Arnold, at the news desk, waiting on first page proofs from the composing-room for last-minute amendments. Two of the Stirling pages were still being made up, prompting Spicer to caustic comment on the sloth of writers, subs, comps, stone-hands and the rest.

'I'd have liked a little more bite to the piece,' Markham said. 'Stirling's arrogance was notorious.'

'Old Bernie always carried a torch for Prince Charming,' Spicer said. 'Nevertheless, it's quite a good piece, considering the time limits.'

'We'll need another year for anything like a detached view. Stirling had too much in his favour for a really objective obit. at this stage,' the editor said, enthusiasm for Roth's contribution undampened by news-room objectivity. 'After all, Stirling was a major influence. Bernie's brought out his strength.'

'And little enough about any little weaknesses,' Spicer said.

'Agreed,' Mason said, 'but at least he's indicated the way he went after the young, pointed out the only way any other worth-while politician will be able to get the voting strength of America on his side.'

'Nevertheless, one can't avoid the thought that anyone might be able to find himself a political idealist with all that lolly,' Markham said.

'On the other hand, with the same kind of lolly you might say balls to the lot of us right here and now and push off to the Caribbean,' Spicer said, looking up from a page proof.

'Would. Not might,' said Reid, taking time off from subbing to join the debate.

Later, after a beer-and-sandwich lunch in the news-room, I went down to the composing-room to see if *Faces & Places* had finally gone away. The editor and Vaughan were ahead. I caught up with them.

'D'you think we've given Stirling enough space, Paul?' Mason asked. 'Until I read Bernie's piece I hadn't realized Stirling had such roots in this country.'

'I don't think schooldays make roots,' I said.

'Mine never did,' Vaughan said.

'Mine did,' Mason said, almost brusquely. 'Perhaps we take these things more seriously in Wales.'

'But Stirling's plainly didn't. Oddly enough, I asked Bernie about that last night and wrote his comment into my page. Perhaps you haven't seen it. Stirling only went back to Scotland once–to Edinburgh University two years ago–and that was by way of building up his image as the international students' friend or the students' international friend. I forget which. And he didn't even go near Loretto. What about that for roots?'

Mason chuckled. 'Very interesting. I'm glad you got it in, but you're almost as hard on Stirling as Dick.'

'I'm not hard on him, as you term it. Neither is Dick. Stirling was a remarkable man in many ways, but there ought to be some kind of metaphysical-mechanical device which measures what rich men would have done without their shekels. I've never been able to get steamed-up over radical millionaires who manage to stay millionaires.'

'Most of the social advances in this country during the nineteenth century were the results of rich men's agitation,' Mason said. By then we were in the composing-room.

'Good work squared their consciences, guaranteed them fame, let them sleep o'nights,' I said.

'Because you've no conscience or political convictions yourself, you discount them in others,' Mason said, laughing.

'Not at all. I can see what Markham means. If I were a rich man with a gift of the gab, a yen for power and looking for a job, I might well take up the cause of the poor myself.'

'I doubt it,' Mason said. 'I sometimes wonder who's the more cynical, you or Dick.'

'Dick. He's older. And he had a more moral upbringing. He's got more excuse.'

Mason smiled thinly. 'I'm afraid age has made me less cynical,' he said plainly believing his own self-assessment.

Vaughan stayed silent.

Faces & Places had gone down to the foundry for plating. We crossed the composing-room and stood together as journalists do, looking down at the leader-page in metal. The stone-hand was locking up the forme for a final proof.

We left the leader-page and crossed to Reg and Tom, the two comps who usually made up the front page. They were working at their normal, swift, imperturbable pace: Tom on the top half of the page, Reg on the lower half. They worked quietly and merrily, always ready for a quip, despite the fact that they were against the clock for every second of their stint. A large five-column half-tone, showing Melanie Stirling, wife, and Clara Stirling, mother, arriving in Los Angeles by air, already dominated the page. Headline type was being dropped into the forme. Linotype slugs were being moved around as if the two men were playing some esoteric parlour game.

I watched them, fascinated as usual, by their expertise. One of the stone subs brought Mason a rough leader-page proof with the Roth piece as lead feature. Mason liked Spicer's heading: PORTRAIT OF A MAN WITH MORE THAN MONEY TO HIS NAME, beneath a magnificent picture by the LSE student showing Stirling squatting on his haunches on a platform, rather like an Indian brave at a peace parley, leaning forward, answering a student's question. Hundreds of students crowded against the platform.

There was little wrong with the page as far as Mason was concerned. Subject to final vetting by Spicer and Reid, the page could go away, he said.

All we had to do, then, was to wait. First for the papers off the rotaries, and then for the news now beginning to come in a rush as America moved into a new day and garnered more news of the tragedy. For the second edition we could remake two pages. For the final up to half a dozen.

That, and waiting to see what the rest of the Sunday press had made of the same basic material, was our programme for the evening and the night.

–9–

There was little need for me to stay on after the first copies of the paper were brought up from the machine-room soon after six o'clock. But I did, for even as the first edition was running smoothly into its first hundred-thousand copies, with no last-minute union demands, no broken reels, no mechanical breakdowns, the cables began to hot up to sensational purpose.

Two young men had been arrested and charged with Stirling's murder. But the backgrounds of the young men made the sensation: two Vietnam veterans, aged twenty-two and twenty-three. They had driven up to the police house of Tylor's Close, about thirty miles outside Los Angeles, left their ex-Army jeep outside, gone in and given themselves up. 'To save everybody trouble,' had been their laconic historic words.

Needless to say, I hung on. Their pictures were on the wire within the hour: two typical young American GIs in levis: crew-cut, square-jawed, heavy-limbed, one with horn specs, the other rather like a rougher, unpolished version of Stirling himself, as Dixon pointed out. They had been ready to talk, it seemed. Explicitly and unemotionally, decrying the publicity attending their arrest, but well able, it seemed, to take it in their stride.

They had served their country well. Both had been wounded. One, John Frederic Kimber, had been awarded the DCM; the other, Alex Ivan Kaminetski, also had a tough combat record. The authorities had certainly been quick off the mark with biographical data. Both had been conscripted, trained as infantry men, lived through Broken Hill and the rest of that monstrous war. Kimber seemed to have been the cool, relaxed articulate spokesman at their first interrogation, made public in that curiously US way, by the police lieutenant of small-town Tylors Close.

People like Stirling, Kimber had said, were the best–and thus the worst – anaesthetics evolved by the Establishment of the Western World. Maybe he was in politics to square his conscience – so what? For him, politics was still a game. The great American scene with its war, wounded, graft, poverty, drop-outs, drugs, squalor, slums, medical privilege still went on. It was too big for Stirling or any one man. The system had got to be busted. People like Stirling, with his patronising patrician Ivy League humbuggery dressed up as new-style radicalism, helped to perpetuate the system. Nineteenth-century paternalism brought up to date. If Stirling didn't win he could go back to his millions, Kimber said, '... but when we come back–and we didn't win anything, man–there's still the same fat old baldies yapping about integration, freedom from poverty, medicare, the Great Society and all that crap while their profits go piling up.' Stirling had never gone hungry, dirty, lousy, wounded to his bed, he went on. 'He just talked. But the time for talk's over. So we shot him just to show we mean business. And if a few other guys who got credits for marksmanship at training school and lived through sniping duties in Vietnam can pick off a politician a week, the way we picked off the VC, the changes'll come p.d.q. We'd like to name six senators a month we're gonna shoot. We shot the best of a bad bunch. You gotta start somewhere. The rest are shit. They'll be dead easy–and real dead.'

Kaminetski had let his buddy do most of the talking, smiling and nodding from time to time. Yet even he, when questioned had apparently answered with the same detached cold-bloodedness that had, it seemed, fairly chilled their interrogators.

One reply by Kimber had a certain promise of immortality about it. Why had they shot Stirling in the back? 'Why not? If you're killing, you're killing. You don't ask a guy to turn around. I wasn't told by my sergeant to tell any VC to turn right round. I got a goddam medal for shooting VCs right in the middle of the back, man.'

'Marvellous stuff,' Spicer said appreciatively. 'What a carve-up. Pity they didn't keep it till next Sunday. All this is too good to throw away in one issue. These characters will have half America on their side. No hippy draft-dodgers, but the real young veteran stuff from the wars. Boy, will this be news till Christmas.'

'Even longer, if their example gets taken up,' Markham said reflectively. 'I wouldn't care to be a fat old right-wing Senator with a bad voting record in the US this week-end.'

'Still less, a lean young senator with a good voting record, it seems,' Spicer said.

We all laughed.

'Well, back to the old drawing-board,' Spicer said. 'I thought we had a front page that would last the whole night through. What a hope! Where's that bloody make-up man?'

–10–

Yet, despite Kimber and Kaminetski, the Stirling killing was little more than a fortnight's story for us, although Mason had other ideas.

The two young killers were taken away. The cops and lawyers moved in. Pretty soon, they, too, wanted their share of the headlines. But that was mainly home-brewed US stuff and not for us.

Yet it was clear that the killing had shaken the United States more deeply than any other political assassination since Lincoln. Far more deeply than the Kennedy killings. After all, as Spicer had said, Kimber and Kaminetski weren't outcasts, drop-outs, misfits, mavericks, druggies, college queers, immigrants, commies. They were two of 'our boys', the young heroes of all America. The groundswell of sympathy on their behalf was immediate and frightening. A nation of emotional thinkers was involved with a paradoxical problem it had rarely faced before: sympathy for both killers and killed.

'These guys are going to be folk-lore heroes along with Dillinger, Jesse James and the Sundance Kid – and with a lot more in their favour,' Spicer said with his usual gift for the sick yet apt summing up.

Nevertheless, for a Sunday newspaper, even a serious liberal-minded Sunday newspaper all out for human rights and the rest, the Stirling story was little more than a two-week affair, trickling on for a month. After that Stirling was a cross-reference, a hark-back, an occasional name in current stories, mostly from Roth. The only headline personalities in any newspaper are live ones. The dead are for inside pages, anniversary echoes, biographies, memoirs, footnotes.

– II –

In any case, we were back to our own domestic turmoil with Mason trying (*a*) to behave like a masterful editor of wide experience and easy authority; (*b*) to hold the peace between Logan and Vaughan; (*c*) to prove himself still young and swinging.

A full-time job for any man. He kept to his room and when he emerged, moved around the office with what seemed his settled mien: heavy frown and would-be springing youthful step. But perhaps I'm unfair. I sometimes get that way. Occasionally, I thought, he was showing signs of wear and tear, especially during those moments in conference when Logan snapped at Vaughan.

It was a situation that couldn't last. Sooner rather than later, Mason would have to choose between the two of them, and if, as I suspected, Vaughan had been wished on him from above, the choice was inevitable: Vaughan would stay. Mason might not like the solution, but it was fixed.

I tried to suggest this to Logan one morning a week or so later when he lingered on in my room after he had dropped in a thought for a paragraph in *Faces & Places*. Vaughan had been about to leave the room as Logan came in. Logan had stood ostentatiously aside. Vaughan left. I sent Pat Gow, my secretary, for some coffee.

'Why do you make your animosity towards Vaughan so very obvious?' I asked.

'Because my animosity towards the little Welsh wizard is so very obvious, a dominating factor in my life and hard times.'

'But why? He does you no harm. He does nobody any harm. You go out of your way to needle him.'

'Old-fashioned chemistry, that's all. We'll never work together.'

'It's prejudice and jealousy on your part, Steve. You think he'd pip you to the editorship if the job fell open tomorrow. I think he was wished on Mason. Against the odds, he's become the editor's white-haired boy. You hate his guts for that alone.'

'That about sums it up. And you think I'm a fool?'

'I think Vaughan's probably got a lot of backing upstairs. If you bring things to a head and make things impossible around the place, I think Mason will have to come down finally on the side of Vaughan—even apart from the fact that he's clearly becoming increasingly dependent on him.'

'Maybe I'll have other fish to fry by then.'

'I hope so. Sometimes, these days, you seem to carry on like a bone-headed Japanese war lord with *hara-kiri* on his mind.'

He laughed. 'Not bad. Anyway, I brought this little item in. Might interest you. Curious story about Arab brides of ten being brought into Malta.'

'Would you put it in under Faces or Places?'

'Dunno. I brought it in because I sometimes think your page should be retitled Curiosa and Erotica. I see this piece under both heads.'

I thanked him and he left.

—12—

For the next couple of weeks Logan seemed less anxious to needle Vaughan or to take umbrage over features that had plainly been previously discussed and set up between the editor and Vaughan. He almost seemed reconciled to the secret bilateral agreements made over his head, all our heads. The rest of us were all relieved. Unrelenting needling matches soon became a bore in any office.

I hoped Logan had seen some kind of sense.

–13–

I continued through the brief Spring into the early Summer, my days and nights divided into three parts. (Perhaps the choice of word is Freudian.) The paper had one part; Helen another; Vicky the third.

It was curious tripartite existence, but it seemed to work–for me. Helen still occasionally murmured about the chances of taking up our married life again; Vicky still occasionally made noises about moving in; Mason still made occasional noises about pushing me off to Europe.

Somehow, like a well-trained juggler, I managed to keep all three propositions suspended and mobile in mid-air; sometimes, in common with even the best jugglers, I doubtless showed signs of strain.

The postponement of the European trip had been due initially to the Stirling story and its aftermath, which had certainly upset Mason's time-table. Then he seemed keen to keep the Stirling story on the boil. He had become strangely preoccupied with the whole traumatic tale as if unable to accept the fact that the American nation could so readily absorb so terrible a crime as it had absorbed other equally horrific murders in its violent history. He wore away at Roth for further elucidation, and Roth, equally fixated, readily responded.

The rest of the paper – at least the opinion side–gradually became more and more the province of Vaughan, and, in an imperceptible but yet quite tangible way, I began to see the heart of the paper slipping into his hands.

For me it was amusing to see how Vaughan, as he began to get a real grip on the leader page, seemed to become far less concerned with youth and all its joys and problems, although he was always prepared to call Youth to his aid to prove a point. Had this been part of his technique for undermining Mason's self-confidence? I wondered as I waited for Vaughan, rather than Mason, to remind me once again to pack my airweight travel-bag for that postponed European roundelay.

But no reminder came, for, after an editorial meeting called suddenly mid-week in mid-July to discuss future features on pollution and environment, I moved into events that for several weeks took me outside the doings of the swinging youth of Europe.

PART III

– I –

After the meeting Pat Gow gave me her usual list of reminders and messages, adding, 'The Ann Toynbee woman said would you call her back before one if you can. She's flying back to New York today?'

'Never heard of her. Who is she?'

'Say's she's an English woman living in New York and has a follow-up to the Stirling story she thought might interest you.'

'She didn't do it by any chance? "I was a gun-toting Kimber-Kaminetski moll and all that"?'

'She didn't say so.'

'Where's she staying?'

'The Westbury. Shall I get her?'

I nodded and sat down to consider the other five items on Pat Gow's list. I tried to recall whether I'd ever met any Ann Toynbee. In common with any other newspaper we had our full quota of nuts ringing to say they had the world's hottest story in their care: did we want to buy it?

Pat Gow broke into the reverie to say she had Miss Toynbee on the line.

Even in that first hearing the voice seemed unusually melodious and assured: an English voice slowed down and faintly tinged with a soft American intonation. She said: 'It's kind of you to call me back, Mr Mortimer. You must get a lot of zany calls to waste your time. I hope I shan't be doing the same.'

She was reading my thoughts too well.

'My secretary tells me you think you can add a few footnotes to the Stirling Story.'

She chuckled, although gurgled might be a better word. 'I like that word footnotes,' she said. 'Nothing like putting the customer at ease straightaway. But I've an odd and obstinate belief that my follow-up is more than footnotes. I know it's a favourite self-delusion, but there it is.'

'Could you give me some kind of outline? Or would you rather call in here and explain more fully?'

I knew the voice had got me. I wasn't usually as accommodating to the world's would-be storytellers.

'I could, but it'd take an awful lot of time. Even an outline as you call it. Shall I start?'

'By the way, how did you get my name?'

'I used to meet your man Bernard Roth in Washington. In and around the Stirling circus. Sometimes even at Stirling dinner parties.'

'And he gave you my name? It seems unlikely.'

'You sound rightly suspicious. OK, he didn't exactly give it. I gathered it. I also gathered you're a kind of features editor. So, I thought, Mr Mortimer's the man for me.'

I was still fairly cagey. All anybody needs to start a con game is somebody's name and a modicum of blarney. She had both. But the voice still held me. And her take-it-or-leave-it attitude was also fairly convincing. Those with a phoney story to tell and sell are inclined to be more insistent and intense.

'Features editor is way off,' I said. 'I run a column. I've now faulted you twice, but OK, press on.'

'He also said you were a man to be trusted.'

Not a bad backhand return I thought.

'Thanks for passing on the testimonial. Why not start?'

'If I get too boring you can ring off,' she said easily. 'Otherwise I'll carry on until I hear the click. Fair?'

'Fair enough.'

'In any case, I'm in quite as much of a hurry as you are, Mr Mortimer. I'm flying back to New York tonight.'

'Right, I'm waiting.'

Her opening sentence was to the point but unexpected. 'You probably knew that Greg Stirling liked women,' she said as if starting on one of those Conrad-type *Victory* sagas.

'Word got around.'

'Well, I was one of 'em. Possibly the last, although one never knew.' She chuckled. 'He had a great talent for making you think you were the first, the last, the best, the only one. There were possibly others around with similar ideas of their own uniqueness in his life.'

'You don't sound very bitter.'

Despite the banter. I was surprised to hear myself answering her seriously.

'One couldn't be bitter about Greg. He was one of nature's charmers as well as womanizers. He couldn't help making women the way Boeing can't help making aeroplanes. And I admired the technique.'

'Scarcely the picture the world had of him.'

'The world always sees what it wants to see. Anyone who sets up as a leader and isn't a downright fraud can get away with it. Isn't that what you think, too, Mr Mortimer?'

I had a fairly confident feeling that she was enjoying her cat-and-mouse game. I was amused but not all that.

'Am I to take it that you'd be prepared to tell something of your friendship with Stirling?'

'I'd want to do rather more than that.'

'Such as?'

'Well, he was a many-sided man, but obviously our friendship is the starting-point of my story, because that's the way it was. That isn't unreasonable is it?'

'Not from your viewpoint. It might be from another's.'

'Such as yours, you mean?'

'I don't know. We haven't come to that yet. But if we did, I take it you wouldn't have any qualms?'

'I love that word qualms. I've never made it yet in Scrabble. No, I don't think I'd have any qualms.'

'What about Mrs Stirling?'

'She knew. All his friends knew. Your Bernie Roth knew, probably better and more than most. Greg was never discreet – at least not in private. No, I think I'd have to leave the qualm side to you. So what about your qualms, Mr Mortimer?'

'It's early days yet, Miss Toynbee.'

As she laughed, I made a decision. Or the voice made the decision for me. If she'd been one of Stirling's popsies she was scarcely likely to be an eyesore. 'Actually, I've got qualms aplenty already. What are you doing for lunch?'

'I was planning to have a sandwich here and then go and buy a couple of dresses at Fenwicks and Jaeger. Then I'll be going out to Heathrow. My plane goes at six.'

'That doesn't leave a newspaper much time for decision-making.'

'I wouldn't expect any decision to be made in any great hurry. If you make one later your newspaper would fly me back, wouldn't it? And forth, of course. Newspapers are very lavish about travel, aren't they, Mr Mortimer?'

I was amused, puzzled and slightly irritated by the way she popped in that 'Mr Mortimer', making me sound like a cross between a family solicitor and a prep school headmaster.

'Well, as I suggested, could you lunch with me today?'

'I'd like that. But we'd have to be fairly speedy. I don't actually need those dresses but I'm determined to get 'em.'

'Meet me at a place called the Etoile in Charlotte Street in twenty minutes. If I can't get a table I'll ring you back in five. Otherwise the Etoile at one. D'you know London?'

She chuckled again. 'I was born and bred in Highgate Village, spent far too much money in Alec Tiranti's shop in Charlotte Street –and still think the Etoile's one of the nicest restaurants in London.'

'You're too clever by half.'

'That's what Greg used to say.'

She was insufferable. Part of the trouble was that I wanted her to go on talking. But I was resolute and said, 'Till then,' and rang off.

Pat Gow, quick off the mark as usual, was already through to the Etoile on the other telephone. Fortunately, they'd just had a cancellation. With a cool customer like Miss Toynbee, I decided, I needed all the appraisal I could get.

I left straight away and was in my seat by ten-to-one.

–2–

I knew who she was the moment she came in: just above middle height, corn-coloured hair, small regular features, an easy smile for the head waiter. I watched carefully as she was shown to my table. Her legs were very shapely.

I put her in the corner chair. She was wearing a fawn linen dress, which well became her hair. She didn't look a love-lorn creature, recently bereaved, as she smiled and said: 'This was the way I'd hoped things would turn out. So much better than roughing each other up over a couple of telephones, don't you think?'

I agreed.

She said she'd like a dry sherry. I ordered a Martini.

We chose our meal plus a bottle of Ürziger. After a few generalities about her trip, England's now quite reasonable summers and so on, I opened up, asking if she'd mind if I started by asking a few questions?

'But of course not.'

'Good. Then I'll begin. First, I gather you're English.'

'Correct.'

'Born and bred in Highgate, as you said.'

She took up the tale of her own accord. 'Educated North London Collegiate School; then the AA in Bedford Square–that's the Architectural Association in case you didn't know.' I nodded. 'Then a two-year fellowship at MIT . . .'

'. . . Massachusetts Institute of Technology in case I didn't know.'

'Fine. I can see I can cut the academic corners. After that I went first to Caracas for a year to study mass-housing, which had begun to be my speciality. Then I joined the *Architectural Forum* as a special writer. Now I free-lance, but I'm retained by the *Forum* for special features.'

'You've never practised?'

She shook her head. 'I'm more interested in theories of architecture than practice. In any case, I think architecture's a terrible profession these days. A lot of blind men working up a lot of blind alleys. I'd stop architecture for ten years and put every architect into labour forces on site.'

'A commissar at heart.'

'Only about architects,' she said in a cool matter-of-fact way.

All the same, I had a feeling she would do just that, given the powers.

'You seem to have crowded in a lot of experience in your young life. How old are you?' I asked.

'Twenty-six. How old are you?'

Men aren't usually faced with that riposte. 'Hitting forty,' I said grudgingly.

'Greg's age, in fact,' she said, as if musing.

'More or less,' I said.

I considered her still more watchfully, but repeated my query: 'Aren't you rather young to have crowded in all this experience?'

'That's not the half of it,' she said easily. 'Don't you think one's got to pile in experience as fast and deep as possible and then sit back around thirty and see if the experience points anywhere in particular?'

'I was never as rational as that about any part of my life. Was your meeting with Stirling part of your passion for experience?'

'In a way. I went to interview him for the *Forum*. I wanted to know where he stood on my subject – mass-housing, as I said – which gets tougher and more important in the States every year. I love these potted shrimps. They're apt to come too big and tasteless in the States – like so many other things in the food line over there. The butter here also makes such a difference, don't you think?'

She had this curious characteristic of talking seriously for stretches at a time and then changing pace and direction with one of those half-schoolgirl, half-gamine asides. But there was nothing arch about her. I was watching for a first false move. So far she seemed genuine enough. But it was certainly turning out to be one of the oddest lunches I'd had in a long time.

'Where did you first meet Stirling?'

'At his New York headquarters. He had a fairly scruffy joint just off the Battery. He liked it down there. So did I. Then he asked me to see him again in Washington. Which I did. A week later.'

'And what kind of story would you want to tell about him?'

'My kind of story.'

She'd finished the first course and sat back considering me.

'Which would be?' I asked slowly and deliberately.

'How I met him, what we talked about, what his views were on some subjects that didn't get overmuch hearing in the Senate . . .'

I interrupted, 'Such as?'

'Oh, mass-housing, multi-racial communities, medicare, the whole process of imposed benefits. Like most liberals, Greg was more than a bit of a fascist at heart. If people don't know what's good for 'em, they've got to be given it and learn later. That kind of thing.'

'D'you think those ideas would have a wide appeal in a Sunday newspaper?'

'If they don't, you ought to move to another newspaper,' she said simply.

The wine waiter came to the table and poured the Moselle. 'I like this,' she said, sipping. 'Delicious! But actually there's a lot else I've put down which would probably meet your wider-angle appeal.'

To my surprise she considered me steadily and then winked, fleetingly but unmistakably.

'Such as?'

'Personal freedom, love, lust, sensuality, the permissive society, the place of pill-armed women in a man-made world. All that kind of thing. Is that the kind of thing you had in mind?' she asked slyly.

'It's the kind of thing that's apt to interest a wider public.'

'I see their point,' she said, smiling.

'Do they play a sizeable part in your memoirs?'

'I guess so. And why not? It's more interesting, isn't it? My housing stuff can be a bit of a bore to the layman. It bores me stiff sometimes. Too many statistics, diagrams, graphs and the rest of the digital, tabulated world I live in.'

'But would you be prepared to put down in black-and-white an account of Stirling's love-life and so forth?'

'Why not? As far as it concerned me, that is. It belongs to me, doesn't it? I've written a hell of a lot of it already. I took notes and sometimes I taped him good and proper.'

'How? Secretly?'

'Good God, no. He'd come to my New York apartment–I'm lucky, I've got two marvellous rooms overlooking the East River on Fifty-Fourth–and I'd say, 'Talk, Stirling, talk. Let's see if your notions today will stand a post-mortem tomorrow. It was a fine way of keeping him from a lot of the bull, pomposity and cant the politicos dish up as their daily fare. I did my little best to wash some of the political hogwash off dear Greg.'

'It still didn't save him from the wrath of youth.'

'Well, he knew it was a dangerous game he was playing, but he didn't think he'd buy it from the generation he went after. It was all sad, strange, awful and ironical. Funny, in a terrible kind of way.'

'How long was he your lover?'

'You make it sound all very formal and Flaubertian, Mr Mortimer. About two years, I guess. And he wasn't my lover–quotes–as you term him. That sounds a kind of trad set-up with me as mistress and all that. The whole thing was far more casual. Actually he was one of my lovers, as you term them. And I was one of his. He didn't go for all this one-man-one-woman stuff. Neither do I. He even said so–in private.'

'I certainly never read anything along those lines in his speeches.'

She laughed. 'I'll bet. I used to throw that at him sometimes. And of course that's the whole ghastly part of politics, the way a man has to lie about his own life, his real life, the ideas he lives by and really believes in. Lies and more lies–even if only by omission. Lies about living, loving, liking, even lusting. Lies about basic major ideas. Hypocrisy's a way of life for a politician. They're all in it together. Nobody blew the gaff on Greg's side-kicks, but quite a lot of people knew.'

'Was Stirling such a hypocrite, then?'

She laughed. 'Of course he was. How else can you be a senator? He said so himself. In private again, of course. He called it part of the bargain any politician strikes with the devil to get nearer heaven on earth.'

'Did his dissembling upset him?'

'In a way. Like any other nicely brought up millionaire-from-birth, he was a tremendous idealist and puritan at heart. But like most puritans he was also a bit of a sensualist. So his hypocrisy was inevitable. No man's pure gold all through, is he? I was lucky to get the off-duty guy. I still think America would have been very lucky to get the politico.'

'He couldn't have asked for a better epitaph.'

'I wonder. All the wheeler-dealing worried him. He wanted to be all one big piece of integrity.'

The waiter brough the *poussins* to the table. 'Golly, that looks marvellous!' she said. The waiter smiled to hear her greedy enthusiasm. Her eyes were lively with anticipation. I could see any man's point in wanting to have her around. As the waiter mixed our salads, I said: 'What form is your record in, Miss Toynbee?'

'Notes, tapes, cuttings, letters, diaries, scribbles, the lot. But, physically, in a couple of monster box files, one of which I've got with me and would be glad to have you take off my hands.'

We began to eat. 'And you'd be absolutely willing to publish these records under your own name so soon after his death?'

'Why not? It would give another view of the man, a far nicer and more human view of him than all this high-flown bogus guff I've been reading about him for the past two months.'

'What about the money?'

'I hope it's a lot,' she said gaily, without hedging.

'It could be. Are you doing it for money?'

'Well, it comes into it, of course. I've lots of things I want to do that need money. Although I believe I was Greg's most recent sidekick, he left me none. Why should he, anyway? *Of course* I'd like the money. But I'd also like the fame, notoriety, infamy, call it what you like.'

'It will be real limelight stuff. You'd have to face that.'

'I don't see it that way. For someone who's a bit of an exhibitionist –and who isn't?–it'd be rather fun to be pointed out for the rest of her life–or at least a couple of years–as a really notorious woman.'

'You'd like that?'

'Apart from a few nuns, most women would.'

'You'd certainly get it.'

'Goody,' she said, severing wing from breast.

'Why does the notoriety angle have such an appeal?'

'Basically, I don't think women have half as much fear of what the world thinks about them as men. For one thing, I don't think they're anywhere near as concerned with concepts of morality and respectability. If a girl's the mistress or part-time mistress of a famous man she doesn't mind if the world knows it. All this secrecy thing is something cooked up by men. They're usually married, frightened of their wives, scared of blackmail, fearful of their public image or something.'

'The public can be very censorious. Even today.'

'Especially in the States,' she added.

'You've considered all that?'

She smiled and nodded. 'I'll wear it,' she said simply.

'What about the widow?'

'She'd be your problem, wouldn't she?'

'It could be quite a problem. At first sight I'd say it could be insurmountable.'

'I can see that. It's occurred to me, too, in more depressing moments.'

'She'd can the whole thing.'

'She'll certainly do her damnedest. It's part of the hazard.'

'Did Stirling share your carefree views on public knowledge of his affairs?'

She laughed. 'You're kidding, Mr Mortimer. Of course he didn't. He was indiscreet, but he wasn't idiotic. I told him more than once, philanderers shouldn't go in for public lives. And vice versa, of course. And he knew I wasn't the kind to go on for ever being a secret little chick on his afternoons off.'

'Did you want to break up his marriage, then?'

'Good God, no. I wouldn't have married Greg in a thousand years. Anyway, his own set-up wasn't what I'd call a marriage, but it suited him. It certainly wouldn't have suited me. A travesty. So why try to emulate it or break it up? Anyway, I don't want to marry yet at all. And Greg would have been living hell as a husband anyway. Any top-line politician would be to anyone who wants a private life. No, it was just that I didn't see why it had to go on being such a hole-in-the-corner affair. I had nothing to hide. Why should he? I used to say. But at the same time I recognised the facts of political life and knew he'd have to hide it.'

'Wasn't somebody likely to opt out of the great conspiracy of silence and shop him?'

'I always thought so; he thought not. But for me it was more than that. I think equality of the sexes might just as well start in the bedroom as anywhere else. No wonder this Women's Lib movement's going like a prairie fire.'

'But Stirling didn't agree with your notions?'

'Well, it was something new for him. He said he'd never had quite such a detached dame around the place.'

'Would you say you were promiscuous, Miss Toynbee?'

'You sound like a doctor in a downtown clinic. Would you say you were promiscuous, Mr Mortimer? Or are?'

I laughed. 'I'd say I was—at your age, for instance—but later became more, well . . . selective's a good word.'

She laughed. 'No, I don't think I'm particularly promiscuous, but I *am* interested in men. And I'm curious. That's apt to lead to bed. Aren't you still curious about women?'

I smiled. 'Very, but, as I said, I do rather concentrate my interest these days, so to speak.'

She rested her left hand gently on my right wrist and smiled. 'Selective; Concentrate. Good man-made words. But not bad in their context. I'll remember them.'

I was beginning to find her an extremely disconcerting guest. She seemed as worldly-wise as a sophisticate of forty with the spontaneity and gaiety of a lively-minded schoolgirl. It wasn't a feminine combination I was accustomed to. I thought perhaps I'd move on to more technical enquiries.

'How much of your story's done?'

'About half, I'd say. Something well over a hundred thousand words, anyway.'

'That's a fairly lengthy narrative.'

'I had a lot to say. And Greg was never lost for words. I'd say it would tot up to a quarter-of-a-million words before it's finished. Perhaps more. I'd want to cut it by at least half. And you'd want to cut it by half again. Some's too personal and a lot's too boring. All diarists are compulsively egomaniacal. But it'll be no struggle to trim. I'm a professional writer, don't forget; a pro with a blue pencil as well as a typewriter. But it's always better if somebody else does the all-too-necessary cutting.'

She dabbed her lips with her napkin. 'I love this poussin, but I suspect it's no respecter of lipstick.'

'You look fine. How soon could you let me see what you've done?'

'Drop me off at the Westbury and I'll give it to you.'

'And then what?'

'Depends if you like it or not, doesn't it?'

'And if I don't?'

"I'll try some other paper.'

'Such as?'

'The *Sunday Times*, the *Observer*, the *Sunday Telegraph*.'

'In that order?'

'I don't know. I'm a bit out of touch, I may hand it over to an agent.'

'And if we like it?'

'I suggest you bring me back in a month's time. By that time I'll have most of the rest done.'

'You seem very sure of things.'

'I told you. I'm a professional. I believe I can complete in six weeks.'

'Has it occurred to you that there might be many kinds of pressure brought to bear on you not to publish? Some very powerful pressures – apart from the widow?'

'Has it occurred to you, Mr Mortimer, there's always somebody who *will* publish? He's the man I'm after. I'd like to think it was your outfit, because I like the paper you print, and now I like you. But, failing both, why shouldn't I try somebody else? It's a good story. Can you recall any other book by the spare-time mistress of a world-famous contemporary politician?'

I agreed I couldn't, especially the spare-time angle.

'Who or what would head your list of the powerful influences who'd try to stop publication?' she asked. 'I've got my own list. Let's compare.'

'First, the widow and the widow's legal advisors. Then the Stirling family advisors. Then the Democratic Party bosses. Then the State Department. Then the US Ambassador here. Then the PM. Then the British Ambassador in Washington. This kind of story in a London newspaper wouldn't help Anglo-American relations.'

'They might,' she said reflectively. 'The younger generation might get a different idea about politicians.'

'You mean if Kimber and Kaminetski had known about his love-life he might be alive now?'

'He might', she said gently, even sadly. 'But I doubt it. They might have done for me, too.'

Then she got back to my list: 'That's quite an obstacle race you've set up. I was a bit weak on the London end. I see your point. But I'd got all the rest. What would any of 'em do if I said I'd sell it to *Izvestia* or *Pravda* and take my roubles in caviar and Russian sables or something?'

'The Russians would probably take it.'

'Then it could come back to Europe by way of Italy – just like Doctor Zhivago.'

'It wouldn't have to. There's always a French, German or Italian outfit that would publish even a rehash.'

She smiled. 'That's better,' she said in a voice so matter-of-fact that it was no good telling myself that I was talking to a pretty but dotty architect-turned-mistress-turned-author. Her vitality, vivacity and general sanity flouted all such fantasies.

Over coffee, I said: 'Were you in love with Stirling?'

'In a way.'

'Desperately?'

'Desperation seems to imply some kind of terrible intensity, an emotional hang-up or blood-bath. It was none of those. I'm not a very desperate sort of person. I loved Greg, and, to an extent, I suppose he loved me. But, no doubt, as the bishop said, there's different kinds of love. I think he loved his wife – or had. He certainly loved his children in his own odd way. He'd probably loved a couple of hundred women in different ways during the past fifteen years. Some carnally, others emotionally, some even intellectually. Above all he loved himself. Any politician's middle name is Narcissus.' She smiled. 'Being Greg, he tried very hard to combine his carnal and intellectual pleasures. Conservation of time and energy. You could call me a typical member of the Stirling circus.'

'I doubt that. The youngest, prettiest and last.'

'Any woman would like to think so. I'll settle for having been the last in a long line.'

She spoke with such detachment that most of my ideas were taking quite a beating. 'What are your feelings for him now?'

'Pleasurable recollection.'

'And you can reconcile that with what you propose to do?'

'But, of course' she said, as if I were an agreeable but pig-headed child. 'Greg's dead. We leave our bodies, our eyeballs and the rest of our bodily impedimenta to the incinerator, the earth or the hospitals. Why not our true stories? If I were to publish a book about how good Greg was with orphans, epileptics, spastics and the rest – which he was – everyone would say how marvellous and how boring. If I write about how good he was with women, a lot of people will hold up their hands in horror – even if riveted. It's all very odd and I'd like to see some of it change or help to change it.'

'And everyone will want to read what you have to say.'

'I hope so.'

– 3 –

Afterwards, out in the sunshine, we began to walk slowly towards Oxford Street. I hailed a taxi, gave the driver directions.

We went up to her room in the Westbury. Her two bags were already packed. She picked up a box-file and handed it to me. 'Take care, but I've got two carbons so it's not the end of the world if you lose it or burn it, although it would be impossible to replace some of the clips and cuttings. My New York address is on the inside lid.'

'And you leave it with me without reservations. Just like this.'

'Just like this.'

'Why?'

'In a way I knew you before I met you,' she said. 'I heard Bernie Roth say once you're one of the few men in the world of words he'd trust with his own words whether in a confession or an interview.'

'He was always one for emotive phrases.'

'He also went on to say he would never trust you with a woman. "An authentic lone wolf, *rara avis* indeed", was his actual phrase.'

'As I said, he likes high-flown phrases. Where did you hear him use it?'

'At one of the Stirling dinner parties when talk turned to the subject of journalists–as it often did.'

'And to the subject of women?'

'Less frequently, Mr Mortimer,' she said, smiling. 'You slip in these sly touches, I notice.'

'And Roth had reservations about my dealings with women?'

'Roth always has to have a reservation about other men.'

'But not about Stirling?'

'That's true. He hero-worshipped Greg to a preposterous, even, to my mind, an unhealthy degree.'

'And you went to parties at Stirling's home?'

'Like a lot of ladies' men, Greg seemed to enjoy flaunting his women in his own home,' she said coolly. 'Less so in public. I used to tax him with it.'

'What did Melanie Stirling have to say about the flaunting in the home?'

'I think she was used to it. He'd been doing it discreetly over a long time. Presumably, she loved him for what he was rather than for what he ought to have been. I never knew. She always put on such a marvellous front, one never really knew the truth about her. At least I never did. And Greg kept pretty mum about his relationship with her, and I never pressed him.'

'So it's thanks to Roth I get this?' I said, taking the file and moving to the door.

'He'd be appalled at what's in there and what his double-edged character-sketch has led to, but there it is. He never really approved of me, anyway. He preferred Greg's more docile chicks. But there it is, as I said: all yours–until you shoot it down.'

Half the time I still didn't know whether she was serious or enjoying a huge secret joke at my expense, but I took the file.

'What's your opinion of Roth?' I asked, moving towards the door.

'I don't like him much. Not at all, really.'

'Because he didn't approve of you?'

'No. Just don't like him. Few women do. He's too heavy-handed and too full of self-pity. And he's afraid of pretty women. And therefore dislikes 'em. But his instincts about men are almost infallible. He's probably eighty-five per cent right about you, I'd say.'

'Not a bad score in a murky light.'

She smiled. 'And he spotted Greg's potential ten years ago. That's when his big hero-worship thing began. I think Greg was everything Roth longed to have been. I may be wrong, but I don't think so.'

'I'd say you were probably right. And now–if I like what I read and we decide to publish, I'll get in touch with you. Otherwise you'll have to let me know whether I'm to send it back or keep it here for you to pick up one day.'

'You may not like all you read, but I think you'll read on. I suppose that's something, isn't it?'

'In my trade it's the main thing.'

'If you do like it, what will you do with it?'

'We'd probably want to serialize it in four or five instalments. But, frankly, I don't think we'll get away with it, if it's all you say. But if we do–by some impossible chance–what about the book rights?'

'I'll be guided by you.'

'The first unashamedly feminine remark you've made today.'

'I'm unashamedly feminine all the time, Mr Mortimer. You just think about it. I'm one of the few women you've ever met who never wanted to be a man. Even, for five minutes. Now I've got to get those dresses.' She laughed as she opened the door.

–4–

I went down by the lift and out into Bond Street and walked slowly towards Piccadilly.

Any number of young women held these libertarian ideas nowadays, I told myself, but I wondered how many lived as fully by them as Miss Toynbee.

In Piccadilly I got a taxi back to Fleet Street. I was tempted to open the box-file and begin reading straight away but forebore.

–5–

Wednesday was usually a fairly relaxed day, free from the higher blood-pressures. I had no great backlog of work to get through. I decided to leave early and start on the Toynbee narrative at length and at leisure.

To that end I corrected typescripts of a couple of stories I might or might not use in *Faces & Places*, answered a couple of letters and cabled Roth: PRAY CONFIDE CONFIDENTIALLY ALL KNOWN ROTH RE TOYNBEE/STIRLING–MORTIMER.

–6–

Ann Toynbee's story, which I began to read that evening, sitting alone in my flat, was a miscellaneous document of great comprehensiveness and complexity: part-report, part-narrative, part-enquiry and part-diary with reflections, confessions, digressions, observations thrown in as the mood had taken her. Yet I could have read five times as much without boredom.

–7–

Her story began in the best Defoe tradition with a bare opening statement under the simple title: A FRIENDSHIP:

> My name is Ann Forester Toynbee. I am an architectural journalist, aged twenty-six. I was trained in London and in the USA as an architectural designer but turned to architectural enquiry as more suited to my talents and interests. I have worked in this manner in Bolivia, California, Puerto Rico and New York.
>
> I first met Gregory van Beinum Stirling in Washington two years ago. He was a likely runner for Democratic nomination in the Primaries for the Presidential Election three years ahead. As he was the son of an internationally known contractor and had himself been trained as an engineer, my editors thought it would be interesting to have his views on mass-housing, urban development, private and/or public ownership of land, roads, airports, conservation, pollution and other matters relevant to our present environmental-architectural condition.
>
> I was deputed to interview him.

The narrative then continued with clips from the three long interviews which the *Architectural Forum* had published. She had plainly conducted a sustained interrogation which wouldn't have disgraced a Spanish inquisitor or a tough prosecution counsel.

The interviews were very long and recorded Stirling's views in a question-and-answer form. The questions–or was it the questioner?–had plainly intrigued him, for he had followed up the published interviews with long personal letters to his interrogator, elaborating and occasionally justifying his expressed opinions. He had also seen, I suspect, that if a sympathetic portrait emerged from these specialized interviews, he would have made a useful mark with a number of highly technical – and normally sceptical – members of the community.

The interviews had provoked a tremendous correspondence. Copies of everything were included.

Altogether it was a rare example of a thorough-going documentation of the beginnings of an intellectual friendship.

Then somewhere around page eighty, the first signs of a change in the relationship appeared.

This episode took its place in the narrative in that matter-of-fact manner I had come to recognise as Ann Toynbee's line. Following an exchange concerning Stirling's reactions to the town-planning theories of the contemporary Greek architect and town-planner, Constantinos Doxiadis in his book, *Architecture in Transition* (which Ann Toynbee had suggested he should read), she had been invited to dine chez Stirling in Washington.

Her entry, in the week following the party:

> I've become increasingly curious about other aspects of Greg Stirling's life. Rumour says he's a fairly consistent womanizer. It's always difficult separating this kind of rumour from fact, especially as there's a conspiracy amongst men not to blow the gaff too often on this side of other men's lives. As I've always been a greater believer in the basic truth of all rumours I'm interested. I noticed last week at dinner how he was most attentive, even gallant towards his wife, Melanie. But that probably wasn't too difficult. She's handsome, marvellously bronze-haired, late thirties, I guess. Fine eyes, good features, but a little loth to smile. Extremely self-possessed. Velvety-smooth. A very cool cookie indeed, I'd say. One thing I did like about her, she didn't play up to her husband as a man of destiny. She had her share of what Roth calls grave charm. They've been married sixteen years, I gather. I should have thought a little more gaiety and somewhat less gravitas in a wife might have suited GS better, but who knows? She's certainly a top-grade hostess: good, but not ostentatious. Good food and well-served. Very civil staff and no sign of fuss or panic. A perfect First Lady in the making, but somehow I don't think her heart's in it. She's a very odd bird indeed. I'm curious about her, but more curious still about her husband.

Ten days later she had asked him to dinner at her apartment.

> I took a big, long-odds chance and wrote inviting him and his

wife to a small dinner-party. He rang to say his wife was down in Carolina. Could he come? Would it mess up my table-plan? I said it wouldn't if I were permitted to revamp the table-plan from six to two. He laughed and said Fine. The ball was plainly in my court.

A fortnight later:

Well, he came, saw, conquered or was conquered. Two-way traffic. As I surmised he is a womanizer. And how! Makes no bones about it. Always has been, he says. Always will be, I say. Well, that suits me. Very accomplished. Said I was, too. Seemed surprised. But why not? I said. Why are men referred to as the competent or lousy lovers but never women? Women are always good or bad lays as if their role was essentially passive. I think that's nonsense and told him so. He laughed and said it was a new experience for him to have the technicalities of performances discussed and analysed. But you'd discuss and analyse an interesting novel, a good concerto, a splendid meal or delicious wine, why not marvellous love-making? I asked. Wasn't transatlantic sensuality as important as gallic gastronomy or contrapuntal harmony? He laughed a lot more. In some ways he's very ingenuous.

We lay talking until three or four in the morning. Then he said he had to go. I asked why. Because he couldn't be seen leaving a girl's apartment, he said. Whose reputation was he thinking of –his or mine? I asked. He laughed and said his own, of course. You'd better go then, I said. Thank God, I've always known men with no reputations to lose. Stung, he stayed. But only till half-past six. I was sleepy and told him it was far more suspicious for him to be seen leaving a girl's apartment at six o'clock in the morning than ten. But he left.

Three days later:

He called me and asked whether he could come and see me again. I said why not? He came. We ate, made love and talked half the night.

He's the most fantastically ambitious man I've ever met. And ruthless. And arrogant. His contempt for all his so-called colleagues, cronies and hangers-on is simply colossal. The only opinions he seems to have any respect for are those of his younger brother, Glen. He seemed surprised when I pointed out these things.

Does contempt really show through as much as all that? Nobody's ever mentioned it.

Who would? I asked. You're surrounded by hangers-on, anyway. You say you are. Perhaps your yes-men and yes-girls are so enamoured they don't sense the chill behind the charm. But they'd be blind if they didn't. Perhaps they're all scared or mesmerized.

He laughed and said he'd never been criticised so nakedly before.

Quite a good pun, I said, the way he was wandering round the apartment, getting himself another drink. So we made love again.

A very highly sexed gentleman, I said.

A very well-matched pair, he said.

He left around midnight.

From then on they obviously became regular and consistent lovers, meeting once or twice a week, usually for a couple of hours or so. Occasionally he stayed overnight. By then he had become 'Greg' in the journal.

Then followed sections in which she carefully but discursively analysed his character as she saw it. I would have been ready to have published some of her comments that week-end. They were a far cry from Roth's piece.

It's far too easy to repeat the old truism that the one thing a rich, ambitious politician can never escape from is his wealth, but it's true. It's a terrifying kind of secret millstone. Greg never lets on about it–at least, not to other men. That would make him vulnerable and the one thing a politician hates and fears in himself is any kind of obvious vulnerability. That might make him human, even bring him down to the level of the rest of us, he thinks. Poor Greg. Born rich and with still greater riches thrust upon him by (*a*) his father, (*b*) his wife, and (*c*) his younger brother who runs that gigantical building business and feels guilty about being the younger brother in command. How pathetically and preposterously Glen Stirling respects his elder brother for opting out of what was, for Greg, the boredom of big business for the heady excitements of liberal politics! And how Glen well-nigh worships Greg's apparent detachment from money-making. The marvellous multi-millionaire irony of it all.

Last night–afterwards–which is Greg's confessional time, he wondered, in a loud whisper, whether he would have been a better politician if he'd been less rich.

D'you mean stinking poor instead of stinking rich? I asked. There's quite a difference between being broke and being breadline stuff. I've lived with both.

If you like, he said. Not very happily.

You're the soliloquizer, I said. You choose: rich, not-so-rich, fairly comfortable, struggling poor, bourgeois-broke, breadline-broke?

He laughed and said I was too heartless.

I said I was only helping him to be honest, a difficult enough task with any politician, even with one who thought of himself as an honest man.

Breadline-broke then.

You wouldn't have been a politician.

Why not?

You're too fond of the good things in life. And wealth fits you like a tailored jacket the way it does anybody born to the stuff. You can't even be divorced from it. Even if you lost it all now, the contacts you've made, the renown of your father's firm, your brother, your wife's relations would rally round to set you on the road back. Inside a year you'd be rich again.

You don't think I know what poverty means?

Of course you don't. You like to think you do–with your imaginative qualities and all that. But it's all only as an outsider looking on. The same way you don't know what being a woman, a homosexual, a cosmonaut, or a giraffe is like. No, you're just plain stinking rich and that's the way things are. You'd better learn to adjust, late as it is.

He laughed. Rather sheepishly. I was enjoying myself.

I went on: Wait till you get to the White House, then give your presidential salary back to the nation the way Kennedy did. That kind of gesture probably helps a man's ego quite a bit, especially if it still leaves a man Kennedy-rich or Stirling-rich.

He laughed again, and called me a malicious little bitch.

Just a little letter-in-of-light-in-dark-places, I said.

He wants reassurance at all times on all things. Last night it was on the fact that inherited wealth has made no difference to him. I suppose most rich sons with worth-while ambitions want the same kind of reassurance.

Why ask me? I said. I was born the daughter of a well-heeled Harley Street cardiographic king-pin.

How did I think I knew what poverty was? he asked.

Only by watching it at work and I've seen more of it than you'll ever see. I've worked in it. I spent a year working in the bug-ridden slums of Caracas where people don't come any poorer. That's a place to learn. But I was still outside, looking on. I could still buy a meal or a bath or an airline ticket home if things got too awful. Finally they did.

Interspersed amongst the diary entries were dozens of comments and asides prompted by the relationship. Thus:

I'm coming to the conclusion that all politicians, however liberal in comment, philosophy or intention, are basically fascists. They all want to impose on us their views of what is right for us, whether we want it or not. Extreme radicals are the worst kind of fascists because they want to change most, impose most, improve most. Oddly enough, the paradox is that extreme right-wingers are lesser fascists. They prefer the *status quo*, which means imposing less. Take your choice. Greg is by way of being an outsize liberal fascist in the making. But he was horrified, needless to say, when I pointed it out.

Again:

I don't think Stirling has one man he can call a friend or one he can really discuss any big decision with on a sincere, dispassionate basis. If he does need help with a decision or what kind of line to take he rings his brother up in Hartford, Conn. One rich engineer talking to another rich engineer about humanity. Marvellous stuff for Swift or Voltaire. But *they're* dead. I'll have to do *my* best.

Again:

My life is people! Greg declared the other night.
How pompous can you get! I said. People as digits or midgets?
He said he thought it was a funny question, but he didn't laugh.
Neither did he answer.

Again:

Dining here with Greg the other night I quoted H. L. Mencken's dictum, which goes, I seem to remember, along the lines that any man calling himself a politician is thereby a self-confessed liar, rogue, thief and scoundrel. Greg didn't know the phrase. After a while he said, Basically I think he's right. One tries to be the exception.

By being a lesser liar or bigger scoundrel? I asked.
Greg smiled but let it drop. Mencken was right.

Again:

I can understand an impotent male wanting power, but I can't understand why anyone as sexually potent as Greg wants power.

He's got it. Right here. But I suppose, ultimately, that's nowhere near enough for any man, although it can be for any woman. Yet the only men women really respect are those who are men at home, no matter what they are at work. When I was at the AA I learned that my father had a considerable renown as a heart specialist, but I'd been proud of him long before I knew about the reputation. He'd been so easily and genially masterful about the house, and my mother, my brother and myself all thought him terrific. About the house and on our holidays at our cottage in Somerset. The hell with the hospital, consulting-room and operating theatre. Yet most men want to be big men around some office or laboratory or workshop or in some political party. Mad mad, mad.

Again:

In theory, liberal politics ought to be the only possible career for a very very rich man. It then becomes what perhaps it ought to be: a hobby, a vocation, even an altruistic game played with understanding and detachment. I suppose that's the way things were occasionally in Georgian and Victorian England. But I wonder. Greg likes to think that his money puts him above the really murky battles. In theory perhaps it ought to. In reality it throws him more deeply into the battle. He has to prove his riches haven't softened him up, that he's as good as any log-cabin type. It makes him that much more rugged and ruthless. And all the time his money is buying him people, power, prestige, publicity. No wonder rich politicos have so few friends outside their own sacred circles of other millionaires, cronies and hangers-on. Perhaps things were better organized or more hypocritical in the eighteenth century.

But the journal wasn't all character analysis and political speculation. Far from it.

Lying awake last night, I asked Greg why he was such a compulsive womanizer? He was appalled to hear himself described in such a fashion—even in the dark.

How can you say that? he protested.

But you are, I said. You've had dozens of women in the past ten years. True or not true?

Half-true.

Does that make it half a dozen or half the number of dozens I first thought of?

He laughed and told me to carry on with the case for prosecution.

No prosecution, I said. I'm merely looking for information. Pursuit of truth and real knowledge.

Genes, he said. It's as simple as that.

Nothing psychological? You're not proving to yourself how attractive you are, day after day, or rather night after night?

You tell me, he said.

I think you are. Any compulsive or consistent womanizer seems in need of that kind of reassurance.

It's obviously a dangerous game for me to play–if you're right, he said.

I think most politicians go in for the business of running other people's lives because they're not so hot at running their own.

He laughed but I went on: They have to keep asking people for reassurance. That's probably one of the reasons politicians are always asking rhetorical questions.

He laughed and we let it drop, for a while, but I think it's true. A politician who's also a womanizer–and there have been several outstanding examples–seems to me to be seeking extra reassurance in his private life. Yearning for acclaim, love, reassurance between four walls and two legs as a change from standing ovations in damned great halls, amphitheatres and sporting arenas. Demonstration of charm of manner and potency as well as power, oratory, administrative efficiency and all that.

After a time, Greg said, as if he'd been reflecting and decided on a modest confessional:

You may be right. It may also be that I don't get all the reassurance I need in my own bed.

It's my sneaky view that your womanizing was one of the things that first upset the arrangements in your own bed, whatever they were or are.

Possibly, but I don't think it was. It was basically politics and it's a long long boring story. And I still say this sex-drive thing is basically a matter of good health and the right kind of genes.

And I still say it's basically a good old psycho-need of reassurance.

Reassure me now, he said.

The woman's not born who could resist that kind of womanizing.

Another entry:

I asked Greg what love making meant to him.

Temporary relief and release from tension, I guess.

Pleasure?

Of course.

Then why don't you spend more time at it?

He was quite surprised. Anybody would think I was a five-minute banger, he said.

Perish the thought, I said, but have you ever at any time during the past ten years spent one whole hot summer's afternoon making love?

A whole afternoon?

That's what I said.

No, but I spend all night–or almost all night–here sometimes, don't I?

That's different. An hour seems like all night. And anyway the day's work's done. But when did you last spend a whole afternoon at it playing hookey from work. Two until six, seven, eight o'clock? Straight after lunch.

Good God, never. Have you?

Often. Especially in Caracas.

What, with a football team?

Only once with a team. Usually with one doctor.

Didn't he have any patients?

Hundreds and hundreds. But he also thought screwing was not only a physical and nervous relief and release but also a great physical art or at least a great craft.

But a concerto only lasts half an hour and you can appreciate a Tiepolo in ten minutes.

Well, there it was. He spent hours at it.

Did you enjoy it?

Of course. Loved it. Are you mad?

What was so special about him?

The way he was concerned to give a woman pleasure.

One is.

Well, for one thing he made cunnilingus something out of this world.

Long silence and then: And after the cunnilingus came the real thing, I take it.

Before and/or after.

Another long silence. At last Greg said.

Good for him. I hope he was a good doctor, too.

He was. And greatly loved.

By patients and popsies alike no doubt.

You took the words, etc. I said.

Greg laughed. He's competitive in most things, but I could see he was willing to opt out of the cunnilingus stakes. Knowing Greg he'll come back to the subject later.

I wondered how many or how few newspapers or magazines in the world would publish that excerpt. I could think of a couple, perhaps, but no more outside the underground sheets.

I went on reading until half-past two the following morning, gripped by the complex and curiously sympathetic portrait of Greg Stirling that emerged from Ann Toynbee's lengthy record.

Yet I was aware that it was Ann Toynbee herself I wanted to learn even more about.

Other readers of the journal might well follow the same course, I thought. They would start reading to learn more about Stirling, continue in order to learn more about the young diarist. And then ask for more. Well, we'd soon see.

What would other women think of her story, I wondered.

Well, I could soon get at least one honest answer to that query, I decided as I put the box-file away in my desk, and set about taking to my bed.

–8–

Whenever possible I lunched, and usually dined, with Helen and Marion on Sundays, either at Milner Street or in one or other of the multitudinous King's Road eating-places. In summer we frequently drove out towards Berkshire or Sussex for picnic lunches on the Downs of either county, returning for the evening meal.

That Sunday I called for them early and we drove out to a place along the river beyond Wallingford. There we had a delicious meal. Helen, unlike most picnic-providers, expertly avoided bread in her concoctions. One wasn't more or less forced to fall asleep afterwards.

Whilst Marion played at the river's edge, I told Helen something of the Ann Toynbee story and then asked whether she would like to read the journals for herself and give me an opinion.

'Can't wait,' she said. 'Why don't you leave them with me for a couple of days and collect them later in the week?'

I agreed. My monthly lunch with Mason was coming up on the Thursday and I proposed to lob my little time-bomb into his lap at a convenient moment during the meal.

Sitting there by the Thames, watching Marion dabbling her feet, I went on with my outline of Ann Toynbee's story. Did a newspaper have the right to publish such a story? I asked.

'Long before a newspaper claims the right, doesn't somebody else–presumably the widow–have the right to say yea or nay. Surely that's reasonable?'

I agreed.

'And she certainly won't give you the OK.'

'I think that's pretty certain. How could she?'

'So you don't have to bother.'

'That's true, too, no doubt. But we shall. Newspapers always press on regardless.'

'But surely the widow's got prior claim on everybody's sympathies?'

I agreed.

'So it's only the immediacy and the fact that Stirling is still headlines that makes Ann Toynbee's tale such a hot property?'

Again I agreed. 'Time will obviously diminish its impact.'

'Its sensationalism, you mean.'

'Probably. But I do also think it's a pity not to back any young woman who's prepared to take such a chance. In her way she's enlarging the scope of feminine freedom. Far more than a dozen Women's Lib congresses, to my mind. Even in this permissive age women still don't have anywhere near complete equality in salaries or sex.'

'I think most members of Women's Lib would contend she was just an outsize high-IQ sexpot. Just the kind they want to polish off, in fact.'

I laughed, but Helen wasn't finished.

'If you think publishing this story might help women in general, you must be mad!' she scoffed in plain disbelief. 'Come off it, Paul.'

'Well, why not? A man can stand up in a witness-box and confess to any number of concubines, and, if anything, his reputation's enhanced. A young woman confessing to fifty lovers would still be generally regarded as a bit of a whore.'

'Whore or enthusiastic amateur, her phone would certainly be red-hot by the evening,' Helen said. 'Perhaps you're right. More power to Miss Toynbee's elbow–if that's the word–if she can get away with it. But I still think the widow's the most important factor. You once told me that widows are remarkably possessive about dead husbands–their money, their reputations, their furniture, their papers.'

'All part of a husbandly image they think they need to keep in good working- and selling-order.'

'I rather see their point,' Helen said. 'A widow's out on her own

–even more than a divorcée. Anyway, it'll be very interesting to see what happens.'

'Damn all!' I said and meant it.

I collected the files from my flat on our way back and left them with Helen.

–9–

Roth's reply to my cable, plainly typed by himself, awaited me at the office when I returned–in the sabbatical newspaper manner–to my chores on Tuesday afternoon.

Dear Paul: I imagine from your cable that you've got hold of Ann T. Or vice versa. I heard she was in London. You don't seem to have wasted much time in picking her brains about Stirling. As you ask for a confidential note you'll get it. First, be very careful how you handle her. She's sheer bloody poison ivy; as clever as a wrangler, as pretty as Grace Kelly, as icy as Mont Blanc and, to my mind, as explosive, potentially, as any H-bomb.

She came into Stirling's life about two years ago. Made a dead set for him. He fell for her in rather a big way, which was strange for him. He usually loved 'em (euphemism, as you've guessed) and left 'em almost immediately. Within very close limits he was mildly indiscreet about women, as you may have gathered from gossip, but, thanks to the general compliance of men and the decency (?) of journalists, the whole thing was kept pretty quiet. In any case, he was never flagrantly indiscreet and I don't think his affairs went very deep or lasted very long. I'm not so sure about this thing with Ann T. She was younger than most, a good deal smarter and cleverer–and prettier.

The real trouble about her is that she was all of a match for Stirling, and would be, will be, for any other man.

She plays 'em at their own game, and any woman who does that well has any man beaten before he starts. I'm sure you'd agree with that rather sweeping dictum. Her armoury's impressive by any standard as you'll agree if you've met her. Top marks for looks, brains and charm. But she has a good deal more going for her which Stirling didn't realize at the beginning. For one thing she wasn't expensive. Never asked for or expected a thing. She wasn't (possibly isn't) one jot possessive. Above all, she did (and probably truly does) believe and practise equality between the sexes. Finally, if she was curious about a man she'd go after him in much the same way that a really skilled and unashamed philanderer goes after women. All this made (and probably still makes, so beware) for a formidable, and, thank God, rare type of woman, although I think we're going to see more of 'em in the future. As a twice-married man I can still watch and learn and thank my native saints I'm not likely to be involved. But heaven help people like Stirling, who do get caught.

She played a subtle game with him. Interviewed him for the Architectural Forum *on one of his intellectual side-issues; mass-housing, technical as well as sociological. Bowled him over by the casual discovery – for him – that they were both alumni of M.I.T. She then followed up the interview by sending him some notes concerning her questionnaire, rather skilfully and flatteringly slanted, I thought, to bring him to architects' notice as one knowledgeable top politician really on their side. Answering that questionnaire enabled him to display his unusual awareness (amongst politicians, that is) of what environmental studies really meant, and what was, in fact, his quite surprisingly wide knowledge of system-building in Russia, France and elsewhere. But he'd trained as an engineer, so perhaps it wasn't surprising.*

He was delighted and flattered by the notice the published interviews received from architects, town-planners and the rest. I saw all this happening because I spent a lot of time with him, partly for the paper, partly because I liked and admired him. I also admire his wife. (Being a loner in Washington makes one a useful standby for hostess's table-plans, so I dined there a good deal.) Stirling committed – for me – the unforgivable sin of bringing his current cookies, including Ann Toynbee, to his table, but Melanie never seemed to mind or perhaps she didn't even notice. A fairly pulchritudinous miscellany passed through her dining-room over the years.

That really completes my knowledge of Ann T. One can't help but be impressed by her. Wells and Shaw would have seen most of their speculations concerning the future of women coming true in the person of Ann T, but to an old Central European-rooted trad type like myself, who likes his women agreeable and reticent in all things (and most of all in the kitchen and bedroom) she spelled DANGER *in very large caps. I think she also spelled ultimate danger to Stirling, too. She seemed to like him, even perhaps love him, but sometimes I thought she was studying him as a kind of a case-history in much the same way that she had studied slum conditions in South America. I sometimes even had the feeling she was just fascinated by the sight of a man of power in the making, wanted to know what made him tick, and wanted to document the story all the way to the White House.*

And all the time, I suspect, he was slipping more and more into a need for her. A physical need and also, more subtly, need for her approval. No other woman had ever had quite the same impact on him. What made her an even more powerful influence on his personal life was that she never, to my knowledge, ever asked for a single favour or privilege on account of knowing him. I give her that. One hundred per cent. But that made her all the more dangerous, potentially. One day she might have wanted to do just that. I always thought that, sooner or later, Stirling would have wanted her for keeps, even thrown everything over for her.

I just don't know. If it had come to that point, I think she would have upped roots and returned to Britain. In any final crunch, I don't think Stirling meant that much to her. Neither was she interested in his ideas of power, his money, or anything that was his. I think she just liked him as a man, a lover, a friend, a companion, a beau to her string, god knows what.

For most women that would probably spell Mr Right, but not for her. In common with the few truly free men one's ever seen, I think she knew that there were other equally interesting, well-shaped pebbles on other beaches. If she's come into your orbit to fill in details on any feature you're planning on Stirling, don't touch her. For one thing she knows too much. For another, it would be sheer dynamite with every kind of chain-reaction. For another I'd be likely to be difficult. I admired Stirling too much to see his name dragged through that kind of mud. All in all, Miss Toynbee spells Big Trouble. In a remote kind of way I suppose I quite like the girl, but I'd prefer her studying the slums of Caracas or Puerto Rico than let loose on any kind of Stirling memoir or biog. He's safer that way. And so are other men. Salutations, Bernie.

—10—

Curious, I thought, that I owed my temporary possession of the Toynbee journals to the casual recommendation he had given her. I wondered whether I'd ever mention the irony to him. I doubted it.

Meantime, I decided to keep the letter, to study it over the week-end or until Mason had had the opportunity to make his own appraisal of the Toynbee story.

I scribbled a fairly long note to Roth, thanking him for the trouble he had taken over his unequivocal views on Ann Toynbee. By that time the usual routine had taken over and I was glad to put Ann Toynbee and all her works out of my mind for a couple of days.

With luck I thought, it would soon be out of my hands and into the hands and arguments of the newspaper's owners, editors, legal advisors and the rest.

But, first, Mason. No, Vicky.

–11–

I'd always had a considerable respect, albeit wary and somewhat grudging, perhaps, for Helen's views on almost any subject. She had a rare talent – in a woman, at least – for cutting through to the heart of the matter and refusing to be bamboozled by masculine persuasiveness.

Nevertheless, I thought I'd get a rather less cerebrated opinion on the Toynbee story from Vicky. After all, she was nearer Ann Toynbee's own age, although, I suspected, any resemblance ended there.

I took her out to supper that Tuesday evening. Half-way through the meal I raised the subject.

I usually went secretly armed with one or two extra-alimentary subjects which I introduced at strategic moments. The stratagem had its advantages. If I had something on my mind I could brood over its manifold aspects whilst Vicky prattled gaily on, turning over the query I'd given her. From time to time she brought my wandering mind suddenly to attention with one of her own peculiarly incisive remarks or rejoinders. Occasionally she was unnervingly, unpredictably acute. Out of the mouths of babes, etc. etc. That would bring me back into the conversation.

That evening I said to her: 'If you were or had been the occasional mistress of a leading politician. . . .'

'What d'you mean by occasional?'

'Well, if you weren't actually living with him. If you weren't, perhaps, his only side-line. If you weren't, shall we say, his sole interest . . .'

'I see. I don't think I'd be around on those terms, but press on until I see what you're getting at.'

'Supposing he got polished off, would you feel justified in publishing your diary of the affair?'

'I don't keep diaries of affairs. I don't even keep letters. Not that you've ever written me a single damn line, anyway.'

'We're straying from my theme; I'm neither a budding politician nor much of a letter-writer.'

'But I am your occasional mistress and I'll bet I'm not your only side-line.'

'We're still straying and still further from my theme,' I repeated patiently. 'If you *had* kept a diary, would you publish it?'

'Depends which paper or magazine. I wouldn't in the *People*, the *News of the World* or the *Mirror*. In that order.'

'Would you in *The Guardian*?'

'They wouldn't play ball. Not with a story like that.'

'They might if the bloke had been a land-owning Etonian Tory and not a great free-thinking liberal with a Manchester Grammar-Redbrick background.'

'You're too cynical. I've a great admiration for *The Guardian*. As a PRO I like dealing with them. One knows what they'll take and so on. I don't think they would take such a diary, so there!'

'Where would you publish, then?'

'Any of the quality Sundays or Colour Supplements. Or the *Weekly Tele*. Or your people, for example.'

'What about his widow?'

'You didn't say he had one.'

'Anyone who wasn't married would marry you on the spot. You're not the mistress type.'

'What the hell am I, then, if I'm staying the night with you? I know I *was* married, but I also know I'm now an occasional mistress. Am I staying, tonight, Paul or is this a very subtle brush-off?'

I laughed. 'I hope you're staying. I bought extra orange juice on your account. Let's call you my intimate friend.'

'I still think I'm an occasional mistress.'

'Sounds positively Edwardian.'

Vicky laughed. 'It's your phrase,' she pointed out. She could never be tetchy for longer than thirty seconds. That was another of her manifold charms. 'All right, my intimate friend,' she went on, 'if he had a widow I'd have to discuss it with her–if she'd known of my existence, that is.'

'Wives merely suspect. Few ever know–or want to know–the real tough truth about these matters.'

'The voice of experience. But I think you're right. Well, presumably, my solicitor or my agent would approach her.'

'Would you feel any compunction about publishing the diaries?'

'It depends what I'd felt about him, I suppose. If the widow didn't mind, I suppose I wouldn't mind. How could I? It would be rather fun to be in the news like that.'

'You wouldn't mind the scandal?'

'I'd like it. All my scandals are so damned secret. I wouldn't mind being in the headlines for a bit.'

'Pointed out as a mistress in El Vino's and the Savoy?'

'Why not? I was once pointed out as a pushover–in the Savoy, too.'

'Are you?'

'You ought to know. I was for you, wasn't I? Why not? If I want a man I don't see the point of playing hard to get. You found me dead easy, didn't you, Paul?'

'Once again, we're straying from the point,' I said. But I was surprised how closely Vicky, so far removed from Ann Toynbee in background, education, work, outlook and the rest, shared the same views. The only differences, it seemed, were such peripheral matters as finding the right man and a talent for narration.

I was quite impressed by the results of this one-man market survey.

–12–

The third of my monthly Mason lunches was, as usual, upstairs at Rules.

Mason was in one of his more magisterial moods, ordering his meal as if dictating a five-line *aide-mémoire* to a Cabinet Minister. As usual I dithered, but, finally, after finishing our Tio Pepe and choosing minute steaks, we got started. Mason said: 'I think the paper's going quite well. What d'you think?'

'I never really know. So many extraneous things seem to come into the estimate of how well a paper's doing. Advertising revenue. Net sales. Rivals' successes or failures. What's being said about us in What the Papers Say. I'm weak on that kind of thing.'

'But the paper itself. How d'you think that's doing–editorially?'

'I think we're overstaffed. Too many people getting in each other's way. Apart from that I think we're probably O K.'

'I can't agree with you about over-staffing. What with the lavish kind of holidays journalists get these days and their vulnerability to digestive troubles – too much sitting, drinking, smoking and motoring–we need every good man we can get. We also need a few more good features. We've had no decent serial since the Russian spy network thing and that was a bit dated. Back to the Krogers and Lonsdale, for God's sake. Now we've only got the Sport Sponsorship piece and that's only worth a week or so. Then there's the pollution and environmental survey, but, that won't stir anybody very much. I don't see anything coming up that'll prove much of a circulation-booster.'

I agreed, and asked what Logan had in the pipeline. 'Little enough,' Mason said almost savagely.

We moved on to discuss, somewhat discursively, a submission we'd had from a hard-hitting history don on *The Decline and Fall of British Foreign Policy*, basically a series of profiles of post-war Foreign Secretaries. I favoured the series, but I'd started out as a would-be historian, so I was prejudiced anyway. As a journalist I doubted whether it would put a thousand copies on the sales. I said so again.

'I, personally, need another hundred thousand copies on our net sales figure,' Mason said. 'P.d.q.'

'Why so personal?'

'Because successful editing is a personal matter,' he said succinctly.

'Where d'you find that number of non-newspaper-readers or how d'you steal 'em from somebody else?'

'Another series like the Flower People survey would help.'

'Why not get a bit fierce with Logan? He's your features editor.'

'I told you when you came back, I wanted your help with features, especially serials.'

'I've got my hands on one human story that might put a hundred thousand on your sales. Even more. But I doubt whether you'd publish it.'

Mason was nettled. 'Who said so? What is it?'

'A two-hundred-thousand-word, blow-by-blow account of the intimate life of Greg Stirling by one of his many mistresses: a twenty-six-year-old English girl. It needs a lot of editing, but it's all there: sex, politics, money, ambition, the lot.'

The waiter brought Mason's melon, my smoked salmon. Mason was silent for a very long moment. 'All authenticated?' he asked at last.

'As far as I can check and double-check. Also pretty well authenticated by Bernie, who knows and dislikes the girl. One called Ann Toynbee.'

'Why dislikes?'

'She's too pretty and clever for our Bernie, that's all.'

'One had heard whispers of Stirling's hobby. Who hadn't?' Mason said. 'I'd always been impressed by the way it was left out of the papers over there. Not their usual behaviour–except, somehow, with politicians. It'd be quite a story if we could get away with it.'

'It is quite a story whatever we do about it. She's a remarkable young woman.'

'You've met her?'

I nodded.

'Does she live here, then?'

'No. New York.'

'When did you see her, then–you won't even go to Paris, let alone New York.'

'I lunched with her a week or so ago.'

'Could you see Stirling's point of view? Could you have become involved, given half a chance?'

'Very willingly, even if a trifle nervously,' I answered, truthfully enough. 'The first truly free woman I've ever met. Bernie thinks so, too–somewhat apprehensively. I suppose a lot more of 'em will be coming along under the aegis of the pill and big top jobs–if they can take the time off, that is.'

'Perhaps that's what the Pope's scared of.'

'He'd better be. He's got one of the jobs they're after.'

Mason laughed. 'Tell me more. Have you got the story tied up by the way–if we want it, that is?'

'As far as I can gather, I'm the guardian-angel of the whole shooting-match. She left me with the first half of the tale. The rest I get in a little over a month's time. If it's half as good as this lot it'll be worth its weight in solid titanium.'

'But it's got some built-in problems,' Mason said. 'I can smell 'em already. But go on.'

Slowly I began to outline the contents of the box-file. The account took us through our steak and salad. At the end I said: 'So there it is. I can't recall anything comparable in quite a lot of years in newspapers.'

'Especially with Stirling scarcely interred, you mean?'

'These tales are usually only heard twenty years after the characters are dead.'

'That's true,' Mason said, ruminatively. 'That Countess of Warwick and Edward the Seventh thing in the *Sunday Times*, for instance, was far too staid and antique. So was the Warren Harding scandal. What a tale the Elinor Glyn-Lord Curzon relationship would have made in the *Pic* or the *People* of the day–on the day!'

'But bitterness and bitchiness would have been keynotes in all those relationships. There's not a pennyworth of bitterness in this girl's story.'

'You think it makes a big difference?'

'Well, it certainly makes for a better tale. She gets on with the story.'

'Was she fond of him?'

'Very.'

'Then how the hell can she tell the tale now?'

'As far as I can interpret her very clear-cut views, her contention is that although we record and discuss the horrors of war, the escapism of drugs, the inevitability of old age, the pains of poverty and so on, once anyone tries to put down an honest view about a relationship in which sex plays a significant part, up go all the taboos. Even today. Especially if a political reputation and public life come into the story. She also contends that men gang up to protect themselves from a woman telling such a tale from her side.'

'She's got a point there. Several, in fact. I'd like to meet her next time she's in London. Meantime, I'd better read the story. The way you describe it, I can't see the members of your board-room being very enamoured of the idea. Frankly, I'm not enamoured myself. I've quite a lot of respect for Stirling's achievements.'

'So I've noticed,' I said, but Mason affected not to hear.

'Anyway, I'll see,' he said in his best editorial manner.

'It's a sizeable venture,' I pointed out. 'The whole thing is probably getting on for half-a-million words, judging by the length of the first instalment, which Miss Toynbee grossly under-estimated.'

'Good God! And on one man?'

'More accurately, one man, one woman.'

'Out of which–if we bought it–we'd want, say, five bites at five thousand words a time. Could you sub the story down to that?'

'I'd have a bash–if you'd give me time and Ann Toynbee were agreeable.'

He wanted reassurance. 'You're *very* impressed?' he demanded earnestly.

I nodded. 'Very. As I said, it's got everything. But I still doubt whether you'd be prepared to publish the really crucial sections as they stand. And there's certain to be a crowd of vested interests ganging up to prevent publication.'

'But if what you say is right, it's a story in ten thousand.'

'Absolutely. But, as I told the Toynbee girl, once the family, the State Department and the F O got wind of it they'd jump on it with everything they've got–from a very great height indeed.'

'That's formidable ganging-up if they decide to work in concert. Of course we might spring it on 'em, but I don't see how we could, if we wanted to get the full sales benefit from it.'

'You'd want to announce it?'

He nodded. 'That's essential. Is she thinking of a book as well?'

'Sure. Especially if we published. Even as it is, she suspects that any number of publishers in the world would jump at it if they had an inkling it's around. Any publisher with the nerve, that is.'

'What's your view of the ethics of the situation?'

'From my fairly conventional, invincibly masculine outlook, the whole thing's indefensible, but, listening to the Toynbee girl, I begin to see her side of the case. I got persuaded. Or almost. This is *her* story. He *was* a womanizer. He *is* dead. Such things were a major part of his character. His wife knew. All his intimates knew. Is he to be presented to posterity as the complete whiter-than-white Sir Galahad?'

'Well, he was a very remarkable man. Unique in my experience,' Mason said.

Had he already had his normal fling as the great go-go editor? I wondered. Had he had his fill of enterprise, and was he already getting cold feet?

I went on: 'If he'd been a homosexual, everyone would have known. The general conspiracy of masculine silence about sex never completely smoke-screens high-placed queers. Yet it does protect high-placed lechers. What Ann Toynbee says, in effect, is that here is a so-called great man as he was to one of his women who also happened to be very fond of him.'

'What about the widow?' Mason interrupted.

'There's only the widow and the children to consider in my view. If we came out bang with the story, she'd have world-wide sympathy, and we'd certainly be in trouble. We've got to get her permission first.'

'Impossible!' Mason said with absolute assurance: or was it absolute relief?

'Not impossible,' I said quietly.

'You mean, if we don't somebody else will. Is that it?'

'That's fairly certain–unless the family solicitors can get a world-wide injunction, which I'd say was impossible. Even if Miss Toynbee's stopped publishing here and in the States, she says she'd let the Russians have it and spend the roubles there. No Washington legal diktat is going to cut much ice in Moscow or Peking. Imagine the fun they'd have playing up the decadence of Western politicians, as if no Russian or Chinese minister had ever had a bit on the side.'

'But we do have to think about that aspect–the widow, I mean.' Mason couldn't leave his escape-hatch alone.

'Of course,' I said gleefully rubbing in the intimidating horrors of the project. 'The family could also probably sue Miss Toynbee for a million–for pain, suffering, malice, the lot.'

'A million, Don't be childish, Paul. These American lawyers only start thinking in terms of twenty million dollars for a killing of this kind–if it's all you say.'

'It's all I say,' I repeated gently.

'As publishers, I'm afraid we'd also be vulnerable to any prosecution of that kind,' Mason said gloomily, but I didn't find his gloom particularly convincing. In fact, I thought he rather welcomed these reminders of the horrors ahead, but I said cheerfully: 'No doubt about that. If it really gets cracking, I'll see you in the witness-box yet. Along with His Lordship and the printers. Would you have to go to Washington for the case?'

'It's not so funny, Paul.'

'It's not so unlikely either. You'd have to face the possibility. Presumably, we'd have every comma checked at our end before we even considered going ahead.'

'I wish it were only the commas. If the story's half as good as you say it is, we'll never publish. I can tell you that here and now. Lawyers, as any editor knows, are the most lily-livered lot of all the many time-servers in and around newspapers.'

'But their job after all, is to keep us out of trouble.'

'Themselves out of trouble and their reputations intact in and around the law courts.'

'And then there's the American lot.'

'As I said. The legal boys on both sides of the Atlantic simply can't lose. I can see it all. Pain and suffering to the widow and children. Imperilling our special relationship with the States. Libel. And the rest.'

I could see the alibis already beginning to be assembled.

'So you think it's a dead duck, already?'

'I'd say so, but I'd like to read it first.'

'Obviously.'

'Then I'll probably have to think again and very seriously. It could be an historic document.'

'It's that already, whether we publish or not.'

'I'd say most history was confirmed by publication,' he said. Rather pompously, I thought, despite the grain of truth.

Finding himself on firmer ground with a fair certainty of rejection ahead, Mason put on his brave new anti-Establishment tone. 'God knows, there'd be nobody stepping in to protect any newspaper editor's secret sex-life. I'd like to see the story as soon as possible, Paul. It'll obviously need a lot of stewing over. But judging from the way you've described it, the whole thing sounds like a major headache all round.'

'With some major returns to ease the migraine.'

He smiled his special guru's smile, as if his cares were way beyond the comprehension of anyone unacquainted with the loneliness of the long-distance editor.

He was very thoughtful over coffee and on our walk back along the Strand and Fleet Street.

I sensed that he already saw that what I proposed to hand over to him was likely to be too hot for him to handle, yet, in his new guise as the swinger's friend, he didn't like opting out of anything that suggested he was chicken. And deep down, like Roth, he yearned to do his bit to protect the Stirling legend. Any Mason comment to the contrary was soft soft flannel, however well-disguised as an old-fashioned abrasive hair shirt.

–13–

Two weeks later, by mid-August, that is, six of us had read the first half of the Stirling story: Mason, Vaughan, Markham, Spicer, Logan and myself.

Mason fixed a meeting for general discussion on the following Thursday, immediately after the editorial conference.

Mason had already seen me about the story. He'd found it wholly hypnotic, he said. 'As any such record is likely to be. But, frankly, as I see things at the moment, Paul, we're going to find it impossible to publish. Unless somebody comes up with some miracle legal device or some oddment of medieval moral sophistry we're cooked. I've never handled anything as hot in all my days as an editor. But we'll wait and see what the others have to say.'

As features editor, Logan was the first to have read the journal after Mason and myself. He came to my room to report. 'I finished your lady friend's journal last night,' he said. 'Three nights of the most entertaining–and concentrated–reading I've ever had, by the way. She's quite a girl. Makes me proud to be English. Not sure

I'd be made keen for either of my daughters to have emulated her, mark you, but there it is. She's certainly got ants in her pants. And she must be the most maniacal feminine journal-keeper since Lady Mary Wortley or whatever her name was. She comes out of it rather a cool little number I thought. I gather we're going to discuss next week.' And then with his usual snide grin: 'When are you meeting her next, old boy?'

Dick Spicer mentioned the journal, too casually, during a Friday afternoon discussion about a piece on *Faces & Places*. 'Oh, by the way. I skimmed through your Toynbee girl's journal last night. Can't say I'm very sold on it. I think these things are best kept quiet. I don't think they'd do us much good.'

'You may well be right,' I said. To his evident surprise.

I also agreed with Markham's similar disparagement. Also to his evident surprise.

He and Spicer would undoubtedly act together in downing and damning the story.

That left only Vaughan to offer his views, before the owners, the lawyers and the rest of the professionally squeamish members of the opposition moved in to offer their views. But, first, we had the general discussion.

–14–

The meeting was opened by Mason.

'We've all read the Ann Toynbee diaries Paul got hold of–he hasn't told me how yet–(laughter) and I'm sure there's one thing we've all agreed on: they add up to an extraordinary and riveting story. What I want us to do now is to discuss the journal–as I'll refer to it from now–as a viable proposition–or perhaps 'buyable' is a more accurate word–for us, or for any newspaper, for that matter. Obviously we'd like such a story for its uniqueness as a record, for its possibilities as a publishing proposition–syndication and so on–and as a sales-booster. On the other hand, we can't afford a major injunction or be forced to call it off after spending a couple of hundred thousand pounds or more on promoting it. The Board wouldn't think it very funny. I'd like to think I've got an open mind on the matter, but I'm prepared to admit, here and now, that I'm a bit dubious about the journal's prospects of seeing daylight. Would you start the ball rolling, Dick?'

Spicer spoke along much the same lines as he had in my room the previous week. He'd been fascinated, much against his will, by the journal, he said. In its own curious way it was undeniably an historic document of a high order, but were we entitled to publish instant history if it also meant instant pain to a lot of innocent people?

Markham backed him up. 'It's fascinating. Agreed. But it would do us no good in the long run–apart from the host of people its publication would hurt.'

'But is it such a lot of people?' Logan asked. 'As far as I can see, it's only the widow. Her vanity would certainly be hurt. She'd be pretty humiliated, that's for sure. And possibly the children. I can't see anybody else being unduly hurt? A lot of American politicians, certainly, but we all know how easily politicians get hurt in any country. Look at the way ours claim parliamentary privilege at the drop of a far-off brick.'

'What about the children? Why possibly? Surely it's inevitable they'd be hurt?' Spicer asked.

'I never really know what is or what isn't hurtful to a child.' Logan said. 'The professional psychiatrists don't seem to know much more than the rest of us. Some children shrivel on being in the news, but most of 'em seem to thrive on it and ask for more. In my experience, there's no special age or sex for exhibitionism. But there it is. Mine are grown up now. I'm out of touch.'

'What about you, Paul?' Mason asked.

'In my experience, any child over eight knows most of the parental secrets, and, generally, they seem more resilient than most so-called adults, but, as an arbiter in these matters, I've no more authority than Steve.'

Logan smiled.

'But do we have to argue the pros and cons of whether widow and/or children would be hurt or not?' Spicer said. 'Simply to publish these journals would be to invade a widow's privacy unjustifiably, and, to my mind, monstrously. Publication would add to her present sorrow, make her future utterly bleak and miserable. Altogether, create an intolerable situation. Of course publication would also upset the lives of the children. Don't let's kid ourselves. More to the point for us, perhaps, is that any US lawyer could bring a dozen child psychologists into court, with an injunction order in his pocket, knowing full well that any US judge would be ready and willing, within the hour, to affirm that the children's lives would be irreparably ruined by publication.'

'I think that sums up the situation admirably,' Markham said eagerly and almost prissily, I thought.

Mason said: 'Undoubtedly it's the most sensationally serious study of an affair in high places I've ever come across. It must break any editorial heart to shoot it down, but I admit I feel much the same way Dick and Gerry seem to feel.'

'But aren't we jumping the gun a bit?' Vaughan said quietly, coming in for the first time. 'We all seem to agree it's a story worth carrying–if we can–legally. Paul reckons the complete journal totals well over a quarter-of-a-million words, getting on, possibly, for half-a-million. We wouldn't want to publish more than say twenty-five or thirty thousand words. Surely we can make extracts; that would be a serious contribution towards understanding the American political scene, its in-fighting, its violence, its wheeler-dealing and the place of one reasonably honest and unusual man –and, as it turns out, martyr–in that set-up. All as seen by a highly intelligent, serious-minded young Englishwoman of fairly remarkable talents and achievements.'

They were all quiet, appraising this new viewpoint. Mason, I think, was momentarily winded by this pragmatic contribution from his white-haired boy. Then he said slowly, 'I think that makes sense–so long as Paul will do the cutting. He knows the girl, and the journal's rather become his thing, whether he wants it or not.'

'Thanks a lot,' I said.

'What makes you think you could still get away with it, even on those terms?' Spicer asked, almost belligerently.

'Why not?' asked Vaughan in return. 'One can imagine the kind of title. Profile of a Politician, subtitled, A study in violence; quote A young Englishwoman's remarkable study of the unknown Greg Stirling. Quote. The relationship could be implied, left to anybody's imagination. The portrait's the thing. I think we could make it.'

'I think it's possible but I also think you're kidding yourself,' Logan said, with what passed for as geniality towards his continuing opponent. 'This journal's only worth publishing with the emphasis on the real heart of the matter, and that's sex. That's the basis of the friendship, affair, call it what you like.'

'That damns it anyway, then,' Markham said hopefully.

' I think Miss Toynbee would agree with Steve's view,' I said.

'You're probably right,' Mason said guardedly.

'How would you propose to cut out the sex?' Logan demanded of Vaughan. 'Would you publish or delete the accounts of Stirling as a performer?'

To my surprise Vaughan said: 'That side of things was very much part of the man, as we all know. I'd be sorry to see that omitted. But there are various references, some less basic than others.'

We all laughed.

'But aren't those just the parts–no pun intended, Tom–that we'd have to omit?' Mason asked. 'I thought we'd all agreed on that.'

'I hadn't,' Logan said.

'Neither had I,' Vaughan said.

I was so surprised to find those two in agreement that I backed their views immediately. The least I could do, I thought.

That made three a side, however carefully Mason sought to cultivate an as-yet-uncommited attitude.

'Primarily it's a job for the lawyers,' Mason said, too casually yet too eagerly.

'Wouldn't the Stirling family want to read every word we proposed to publish, anyway?' Spicer asked, plainly dead set against the whole idea. Despite his daily cynicism, a sacerdotal upbringing and naval training inevitably triumphed over Fleet Street scribbling when it came to a question of a boss man's honour, however dubious, and a widow's pain.

'They'd try, that's certain,' Mason said.

'But somebody's going to publish the lot, within the year, without reference to the family and then sort out any consequences afterwards–unless Miss Toynbee's a very different bird from what I take her to be,' Vaughan persisted.

'Then let 'em,' Spicer said curtly.

'They certainly will,' I said. 'Somehow. How shall we feel then?'

'Very relieved,' Markham said briefly.

'I'm not so sure,' Mason said hurriedly. 'I'm not altogether certain we'd be so relieved, Gerry.'

'Public opinion would be on our side,' Spicer said.

'If public opinion ever knew of our altruism,' Mason said.

'Miss Toynbee doesn't give a damn for public opinion,' I put in. 'In her view, public opinion is usually masculine opinion. I'm rather inclined to agree. Apart from which, she knows she's got a story in a million.'

'And there's also the money!' Spicer scoffed.

'And why not?' Vaughan broke in. 'Authors deserve payment don't they? Is your idea only to pay writers for writing about subjects that please you? Gide got paid for writing about buggery. You'd have had the whole thing hushed up, no doubt. We get paid for writing journalese, which is whore-writing half the time. Why shouldn't a girl get paid for writing about her spare-time screwing if she's serious about it?'

This was the first time Vaughan had used his whip-lash television technique in the office: it was very effective.

'So you think I'm a kind of Franco of Fleet Street?' Spicer said, smiling thinly and dead-serious.

'Heading that way unless somebody calls a halt,' Vaughan said, also smiling, breaking the sudden conflict.

'We're all talking as if *we've* got this thing sewn up,' Logan said. 'Supposing Epoca or Spiegel got on to this. Either would pay a damn sight more than we could.'

'Paul swears it's all ours–or his,' Mason said.

'When do we get the other half?' Logan asked.

'By the end of the month.'

'Supposing we decide to publish, when would we?' Spicer asked despondently.

'Cheer up, Dick,' Mason said.

'Sooner the better as far as I'm concerned,' Logan decided.

'If we do–and it's still a sizeable if–it would probably be in late November,' Mason said. 'Might even have to be early next year. The circulation people would probably prefer that. That's when we shall need a lift. We could certainly get half a dozen *Review* leads out of it.'

'I'd like to know we'd really got it,' Logan said. 'It's a million light-years better than anything else in the pipeline.' He turned to me. 'How do we get hold of the second half to see whether it's as good as this?'

'We can ask her to send it over or ask her to bring it over.'

'There's not much point in that at this stage, is there?' Spicer asked dyspeptically.

'Don't we all want to meet her?' Vaughan asked, smiling. He was a very different man from the one we'd been dealing with for the past three months. This was the television personality, confident, relaxed, articulate. I began to wonder whether he'd now decided that he'd fully sized up the proposition and/or opposition and now felt ready to go.

'We don't have to,' Spicer said. 'I'm not particularly sure I want to, anyway. And I still think you're making the whole thing sound too easy. In my experience, one never keeps this kind of thing secret, and the moment the whisper gets around, the Stirling family lawyers will be down on it and us like a ton of bricks. I know these New York attorneys. If they're acting for anyone who's loaded and prepared to pay, they're nothing but a crowd of legalized mobsters, bully-boys and blackmailers. They'd silence anybody–especially a girl with the truth to tell about a millionaire playboy-politico.'

'I think you're overplaying the mobster touch in this case,' Vaughan said. 'In any case, mightn't it be a better idea if Paul were to collect the rest of the journal from Miss Toynbee in New York, see what Roth thinks of the whole project anyway . . .'

I interrupted. 'I can tell you here and now what Roth thinks. He thinks it stinks.'

'He always carried the world's most flaming torch for Stirling,' Logan said.

'And why not?' Spicer said, almost spitting out the words.

'I'm not optimistic, but it's a thought,' Mason said in his smoothest judicial manner. 'As you've gathered from Paul, Bernie doesn't take to Miss Toynbee. In a confidential note to Paul he made it quite clear he thinks she's sheer poison ivy. He admits she's clever and so on, but obviously her journal does rather cut Stirling down to mortal size.'

'I'm all for that,' Logan said.

'Shouldn't we take Roth's advice?' Spicer asked, almost pleaded. 'After all, he's our man. He should know.'

'He might be prejudiced' Vaughan said. 'I still think someone from here–obviously Paul–might sort things out a bit, look around, get the feel in the States about Stirling. Even take a peek at the widow if Roth can lay it on. After all Roth's always been regarded as a very close friend of the Stirlings, hasn't he?'

'Their very closest, according to Roth,' Logan said, grinning.

Vaughan had spoken as if he were already editor. Mason seemed hypnotised and by-passed. 'That makes sense,' he said. 'What d'you think of the idea, Paul?'

'I don't think it's essential, but I'll go if you think it might be useful.'

'I think it would,' Mason said. 'It'd be a lot more sensible than bringing Miss Toynbee back here.'

'I think it might well,' Spicer said. He turned to me: 'You might even be persuaded of the madness of the whole idea once you get into the climate of opinion out there.'

'Let's hope so, anyway,' Markham added.

The rest of us laughed at their determined dolefulness, but, on the understanding that I'd go to New York and Washington before the end of the month, the meeting broke up.

Mason, Markham and Spicer were plainly relieved to see the meeting at an end.

–15–

I went back to my office and dictated a brief note to Ann Toynbee in New York.

Dear Miss Toynbee: I have to see Bernard Roth within the next week or so. If you could let me know when the second part of your journal will be ready, I could combine the two jobs. It would be pleasant to see you again.

We all like your journal, although, as you may imagine, it has certainly set the cat among the pigeons.

Perhaps you'd let me know.

The letter went that day. On Friday I had a cable: COME AND COLLECT TOYNBEE.

–16–

On Sunday morning ten days later I flew direct to Washington. Roth had booked me in at the Madison. A note awaited me.

Dear Paul: After you've had a decent rest, ring me and I'll come and pick you up for a meal. It's hell getting a taxi in this city. Ever, Bernie

I took his advice, woke a couple of hours later and rang him to say I'd be presentable in about an hour. Then I rang the New York number Ann Toynbee had given me.

Her greeting was warm and her regrets that I was in Washington sounded agreeably sincere. 'And when do you get to New York in this schedule?'

'In two or three days' time. I have to see Roth and then–take a deep breath–I aim to go down to Louisiana to try my luck with Mrs Stirling.'

'You don't stand a chance. I might as well sell my story to the Russians today. What chance d'you think you'd stand with any widow in this kind of situation, let alone a rich dame who's had her own imperious way all her life?'

'She didn't with Stirling,' I pointed out.

'That's true,' Ann admitted.

'Anyway, it's a job that's got to be tackled at some stage. Better that I should do it than anyone else. Better, too, to do it now instead of crashing on regardless, committing ourselves all the way and then getting busted.'

'You'll get busted all right, and what about my book then?'

'I think it'll be caput–as far as we're concerned. There'll be plenty of other takers as far as you're concerned.'

'I'd rather taken a fancy to you and your lot,' she said, chuckling.

'Apart from Roth, no doubt.'

'That's true. But I just don't want to have to go all the way to Moscow to sell my story. I'd probably have to spend eighteen million roubles on caviare. All in a week.'

'There's always a magazine or publisher or agent in Milan or Rome who'd work something out for you.'

'I don't want that either,' she said in mock-plaintiveness. 'You'll have to work hard on that there Melanie, but I know it's hopeless even as I suggest it. She's the coldest cookie in the fridge.'

I laughed. She laughed too, resigned.

'Well, I wish you luck,' she said gloomily.

'What about the rest of your compilation?' I asked. 'Finished?'

'First, "qualms" and now "compilations". You do use some truly horrific words. "Compilation" sounds like a scissors-and-paste job, instead of the flesh-and-blood masterpiece–or mistress-piece–it really is. Well, it's done and ready. You can collect any time. Give me a day's warning and I'll have everything ready.'

'I'll try to reach Melanie Stirling this week. She'll probably shoot me down, so let's say Friday, in New York, but it may be Saturday or Sunday. I'm somewhat optimistically booked in at the Barbizon-Plaza from Friday on.'

'I'll keep the week-end free, but you'll probably be here on Thursday. She'll finish you off in three minutes on a long-distance call, but I'll cross my fingers for you.'

I thanked her, said my fond farewell, to which she replied, 'Bye, Paul.'

First use of a Christian name in a developing friendship is one of those subtle ties that sorts out the innocents from the sophisticates. I gave Miss Toynbee full marks for her well-timed ploy.

–17–

Roth had a pleasant office in the *Washington Post* building, one of a suite of three rooms which the group rented. With uncommon skill–uncommon in a journalist, that is–he had managed to make his own small room more like a scholar's hide-out than the workaday office of a busy and conscientious foreign correspondent, first for the daily and now, additionally, for the Sunday. After all, he had been Mason's discovery.

He was about fifty, a bear of a man, about six-foot-three or four, girth to match. With his ill-fitting clothes, thinning dark curly hair, sad pale face, treble chin and five o'clock shadow five minutes after his morning shave, he looked less like a journalist than a couthless giant out of some Black Forest hobgoblin tale. He had been born in Warsaw, of mixed Polish-Austrian parentage, the only child of a runaway marriage between a young dancer in Vienna, more or less willingly abducted by a much older Polish music professor with a modest estate south of Danzig. His mother's Jewish blood, had caused Bernie to be sent from Warsaw to friends in London in the late 'thirties. He had finished his schooling at the French Lycée in South Kensington and then served throughout the war in the Pioneer Corps. He had never heard of his parents again, despite protracted and distracted post-war journeys and enquiries in Poland and Germany.

After the war he'd gone up to Christ Church on an Open Modern Languages Scholarship and had then joined the monitoring service of the BBC and, two years later, the foreign news service of *The Times*.

He'd had two disastrous marriages and bitter divorces, first to a fiddler in one of the London orchestras, then to a pediatrician in a Birmingham clinic. Perhaps his unrelenting persecution-mania had worn them out. The ex-wives had retained two children apiece, and Roth supported them, I gathered, generously enough. Meantime, he lived a life as part-exile, part-recluse in the Washington diplomatic-journalistic goldfish bowl.

I had first met him five years before, soon after he'd been taken on by Mason, who had sent him to Washington. There he'd made quite a name for himself as an alert and sympathetic interpreter of the American political scene.

I'd always found him an agreeable but exasperating creature. He wore his sorrows as if they were medals, unable to see that, compared with many of his own generation with a similar eastern European Jewish background, he had been exceptionally fortunate. But he could only think of lost opportunities, lost parents, lost wives, lost children. Perhaps his was basically a case of lost identity. I'd always found his built-in determination to make sure that everyone knew the fates had treated him real bad was too strong a potion to take at all frequently. He saw unseen slights, oversights and the rest of the world's negligences the way other kinks see UFOs.

With his usual vicious punctuality, Roth picked me up on the dot. We exchanged the usual civilities. I'd brought him good wishes, books and two new briar pipes from Mason and a couple of Turnbull and Asser shirts from Markham, who had the useful knack of remembering personal minutiae relating to his more reliable, long-suffering, long-serving oversea correspondents. As a race, they're apt to cultivate a deep sense of neglect by those back home.

After our initial exchanges and some fairly general chit-chat in the car, we got to a small Italian restaurant in Georgetown. After we'd chosen our meal, Bernie said: 'What brings you here? Something tells me the Toynbee girl's involved.'

'Your extra-sensory antennae are in sound working order.'

He smiled thinly. 'I was afraid of that. I suppose she's tried to sell you her version of Stirling as Nelson and herself as Lady Hamilton.'

'I never quite saw Stirling as a one-eyed Nelson-type figure and I certainly don't see Ann Toynbee as a dairymaid at Uppark *or*, for that matter, ending in the gutter.'

'I sometimes forget your interest in the by-ways of history,' he said, smiling again.

'I'm apt to think we're more likely to find any great historical truths tucked away in by-ways rather than High Streets.'

'Sometimes, perhaps. Not always,' he said guardedly, suspecting a dialectical trick. 'But tell me more.'

'We're interested in what we all agree is a remarkable document...'

'As I said,' he cut in: 'Her version of her liaison.'

'I always understood liaisons took two,' I said. But he was too angry to listen, his ego too outraged. 'Why couldn't she have brought the document to me?' he said shrilly. 'She knows me well enough. She knows my position here.'

'She also knows she's not your favourite citizen. And she probably knows you carry something like a flaming torch for Stirling.'

'That's true on both counts,' he admitted ruefully, calming down, almost smiling for once.

'The document was left with me on the understanding that it wasn't to be shown to anyone close to Stirling until after our decision had been made. Half a dozen of us have read the story.'

'Half a dozen! What's the good of having a Washington correspondent if you can't even take him into your confidence on a major Washington story?' Roth asked irritably, the well-known and, I sometimes thought, well-practised hurt look back in his vulnerable brown eyes.

'I've just told you. This is a young Englishwoman's story of an American politician. You were too close to Stirling. Too parti pris by half.'

'I also hope I've got something of a trained journalist's detachment.'

'Relax, Bernie. Forget the agony and aggro. Any American political story gets referred back to you before publication, as you know. Even if things went our way we couldn't publish for at least another three or four months, probably six. You'll see the Toynbee story long before then.'

'Better not at all,' he said gruffly. 'Ann Toynbee's a demoniacally ambitious, self-seeking little bitch–and anybody's tart.'

'Have you had her?'

'Neither the offer nor an acceptance is the remotest possibility.'

'Why the vehemence, then? Or is that the reason.'

'If you must know, it's for the simple reason–which seems to have escaped you–that, in one week, she could, with her updated Fanny Hill, bring down all that Greg Stirling built up in ten years of super-human effort.'

'He still found time for her–and a few others. His amours were a sizeable part of his life.'

'What of it? Since when are a man's peccadilloes to be weighed against his contribution to mankind's welfare?'

'Since when are they to be suppressed as if unwholesome? Actually, the Toynbee girl gives him full marks on both counts. She thinks they're part of the same man. Why praise one quality and hide the other? She may even be nearer the true man than you, with your well-meaning smoke-screen.'

But Roth was in no mood to practise the detachment he apportioned to himself.

'Greg Stirling was the most hopeful thing that's hit this city and this nation in a century or more. He was far bigger than either of the Kennedys. He was younger, he was more radical, he was less equivocal, he was more dynamic. He had a more positive and worthwhile programme. He was the only hope against the galloping fascism of present-day America. Why smear the image now?'

'If you're so keen on his virtues, why not mention one or two of his failings–if failings they are? I certainly don't see them as that. Having met Ann Toynbee. I can't see her as anybody's failing. Rather the reverse. Isn't the man, the myth, the image, or whatever you call it, big enough to take it? It's part of Ann Toynbee's outlook that any man, especially a public figure, ought to be seen whole, not doctored or fixed for admass consumption, the way you seem to want to doctor him.'

'The image has become more important than the man ever was,' Roth said, as if reciting an induced belief. 'Assassination is apt to do that kind of thing. Lincoln's the best example. The Kennedys and King are others.'

'Is it the man or the legend you're so keen on preserving like some Egyptian mummy.'

'Both.'

'Well, Ann Toynbee gives full value to both.'

'She reduces him to any run-of-the-mill politico. Of that I'm quite certain. Anything she's written will denigrate the man. Am I right or wrong?'

'Wrong! If he's so much larger-than-life why are you so keen on whitewashing him? Or, at least, his sex-life?'

'Because he was a friend. Because the sex thing distorts the rest, overpowers the man and all he stood for. He was the hope of the young, the have-nots, the blacks, the poor, the sick–all the great underprivileged masses of this nation that the rest of the world still knows too damn little about.'

'Wouldn't all that sunlight stand a little shade?–if sex is shade. And are the young quite so censorious as you seem to be?'

'You're hairsplitting.'

'I don't think so. I don't see why these great shining white hopes of mankind shouldn't be shown to have a few little soupstains, like the rest of us. Generally, I'm against any personality cult, good or bad, Left or Right, angelic or demoniac. Ultimately it only makes for trouble.'

'You don't believe in men of greatness.'

'Basically, no. Average men in jobs too big for them is the usual thing. And some men have greatness thrust upon them. Assassination's a great help. I'm still suspicious of any man who's so convinced he knows the answers to all man's ills that he's prepared to offer his personal formula to two hundred million people. Apart from that, I also think such men are occasionally mean-gutted, spiteful, lecherous, envious–in common with the rest of us.'

'Lechery is the one that always get the headlines,' he growled.

'It's where most of us came in.'

Again he smiled thinly.

'So far,' I went on, 'all you've been concerned about is the possibility of damage to the Stirling image. What about the pain and suffering to his wife and children.'

'Of course there's that, too,' he said too quickly.

'You're so preoccupied with Stirling, you make the widow sound like an afterthought.'

'Of course she's not an afterthought, but, in the historical picture, it's Stirling who is irreplaceable. In five or ten years time she'll probably be remarried, have a new way of life and a new name. She's attractive enough–and rich enough. His name–and all he stood for–will live for half a century or more. He's as powerful in his impact at this moment as he ever was in real life, perhaps even more so. In a ghastly kind of way, as you say, assassination helps. If you'd grown up, as I did, Paul, as a Jew under the shadow of the SS, you'd clutch at any man who offered some hope to the world's underprivileged.'

'Maybe, but I don't think anything's to be gained by doing a Goebbels-in-reverse on your hero. Making him out to be a cross between the archangel Gabriel and Sir Galahad himself.'

He laughed. 'I see your point, but I can't accept your description.'

'What's the difference, then?'

He shook his head, refusing to be drawn into any further hair-splitting exercise–as he was apt to term other men's views.

'But what about Melanie Stirling?' I persisted. 'Tell me more about her.'

To my great surprise, he said slowly and as if reluctantly, 'I didn't take to her.'

'Why not?'

'She didn't go along with a lot of Greg's beliefs.'

'Are wholesale agreement and full-time co-operation so essential for a wife, then? She seems to have gone along with him in most ways.'

'She was a loyal and marvellous wife.'

'Sounds like an epitaph for a gentle, lovely lady now dead.'

'She's none of those things, actually,' Roth said, relaxing slightly, now that he'd committed himself. 'Her marriage didn't turn out the way she thought it would, that's all.'

'Most marriages don't. How did hers go wrong?'

'Well, for one important thing, when they married, Greg was indistinguishable from any other extremely well-heeled Ivy League young man. His future in the family business seemed certain. She could have looked forward to forty or fifty years of rich and self-indulgent domesticity. Greg changed all that–suddenly and dramatically. She stood by him.'

'Well, she'd married him for better or for worse.'

'This was a lot worse than the worst she could ever have dreamed about. She had no interest in politics of any kind. Deep down, she hates the poor.'

'And you didn't like her. That makes a difference, too.'

'Not really,' he said, and then added quietly, 'Yes. I suppose it does make a difference.'

'You don't want to talk about her?'

'You're crowding me, Paul. Stirling was the only Stirling as far as I was concerned. I would have followed him to the barricades, anywhere he wanted to go. I worked for him. Wrote half his speeches, if you must know. For me he was one of the few hopes for mankind. To me she was his wife and that was all. I had no time left for her.'

'From your letter I gather you had.'

'I admired her loyalty. Taken over the years, it was a remarkable exhibition of selflessness. Remarkable.'

'You didn't take to Melanie Stirling; you don't like Ann Toynbee. Were there any Stirling women of whom you did approve?'

By this time our exchanges were again becoming fairly sharp.

'You think I was jealous of them or something?'

'Something like that. It's been known.'

'*Homo manqué*? Something like that, you mean?'

'You'll have to find the right word or phrase for it. If there is one. I'm only on the outside, guessing.'

'You're like the rest of your countrymen,' Roth said suddenly, venom breaking out. 'You can never understand enthusiasm for anything or anyone who isn't a teenage sportsman or an octogenarian littérateur.'

I laughed. 'Not bad,' I said. 'A bull's eye, in fact.'

He smiled, but not in humour. 'And like the rest of your countrymen you enjoy jokes against yourselves. Sheer inverted vanity and arrogance.'

'Probably,' I agreed. 'It's been said before. But let's get back to Stirling. I never knew him. Perhaps he would have brainwashed me the way he seems to have brainwashed you.'

'Brainwashed! You must be mad!'

'Brainwashing's not just a communist-fascist work-out as I see it, Bernie. I think it's just as easy to brainwash liberally, so to speak. The English brainwashed the world for years into believing we'd established a Parliamentary democracy. What's so democratic about an aristocracy that's scarcely changed in five hundred years or an Upper House mainly still based on accident of birth and ownership of land. What's so democratic about a nation in which the rich get richer and the poor get poorer? All the time. If that isn't brainwashing the world on the theme of so-called democracy, what is?'

'It's still a lot better than any place else I know,' he said defiantly.

'For me, too. I'm not criticizing. I'm observing.'

He smiled thinly. Gradually we returned to a more equable exchange. Neither of us seemed to be enjoying the way our words and meanings were getting entangled and mangled.

'What d'you think my chances are of seeing Melanie Stirling?' I asked, changing direction.

'Not very rosy. She retired to her ancestral home in South Carolina immediately after the memorial service and hasn't been seen since. I doubt whether anybody in the news business will see her again for a long long time. Not even *Time-Life* or *Newsweek*'s been able to get anywhere near her. Certainly none of the networks.'

'Should I ring her?'

'You can try, but I wouldn't if I were you. You'd get a fairly decisive brush-off. Your best chance – in fact, your only chance – is to fly down there and then try you luck on the doorstep.'

'But you still think my chances are nil?'

'I'd say so.'

'Could you give me a letter of introduction?'

'I suppose I could. With some reluctance, mark you. And it wouldn't cut much ice. As I've intimated, I don't think I was her favourite house-guest, but she knew the kind of regard I had for Greg, and I hope, vice versa. It might help, but I doubt it. And I still don't see why I should.'

'You might get double satisfaction if I get the brush-off, decisively and forever, direct from the widow herself.'

'Satisfaction doesn't come into it,' he said stiffly.

'All right then. I'll fly down, armed with your note. If I do get in to see her, what d'you think she'll really have to say about the Toynbee tale?'

'I think she'll have you thrown out of the house.'

'She's got some big retainers?'

'Big and black. She's old-fashioned southern style, right through,' Roth said, smiling his chilly smile again. 'Not a style I like.'

'Too anachronistic?'

'Anachronistic, monstrous, intolerable.'

'How did Stirling square all that with his views?'

'He never did. And she never did. That's why he went there less and less.'

'Sounds cosy.'

'It was sometimes very difficult for both of them.'

'All the same, I think I'll go,' I said. 'Let me have the best letter you can pen in the circumstances.'

'We'll drive back to the office and I'll write something now. I can't promise it will be very convincing.'

'I'll take what comes out of the ball point.'

Again he smiled, more thinly than ever, and called for the bill.

We drove back to his office. And while he wrote at his desk, I ranged along the shelves of his bookish room, as orderly as an ocean-going chart-room. He must have had a couple of thousand books housed there in his compact library of Americana: Bryce, Emerson, Whitman, Melville, Mencken, Nathan, Frost, Wolfe, Santayana, Weller, Brogan. Roth certainly worked close to his check-points.

A quarter-of-an-hour later he stood up and handed me a letter on his own die-stamped Georgetown writing-paper. I read:

Dear Melanie: This note introduces a friend of mine from London, one Paul Mortimer. I have known him for many years and he remains the Englishman I would most readily trust. He is travelling to Athens especially to see you with what seems to me an extra-ordinary proposal. I have told him you will turn the whole matter down flat, but he is not to be deterred from making his journey. Will you see him?

I can at least say in his favour that he will take your yea or nay immediately, will not argue, will not pester. Please see him, so that he will know that I spoke out of some knowledge of your dear self.

I hope many things for you, but the hopes are too large for words. Ever, Bernie.

'If any letter could get me into the house this might,' I said gratefully.

'The professional persuader got the better–momentarily–of my emotional convictions,' he said, almost sheepishly.

'Well, thanks a lot.'

Bernie smiled. With permissible pride he said, 'The word "extra-ordinary" should arouse any woman's curiosity. I've also implied that I've made a decision on her behalf, which she'll resent, anyway. Finally, I suggest that you're something of an olde worlde English gentleman which still means something down there.'

'I hope she reacts to your reasoning, and I match up to your implications.'

'Don't set overmuch store by it,' he said dismally. 'My would-be readings of the female mind have so far been consistently disastrous –to me and to them.'

'Well, thanks again. I'll let you know in due course if you've read her right. I hope so. Can your girl book me a return flight to the nearest airport to Athens and charge to London?'

He picked up an air time-table, flicked through the pages and said: 'There's a National Airlines flight out of here to Charleston at ten-forty in the morning. We'll see to your ticket. Could you call in on your way out to the airport? Say ten-thirty. I'll take you back to the Madison now.'

We took the elevator down to the hall and walked through to the car. We drove in silence. Outside the hotel I thanked him, went to my room and in ten minutes, no more, was asleep, air-conditioning notwithstanding.

PART IV

– 1 –

The flight took an hour. We landed at Charleston in what seemed to me fully fledged tropical conditions: the heat of the day burned into face and eyes and feet. Already my clothes were clinging like seaweed.

Athens was over ten miles away. I was tempted to stay in Charleston overnight, for it had been one of the most memorable places I had visited as a young man. I would have given a lot to see once again the balustraded and canopied pleasures of the city, but time was the one intangible I couldn't give. So I took a taxi from the stand outside the airport and asked the swarthy, unshaven, cheerful driver where I ought to stay.

'Classy or ordinary?'

'Midway,' I said and he suggested the Turnpike Inn, about eight miles out of Charleston. I said I'd want a driver for the rest of the day: was he game? He said, no, if I didn't mind; he preferred sitting around the airport, his daily routine.

I liked the look of the Turnpike Inn, booked in for two days, paid off my driver, took a bath and then had an omelette in the so-called Battery Bar.

Afterwards I booked a local taxi from Athens.

When I went out, my driver was waiting. This one was spruce, shaved, ready to go. I asked him whether he knew where the Stirling house was.

'Lake House. Where Miss Gardner lives, I guess you mean, mister,' he said, almost surly on the instant. 'We never went for that nigger-loving husband of hers a great big bundle down here.'

Somewhat shaken by the brusque and brazen come-back, I said, 'I've a message for Mrs Stirling and I'd like to take it out there.' I half-expected him to drive off in a flurry of fury and dust, but he waited. I got in. His surliness still burned. I wondered how frequently – or infrequently – Stirling had ventured into this hostile territory.

'Miss Gardner's a fine lady,' the driver muttered as we started. He seemed to be talking to himself. 'I never could understand how she took up with that bum.'

Once again I was surprised by his outspoken aggressiveness, but,

I reminded myself, from memories of Chicago and New York, American taxi-drivers had always been that way. I stayed silent.

'She spends most of her time here now, I guess,' he went on. 'Nobody ever sees her. She keeps herself hidden away in that great house.'

We were silent for the rest of the four-mile journey, skirting the township of Athens to judge from signposts via a clover-leaf into a country road.

Gradually, the landscape changed. Soon we were amongst woodlands; high, dark-foliaged trees, crowding in upon the narrow road, keeping the sun from the track, darkening the day.

The taxi turned off on to a lesser track and then, coming to a clearing, swung round before vast iron gates with a couple of white octagonal clapboard lodges with small cupolas, recently painted.

The driver used his klaxon twice in short quiet honks. A tall Negro, in white shirt and black trousers, as spruce as the lodge, came out towards the car via a small side gate.

'I gotta gentleman here with a message for Miss Gardner,' the driver said.

'Does he have an appointment with Mrs Stirling?' the lodge-keeper asked, stressing the 'Stirling'.

I spoke up: 'I've no appointment. I've a letter of introduction from a mutual friend.'

'Shall I give your name, sir?'

'Mrs Stirling wouldn't know it from Adam. I'd better leave the letter. I'll scrawl a note on it.'

'I'll willingly call Mrs Stirling, sir.'

'No, I wouldn't want to bother her. She can call me if she feels like it.'

I took out the letter, wrote across the envelope: *I'm staying at the Turnpike Inn. I would take it as a privilege to get a call saying that I could call again. PM*, and handed the envelope over.

'As you wish sir.'

I thanked him, got back into the car. As the taxi turned, I looked back into the gravelled drive, hemmed in by vast rhododendron and azalea bushes, all against a background of gigantic dark-leaved trees. I hoped I'd get a chance to see them again, preferably at leisure.

Meantime, we were on the track again.

'You shoulda waited, mister,' the driver was saying. 'These niggers like coming the major-domo in these outfits. They get uppity if you string along with 'em in the kinda way you did.'

'He had a job to do. You said–and I know–Mrs Stirling wants

her privacy protected. I thought he did a good job. He was efficient, polite, pleasant.'

'You sure got strange ideas about politeness, mister.'

I had no more words and once again we finished the journey in silence. I paid him off. He swung his big Buick round and went off in a flurry of dust that presumably echoed his feelings.

I went in and had another bath. I felt as tacky as flypaper. Lying dispiritedly in the bath I wondered why I'd agreed to make the trip. The whole project now seemed unreal, unprofitable. Four thousand miles from Fleet Street, Ann Toynbee's extravaganza seemed like a zany fantasy.

Around six o'clock I changed into a light-weight blue suit and went along to the residents' lounge, a comfortless room with large-screen television and an assortment of black vinyl-covered arm-chairs. I was a long way from Fifth Avenue or even Charleston.

I sat reading a paperback I'd bought at Kennedy airport; a long-ago novel by Compton Mackenzie. That passed the time for an hour. By then I thought I'd have an early supper, watch some of the local TV and turn in early. I was finding the humid heat fairly wearing.

I'd given Mrs Stirling a couple of hours from the time I'd called at Lake House to call me if she had a mind to. After seven hours I began to face the fact that my chances of a meeting were zero. By then I was chiding myself for having been too considerate and reticent at the lodge gates. I should have at least have chanced my arm.

I had a pleasant enough supper, along with a dozen travellers in and out of Athens and a rather sad young honeymoon couple who bickered all through their meal. The chances for their way ahead seemed pretty dim. Afterwards, I checked that the first plane out of Charleston to Washington was at 08.25; thence to New York. A bit early, I decided, and opted for New York direct at 12.30. I also checked that I could have coffee and a miscellany of wheat cakes, griddle cakes, muffins and honey in my room at eight sharp.

I went back to my room about nine, wrote a few notes so that I'd be able to keep my memory fresh under enquiry in London and turned in to read. It had been a thoroughly desultory day and I looked forward with some anticipation to escape in either of those north-bound planes. Meantime, I damned Roth and Melanie Stirling, but not, strangely enough, Ann Toynbee.

—2—

But Melanie Stirling rang at nine the next morning.

'I got your note or rather Bernie Roth's,' she said after announcing herself briefly. 'I decided to sleep on it. I suppose I also hoped you'd be gone by the time I rang. Are you an English newspaperman, Mr Mortimer?'

'I'm afraid so.'

'As I guessed. A journalist so far from home means a story and that's what I don't want.'

She had a slow-speaking, deep-toned voice, agreeable to listen to.

'I see your point.'

'If you see my point, why are you here?'

'Because I think I've got a point, too.'

She laughed. 'What's your point in ten words flat?'

'To tell you about a story that's already written and see what your views are.'

'I'm against any kind of meeting. It's sure to do with my husband and I'm tired of all that. I want to forget it.'

'The story I want to discuss concerns you a good deal more than your late husband. If it's published you might well come to wish you had seen me.'

'That sounds dangerously like an ultimatum.'

I took a long chance. 'It may sound like one, but, oddly enough, it isn't.'

'Does that mean that if I see the story and don't like it, it gets torn up.'

'Not quite so final as that, but I doubt whether it would get published quite so soon or in quite the same form as the writer would have wished.'

'It's an English story?'

'In a way.'

'And you think I wouldn't like it.'

'I'm sure you wouldn't.'

'Then why, in Heaven's name, come four thousand miles to tell me that? You're scared to publish as it is; is that it?'

'Partly, but not wholly. If my paper doesn't publish the story, another paper–probably a good deal less respectable and responsible –will publish. That's for sure. And it'll go around the world with what I think would be an altogether wrong emphasis.'

'No story like that would go in any newspaper without my OK. That's why one hires lawyers, Mr Mortimer.'

'I don't think even US lawyers move as fast as some European publishers.'

'So you think I'm caught either way.'

'Not inevitably.'

'You're back to your ultimatum?'

'Not even that. At this stage all I'm suggesting is that you consider the story I have. I'm not sure any other publication likely to get hold of the story would do the same.'

'If that's not an ultimatum I've never heard one before,' she said bitterly. 'Well, you'd better come on up. No wonder I hate all journalists, feature writers, photographers and the rest of your so-called profession, Mr Mortimer. In my experience they're either unctuous sentimentalists like your friend Mr Roth or just plain cut-throat thrusters.'

'It's not much of a choice you offer,' I said, 'but if you're right, don't you think it's strange we should be the first people dictators slap down and shut up, Mrs Stirling?'

She laughed shortly. 'I see you not only *write* words, Mr Mortimer, you split 'em. Then, to my astonishment, she said, 'Would you care to come to lunch if you're free. How long are you staying?'

'I was taking the midday plane out.'

'I should have let you go. I woke up thinking you might be a doorstep-squatter and I'd have you around for a week.'

For a moment I almost told her what to do with her lunch. If this was the Southern hospitality I'd heard so much about, I didn't think much of it. But when in Athens do as the Athenians do, I told myself and thanked her for the invitation, and left it that I'd be at Lake House around one o'clock.

As things were turning out I didn't think I was likely to find myself on Melanie Stirling's side. Or she on mine. And I didn't see my stay dragging on.

–3–

Nevertheless, I cancelled my flight, asked the girl at the desk to order a taxi to take me out to Lake House at twelve-thirty and then went for a walk. But it wasn't walking country. I found myself at the end of a soggy lane with weeds growing thickly and dankly. I turned back.

I sat on a bench out in the clearing behind the motel and sought to picture what kind of woman Melanie Stirling might be. I recalled pictures of a handsome, fine-boned woman with dark eyes and a long slim neck. But pictures never give hints of colour, voice or manner. I'd liked the voice, but I wasn't mad keen on the sampling I'd had of her olde worlde Southern-style courtesy and all that. But why should she be so mannerly? In her eyes, wasn't I a boorish, uninvited, unwanted, unwarrantable intruder into her mourning?

The taxi came. The same Buick and the same driver as on the previous day. We were going out to Lake House again, I said.

'You shoulda done what I said yesterday, man, and gone in over that coon's dead body and saved a day.'

'My own way seems to have worked quite well.'

'A sight slower, mister.'

'It takes all sorts. You bust 'em, I trust 'em.'

He looked round, but decided to leave it alone. Again, in tacit agreement, we journeyed in silence.

–4–

This time the lodge-keeper had the gates open and let us through. Looking back I saw that he was swinging them to again. All very Deep South Trad, I thought, and more than a touch antediluvian, although I suspected that the scene could probably have been paralleled a hundred times on other estates well below the Mason-Dixon line, despite Kennedy-Johnson-Stirling and the Greater-than-Great Society.

The drive continued for well over a mile through what seemed like barely tamed jungle; oleander bushes at the edge, giant trees beyond.

The car was hot, the drive was bumpy, the day oppressive. Then, suddenly, round a bend, the house, built on a knoll above a lawn sloping down to a lake, came into view; a colonnaded Palladian mansion, curiously two-dimensional at first sight, rather like a stage-set painted on great flats.

The drive curved up to the house. I got out, paid off the driver and asked if he'd call back for me in a couple of hours. He agreed. I went up the wide steps to the doorway beneath the vast portico.

Through the half-glazed door I could see a marble hall with another glazed door at the far, very far, end. Lake House was quite a place.

I pulled at a cast-iron bell-pull which seemed the only possible way of announcing my arrival. Even as I listened to the far-off tinkle, a young Negro was opening the door. Fine features above a grey-and-black striped seersucker jacket over a black tie, black narrow, knife-edged trousers. The Stirling livery was probably an emancipated advance on stiff collars, doublet and hose, but it still had overtones of a distant past.

But that was only the beginning.

I was taken across the hall and shown into an enormous drawing-room. 'I will tell Mrs Stirling you are here, sir,' the youth said and left me to my curiosity.

The house was built, it seemed, on conventional Palladian lines, varied to taste: a central hall, rooms opening off, but no grand staircase. The drawing-room had high windows on three sides: one overlooked the forecourt and lake–or was it a southern bayou? –and, beyond, grassland dotted with oaks and chestnuts. The two side windows overlooked a vista of hillside and woodland, background for the nearer parkland. A setting by Capability Brown straight out of Oxfordshire or Derbyshire translated into the Deep South with an improbable luxuriance of growth and dark glaucous foliage thrown in for good measure. I turned from contemplation of this peaceful panorama as a voice said 'Good afternoon, Mr Mortimer,' and I turned to meet a young woman in a brown cotton dress.

I thanked her for letting me visit her. She suggested that we sat down. Facing me on one of the sofas, she said: 'In a way I had no option, had I? I couldn't let Mr Roth make decisions for me–which may have been his or your calculation. Your virtual ultimatum clinched it.'

'No ultimatum,' I repeated patiently.

'A choice between inevitabilities, then,' she amended.

'Not even that,' I said lamely. 'A consideration of alternatives, I'd say.'

'Prettily put,' she chided, 'but I imagine it amounts to the same thing.'

I'd expected a dark-haired youngish woman, for that was the way her photographs always seemed to reproduce. But her hair was dark bronze-auburn, very striking, especially in alliance with her fine brown eyes and a dark vivid complexion that I could only relate to a gypsy. She was about middle height, which means, for an American woman, five feet six or so, and very slim. Her brown sleeveless dress well became her colouring.

'We usually lunch here rather later than New Yorkers,' she said. 'Two o'clock sharp. I hope you're not too ravenous. I'm afraid it's little more than a snack. I've a dinner party tonight, but we'll do our best.'

She was friendly but distantly so. I was being summed up. And why not? More than most professions, trades, or jobs, journalism includes the full range of humanity from horrors and hogs to boors and bores. Apart from that, they spell danger to those who prefer privacy. And Melanie Stirling plainly did.

She asked what I'd drink. I chose Dubonnet and tonic. She laughed. 'One always thinks of journalists as such hard-drinking men,' she said, pouring Bourbon for herself.

We sat down again. 'We've got the best part of an hour,' she said. 'Why not outline your ultimatum – or is it ultimata? – and let's see where we go from there. Do you smoke?' I declined. She took a cigarette. I lit it for her, returned slowly to the sofa, sat back and took a deep breath. Having a large cold tumber in one cold hand helped. We were silent for a long long minute before I began: 'You and your husband knew a girl called Ann Toynbee ....'

'I knew her socially; my husband knew her – well, biblically – to put it politely.'

She was leaning back in her sofa, relaxed and watchful, but giving out a kind of intensity of concentration that rather unnerved me. I knew that I was involved with a very wary and steely numero indeed, a sophisticated tigress. Casually she added; 'A clever girl and a good-looker.'

I nodded and said. 'Ann Toynbee kept a journal of her friendship with your husband and now wishes the journal to be published.'

'Rather more than schoolgirl-diary stuff, I take it?' she queried.

'A good deal more.'

'And you've come four thousand miles to tell me this and get my views,' she said with a contemptuous, incredulous smile. 'What on earth did you think my reply would be?'

I knew I'd have to live through one or two moments and comments along the same lines. I kept to my point.

'The journal is pretty comprehensive,' I said.

She laughed briefly. 'Diction is de choice of woids, as they say in the Bronx. Comprehensive seems a careful word. Give it to me straight. It's the lot, I take it.'

'I don't know what the lot would take in. I'll stick by my word.'

'Have it your own Doctor Johnson way. Why does she want to publish it?'

'Because, like most other diarists, however secretive, she's an exhibitionist at heart. Unlike most of the world's better-known diarists she wants her exhibition while she's alive.'

'What about money?'

'Of course she'll clean up, but, oddly enough, I don't think that's the major, impelling force. I think the driving-force is her yearning to be famous, infamous, notorious, call it what you like.'

'Could she be bought off?'

'Not a chance.'

'Every woman has her price, Mr Mortimer.'

'Not if she'll get more than anyone could ever offer, plus what may well be her even more important objective–fame or notoriety.'

'She'll live to regret it.'

'I'm not so sure. A few people–including yourself, I imagine – genuinely have no wish for headlines. Most people yearn for them, and, if they get 'em, thrive on 'em and never want to be out of the news again. I think Miss Toynbee–embryonically so far–is like that.'

'It's true,' she said, as if she'd decided to act like a human being. 'Greg was like that. Being in the news was a kind of drug to him. Wholly and utterly addictive.' She smiled. 'Perhaps he was a carrier and passed it on to Miss Toynbee. The bug certainly by-passed me. Tell me more about the journal and what you'd like to do with it, Mr Mortimer.'

'Well, as it is, the whole thing's far too long. Well over a quarter of a million words. . . .'

'That's quite an output for someone in her twenties.'

'It is indeed.'

'Have you got any of it with you? The less comprehensive parts, that is?'

I shook my head. She said 'Sorry to interrupt.' I said, 'Not at all,' and went on: 'I must tell you straight away Mrs Stirling, that half a dozen experienced journalists as well as myself have read the first half of the diaries and find them of extraordinary, even hypnotic, interest.'

'They ought to, if she's told the truth.'

'We'd like to publish an edited version of the journals.'

'I suppose–unlike the publishers of my girlhood editions of Boccaccio and Casanova–you're proposing to leave in the purple passages and expurgate the dull stuff?' she said, smiling.

I laughed. 'Little enough is dull. At least, that's my view. It's just that we couldn't run the full-scale job.'

'I could get an injunction against your outfit even on the little you've told me so far,' she said quietly. 'You must realize that, Mr Mortimer. And I could probably file suit against you for a hundred million dollars for damages if you published without pre-announcement.'

She spoke agreeably and assuredly as if she'd just finished a leisurely four-year stint at the Harvard Law School and done quite well. 'American lawyers can be very quick off the mark, Mr Mortimer, despite what you said on the telephone–and Americans, generally speaking, are an extremely litigious lot.'

'I'd agree on all counts.'

'Then why are you here?' she said, the quiet reflective tone gone and a sharp edge back in the voice.

'Because I think the Russians–and/or the Chinese–could do a Pasternak-in-reverse on your husband *and* the United States by publishing the journals and letting translations seep into the West. It would be sensational, to say the least, and they'd get a fantastic coverage with nobody needing to pay for any syndication rights.'

She was silent.

'I see that,' she said at last. 'This is the ultimatum, then. But do you think Miss Toynbee would do this? *She* may be bluffing. *You* may be bluffing.'

'I assure you I'm not, Mrs Stirling. Miss Toynbee would be even more notorious if that were the way her journals got published. As I told you before, I don't think money's her driving-force. She's got a very good job. Her family's quite well-off. Her future's quite cosy.'

'Cosy! What an odd English word to hear in this context. But I see what you mean.'

'I think you'll find that Miss Toynbee wants her name known throughout the world. In a way she's just doing what many ambitious men have done as a matter of masculine course throughout history. She wants great fame or great notoriety and she wants it young. Let's call her a female Byron.'

'So, basically, you think she's got me over a barrel. What about the International Court at the Hague? Couldn't they do something about it?'

'I doubt it. They're OK on oil royalties, boundary disputes shipping lanes and the rest of the international legalities between two parties, both equally prepared for arbitration. I doubt whether they'd cut any ice at all in a matter of this kind or even whether they'd be quick enough off the mark. The Russians would just let it happen and then express surprise at the happening, call on the civilized world to join them in horror at the revelations.'

To my surprise Melanie Stirling said, smiling, 'Ann Toynbee would have the devil of a job spending all those millions of roubles in Russia. One sable coat's enough for any woman and I don't remember her as a sable-type girl.'

'That's true,' I said. 'I happen to know she shops at Fenwick's and Jaeger when in London.'

She laughed. 'So what would you advise me to do, Mr Mortimer?'

'I'd suggest you made no decision of any kind now, but waited and let us show you an edited version of the journals.'

Again she was silent.

'I'm not so sure about that Russian angle,' she said at last. 'A lot depends on the climate existing between the two nations at the time, don't you think?'

'A lot. But the Russians are always ready to upset a climate and then disclaim all official knowledge. Moscow students can bust up a foreign embassy whilst the authorities deprecate the whole affair whilst it's still going on. They've made dissociation a major diplomatic ploy.'

'But I could get an injunction against any publishing house in the world outside Russia or China?'

'But that's leaving out half the world at one go.'

She smiled.

'Italian publishers, can also work very fast and surreptitiously when the heat is on.'

But she hadn't given up. Like any other rich woman who'd had a lot of things their own way all their lives, she couldn't believe that there wasn't a way out for her. She said again: 'If I decided to fight your newspaper, Mr Mortimer, you wouldn't stand a chance in hell. And if I defeated you, who else would have a go?'

'I come back again to the Russians and the Chinese and to the fact that even to file the injunction would make a lot of people very inquisitive.'

As I took another gulp of my Dubonnet, I heard my hostess say, to my very great surprise, 'Would you care to join my dinner party this evening, Mr Mortimer?'

'Very willingly, but I'm afraid I've no formal clothes.'

She gave me a quick glance, as if appraising my height and weight.

'That can soon be sorted out, I'm sure.'

'What about your table-plan?' I said, smiling. 'Reflect carefully. These spontaneous and generous invitations can cost a hostess deep regrets six minutes or six hours later.'

She laughed as she got up from the sofa, smoothing down her dress over extremely shapely legs. I stood up, too. Gaily and without reservation she said: 'On the contrary, Mr Mortimer, it would be a great relief and privilege for me and you'd be helping me out. Frankly, I'm a man short, if that eases your conscience. In any case I need more time to think over all we've been discussing. Tell me more about Ann Toynbee's journals.'

During the ensuing ten minutes, I gave Melanie Stirling the most concentrated rundown of a quarter-of-a-million words I or perhaps anybody else has ever essayed. She sat silent through the disquisition.

At the end she said: 'It sounds quite a portrait. She seems to have got him fair and square. As far as I was able to judge at the time, and reflecting on the relationship since, I think Miss Toynbee had the rare talent or rare good luck of not getting emotionally involved with Greg. Most of his other women did. He seemed the answer to so many feminine yearnings.'

Her own words seemed so detached, especially from a widow so recently bereaved, that I looked up sharply, but her eyes were so intensely set on myself that I turned away to stare at a pair of three-quarter-length portraits hanging either side of the door.

'My forebears,' she said evenly. 'There are dozens of others around the house. Mostly painted by French artists who used to come over here for a couple of seasons and clean up. As now, people wanted to leave replicas of themselves for posterity. Instead they've become elements in my colour scheme. As you see, the room is decorated around the reds and blues in those enormous portraits. A salutary thought for anyone who wants to leave his mark on posterity. I imagine they're a lot less searching as portraits than Ann Toynbee's journal seems to be.'

'I rather like them, all the same,' I said. 'An indulgent and superficial appraisal's a great relief sometimes.'

She nodded, and pointed to the large portrait above the chimney-piece on the one windowless wall: 'My great-great-great-grandfather. He came here post-Revolution and made a fortune in sugar and tobacco. Why don't you stay here for a day or so, Mr Mortimer?'

'I call that the hospitality of the South ever-extending itself, Mrs Stirling,' I heard myself saying as I puzzled over her *volte face*. She smiled 'Not a bit of it. I've been cut off from everything for a couple of months. I thoroughly enjoy my privacy and I've lots of friends, but a voice of sanity from Europe is a gift not to be spurned. Will you?'

I said I'd like to.

'Then I'll get your things brought up from that crummy motel.'

'They're very conveniently packed and my bill's equally conveniently paid. But I'd better tell the girl there to try to tell the taxi man not to call this afternoon.'

'You expected short shrift, then?'

'Very.'

She tugged at a bell-pull. The young Negro entered and took instructions.

– 5 –

I enjoyed the meal and my introduction to a way of life persisting so improbably into the twentieth century. A way of life, I imagine, more likely to be encountered in the Deep South than anywhere else in the world today.

A couple of white-gloved Negroes, in the Stirling – or was it Gardner? – seersucker livery, waited at table, serving a three-course meal – fish soufflé, roast chicken, pineapple au kirsch. Some snack!

Afterwards, again in the great drawing-room, taking coffee, Melanie Stirling, seeming to read my thoughts, said: 'As an Englishman interested in various aspects of history, Mr Mortimer, you must find this southern way of life a curious relic from the past.'

'The word "relic" always suggests death and decay. This set-up seems very much alive.'

'Greg hated it. He was here only once in the past two years. He couldn't bear to think that the system still worked and that people didn't seem to object.'

'All systems work – for some.'

'I suppose you're right. Even Stalinism – for some. Greg wanted a world and a system that worked for all. He hated everything Lake House stood for. Stands for still, I suppose.'

'In his position, and with his political philosophy, I can see why.'

'More a programme than a philosophy,' she said dismissively, and then asked what I'd like to do for the rest of the day. 'Old customs die hard,' she added. 'I usually rest.'

I said I'd rather not interrupt her routine, adding: 'I'd like to wander in the shadier areas of the grounds along the lake for an hour or so and then, perhaps, also rest.'

She seemed relieved to agree. I wondered whether she was already regretting her hospitality as she showed me my room and wished me well in my wanderings.

Lake House and its plantations seemed to stretch for miles. First, I inspected the house more closely, taking pleasure in the curious and determined way that the architect, with his mansard roof and parapet, had grafted French characteristics on to a Palladian prototype. Afterwards, I wandered slowly along the lake, making a wide detour to return through the magnificently landscaped – and maintained – parkland. The air was heavy and damp. The day's heat seemed to burn from both cloudless sky and weedless grass; a walk through a vapour-bath.

I was glad to be back in my air-conditioned room. Lying on the bed were light-weight dinner jacket, trousers, black silk socks, white silk shirt, black tie. By the bed were black patent shoes, modestly buckled. I tried the jacket on for size. A well-nigh perfect fit. So, even more curiously, were the shoes.

I had no doubt that I was about to wear part of Greg Stirling's rarely worn home-based wardrobe. He'd certainly had an eye for gear I thought, appraising the watered silk facings. I remembered, as I hung the suit in the wardrobe, that Ann Toynbee had said as much here and there in her journal. But the day was too hot for overmuch speculation. Within a minute I was undressed and under a single cooling linen sheet. Within another minute I was asleep.

–6–

I awoke a couple of hours later, soon after six, lay there wondering where I was; then, coming to, what the house-drill was. Melanie Stirling had said dinner at nine, but presumably I was meant to surface before then and make my number in the drawing-room.

I shaved, bathed and dressed in leisurely fashion and went down some time after eight. A dark, broad-shouldered man was alone in the drawing-room. He said, 'You must be Paul Mortimer. Melanie called me and told me you were here. I'm Louis de Marais, usually known, I need hardly tell you, as Lou Murray around here.'

I shook hands, puzzled momentarily by the gallic name allied with the deep, thoroughly transatlantic voice. Then I recalled that any number of French families had been here for almost two centuries. As Melanie Stirling had said earlier, her own background was similar. And wasn't Lake House the work of a French architect?

De Marais began to talk about the house as if in pride-by proxy. 'I find it fascinating,' he said, 'to think of these French and English architects, most of them sons of builders and carpenters back home, coming out here and providing plans and elevations for the planters, the *nouveaux riches* of the times. They certainly knew their stuff, but I suppose they had good models to work from. I suppose that's one of our troubles today. We seem to have lost any interest in earlier models of anything.'

He was in his early forties, I judged; tall and handsome; black hair flecked with grey; grey eyed; broad-shouldered, but running to fat the way one-time athletes are apt to go in post-glory days. I could imagine him on any US college squad. Thirty pounds less and he'd have been likely Hollywood material.

I asked whether he lived locally.

'Ten miles off. I grow cotton. My people came here around the time Melanie's family settled here.'

'From which part of France?'

'Dijon. They must have had a sixth political sense. They skipped the Revolution when they saw it coming.' He said the words so smoothly he'd plainly said them a thousand times before.

'Do you still keep any contacts with France?'

'I spent two years reading law–French Law, of all things–at the Sorbonne. Apart from that I'm an American citizen through and through. I was even a lieutenant in the US Navy.'

He was agreeably communicative. I asked how many were dining.

'Around eight, I guess. That's Melanie's favourite number. I hear you saved the table-plan. One of our aged bachelor friends got himself caught up in a Washington command performance.'

Half an hour later, eight of us were sitting in Empire chairs around the large circular pedestal table. Chairs and table of amboyna, with faded gilt embellishments, were set under a chandelier *à la Malmaison*. Walter Reuther, John L. Lewis, Luther King need never have lived for all the impact their lives had made on such a setting. Negroes in white linen jackets, black trousers, black bow ties, served the meal.

The guests were from plantations twenty or thirty miles around, I gathered. Talk was of US politics *vis-à-vis* Vietnam. Russia, Europe, China cropped up–in that order. Politics, interlaced with gossip concerning crops and neighbours, was the order of the day, or rather, night.

The whole set-up was like a colour-page feature out of *Vogue* showing how the Beautiful People lived–except that, apart from Melanie Stirling, there weren't any particularly Beautiful People around the table. De Marais might have made it if he'd had laid off food and wine for a time, but the two elderly couples and an earnest, bespectacled, youngish, spinsterish research lady from the University of South Carolina were just plain ordinary folk. I had the researcher on my right, Melanie Stirling on my left.

I made and listened to polite conversation and thought how exactly right so discreet a dinner party was three months after a husband's death. My own historical interests were quickly discovered and dismissed by Teresa Cross. From then on I was doused in a lecture on every aspect of Norman influences in Sicily, Miss Cross's subject. She was certainly making it her very own and I wasn't surprised to learn that a doubtless well-footnoted scholarly monograph was in production at the University Press.

Afterwards, in the drawing-room, the dull, discreet exchanges continued. Dull to an outsider, but enthralling, no doubt, to the intimately initiated and involved. Neverthess, I had to admit it was an advance on anything the Turnpike Inn could have laid on.

The party broke up around half-past eleven, with warming displays of tenderness and consideration for Mrs Stirling. De Marais was last to go. I overheard him say he'd be over the following day for lunch. Then the great house was suddenly quiet again and I was with Melanie Stirling, drinking a last whisky and thanking her for a very pleasant evening.

'The kind of evening that I love and the kind which drove Greg absolutely screaming mad.'

'I can see it was scarcely the kind of evening for a man dedicated to a Greater-than-the-Great Society.'

She smiled. 'But it's the way I grew up. It's the life I know: a way of life I like.'

'You do it very well, if I may say so.'

'You disapprove!' she said, accusing but unconcerned.

I laughed. 'I thoroughly enjoyed the experience and it was kind of you to let me come.'

'You sound like Eliza Doolittle,' she chided.

'I feel rather like Eliza Doolittle,' I admitted.

She laughed and then said suddenly, 'About Ann Toynbee's journal.'

I put up a restraining hand. 'Let's forget it. I understand.'

She got up from the sofa and crossed towards the fireplace filled with flowers in a great bronze urn. She still held her tumbler and her back was towards me.

'But you don't understand!' she snapped. She spat out the words: 'Not one damned footling thing!'

'All right, then,' I said. 'I don't. Fill me in.'

I sipped and waited. To my disbelieving astonishment, she swung round and I heard her saying–and the words seemed, to me, to come from a long way off: 'I want Ann Toynbee's journal published. As soon as you like. As much as you like. I'll give you my O K in writing. Now if you like.'

The shock was so sudden and complete that I think I nodded dumbly as one does in dreams. She wasn't drunk. She didn't seem doped. Yet the outburst was so unreal that I expected to wake in the Turnpike Inn or an aeroplane and find I'd dozed off. But I still thought it was no time for comment from me.

'Of course you don't understand,' she went on. 'How could you? How could any man?–except Louis.'

She moved from the fireplace and stood by the armchair, looking down at me. She spoke quietly yet with fierce intensity: 'Mr Mortimer, I want this saintly image of Greg Stirling that's building up fast, destroyed, utterly and completely. Unless that happens I shall be the prisoner of his life and death for the rest of my days.'

'Sit down and explain. Please!' I begged, sounding I thought, even as I said the words, like a cross between a good uncle and a bad psychiatrist. But the words worked, or rather half-worked. She didn't sit down but she did explain.

With her back to the flowers in the fireplace, she began: 'When I married Greg Stirling, Mr Mortimer, he lived much the same kind of life as I did and now do again. I was more or less unofficially engaged to Louis when I met Greg at a Harvard dance. He swept me off my feet–as he did countless other women–and we were married within three months. Louis was shattered, but there it was. I was deliriously happy. I adored Greg. I went to India with him. Then the children came. My cup seemed full. I had them. I had Greg. I had the undying troubadour devotion of Louis. We had this place, Greg's place in New England, marvellous holidays abroad. What more could any woman want?'

'So far, it's fairy-tale stuff.'

She laughed, almost lightheartedly, although the laughter was a trifle high-pitched for gaiety. 'Thank God I can at last talk *about it* all to someone. I talk *round and round* it with Louis. All the time. But it's never quite the same thing. In fact, it's very very different. Heaven knows why, but I'm telling you things I've only brooded over during these past years. We'd been married about six or seven years before I discovered that Greg was involved in half a dozen affairs, a couple of which he'd casually continued since his Harvard and MIT days. And he was replenishing the stock, so to speak, all the time. It was a shattering discovery. I was pregnant with our third child. Wives usually are, I gather, when they make these discoveries. Greg was quite unabashed when I taxed him. Said that was the way he was. I said he'd never told me. He said it was scarcely the thing one told a bride-to-be. I suppose I'd have got over that side of things. Thousands of wives do. No matter about the gossip, the rumours, the phoney pity and the rest. No matter about the wife's name being dragged through all the mud. But the worst of that came later–after he got his political thing. That was infinitely, fiendishly worse. For me, anyway. There's nothing quite like Washington dirt and scandal.

It's obscene. For Greg it was OK. He was off on his life's work. For him it was a kind of religious mania. A revival meeting conversion. Real Shaker stuff. He really thought he'd found the light. All his guilt feelings about being a millionaire's son married to a millionaire's daughter were suddenly sublimated. He could now persuade himself that his flips with women were a necessary relief from the hard grind of his dedication. He was the greatest self-persuader in the business. Within a year he believed it all. He really reckoned he was the new Messiah.'

'But you stood by him.'

'Nominally, yes. For one thing, I'm a Catholic, although Greg wasn't. I could have called my Church to my aid, no doubt, but one doesn't. In any case, women of the South are apt to be preposterously loyal in that sense. We've never been brainwashed the way the women of the North have been. We've been too used to our men having their black bits on the side. Generations of it. We're no good for any Women's Lib-type propaganda.'

'You mean you could have forgiven him the women, not the politics?'

'I suppose, in its bluntest form, that was it.'

'But you put on a good show?'

'So I'm told.'

'Yet you're free now,' I said, seeing my chance.

'How can I be free. I'm imprisoned by his image. Now he's a saint for millions of people in this country and abroad. And from now on, whatever I do that's normal and natural is a kind of chiselling-away at his sainthood, saintliness or whatever the word is. I'm supposed to look as sorrowful as only a good widow can, appear at Washington functions I hate. I'm supposed to recover in time to attend fund-raising Democratic jamborees and look beautiful and bereaved. And because I don't, because I've come and stayed back home and word gets around that I have Negro servants again–which Greg wouldn't have–I'm told I'm smearing his death-mask, or whatever it was some damned New York hack wrote a week ago. Currently, I'm the one who gets the brickbats and the snide remarks.'

'I understood from Roth that you were being left alone.'

'Roth as usual is a month out of date. Pressure is building up. I've had my spell of mourning. Why don't I come out and help the Party? The criticism's getting up steam all round. Everyone's for Greg and I'm the outcast, the one who's letting him down. What's so terrible about Negro servants if I prefer the way they do the job and they quite like the job? Why is it demeaning for a Negro to be a servant and not a white man?' Her voice rose with her rhetoric.

'Relax,' I said gently.

'I'm sorry,' she said. 'It gets bottled up. This is the first chance I've had to let off steam since Greg died. I used to flay him alive sometimes, poor man. I'm sorry you're the innocent victim now.'

Not so innocent, I thought, but said: 'What's the one particular thing that's persuaded you about the Toynbee thing? There's always one reason above all others for such a change of heart.'

I thought I knew the reason, but I wanted confirmation.

'Not one. A dozen. Because I want to be free of Greg Stirling in every possible way in every degree. Because I want my own life back again.'

'And because you want to marry de Marais,' I said, the words sounding like an absurd nursery jingle.

'Because I want to marry Louis,' she said quietly, whispering the words slowly as if relieved to get the confession out. 'This year. Because I want Louis's children. Children he's always wanted. Children he'll love. Greg was so damned concerned with the children of the world's horny-handed workers he only saw his own three brats two or three times a year and then took damn good care to have a *Life* photographer around at the time. For ten years I was loyal to him, watched his women, suffered his politics, played his hostess, strung along with his ambitions . . .'

'Supposing he'd made the Presidency, what then?'

'I'd have stayed loyal and done the best job I could, but I don't see why I have to go on carrying a spluttering wet torch for him now he's dead. I sometimes suspected he had an outsize death-wish.'

She made him sound like a wilful suicide, which, in her eyes, I daresay, he almost was. She plainly wanted to be rid of him pronto and forever. But I didn't want to make things difficult for her or for myself, now or later, as far as the Ann Toynbee journals were concerned. I wanted her to be clear in her own mind about what she was doing, and the likely consequences. I said, 'People will know you've approved publication. You'll be Mrs Stirling reviled.'

'Only by those I've no time for. Only by a lot of phoney Democrats and professional radicals. If I have any politics at all they're far away to the right of any right-wing Republican, you ever met. As you've probably guessed. Why should I worry? My life's here. Everybody round here would approve once they'd read this Toynbee thing. In any case, I shall be married. Don't you understand? I hated, hated, hated everything Greg crusaded for. Finally . . .' She paused as if trying to halt what she was about to say, but then burst out: 'Finally, I hated Greg. And that's the ghastly truth. I hated everything about him.' She paused as if out of breath. In a low voice she said: 'I'm sorry Mr Mortimer, but ten years' unwishful loyalty makes for a lot of bottling-up.'

There were few bottled-up signs around at that moment, I thought. Her outpouring bitterness was dreadful to watch and to hear; its enormous intensity distorted her fine features into an unworthy mask.

'You've discussed all this with de Marais, I imagine,' I said as she took breath.

'For two years past and for two solid hours this afternoon after lunch. Then he went back to La Falaise–that's his plantation. Then for another couple of hours this evening before dinner. He absolutely agrees with me. Backs me to the limit.'

I'll bet he does, I thought. Wouldn't any man proposing to marry his childhood sweetheart, who also happens to be the widow of one of the world's current semi-saints, want a little hatchet work done on the immaculate image? I would have liked to have known more about de Marais' role as comforter during Melanie Stirling's decade of disillusionment. Had he really been the troubadour-type, the soul of Southern honour and loyalty, the complete olde worlde gentleman Melanie Stirling would have had me believe? Well, I'd never know, so I let the speculation die.

Meantime, there were more important matters. I took a chance, a big chance. 'Why not sleep on your decision?' I asked.

'I'd rather not,' she said. 'I'd rather sleep on the note I'll give you now.'

To my further surprise, she crossed to a high mahogany bureau-bookcase standing to one side of the door and came back with an envelope with my name written on the front. I took out the folded sheet of writing-paper. Under the die-stamped heading of *The Lake House*, she had written:

> *Dear Mr Mortimer: Thank you for being so frank with me concerning the matter of Miss Toynbee's journals and their references to my late husband. Greg Stirling was a man with a passionate regard both for the truth as he saw it and the truth as other people saw it. If Miss Toynbee's journals are true by her lights she has every right to publish her record if that is her desire. My husband's reputation and record suffice to stand against any possible calumny. Melanie Stirling.*

Well, it was a blank cheque worth a mint in any of the law courts of the world.

'A noble letter,' I said in genuine admiration. 'Rather shorter and more to the point than any number of essays on the nature of truth and freedom of speech by the world's philosophers.'

She smiled. 'I have to confess, Mr Mortimer, that Louis de Marais had a hand in it.'

'His Sorbonne studies weren't in vain,' I said, wondering whether he'd also had time to take instruction in swordsmanship as well as sophistry whilst there. His sabre work seemed to have quite an expert flourish to it.

We talked for another ten minutes or so, but the day was done.

Would I stay on for a couple of days? she asked, the gracious hostess smoothly ousting the outraged wife and widow.

I had to make a quick and decisive gamble. I had the note. The great thing now was a quick getaway. Yet if I pushed off first thing on the following morning, mightn't she later recall my visit as some kind of hit-and-run raid? Especially if things got a bit tricky. There was no goodwill for the future in that.

Could I stay another day? I asked. I had a good deal to do in New York, but extra time at Lake House would be marvellous.

'But of course,' she said. You'll be able to talk things over with Louis at luncheon. I'd like that. And so would he.'

On that note we made our fond good-nights.

Upstairs, undressing, reflecting on the strange evening, I wondered how Roth would take Melanie Stirling's decision and her note. As a journalist he ought to approve, I gingerly decided. After all, he was always quoting Nietzsche along the lines of 'That may be your truth, Paul. Now I'll give you mine.' But I doubted whether he would be prepared to listen overlong to Ann Toynbee's truth, even with Melanie Stirling's OK.

Nevertheless, I decided there and then to by-pass Roth on my way back and to return directly to and through New York. I doubted whether he'd be full of good cheer when he realised what his letter had produced.

–7–

I spent most of the next morning putting down my view of the previous evening's events; a kind of *aide-mémoire* to myself, and, perhaps later, for Mason and other potential disbelievers. The previous evening's session had had such an unreal touch about it that I thought incredulity might set in at any moment. Ann would find it interesting, anyway.

After that I went for another perambulation of the park, seeking to evoke in myself some semblance of the feelings of that long-ago Frenchman who set himself up here in emphatic distaste for *égalité fraternité liberté* and the rest. He had a point, I thought.

When I returned, de Marais was in the drawing-room, alone. After a few pleasantries about the weather, the house and the previous evening's dinner party, he began:

'Melanie told me something of her talk with you last night after we left. As you know, the words of the letter were mainly my responsibility, but we are absolutely as one in our reaction to your proposal.'

'I see your point,' I said fairly pointlessly, but I wanted de Marais to go on. He did.

'I gather you know our situation. It's very difficult, although our mutual friends in these parts are very understanding. I want to marry Melanie as soon as possible. Today, tomorrow, next week. I've loved her for over twenty years. We've both lived through a purgatory during the past five years. If we were to marry as things are, Melanie would immediately become one of the most hated and maligned women in America. And American women's malice can be a very alarming force, believe me. Publication of Miss Toynbee's journals would give us the chance for an immediate go-ahead in a way no other single act could possibly do.'

And so on and so on. He had a lot to say. Stuff he'd obviously been brooding over for years: his love for Melanie Stirling, his hatred of Stirling festering under Stirling's growing renown as the greatest of all liberals; his own and Melanie Stirling's religion; his desire for children; the lot.

I listened, sensing that I need have no worries about Melanie Stirling going back on her letter. De Marais would be my ally through and through.

Lunch was much the same, with both of them talking over the *homard thermidor* as if I were the Great Deliverer. And all without having seen a word of the journals. Not that that would have made much difference, I imagined. The more explicit the journals, the more complete Melanie Stirling's escape from a legend.

Dinner, a repeat performance, relieved by the later appearance of a married couple who'd been to a concert in Charleston: a biologist from the University of South Carolina and his musical wife. Altogether it was a very neighbourly, homely and agreeable evening, which would undoubtedly have driven Stirling, as I had come to know him through the journals, stark raving mad. But *chacun* . . . as somebody once said.

And, later, after the others had gone, a final summing-up from Melanie Stirling, more thanks to me and the day was done.

–8–

Driving out to Charleston airport the following morning, Melanie Stirling said, 'Don't get ideas above your mortal station, Mr Mortimer, but in a strange and, I suppose, terrible kind of way, your coming here seems to have been a stroke of providence for Louis and myself. It really did bring all our endless and bedevilled discussions of the last few months out into the open. You've been a marvellous catalyst.'

'It's a new rôle.'

She smiled and went on: 'There's another thing: I don't know whether you're at all religious, Mr Mortimer–I have a feeling you're not–but I am. With some fairly out-dated beliefs. At least they're out-dated nowadays. I was brought up to believe that we reap what we sow. I believe this Ann Toynbee thing is a kind of divine corrective to Greg's overweening hubris. I know it sounds old-fashioned and presumptuous, but somewhere along the line I sincerely believe that it is God's will that Greg should not be built up into some kind of saint by the masses.'

I had several alternatives open to me on hearing the words: I could have burst out laughing; I could have argued the toss about God and his mysterious grinding ways; or I could take a grip on myself and sit in silence watching the needle steady at seventy, the cotton fields slipping by and/or Melanie Stirling's profile.

Or do what I did, which was to make some poltroonish comment that these things were way beyond me.

I wish, of course, that I'd been made of sterner stuff, and asked in conversational tones whether she thought it was God's will that she should own several million bucks, Lake House and its many acres and be attended by a score of black servants. But I'm no good with anyone with a private hot line to the Holy Man. And not so deep down, I suspected she'd say, in all innocence, that it was God's will, of course. That she might, equally equably, have been accepting God's will as a Japanese nun in a leper colony or as a thirty-six-year-old shrivelled Bengali grandmother on the breadline in Calcutta.

So I let my cowardly ways take over. I didn't even make my own simple views clear: that I'd made a remarkably opportune appearance to suit the desperate yearnings of Melanie Stirling and Louis de Marais to get this present and still-censorious corny world well on their side. With Stirling's name well smeared they'd be sitting pretty. I could even imagine the commiserations of the most venomous old bags in Washington. That poor Melanie Stirling! What she must have suffered all those years from that hypocritical whore-master, Stirling! Good for her if she's found peace at last with one of her own kind! These damn rich rads! I never did go for them! Sex-maniacs, sadists, scabs, the lot of 'em! And so on and on. Ninety-nine tongues wagging in her favour to every one against. And all the coiffured heads of the daughters of the American Revolution nodding fierce approval with each blue-rinsed curl.

She drove well. I was silent, admiring her skill. 'There's something else, Mr Mortimer. Partly due to what Bernie Roth said in his note about yourself and partly due to this Ann Toynbee thing, I've told you things about my private life known only to Louis and myself – although several loyal friends have their own ideas, no doubt.'

I put up my hand to slay the expected words, but she went on: 'If the American press were to get the merest whisper of the situation I've discussed with you, my life wouldn't be worth living. You've no idea – but you probably have – what the American press is like when it's on to a story of that kind.'

'Fleet Street isn't crowded out with canonised curates,' I said. To my surprise she smiled, and went on:

'So I must ask you to treat all I've told you with the utmost discretion. Obviously, I can't impose a condition of absolute confidence – you have others to consult – but I beg of you to take care. I have done a dangerous, possibly a foolish thing. I hope it works out for me and for you. You do understand, don't you?'

'Of course', I said and repeated.

During the hours I had spent with her I'd gradually, unwillingly perhaps, come to have a good deal of sympathy for her present situation. Her good looks helped, of course. It's always easier to be sympathetic to a young and beautiful woman than a cracked old crone. Life is very unjust.

I muttered again that I fully understood.

As, indeed, I thought I did.

By then we were turning into the airport compound. I thanked her for her hospitality and the note, took my case from somewhere in the cavernous depths of the Cadillac station wagon, waved farewell, watched her turn and drive away.

I made a thoughtful way into the airport, patting the note inside my breast pocket for reassurance.

I'd never expected a return journey like this. Not in a thousand lifetimes.

—9—

I checked in at the Barbizon-Plaza, my long-time favourite New York Hotel, took a bath, had a drink and rang Ann Toynbee.

'Good, so you made Thursday, after all. Are you taking me out to dine or coming to my place?'

'I'll take you out and then come back to your place and collect the documents in the case.'

'You sound (*a*) like a Scotland Yard man, (*b*) like a man catching the next plane out of Kennedy. I hope I'm wrong on both counts and that you're not quite so relentless.'

'I'm probably the most relenting man you ever did meet.'

'I'd almost forgotten you were a man who's paid to play around with words. All right. Come and collect me. I'm not so far from the Barbizon-Plaza. Walk down Fifty Seventh Street, cross and you're almost there.'

I nodded. 'Around eight, then.'

—10—

'You must have a lot of news for me, and most of it bad, I suppose,' Ann Toynbee said after we'd ordered our meal at Haggerty's.

'Not all bad,' I said. 'In fact very little that way. In fact, nothing.'

'All right, then, let's go. How did you find Melanie Stirling?'

'A lady of emotional extremes.'

'How come? I only found the coolest goldfish in the tank.'

I outlined my emotive times in Athens.

Ann Toynbee was plainly shaken by this new aspect of her journal.

'So she sees my story as destroying Greg. I'm to carry out her revenge-by-proxy on poor dead Greg.'

'How else did you ever see it—if she were to approve the tale?'

'Not quite like that. I certainly didn't.'

'What did you believe, then?'

'What I told you. I really did. That it would give a more human image to a man I loved and still do—in my own way.'

'But the tale you propose to tell would be enough to destroy the image of any man who'd set himself as one of the world's supermen –and super-goodies.'

'Greg didn't!' she said, almost sharply.

'All right, then, the world did. But he didn't disabuse them by taking you out and about in public.'

'Che Guevara's complicated sex life hasn't detracted from his achievement or significance, has it?'

'He was a revolutionary. He needed to destroy every kind of bourgeois standard to set up his alternative society. Stirling called himself a democrat. He still wanted to prop up the status quo. Anyway, all these leader-figures are outsized paranoic monsters as far as I'm concerned. Roosevelt, Churchill, Stalin, Nasser, Castro, Guevara, the lot. Even Stirling.'

She shook her head. 'Greg was different.'

'You stay with your beliefs, I'll stay with mine.'

'You're out to undermine my belief in Greg's essential worth.'

'Nothing of the kind. How could I?'

But she was unconvinced.

'Shall we now leave you and your idealistic beliefs concerning Greg Stirling and get back to his widow and your great and genuine surprise that publication of your journal might conceivably smear your lover's image?'

She laughed. 'I still don't think it would. Not amongst the young and the rest of the world's have-nots.'

'A lot of old men and women, who, by natural processes of physical decay, have become sexual have-nots, will do their antique best to distort your picture of the saintly sexy Stirling.'

She laughed. 'Now you're being plain nasty. But I don't care. My money's still on my belief and my story.'

'And why not? Conviction's the first requirement in any artist, writer or musician.'

'Fine words, but *you* don't sound very convinced, all the same.'

'I'm neither artist nor musician and, as a writer, a paid hack. In any case, I'm convinced more by your narrative skills than by your arguments.'

'Not even by my sincerity?'

"Yes, I give you that.'

'And my genuine fondness for Stirling?'

'I give you that, too, although I'm doubtful whether I'd be posthumously very pleased to find myself as well and publicly documented by someone I had come to love and trust.'

'You really would mind!'

'I really would.'

'I do believe you would.'

'Thank you, Ann.' I bowed my head in mock-appreciation of this tardy acceptance of a viewpoint.

'Lunch, dinner, letters, cables–and only now am I Ann.'

I laughed. 'Perhaps I was disconcerted, knowing so much about you from your journals.'

'Too much?'

'Not too much, but you are rather laid bare, so to speak. When I look at you, I have a kind of double vision: the girl before me and the one in the book!'

She laughed. 'D'you think I'll get many offers of marriage if they're published?'

'Thousands, especially from east of Suez.'

She smiled. 'What d'you think Roth will have to say about your success down South?' she asked suddenly.

'I haven't told him yet. I think I'll ring him and tell him tomorrow morning before I leave.'

'You're not leaving so soon!' she said with sudden, flattering concern. 'I'd hoped you were here for a week.'

'This is a working week for me.'

'Must you underscore the fact I'm just a job of work for you? But what will Roth say? After all, Greg was his hero. Greg stood for all he thought the US ought to be. Melanie's OK will break him in small pieces.'

'I've thought a lot about that, but there it is: a fact of life. He wrote the note that got me into Lake House, although hindsight tells me I might have got there under my own steam. Anyway, Bernie loves being one of the world's sufferers, so he'll have a field day. He suffers from his race, his beliefs, his ex-wives, his children, his hopes, his lot.'

'Poor Bernie,' she said and seemed to mean it.

From then on it was a merry meal.

–II–

Afterwards we walked back to Ann's small two-roomed apartment down by the East River, on the eighteenth floor of a tall narrow block.

As somewhere to live in a city I would have put her small pad amongst the half-dozen most agreeable places I'd ever seen. Not only for the spectacular view–'Unaccountably not charged for in my rent,' Ann said, taking me out on to the small balcony perched high above the river–but also for the interior where her skills as a designer had been given full scope. Her small living-room ('I'd have called it a white cell inhabited by a rather bookish nun with a taste for creature comforts,' I said–'if I hadn't read your journals') opened into a small brightly coloured bedroom with little more than space for a divan, built-in wardrobe, built-in desk and more bookshelves.

'Quite an eyrie!' I said as we sat down in a couple of tubular-steel-and-leather armchairs, which I found, rather to my surprise, quite comfortable. 'No wonder you don't want to come back to London.'

'Oh, but I do. I want two-room homes like this in London, Paris, Venice, Rio, Istanbul, Hong-Kong, Tobago, Ibiza and County Kerry. I want lots and lots of small apartments in great cities and small cottages overlooking rivers, seas and mountains throughout the world.'

'How many have you got so far?'

'Only this.'

'You'll probably be able to get yourself a flat in Leningrad and a dacha on the Caspian Sea if we can't publish your story.'

She grimaced. 'Not my scenes.' She reached forward to the coffee-table, took a foolscap box-file and handed it across to me.

'Second and concluding instalment of the Moll-Flanders-Toynbee story,' she said. 'I hope B O A C won't charge you excess. It seems to weigh a ton.'

'I'll get by. When, by the way, did you first start keeping a journal?'

'During my first real love affair–when I was fifteen.'

'Why do people keep journals?' I asked. I was deeply interested.

'All children do spasmodically, I suspect. Didn't you?'

I shook my head.

'Well, for me it was a kind of identity-pursuit at first, I imagine. Then it became a habit.'

'In the process did you find the identity you were pursuing?'

'I can't have, can I? Otherwise I'd have stopped, wouldn't I?'

'And you'll never stop?'

'I doubt it. All adult diarists are compulsive if secret exhibitionists. It's a drug.'

'Did your previous journals deal with your love affairs as well as your work?'

She nodded. 'And your current journal?' She blushed and didn't answer.

'Isn't this Stirling effort a fair sample?'

She laughed. 'In a way, but far more comprehensive, of course.'

I laughed and told how I'd used the same word in the same context to Melanie Stirling. She was amused.

I went on:

'Why? Because he was a big figure in the world or a big figure in your life?'

'Both. It's not often a girl has an affair with a man in that kind of set-up.' She smiled her gamine smile. 'I thought it deserved the full treatment.'

I laughed. 'At the expense of sounding like a telly interviewer, don't your working-life and sex-life seem inextricably involved?'

'Aren't yours, too?' she answered in genuine surprise. 'Memories of working in the slums of Caracas come alive for me because I remember the marvellous doctor I worked with and slept with. Memories of last winter's ski-ing in Plymouth, New Hampshire, are more vivid because of a marvellous flip I had with a French-Swiss instructor there. Aren't your memories equally involved?'

'Possibly,' I agreed, remembering, Helen, Molly, Vicky, and a dozen others during recent years. 'But there's one big difference: I don't take out a pen and exercise book or a Grundig every night to put it all down.'

She laughed. '*Touché*,' she said, got up from her chair, crossed to mine and kissed me lightly on the cheek. 'I've put the Grundig away for the night, I swear. And I've put away all my exercise books until next week. And what would Paul like to drink?'

—12—

I could justifiably claim that I had other rather more official reasons for staying on in New York than my too-few hours of Ann's companionship. For one thing I had been asked by Mason to check the small print in the British serial rights we had bought in two forthcoming American books. I was also to discuss with one of the New York dailies our planned series on the Decline and Fall of British Foreign Policy, 1900-1970, in which they'd shown interest. Dixon had also asked me to try to negotiate lower rates from one of the picture feature agencies. Vaughan had also asked me to discuss with one of his friends at CBS a TV series on the *Great Nineteenth-Century Radicals*, in which he was to be involved during the autumn. All in all, I had some busy hours, apart from domestic shopping.

I also had some brooding moments concerning Roth, unable to make up my mind about the best way of giving him the news from Melanie Stirling. To telephone him would, I knew, prompt an extended whine over the wires. To let him know I was at large in New York with information he thought he ought to share would have brought him flying in within a couple of hours.

Yet I owed him some kind of acknowledgment of the results of his introduction to Melanie Stirling, even though he had undoubtedly thought her refusal a foregone conclusion.

After a good deal of reflection and discussion with Ann, I finally decided that a note to reach him on the morning after I'd left would be the best way out of the problem. Accordingly, readily persuading myself that Friday and Saturdays were his busiest days, answering London's demands for explanation, elucidation, speculation and narration concerning the Washington scene, I didn't contact him.

A too-discreet way out, no doubt, but, I told myself, why should I put Roth in the picture before explaining the situation to Mason? So I cabled Mason saying that I would return the following Tuesday or Wednesday. Meantime I was carrying out his extra-mural tasks.

After which I thought I could devote the rest of my time to the *raisons d'être* of my visit: Miss Ann Toynbee and her journals.

I wrote, as non-committally as I could, to Roth:

> *Dear Bernie: Thanks to your note I was allowed into the Stirling presence. To my surprise I was asked to stay. All in all I found her pretty reasonable. In fact, I rather took to her. Her reaction to the Toynbee project was thoughtful to say the least, and she has given me a note for the Editor. You will be kept in touch, of course, and I shall certainly tell Mason how helpful you've been throughout. Many many thanks. Paul.*

I returned to London, the following Wednesday, arriving in Fleet Street just before midday.

—13—

Mason had kept his Thursday lunch date open. Rules as usual.

After ordering and a few general enquiries about Roth, the chores he'd given me and my superficial views and news concerning the state of the United States after my one week there, he said: 'And what about the Toynbee story?'

'I've got the rest of it with me.'

'Had time to dip into it?'

'Here and there. I've jumped about a bit. To me it seems even better than the first half. Stirling's growing dependence comes through. He was seeing her most days he was in New York and she spent a good deal of time with him in Washington. My own view is that by that time he'd really fallen for her, had found her the most entertaining and elusive of all his women and couldn't bear the thought of her disappearing from his life. In a way it's poignant stuff, and one can't help but wonder what the outcome would have been. I think he really had fallen for her. His scribbled notes to her prove that – to me – pretty conclusively.'

'He'd have been in real trouble if he'd made the Presidency.'

'One or two of our own PMs have managed it?'

'We have a greater respect for privacy,' Mason said. He really believed that kind of thing.

'Ha! Ha!' I added mirthlessly.

'Well, go on,' Mason said, unamused.

'Stirling's death and its aftermath are the most extraordinary sections I've read so far. Here was this girl – probably closer to him than anyone he'd ever met, apart from his wife in the early days of their marriage – and suddenly it's all over and she can't get near him. Nobody knows how close they were and even if they did, nobody cares and certainly nobody wants to know her. Whatever her feelings she's got to work them out in private. As far as dead Stirling was concerned she was just another newspaper reader or goggle-box viewer.'

'D'you think she took it badly?'

'There's a good deal about her reactions. Quite extraordinary some of it. So detached and analytical, it's scary. She's an odd numero. It's a good job she was so much more self-sufficient than anyone I've ever met.'

'Well, if *you* say so, she really is. I always thought the label belonged to you.'

'I'm not in the same league as Ann Toynbee.'

Mason listened thoughtfully as I went on with my reactions to other parts of the journal. At the end he said, 'And Mrs Stirling won't let us publish a word of it is, I suppose, the grand finale to your story?'

I reached inside my jacket and took out the letter.

He read it through and took a deep breath. 'My God, that's a turn-up for the book. Can I keep this? It had better go in the strong-room straight away.'

I nodded. 'It shook me, and it'll probably give Bernie apoplexy.'

'He doesn't know yet, then?'

'I thought you ought to know first. It might be a lot better if the news came from you.'

He nodded his gratitude for this dutiful thought, and then: 'Tell me about the trip–and Mrs Stirling.'

I outlined my journey: from my session with Roth in Washington to my brief sojourn in Athens. I omitted one or two episodes, including Melanie Stirling's relationship with Louis de Marais and her after-dinner diatribe, and my evenings with Ann Toynbee. I thought the former had better come out bit by bit–as it did–and the latter never.

'Why d'you think she's taken this step?' Mason asked, half-suspiciously pocketing the letter. 'Does she want a cut of the profits?'

'I doubt it. She didn't even mention lucre. It's not her line. My own belief is that she wouldn't mind the Stirling image being tarnished a little. A little roughing-up might well suit her current way of life.'

'Why, for God's sake. Wasn't she the ideal American wife and now the ideal widow?'

'I got the impression she'd like to marry again and pretty damn quick. There's a long-time admirer hanging around. If she does it too soon and while Stirling's still a dead saint she'll be fairly well ostracized. That's for sure. Not exactly in her own home town where Greg Stirling is still a dirty name, but certainly in most other places? And like most dames of her kind, I'd say she's fairly concerned about her social standing anywhere in the States, although she affects to be concerned only with the opinions of her neighbours.'

'And if we publish the Toynbee tale, we'll be doing her dirty work for her?'

'More or less. The true story of Lecher Stirling will bring her the sympathy of every virtuous wife in America, all the daughters of the American Revolution, her own Church, the lot. Especially if the man she wants to marry is a Catholic–which Stirling wasn't. Especially if the man she wants to marry is a childhood sweetheart who's waited for her all these years. Especially if she showed herself a loyal wife to Stirling and a devoted mother all these years–as she did. Especially if we published that letter. She'd have every man and woman in the Deep South on her side and most of the rest. And not even the radical intelligentsia could object to that letter.'

'You seem to have dug out a lot of data. Did you dope her or screw her? She sounds pretty formidable.'

'She is. And the childhood sweetheart's a tough nut, too. I was told most of these matters in the utmost confidence, by the way.'

He nodded. 'I can see it's dynamite all through. But let's get this quite clear: as you see it, our job is to reduce the Stirling image to rubble for her benefit?'

'And the benefit of your net sales figures, don't forget?'

'I'm certainly not forgetting those. But it's all building up to be a bit of a bastard.'

'Wouldn't any story of these dimensions prove to be?'

He nodded and then said, 'Probably.' And then, after a pause, 'Have you ever thought, even once, that it's all getting a bit nasty?'

'It's got its more grotty moments, but what story of lust and power in high places hasn't, starting with Antony and Cleopatra, moving on to Henry the Eighth, Edward the Seventh and Mussolini to choose a random sample? This may be too nasty for us–or for you–to handle, but somebody's going to do it even if we don't. We may be a great quality Sunday newspaper and all that, but there's plenty of go-getting hacks around, a lot less squeamish than us, who'd treble whatever we'd offer and get cracking.'

I began to detect the Mason signs I knew so well: the gradual withdrawal from the necessity for unwelcome personal decision; the step-by-step shifting of the responsibility to others; the call to decent behaviour. And all under the guise of the rugged liberal man of action. He said: 'We've got to be squeamish–occasionally. But that's no justification for milk-and-water journalism. If this Toynbee tale stands up under your subbing and Lovell's legalizing, we'll go ahead.'

'My editing will still leave a good deal in that the lawyers will want out. You'll have a major fight on your hands before ever we get to the story. You'll have to take a sizeable chance, whatever we do.'

'I'll meet the legal queries when we come to them,' he said. Then came the gimmick he was so good at and which I'd been expecting. The combination of decisive-man-of-action-and-decent democrat. He said: 'We'll have a meeting this afternoon and throw it around a bit. I'd like to hear what the others think. They've all read the first part: you can give a rundown on the rest of the record. Then we'll see.'

So we finished our meal and wandered back along Fleet Street to Fetter Lane. I had work to do before the meeting.

–14–

Soon after four o'clock that afternoon, five of us pulled chairs around Mason's desk: Vaughan, Spicer, Markham, Logan and myself.

After words of welcome to the traveller returned, Mason said, 'I'm happy to tell you that Paul had a good trip. He's got the rest of the Toynbee tale, which, he says, is even better than the first part. He's also got what appears to be a letter from Stirling's widow which is virtually a copper-bottomed O K to go ahead.'

The ensuing expressions of incredulity were well-laced with ribaldry concerning my method of getting the note.

'Paul assures me not,' Mason said, grinning. 'And it certainly doesn't read as if sex came into it at all.'

He took out the note and read it.

'Why, for God's sake?' Spicer asked.

'Paul has a theory that she was never very enamoured of the Stirling image and, more recently, of the man himself. The Toynbee journals show why, perhaps. Paul also thinks she wants to get married again and that she'd be in a far stronger position, socially and the rest, if she could tarnish the Stirling image quite a bit. She's also a Catholic. These clean starts seem to mean a lot to them. As a one-time Welsh Methodist, the subtleties escape me. Does that more or less sum it up, Paul?'

'Very succinctly.'

'Good. Has anybody any views?'

Spicer started: 'Are we justified in publishing the Toynbee tale in order to make Mrs Stirling's fresh start that much easier? I don't see why we should. I've never been very keen on the project anyway. What you've said makes my feelings all the stronger.'

Logan said: 'Any story has to stand or fall on its own merits. As far as I'm concerned the Toynbee story is one of the most riveting documents I've ever read. We'd be falling down on our job if we passed it up, especially now we've got over what we thought would be our biggest obstacle.'

'What about it, Tom?' Mason asked.

'I'm with Steve,' Vaughan said. 'It's preposterous to have a story of this quality and uniqueness and then hand it on to other people. Which is what we would be doing–make no mistake. I think Dick is bringing what is basically a non-starter into the discussion. Mrs Stirling's reasons for allowing us to publish are her affair. Her permission is our affair. Now we've got it, let's publish–the sooner the better.'

The television features man was well-to-the-fore again in that contribution. Mason turned to Markham. 'And what about you, Gerry?'

'I don't think it will do us any good at all,' Markham said coldly.

'It will destroy our contacts amongst politicians throughout the world; it will lower the standing of the paper; it will discredit us in every way.'

Mason reflected on that for a moment and then turned to me: 'And you, Paul?'

'I'm for publishing. It will take nerve, but I think we should have a go.'

Discussion then broke out. Heatedly. The curious situation that had arisen in the previous meeting–Logan and Vaughan opposed to Spicer and Markham–persisted. Logan was intolerable: bitter, personal, almost abusive towards Spicer, which he'd never been before. Vaughan was cool and assured. Markham was rather disdainful about the whole project. Mason watched the battle, not altogether relishing some of the exchanges, I thought. I had a strong feeling that he could have wished that Vaughan and myself had shared the distaste Spicer and Markham had for the story. He could have dealt easily enough with Logan. As the tale-bearer, so to speak, I was rather an onlooker, after I'd made my own views clear.

The argument, which had started supposedly as a discussion, went on until six. At last Mason said: 'Well, I've certainly got all your views. I'll have to canvass one or two others, of course, but I'm glad to know where you all stand. Now it's up to Paul, then the lawyers. How long will you want for your editing job on the journals, Paul?'

I said I'd need at least a month.

'Try and have the first two sizeable sections ready in a fortnight, could you? I want to get it under way with the lawyers as soon as possible.'

I said I'd try.

With unconcealed hostility Spicer almost barked to Mason: 'How many weeks d'you propose to run it?'

'We've never run any feature for more than four weeks. Not even the A-sub story. But I think I'd run this for five or six. The material will certainly stand up to it.'

'I'd back that,' Vaughan said, 'Starting with a bang over three pages. We might even get it off to a flying start in the colour magazine. We've got the time.'

'No. I want to keep it in the paper,' Mason said decisively. 'Too many people will get to hear about it with time-lag involved in the magazine's printing schedule.'

'That's true,' Vaughan agreed, obviously annoyed with himself for not having thought of that one.

'In any case, all Ann Toynbee's photographic material is black-and-white,' I added, 'apart from a few fairly ropey transparencies and polaroids.'

'How much are we paying the little whore?' Spicer asked, bitterly.

'I'd thought around a thousand for each instalment. Do you think she'd agree to that, Paul?'

I thought so.

'She wouldn't find it difficult to treble or quadruple that, if she shopped around a bit,' Logan opined. 'Aren't we counting our chickens too soon at that kind of chicken-feed for this kind of material?'

'Ask Paul,' Mason said.

'I doubt it,' I said. 'She'll clean up over the book and syndication rights. I think she'd agree.'

'I suppose we've never had a feature so ready-made for the upper-middle-class women of Britain.' Spicer said, returning at last to his more normal manner now that the battle was seemingly lost. 'One of their own class having it off with a US Senator, probably booked for the Presidency. In a permissive age and stringing along with current Fleet Street standards, I suppose this thing could be considered a gift for a quality newspaper.'

We all laughed. All, that is, except Markham. His disapproval and opposition were more obdurate and refrigerated than Spicer's.

The meeting broke up around half-past six. I still had a couple of hours work to do, getting a US-slanted *Faces & Places* into final shape.

Reflecting on the meeting afterwards I retained a firm impression that Mason was still far from happy with the prospect of publication.

–15–

That evening I dined with Helen and Marion in Milner Street.

I was late in arriving, but I had warned Helen. In any case, I arrived bearing gifts; dresses for both from Saks and Lord & Taylor; kitchen gadgets from Hammacher Schlemmer. I was an out-of-season Father Christmas, who, fortunately, had made apt choices in size, style and the rest.

An extremely talkative meal ensued. Although I'd only been away just over a week, it seemed a month. We had a lot to catch up on.

After supper and skilfully prolonged good nights from Marion, strung out by exuberant thanks for my gifts, I returned to the sitting-room for coffee and Cointreau.

We talked about Marion, her school life at the Lycée, the chances of a late summer holiday, finally my trip.

I've always respected Helen's worldly know-how and put the whole thing to her: Ann Toynbee's journal; Melanie Stirling's agreement; Roth's misgivings; the divided editorial opinions; my own doubts. How did she see it all?

'I see it as something men would take in their stride if it were one of their own sex publishing a journal about his intimate affair with a world-famous actress; even, possibly with a woman Cabinet Minister, although few of those seem likely propositions for the job.'

I laughed. 'Come off it: it's not as simple as that.'

'Basically it is. The whole thing is about the freedom of a woman to write about things that men still consider *their* very own particular province. Look at the commotion that that ex-mistress of Picasso caused when she published her memoirs?'

'Françoise Gilot, you mean. But she had a child by him.'

'Any man could have written about a flip with Bernhardt, Isadora Duncan or Sylvia Pankhurst, fathered a child by any or all of them, and it wouldn't have caused a ripple.'

'His versatility, virility and mobility would have caused more than a ripple.'

Helen laughed, but went on: 'It's just that it's still simply not done for a young, well-brought-up girl–an intellectual to boot–to confess that she likes sleeping with men. Intelligent men. If she'd slept around with Pop Groups and told her story–as I believe some of the groupies have–it'd be forgotten in a week. It's just that this Toynbee girl is pretty, upper-class, intelligent and slept with a high-placed, handsome political legend–it's all that that's giving you the vapours.'

'So you think a responsible newspaper would be justified in publishing.'

'Newspaper men are incredible,' Helen said. 'Only the Pope and newspapers have the nerve to call themselves responsible every time they want to do something pretty dubious. You know jolly well that if you can get the story OK'd by your lawyers, you'll publish.'

I smiled, but Helen wasn't to be denied. 'Personally, from what I've read and from what you've told me, I think Ann Toynbee's tales out of school will be a pleasant change from all this heavy-handed responsibility line you've been dishing up recently for your poor benighted readers. *Faces & Places* excepted, of course, my sweet.'

'Thanks for the afterthought. I'll tell Mason about the rest.'

'You do that. Tell him I'm all for the confessions of your A-level tart on Capitol Hill. Isn't that the place?'

'It is, and I'm very impressed by your general knowledge.'

'Balls,' Helen said succinctly. We talked about going to bed.

–16–

Pat Gow spent most of the following week in the copying-room, xeroxing every sheet in the Toynbee journals; text, pictures, clips, the lot.

She made three copies. The original compilation–and it was the best word, despite Ann Toynbee's protest–went to the office strong-room. One of the copies went to Mason and two to myself. Why I fixed two copies for myself–six hundred pages apiece–I don't know. One was to be a working copy. Why the other? I would need a lie-detector and psychiatrist to help me out on that one. I took both copies back to Swan Court.

I started serious reading of the second part that evening.

I'd arranged with Mason that at a convenient moment in the very near future I'd take a couple of weeks off to start editing the journals. I'd decided to go to Ireland and had booked hotel and passage for a fortnight ahead.

The following Tuesday morning, I received a letter from Roth.

Dear Paul: Thanks for your note. Reading between the lines I gather that you had rather more success with Melanie Stirling than you or I had allowed for. I also suspect that you deliberately bypassed Washington on your return and didn't call me from New York to avoid hurting my feelings. Melanie's reaction–if I'm right as I think I must be–astounds me. When I gave you my note of introduction to her I'm afraid I didn't rate you a chance in a million. I thought you'd get a downright point-blank, all-time refusal. If you didn't get that you must have got something very different. If you did, it means that the Ann Toynbee outpourings could be published, which brings me to the gist of this letter. If, as I suspect, the paper is beginning to make arrangements to publish these so-called journals, I shall do my best to see that publication is stopped. I do not intend to have Stirling's struggles smeared by this nymphomaniacal chit of a girl, even though I gave you the note to Melanie S.

You may think that I am going far beyond my position as the paper's Washington correspondent, but I see certain duties as transcending the demands of this—or any other—newspaper or any other newspaper job. As man to man, Paul, I must ask you or the Editor to let me know to what extent Melanie Stirling is playing along with your project. If I don't get what I regard as a reasonable reply to what seems to me a reasonable request within reasonable time, say two weeks, I propose to resign from the paper forthwith and to devote myself to the task of putting paid to this Toynbee project.

By all means discuss this letter with the Editor, but I hope and expect *to have an answer within that time.*

In my view Stirling was one of this century's great men (pace *your own views on this matter) and could have been the greatest, possibly, after Gandhi. That is, if one thinks of greatness in terms of one man's work in seeking to meet the world's longing for peace and goodwill and in helping the oppressed and needy. I do.*

I write to you because you wrote to me and in some ways a letter of this kind, which is ultimately addressed to the top brass, is perhaps better addressed obliquely rather than directly. Show the letter to the Editor if it helps to explain my position as I see it.

I hope you are well. I'm still sorry you by-passed Washington on your way back. And thanks for being so patient last week over dinner. I can see that some of my views may seem ingenuous, even jejune to you, worldling that you are, but you were very kind and indulgent. Which is, perhaps, the reason why I am writing to you rather than to anyone else at this stage. Ever, Bernie.

Well that was sand in the works, I thought, putting down the letter and yearningly considering a picture of Waikiki Beach on the Pan Am calendar, behind Pat Gow's desk.

I took up the letter and went across to Mason's room. He was free and restless as he usually was on Tuesday morning, still finding the transition from daily to sabbatical journalism a somewhat irksome business early in the week. He was in an expansive mood. 'Hello, Paul. Come in. I'm bored to the back teeth. How I hate Tuesdays and Wednesdays! I'm not an editor then. Just a bloody executive.'

'This should dispel executive boredom,' I said, handing him Roth's letter. He read it through. When he looked up his lips were pursed and his eyes grim.

'When I think of all we've done for that son of a Polish pastry-cook.'

'Take it easy,' I said. 'His father was a notable professor of music. And by education and upbringing Bernie's as English as you or me.'

'No true-born Welshman is ever English by education or upbringing. Neither is any Pole.'

'Well, he's an idealist. How does that leave you?'

Mason relaxed slightly. 'In common with the rest of mankind, I'm a selective idealist,' he said. 'My idealism is reserved for Liberalism; unmarried mothers; Welsh rugby; freedom of the printed word and Bangor University. None of 'em ever gets enough honest-to-god publicity. Anyway, it's not a bad list for a start. What's yours?'

I doubted whether I had any, I said. 'I think I brood on horrors to escape from rather than ideals to fight for. Old age, marriage, opera, youth, men's clubs.'

Mason laughed. 'Nothing you'd back with fervour or even modest enthusiasm?'

'Nothing much, apart from more and better wife-swapping.'

Mason laughed again. 'You're an unmitigated liar and dissembler. You're probably the most sentimental romantic around the place.'

'I doubt it, but I'll bow to your uncanny Welsh insight. What about Bernie? He seems to mean business.'

'I think you're right.' He then fired a question which I didn't take seriously for a moment; a man can play parts too far out-of-character to be convincing. He said quietly: 'We might have to rush the series through pretty quickly. Supposing I decided to start publication in a month's time, could you make it?'

'I'd have to, wouldn't I? It would be editing on a Dickens-Thackeray basis with a couple of copy-boys writing at my elbow for the next instalment but I might be able to make it.'

'Good. I like to know where I stand.' He was quiet for a moment and then spat out the words.

'Who the hell does Roth think he is?'

'Your man in Washington, presumably.'

'He's beginning to make it a very tenuous appointment.'

I didn't believe that for a moment, but to keep the game alive, I said: 'He's also what I said earlier–an idealist.'

'Like most of his breed he thinks his ideals give him the right to run the rest of the world.'

'Surely that's always been the idealist's self-imposed prerogative.'

'Maybe, but if Roth thinks he can do as he likes around this office, he's mistaken.'

'Isn't that why he's prepared to bow out?'

'And busting our serial en route. The best series we've had in years. Not on your life!'

'I doubt whether Bernie's as preoccupied with our net sales figures as you are.'

'*His* dispatches certainly never sold an extra copy for us.'

'Come, come! Give him a break. He did a first-rate job on the last US elections. He wasn't too bad on Stirling, considering his hero-worship. You said so yourself.'

'That's past. He seems to have you on his side, anyway.'

I grinned. 'I like him–in a curiously twisted kind of way.'

'Well, what d'you suggest we do now?'

'Why don't I write him a stalling letter, taking the whole thing a stage further, implying we're keeping him in the picture, that he's blasting-off too soon and so on. We'd at least see how determined he is.'

'OK. Do that. But I still think we're giving the naturalized Polak too much rope.'

I said I'd bring in a draft later and left.

Somehow Mason's flare-up didn't ring true. When thoroughly thwarted, even momentarily, he was apt to brood silently and darkly. Now he was too vocally and belligerently cheerful. I put the cheerfulness down to the fact that he probably thought Roth's letter could prove another useful obstacle to publication of the Toynbee journals. With that letter around he could play the thrusting, busting, swinging editor with even greater flair.

He was unusually cheerful throughout the editorial conference an hour later. Further confirmation of my continuing suspicions, I decided.

–17–

I wrote to Roth:

Dear Bernie: A good deal of what you surmise is correct. I did get on a good deal better with Melanie Stirling than I'd expected, and she was a good deal more accommodating than you'd anticipated. But that doesn't mean that we propose to print a sensational exposé of Stirling as a kind of Capitol Hill Casanova. Far from it. Ann Toynbee's journal gives a compassionate, even affectionate, portrait of the man. Admittedly not the conventional, sentimental slush that's usually dished up about public figures, but infinitely better for that reason.

I've shown your letter to the Editor and we've discussed it at length. What we'd both like you to do would be to delay making any kind of decision which we'd all regret sooner rather than later. I'm off to Ireland next week for a couple of weeks. By the time I return I shall have the Toynbee journals reduced to less than ten per cent of their present length, i.e. from well over 300,000 *words to between* 25,000 *and* 30,000, *and roughly in the form in which we'd like to publish them as a five- or six-part serial in the Review Section. A copy of this edited version would be airmailed to you at the same time as copies to Ann Toynbee and Melanie Stirling. If Mrs S. approves, I don't see how you can disapprove. Do you, frankly?*

Will you do this? The Editor would appreciate it. He's not writing you on this matter at the moment as he thinks it's strictly my pigeon. He'll write later. Paul.

I showed the latter to Mason. Apart from adding a couple of commas in his rather Proustian passion for those grammatical ornaments, he approved.

–18–

I'd neglected Vicky for over a week after I returned from New York. I was too busy soaking up the Toynbee journals.

Finally, however, whilst Pat Gow was getting coffee, she got through my evasive defensive stonewalling.

'Hello, Paul. Vicky here, but perhaps you'll remember me better as Mrs Holt, that PRO girl you used to take out. How long have you been back?'

'Yesterday.'

'Why no call to your intimate friend?'

'Have a heart. I've been working round the clock trying to get my US stuff into some kind of order.'

'I read it in last Sunday's paper.'

'Cabled it,' I lied. 'A round-the-clock job.'

Any reference to midnight oil in the cause of true journalism always had Vicky immediately on one's side.

'Poor thing. But now you're back. And a man must eat, surely? His woman, too, if you can take a direct hint.'

I caved in. 'Why not have supper with me tonight, then? Or are you bespoken already?'

'You know damn well I'm not if there's any chance of your being around. But it's certainly a full-time job tracking you down, let alone getting you to a meal.'

'Let's meet at the Savoy at nine, then. Grill Room.'

'Lovely!' said Vicky. Her yen for that place was almost pathological.

So we met, and after we'd ordered our meal and I'd handed over the savagely modern armlet in gold and silver I'd bought in some savagely modern jewellers on 57th Street, resentment was a mood of the past. And as she settled those endless legs under the table I wondered how I could have been such a fool as to have left them unopened for a week.

She wanted to know all about New York, of course. One of her many career-daydreams was to work in an advertising outfit there. She believed–probably with some justification–that Madison Avenue was just her scene. After all, she was beautiful, bright, bursting with energy and a believer in all the craft and so-called arts of commercial braggadocio.

I talked for a while, but, basically, I preferred to half-listen to Vicky's views on this and that: it was a very restful way of sorting out one's own thoughts.

She said at one point, casually, that she'd been seeing her one-time husband.

'Is he making a play to get you back?'

'In a kind of way, I suppose.'

'Where did he take you?'

'Here, oddly enough. In the restaurant. He likes to dance.'

'How often?'

'A couple of times. Last Friday and Saturday.'

'Will he get you back?'

'Not in a million years.'

'Why not?'

'I've told you before. Because he's thick. Because he snores. Because he's running to fat. Because he whines. Because he's got the finesse of an ostler–in bed. On the job. And because I'm after you.'

'Is "on the job" an expression of your own finesse?'

She laughed. 'I've never claimed finesse as one of my bed-time virtues.'

'Wasn't he ever any good?'

'I've told you. Never.'

'Not even on Friday or Saturday nights?'

She put down her knife and fork.

'You're so damn sordid, sometimes, Paul. But you can't rile me tonight, what with this divinely pagan armlet and this smoked salmon.' Her knee touched mine: her hand moved slowly along my thigh.

Poor Mr Holt. I could quite see how images of Vicky could drive a fond lover mad with jealousy were he to be so misguided as to start thinking of those fabulous limbs entwined about a rival.

'Supposing,' I said, keeping her hand in position, 'instead of all those defects you just loaded on to Mr Holt, he'd had every kind of virtue and then got killed; supposing you then wanted to marry a somewhat lesser man very quickly, would you consider it justified to play down your late husband's virtues?'

'Quite unjustified. Utterly. Speak well of the dead is my motto, especially if he'd been good to me. Anyway, why bash someone who can't answer back? A new marriage would be a new chapter.'

'No vilification of a saint to marry a sinner?'

'Tony's no saint and he's not dead yet,' Vicky said easily, 'although by any standards I suppose you could be reckoned a bit of a villain, especially the way you've been giving me the run-around. By the way, I found out you came back last week. So there, you congenital intimate liar.'

She was delighted with her comment. I could see that as far as the Melanie Stirling situation was concerned, I'd get no subtle pragmatic advice from Vicky.

I dropped the subject. In any case, too many of Vicky's current quips had either too pertinent a point or highly distasteful marital overtones.

–19–

Roth's reply awaited me on Friday morning.

Dear Paul: Thanks for your letter. I'm not convinced. As you said in Washington I'm extra-sensory about some things and Stirling is one of them.

My suspicions are–and your letter does nothing to dispel them –that Melanie Stirling wouldn't be unduly upset if her husband came out of the Toynbee story as something less than a golden boy. A good deal less. She kept her opinions on Stirling's radical views very much to herself, but Stirling once told me, in an evening of qualified revelation, that they were far far different from his own. By now you may know more about those views than I do. So be it.

I'll wait until I get a copy of your version of the Toynbee journals, but what I wrote in my earlier letter still stands. If I think the journals diminish Stirling's character and achievement in any degree

I shall quit the paper forthwith and do my best to stop publication.

If I see nothing objectionable in the draft, I'll let you know within forty-eight hours. In any case, of course, I'd return the script to you. Bernie.

I smiled, noting the unconscious pomposity of the letter. Bernie was plainly already seeing himself as Keeper of the Golden Stirling Image.

I thought Mason ought to see the letter straight away.

–20–

'By which time he'll know every bloody word of what we intend to publish and have six weeks' start on blocking publication,' Mason said after I'd shown him the letter. 'Bloody man. He's full of every kind of moralizing ultimatum.'

'But as our Washington correspondent, hasn't he every right to see one of the biggest-ever Washington stories before publication?'

'I see that and accept it, but I wonder whether we've done the sensible thing in offering to show him a copy of the typescript.'

'It's a chance we had to take.'

'He says he'll return the script. If he's as dotty about the Stirling image as we know he is, he'll take a copy. When these idealists get weaving they're pretty smart at skipping the ethical conventions.'

'So I've noticed.'

'Even if he didn't use it openly–and even that is doubtful–he'd use it to refresh his memory.'

Vaughan came in. Mason gave him a recap of the situation and passed him the letter. 'Any suggestions?'

We were silent whilst Vaughan read slowly through the letter.

'I didn't know you'd promised to show him a copy of Paul's version,' Vaughan said, almost sharply, turning to Mason.

'Oh, come, Tom, we had to,' Mason protested.

'Unfortunately, we now seem honour-bound to send our fifth columnist in Washington a draft of a major Washington story,' Vaughan said gloomily. 'I suppose it was inevitable and unavoidable, but it's a bore.'

'We've just come to the same conclusion,' Mason said.

'Would you trust Roth, from what you know of him?' I asked Vaughan.

'I interviewed him on the box last year when he was over here.

I found him excessively emotional about Stirling. He seemed to me to be investing far too many fond hopes in what he believed Stirling would achieve after he got power. I also got the impression that he was somewhat unbalanced about his hero–to put it mildly. This letter confirms it.'

'I remember the interview very well,' Mason said, as if to close the recollection. But Vaughan went on: 'I asked him, at one point, didn't he think he was being rather unfair to Stirling to pin so many hopes on him? He said Stirling was big enough and willing enough to accept the responsibility. Didn't that make Stirling a bit of a paranoic? I asked. Why must the power for good carry a label normally reserved for the power for evil? he countered. Good hair-splitting stuff but it didn't answer my query.'

Vaughan didn't often talk at such length. I was invariably interested in his references to his television life and would have listened to more, but Mason, as I'd noticed before, didn't take all that kindly to references to Vaughan's earlier career, which was beginning to be mentioned again as a collateral career for the winter months ahead. Perhaps Mason still remembered that elderly editors programme and suspected Vaughan's hand in it.

'So you'd say he was a dicey prospect?' Mason queried.

'I'd say so, but, as things are, you're plainly honour-bound to let him see the typescript.'

'Or the galleys,' I said. 'We'd be that much nearer publication and they'd show we meant business.'

'He'd say we were trying to jump the gun,' Mason said. 'Leaving things too late and all that. Forcing his hand. No, we've got to give him the typescript and take a chance.'

'How d'you think Roth would react to that splendid early reference to Stirling as it stands now?' Vaughan asked, quoting: 'I was never Greg Stirling's mistress in the conventional manner. I suppose I was what a Parisian friend of mine once called a girl friend of his –*une amie poste restante*.'

I smiled. So did Mason–very thinly.

'I love that phrase,' Vaughan said. He turned to Mason. 'I'd far rather you sacked Roth than take that out' He went on: 'Why not deny Roth the script and tell him we wanted to keep him out of the whole thing? Let him resign if necessary.'

'I've thought of that. It wouldn't work. And he'd cause too much trouble,' Mason said flatly. 'Besides, I've given my word.'

'Especially with a persecution-maniac like Bernie,' I added for good measure.

'So he'll have it, use it, kill it. Stone dead,' Vaughan said.

'One hopes not,' Mason said.

'Roth's certainly making things easy for anybody who's squeamish about publishing the story,' Vaughan said pointedly.

'Who d'you mean?' Mason asked quickly.

'Dick and Markham, for two,' Vaughan said evenly.

Mason reflected. In his best liberal–oracular style, he said: 'We have to respect and try to understand other people's reservations as well as their enthusiasms.'

'That presupposes one has learned a technique for respecting,' Vaughan said, smiling. 'It always eluded me, from schooldays onwards.'

Mason gave a somewhat defensive smile. With his curt and cutting comments Vaughan had unsettled him.

'I think you sometimes overdo this *enfant terrible* line of yours, Tom,' he said, with another would-be avuncular smile. 'A carry-over from your TV life. When it comes to the point you're as responsible as anyone here and as respectful of other people's views.'

'I don't think I've come to that kind of crunch-point here. If I did, I think you'd find me among *les irresponsables et sans-culottes*,' Vaughan said.

He made his remarks with such disarming light-heartedness that an uninitiated listener could easily have dismissed them as the everyday banter of an easy-going, not-too-serious young man; but, for me, the interplay had now acquired a tougher probing quality, absent two months earlier. At a certain point during the past few weeks, Vaughan seemed to have decided that his three-months-tight-lipped-survey of the situation was over. He now queried the paper's contents, conventions, attitudes far more frequently. He was more critical of people and notions that Mason plainly admired. The transition had been slow and subtle, but was now clear-cut. At least it was to me, probably because, ultimately, I was watching from the touchlines, as it were. Apart from Paxton, perhaps, but he was pretty poor *voyeur* material by my standards.

'What would you do then in the circumstances – in your own inimitable, irresponsible disrespectful way, of course?' Mason asked, heavily jocular, but extremely wary.

'Bring him back here for a week, shut him in an office with the script – which I'd have him return to Pat Gow every evening – and then, at the end of his reading, ask him what he proposed to do. If he said he was against the story, proposed to try to stop it, I'd have him sign a paper saying he'd retained no notes and so on, pay him off there and then and close the Washington office to him. He could go and collect his books and personal items at his own expense. I'd also send a replacement out pronto. Roth would soon begin to look like any other unattached British scribbler with an American bee in his bonnet.'

Mason slowly bit on his lower lip and turned to me, 'What d'you think of the idea, Paul?'

'It certainly gets over some of the major problems. Keeps the typescript here and not floating about at Bernie's discretion in Washington. And it would certainly keep Bernie from doing anything decisive–without our knowledge–over there. I like it.'

'It seems there's a lot to be said for the idea, Tom,' Mason said magnanimously. 'Meantime, I could drop him a note saying we've discussed his letter and that I'm now taking over the correspondence and I'd like to see him here in, say, three weeks' time for full discussion.'

'Full and frank discussion, don't forget,' I said, smiling. 'Bernie likes phrases like that.'

So, too, I recalled as we broke up, did Mason.

Out in the corridor, Vaughan said, 'My view is still that Mason doesn't want to publish the story one little bit and is running all ways looking for a face-saving way out. What's your view?'

Vaughan was certainly stepping out of that web of discretion he'd spun and wrapped himself in for three months.

'I think you may be right. But in that case, why did he agree to bring Roth back?'

'Because the idea was too simple, logical and incontrovertible to oppose,' Vaughan said smoothly. 'He had to agree. It also has the advantage for Mason that if he's as chicken as I suspect, he can rope in Roth as yet another ally. In a subtle roundabout way, of course. It was a chance I had to take, but I could see by the glint in his eyes, he'd made a note of it.'

'But it does mean, of course, that you'll have 'em both under your personal supervision.'

He smiled. 'That's a very snide remark and I appreciate it, Paul. It also happens to be true.'

'Machiavelli, thou should'st be living at this hour.'

'He'd have found plenty of scope in Fetter Lane,' Vaughan said, departing. 'Be seeing you.'

—21—

Despite the fact that Friday was one of our two busiest days of the week, Mason thought the others should be made aware of the Roth situation. Especially Markham, the Foreign Editor. After all, as Mason said, Roth was, nominally, a member of Markham's staff, even though Roth frequently insisted, touchy as he was, on dealing directly with the editor.

Half an hour after I'd returned to my room, I had a house-call: would I go to the editor's room?

After we'd taken our usual chairs round his desk, Mason read Roth's letter.

'What would you do, Gerry?'

'In your position I'd ask him to come over for a week or so to see whether he could be dissuaded from his headlong course, although I must say I admire him for having the courage of his convictions and all that.'

'Sure you haven't been talking to Tom?'

Markham, surprised by the question, said 'Good Heavens no. Why?'

Mason laughed. 'I'm sure you haven't, but great minds and all that. . . . Tom suggested much the same kind of action an hour ago. Failing satisfaction, Tom wouldn't let Bernie go back–only under his own steam. Would you go along with that idea?'

'I'd need notice of that, but I doubt it,' Markham said coldly.

I wondered whether Markham's quickness off the mark was also due to a sudden desire to get Roth back as an ally in shooting down the Toynbee project. Markham wasn't the kind of man to take defeat in his stride. He'd always been something of a snapper-backer.

'Mightn't he resign rather than come back?' Spicer asked. 'He might prefer not to have his hands tied for three or four weeks back here.'

'I need four weeks,' Mason said. 'Paul thinks he could have finished editing the journals by then. He starts this week-end.'

'I see,' Spicer said thoughfully.

'Has he any personal reasons for wanting to come back here?' Vaughan asked. 'You all know him a lot better than I do. Any family and so forth?'

I said: 'Two ex-wives and four ex-children. At least, I suppose one could call 'em that. But he still loves 'em all.'

'But both wives have remarried,' Markham said.

'Nevertheless, he usually goes to see 'em to shed the odd tear or two. He's a great one for going over, *ad nauseam*, what might have been.'

'Come now, Paul, that's not worthy of you,' Markham said tutorially.

'Oh, come off it, Gerry. You know it's true,' Logan said.

'I'm afraid it is,' Spicer agreed.

'Why did they leave him?' Vaughan asked, interested. I was always amused to see how quickly the television interviewer took over. Possessed as I was of similar curiosity about other people's lives, I rather shared his point of view and found his unabashed inquisitiveness quite entertaining. So I replied, giving the answer to what I had always seen as his two greatest demerits in any kind of relationship, from marriage to friendship. 'I always suspected a combination of his enormous self-pity and the way he sweats all the time.'

'Paul!' Markham said, genuinely shocked.

'But why not?' Vaughan said quickly. 'Why not?' 'If Paul had said it was Roth's too-extravagant interest in glow-worms or Carpathian folk-music, it would have been OK, I suppose.'

Everybody laughed, except Markham.

'I don't go in for this particular emphasis on our emotional and physical shortcomings,' Markham said, somewhat prissily. 'I think we're all too vulnerable.' He smiled thinly. 'I should hate to think my wife might opt out on account of my undeniably thinning hair.'

'She's far more likely to stay if she notices, as I do, the added distinction it brings to your visage day by day,' Vaughan said, grinning, making 'visage' sound like a synonym for a death-mask.

Even Markham smiled at that bland insincerity.

'Supposing Roth's already gone ahead and tipped off one or two people that the Toynbee story's in the wind, what then?' Spicer asked.

'We'd probably know soon enough,' Mason said. 'I think bringing him back–if he'll come–is the most practical idea.'

As if he'd already made his irrevocable decision he added: 'It makes more sense all along the line to have him back here.'

'Why not speak to him this afternoon?' Markham said. 'We'd know where we were then.'

'OK,' Mason said. 'Get your girl to get him. What's the time in Washington now?'

'Too early,' Markham said. 'It's only about five in the morning. We'll get him at home later. He's rarely in his office before midday. I've got one or two items to discuss with him, anyway. I'll try this afternoon and switch him through to you, David.'

'Right,' Mason said. He was plainly pleased by the way the meeting had gone.

–22–

'What will we do if Roth were to pull out now?' Markham asked.

'Wouldn't you want to move Daniels up from New York?' Mason asked.

'He's not the political animal Roth is. It would take months to build up those contacts again.'

'It's a job any journalist has to be prepared to do and any Foreign Editor ought to be ready to master-mind,' Mason said augustly. He thrived on this kind of magisterial opining. 'We all have to bone up on new studies from time to time. You speak like a man who's been so exclusively preoccupied by foreign affairs all his life that he's come to believe there's some mystique about it all, Gerry.'

'Possibly. But even getting a superficial view of things out in that complex set-up takes time,' Markham said primly.

'I saw a good deal of Daniels while I was in New York,' I said. 'Although he'd be pretty young for the job, I found him unusually well-informed on the scene generally, and with an unusual interest in American history. And knowledge of.'

'I thought so, too,' Spicer said. 'I think we underrate Daniels. Everything he files is readable, which is more than can be said for some of Roth's more extended *tours d'horizon*.'

'You seem to imply I'm overlooking the prophet in our midst,' Markham said sharply.

'You may be, Gerry. Others aren't, it seems,' Mason said pointedly. 'Think about it, in case you have to move quickly. Meantime, I'll talk to Roth this afternoon.'

We broke up, Markham looking distinctly put out.

–23–

Later that afternoon Mason came into my room as I was going over the first rough proof of my last *Faces & Places* for a couple of weeks, for I was to leave for Ireland the following morning. Vaughan was with me, having a vested interest in the page that week. I'd included a piece on a Singhalese jewellery designer he'd met a couple of weeks before.

Mason seemed very pleased with himself. As Vaughan got up to go, he waved his hand, 'Don't go, Tom. I've just spoken to Bernie. He's coming over as you suggested. In about a fortnight's time. Seems quite pleased at the prospect. I suspect he thinks he's pulled off a bit of a personal coup. Making us aware of Bernie Roth. Keeping us all on our toes and all that. Free trip and the red carpet out when he gets here.'

'He may well prove a difficult so-and-so when he does get here,' I said. 'He's got a real bee in his bonnet over this story. Sees himself as Stirling's John the Baptist.'

'All the worth-while posthumous propaganda was done by your namesake, Paul of Tarsus,' Mason corrected benignly. 'I think you'll find he's the chap Bernie's identifying with.'

'Maybe, but I still think you're going to find Bernie an outsize irritant.'

'Saint Paul was too,' Mason the Methodist had to put in, and then: 'But aren't we buying time. If I can delay him for three weeks from now, stifle some of his misgivings and keep him another week while he reads your edited version or, better still, try to send him back to Washington without having seen it with the promise that he can see it well before any publication date, we'll be in a far better position than we are now. D'you agree?'

'He'll certainly want to wait for my return, from Ireland,' I said.

'He will, indeed,' Vaughan said. 'That's for sure. And supposing he won't be stifled anyway? When I interviewed him last year he didn't seem like one of nature's stiflees, to coin a word. He'll insist on seeing something before he'll even consider going back'.

'Oh, well, I'll have to play it by ear. I see what you mean. Time is what we need. What I don't want to happen is to be rushed into one of the biggest things we've ever attempted without due time for preparation or reflection.'

Perhaps it was a reasonable statement of the situation, but Mason was beginning to make it too often.

'How much time for preparation, how much for reflection?' Vaughan asked quietly.

'I don't know. The most important thing is to have Paul's typescript here in front of us, with copies for ourselves–and Bernie, I suppose–as soon as possible.'

'How many copies?'

'That's a point. I'd say four of Paul's edited version. It does sound rather apostolic, put like that, doesn't it?' He turned to me. 'You've got the only other copy of the full text, haven't you, Paul and I've got the other? And the original's in the strong-room.'

I nodded. I thought that was enough. Mason, the man of decision, went on: 'I'd say we need four copies of your edited version, then. Make a note, will you, Pat?'

Pat Gow made the note.

'When will you start the job?' Vaughan asked, turning to me.

'First thing Monday.'

'Where are you off to? Which part?' Mason asked.

'County Kerry. Pat's coming over mid-week with her portable.' I turned to the editor. 'I hope that's OK.'

'Fine by me. How long will you be away?' Mason asked.

'A couple of weeks.'

'You've made all arrangements here?'

'Everything's under control. Floyd will look after *Faces & Places* with Tom looking over his shoulder. We were just discussing that when you came in.'

'Well, I'll leave you to it. Have a good time. Bring us back a journal fit to print.' He laughed. 'You'll want another holiday to recover. Take a week or so's real holiday in a month's time. Italy or something. I'll see about it. See you later.'

He turned and went. 'D'you think Pat could get us some coffee?' Vaughan asked.

'Why not? Three cups, Pat and take your time.'

'D'you think Mason really wants to publish this damn thing?' Vaughan said, mock-wearily, as Pat left the room.

'If he doesn't, he's putting on a pretty good show.'

'All Welshmen are actors. I ought to know. You, too, with a name like yours.'

'My mother was a Scot, a sound corrective.'

Vaughan smiled and went on: 'I can't make it out. At first he was dead against it. Now he seems all for it. Even falling in with my notion to bring Roth over. But I don't read his temperament, character, experience, career and the rest thataway.'

'Perhaps you've fed the wrong data into the Vaughan computer.'

'I don't think so. There's something fishy in this new determination of his to go ahead. After all, for him, it's sheer sensationalism – despite all Stirling's high-sounding blue-blooded political-intellectual connexions. All in all, Mason's current behaviour doesn't ring true.'

'Perhaps he's trying to break out of your character-casting system,' I said gently.

'I accept that, and I probably deserve it. You think I'm setting up as a tame astrologer or palmist or something.'

I grinned. 'I'd say you were just setting up to be the king-pin himself.'

Vaughan let that pass as if he hadn't heard the words and went on calmly: 'I've always acted on my character estimates, judgments, assessments, call 'em what you like. So far they've never let me down. Basically, it's my stock-in-trade – Intuition.'

'You're overlooking the fact that Mason may be going through his equivalent to the female change of life – climacteric's the word, isn't it? Some women, I gather, go all out for young men at such times, I'm told. Maybe that's why Mason's trying to act like a young editor.'

Vaughan laughed loudly. 'If so, it's the first time in his life. But have it your own way. Not that you believe it. My belief is that I'm dealing with the same old crafty manipulator he's always been. He's never gone overboard for anything in his life. I've been going through the daily paper he edited for ten long years. Not one really *surprising* feature. Nothing in the same league as this Toynbee thing. If ever there was a middle-of-the-roader it's Mason. Why he even took *Faces & Places* over from *New Sunday* in toto. Did he ever give you a similar chance when you worked with him on the daily? Did he ever have such a feature in his mind before?'

I smiled. 'I was the industrial correspondent,' I said, trying not to laugh my head off.

Vaughan laughed in triumph. 'With a talent for writing about other people's talents. Spurway spotted it, not Mason.'

'Why, then, did he choose you as his one and only whiz-kid?' I asked.

'I was wished on him,' Vaughan said simply. He got up. 'Tell Pat I skipped the coffee. Well, have a good time in Ireland if I don't see you again. I'm on the box tonight. Don't work too hard. I can't think we'd need all thirty thousand words at one go.'

'Or even one thousand if your palm-reading's in sound working order.'

'Never let me down yet,' he said modestly.

Pat Gow came in with three cups of coffee.

'Looking forward to Ireland, Pat?'

'Madly, Mr Vaughan.'

Vaughan sat down again, took a cup and began bravely to sip the brew. 'What kind of working programme d'you envisage, Paul?'

'Ten till three and then call it a day. By the time Pat comes over I'll hope to be far enough ahead to keep her to the same working arrangement.'

We nattered about Ireland until we'd finished the coffee.

–24–

The following morning, the first Saturday in September, I packed my bag, went down to the car and drove round to Milner Street to call for Helen and Marion. Thus we began the long journey to County Kerry, by way of the A40 to Fishguard, thence by Sealink to Rosslare.

The previous summer, whilst writing a piece for *New Sunday* on the work of the younger Irish architects, I'd come across a small modern hotel on the outskirts of Dingle. I'd liked the hotel a lot during the one night I'd stayed there. Now I thought I'd test its worth as family hotel and working retreat.

In the event the whole project worked remarkably well: hotel and weather, for we had brilliant sun on most days during our fortnight there.

My daily routine was simple, but different from the programme I'd outlined to Vaughan. I tried to put in between five and six hours a day on the journals, rising at six for a two-hour stint. Then bath and shave. Then breakfast *en famille* at nine. Then back to work until lunch-time.

That gave me the afternoons free. I did another hour or so in the evenings. Helen and Marion wandered around in the mornings, even occasionally swam the boisterous seas. Marion also did some holiday prep, particularly as she was to return, by special dispensation, to London after the Lycée had restarted term.

After lunch we were free for holiday excursions, driving over to Inch to swim and laze on that great sweep of beach or driving on to the Killarney lakes.

Preparing 'Toynbee' (as I'd begun to term the whole project) for publication as a five-part serial was a mammoth but absorbing task. I found that I had sizeably underestimated the contents of the two box files. I reckoned that Ann's records, including relevant cuttings, letters, notes and the rest, totalled well over three hundred thousand words. Reducing this to between twenty-five and thirty thousand words was the most concentrated editing I'd ever undertaken. All the printed material went first. That helped. But it all had to be read. A feature article frequently needed to be reduced to a five-line precis.

The problem had something of the challenge of translating a poem from a foreign language into one's native tongue, with the same urge towards giving a coherent shape to the result. I never had to flog myself to get down to the task. The background of the great early morning skies and rugged mountains helped, of course. Plus that first gulp of black coffee from the thermos I always had filled overnight.

I started the job on the Monday morning following our arrival on the Sunday afternoon, for we'd stayed over Saturday night at the motel near Rosslare.

Pat Gow came over on the Wednesday. Helen and Marion drove up through Kerry and Limerick to meet her at Shannon, thoroughly enjoying the excursion. The West of Ireland was at its glorious best: shafts of sunlight between great banks of cumulus with occasional showers. Then sunlight again.

Before Pat arrived I'd worked steadily away in my room, making half-hour breaks every two hours for a walk along the shores of Dingle Bay. From Thursday onwards Pat Gow worked steadily through the material on which I'd made a head start. She started work after breakfast, taking over what I had ready and worked again for an hour after lunch.

A long trestle table had been moved into a spare room and there we worked, overlooking the bay. Perfect working conditions, apart from the fact that the temptation to move outside was always building up, especially as that year's Irish-Indian summer continued day after day.

Problems usually inseparable from having a secretary with us at meals and in the evenings never arose. Pat Gow was soon taken up by a coterie of Irish TV camera-men from Dublin busy making a documentary based on some of John Synge's Kerry pieces. We scarcely saw her outside working hours.

–25–

Although, as I've said, the task of editing the journals was challenging and engrossing, it was also impossible.

In common with all other good diarists, Ann Toynbee had an insatiable eye for detail which quickened her recollections of people, places, scenes, happenings. In the light of my own recent meeting with Melanie Stirling, the journal now had even greater interest. Inevitably much of what Ann had written about Melanie Stirling was unpublishable and instantly deleted. Such entries, I decided, could await some curious researcher a century hence.

For example:

I asked Greg whether Melanie knew of his affairs. He said she'd found out over ten years before, had never forgiven him and had never slept with him since. I said this might have started out as a sulking gesture: had he tried to win her round again by chatting her up as if she were a new bird in his life. He said no, there had been religious beliefs involved, an abuse of loyalty and all the rest of it and that her decision had had such a finality to it that he knew it was hopeless. But had he tried? I persisted. Finally, he agreed he hadn't. I said any woman was entitled to play her big tragic scene at such a time: and that it was up to the man to string along with her. He smiled as if he knew a trick worth two of that. Secretly, I think he'd probably been relieved. She'd given him his children of whom he's very fond in a possessively paternal but scarcely emotional way and her decision has given him a fairly carefree conscience ever since.

(Wholly deleted)

Again:

Melanie Stirling is the most accomplished hostess I've ever encountered. Even amongst the streamlined-Washington-political-diplomatic-journalistic-set she's outstanding. Not a thing ever goes wrong. Everything has a mechanical perfection about it, but, unlike a lot of American homes, the food and wine are first-rate. And she always looks the part. I feel positively dowdy sometimes, even when I've taken pains. But all this perfection is apt to demand perfection in the guests, who scarcely ever unbend. Nobody ever raises a subject with tongue in cheek. Nobody ever treats serious subjects lightly. It's all so damned earnest. Main discussion and argument always come back to Vietnam, of course, but as all the guests are invariably liberal-radical there's ultimately only one theme—withdrawal. But how complete a withdrawal? When I said why not complete and utter withdrawal in one month flat, everybody's aghast, even the so-called radicals. Scratch any good American radical and you'll find a frontiersman just below the epidermis.

(I retained the second half.)

Or again:

The real and incurable trouble about politicians the world over is that all their friends are politicians. And this is particularly so with rich radicals. All their friends are rich radicals. A few poor artists or arty-fringe-type people like myself are occasionally roped in, but we're there as decorative oddments, court jesters, horse-painters, frills around the table cloth.

(Retained)

Again:

Knowing what I do about Melanie Stirling I watch her with obsessive fascination. She has a marvellous bone structure which any woman's got to have if she's going to stay the course as a good-looker after thirty-five: A beautiful jawbone from ear-lobe to chin-point. Her hair is fabulous: straight out of an old Venetian fresco: thick, lustrous, dark bronze. Fine eyes: dark, deep, umber. A mildly imperious nose. Good mouth, well-shaped lips, with a pouting underlip. Altogether very handsome. About five feet six. Good legs. Flat belly. She and Greg make a remarkably handsome pair. Little wonder they've been trailed by all the cameramen for years. How odd, that so randy a man has left her untouched for ten long years. She looks sexy, but he says she isn't (I've usually found husbands only too ready to discuss their wives' performances, usually with the implication that their own prowess was too much for the little lady. Hence, the necessity for their own predatory careers). But I can imagine that Melanie regards the whole sex set-up as basically a means to an end, and probably never even spent half an hour in a session. Greg swears she didn't, but married men, I've noticed, are determined not to remember what must have been thorough-going–even if only occasional–sessions in the ardent days of their early marriage or on the sensual nights of second honeymoons. What scum men really are. If only one didn't like them so much one could really accomplish miracles of work.

(I retained the physical description of Melanie Stirling–no woman would object to that?–but deleted the rest.)

Again:

Watching Greg dress this morning I asked him whether he ever thought he was too good-looking to be a successful politician. It appeals to the women, I said, that's certain, but do you ever think it might antagonise a lot of pot-bellied stockbrokers and all those ugly-looking brutes in the working classes? I'll stand on the record, he said, with typical masculine conceit. But he did laugh as he said it. I'll give him that.

Retained(apart from the first five words).

Again:

A merry evening. Half-way through, Greg laughing, asked whether I thought I had any nymphomaniacal tendencies. First, what was the masculine equivalent of nymphomaniac? I asked. *L'après-midi d'un faunomaniac? Pornomaniac?* He laughed, but admitted he didn't know of one. Philanderer, he offered. I scoffed. 'Nymphomania' sounds like a disease; 'philandering' sounds like a vocation. Whatever its medical provenance, nymphomania has somehow become a term of man-made semi-abuse. But philanderer remains an indulgent, genteel, soft-soap word. Trust a man to think that one up. Must look up etymology of both words. I then told him a good word for such occasions was satyriasis, which he suffered from. Look it up, I said, it's in all the good dictionaries.

(Deleted.)

Again.

I find it very odd to have Greg wandering round my apartment at half-past six in the morning looking like a leading character out of a Henry Miller set-piece and to know that sometime later that afternoon he'll be on a platform looking like the All-America dream-boy as if butter wouldn't melt in his mouth, and every American mother's dream-son. Yet here he is, one of the most accomplished lechers and/or philanderers of his time, with every detail worked out to the last second. Even his getaway car from my apartment. A small Volkswagen beetle he keeps in a nearby garage registered in the name of one of his secretaries. No smooth Cadillac for him on these occasions. He can park it and he can take it out to Kennedy and nobody spots him. He loves the headlines, but, my, how well he can practise anonymity.

(Deleted)

And so on and on.

–26–

By the day before we were to leave Dingle the job was more or less done. I could return to London with the certainty that copies of the draft, retyped and xeroxed, could be put before the editor, Ann

Toynbee, Melanie Stirling, Roth and the others, including the lawyers, within a week.

We sent Pat Gow off to Dublin with the film technicians for a couple of days let-up and then drove back across Ireland to Rosslare, crossed to Fishguard and then back through the West Country in a fairly lighthearted mood.

'How odd we never had half so much fun on holidays when we were officially married,' Helen said as she undressed the night before we left.

'Yet you'd take that old life up again?'

'If you agreed.'

'In spite of what you've just admitted?'

'Right.'

'Why?'

'I don't know.'

'Because you're a woman and want the worst of two worlds rather than the best of one.'

'Nonsense. I want the best of several worlds.'

'Such as?'

'The security of marriage. Not just the economic set-up, the status or any of those things–you take good care of those things, anyway –but the mere fact of knowing one's married. Plus the carefree days we've had here.'

'Perhaps our present state is the one to aim for. Perhaps the ideal arrangement is first, to marry, then divorce, then unite again without sanction of Church or State. It might suit quite a lot of people.'

'It would suit more men than women.'

'Come, come, even in these days of Women's Lib?'

Helen nodded. 'Anyway, isn't the new Divorce Bill aimed to do just that?' she asked from the bed.

'I doubt it. That's for those who long for full release. I'm obviously the type who yearns for a kind of demi-semi-release and/or a demi-semi prison.'

'On *full-pensione* terms. I'll give you that,' Helen said, laughing. 'Come to bed and sample the landlady.'

Fortunately, Marion, in common with most twelve-year-olds, was able to take our curious non-marital set-up in her leggy stride. She might have thought our arrangement somewhat strange, compared with those of most of the parents of her school friends, but she gave no sign of any hang-up over the matter. Perhaps she never even thought about it. Perhaps she even thought we were married. Or never had been.

As I've said before, the only contribution I can make is that children seem to be extremely resilient in their social attitudes. But maybe I kid myself. I often do.

–27–

I returned to London to find Roth had arrived two days before, but had been persuaded by Mason to take ten days off to visit the paper's correspondents in Paris, Bonn and Rome.

He hadn't taken overmuch persuading, Vaughan added, filling me in on the details.

'How was he?'

'No different from the way I found him last year. Touchy, opinionated, self-righteous, and, as usual with that kind of man, utterly lacking in self-confidence. No wonder he fell for Stirling the masterful spellbinder. The Roth kind of man is always looking for a leader to cling to.'

'Vaughan's instant-character-chart's had plenty of scope, I see.'

He grinned. 'Roth offers too little scope. That's part of his trouble: he's so damnably appallingly obvious. How did you get on?'

'Quite well. Reduced the masterpiece–or mistresspiece–to something well under forty thousand words. Somebody else can do any further cutting that's needed.'

'Curious we have masterpieces but no mistress-pieces. Not even *Wuthering Heights* or *Pride and P*,' Vaughan said, thoughtfully.

'You can introduce the subject on one of your telly quiz programmes. Miss Toynbee's always chiding at our masculine-slanted language. She wants a masculine equivalent for nymphomaniac? Or saviour? She says that even when we do use feminine affixes they sound like apologies: authoress, poetess, editress.'

'What about tigress and lioness? Nothing apologetic about those, surely?'

Vaughan was plainly entertained by the turn the conversation had taken, having to the full the television man's delight in digressions. That alone made him, for me, one of the more agreeable people on the paper.

We discussed the subject for some minutes.

'Another reason why I'd have liked to have met your Miss Toynbee,' Vaughan said. 'Just the kind of girl I'd liked to interview in the good old days.'

'You're too young to be getting nostalgic,' I said. 'Ann Toynbee will certainly come your television way if her story comes our newsprint way.'

He laughed. 'Where's Pat?'

'I gave her a couple of days off to spend in Dublin. Needless to say, she met a heart-throb in the West of Ireland who offered to show her the city.'

'Good idea. When do we get a chance to look at your handiwork?'

'I'm handing it over to the editor in about an hour's time. I've a few corrections to make and then, as far as I'm concerned, it's terminado.'

'Was it tough going?'

'Tough and frustrating. I scarcely wanted to cut a single page yet had to cut ninety per cent.'

'She'll get it all back in the book, presumably.'

'So I kept telling myself every time I put my blue pencil through another entertaining passage. But it had to be done.'

'When will she get her copy?'

'Next week, I imagine.'

'I suppose she can always shoot the abridgement down.'

'I doubt whether anybody would publish the journals in full. At least, not in her lifetime. It's one of those jobs some history professor at Johns Hopkins or Princeton will take on a century hence.'

'Even Ann Toynbee won't be alive then, you think?' Vaughan said, smiling.

'She might if the quacks speed-up the longevity genes. Or her own vitality and a little yoghourt might well see her through,' I said and meant.

–28–

I handed Mason my Toynbee adaptation later that afternoon: one hundred and fifty pages of double-spaced typing beautifully tapped out by Pat Gow.

I also began a letter:

Dearest Ann: I've just returned from the West of Ireland where I've been abridging Toynbee, without, I hope, unduly expurgating or bowdlerising Toynbee. Your copy will be sent over next week.

I found it an impossible job, but one that had to be done. Anyway, let me know what you think. Roth is here or, at least, in Europe somewhere, catching up on the international scene. He returns next week and will probably be permitted to see a copy of the edited version.

He may still prove difficult, I suspect, despite Melanie S's agreement. We'll see.

Also, at the risk of this letter appearing as a footnote in the contents of some future box-file, I should also like to tell you that I think, quite frequently, of those delightful hours in your New York eyrie, and wish that I could be working on a scheme to get to see you in one of your future eyries. That one on the Bosphorus would be nice.

My letter went on and on until my final suggestion that the best thing to do with such effusions is always to burn after twice reading.

–29–

By the following Tuesday afternoon, half-a-dozen numbered copies of my edited version of the Toynbee journals had been made for discussion at the editorial conference a week ahead.

Three were handed to me, one to be sent to Ann Toynbee herself, the other to Mrs Stirling. I was to retain the third for further work if deemed necessary.

The editor retained two: one for his own use, the other for circulation to Markham, Logan, Spicer and Vaughan. Copy No 6 was handed to the paper's lawyer, Grant Lovell, for his views.

I sent the two copies off that evening with covering letters:

Dear Mrs Stirling: I am enclosing an edited version of Ann Toynbee's journal which I discussed with you in your home last month. This represents the material that would be considered as potentially publishable. Even this edited version (which represents no more than one-tenth of the original) may prove too long. Any observations you care to make can, therefore, be based exclusively on the enclosed typescript. If the journals in full are considered for publication that would be an entirely different matter, unlikely to be in my hands.

If necessary, I would be prepared to come to Athens to discuss further with you.

Lovell approved the letter; it was agreeably non-committal as far as he was concerned, he said. He didn't see my letter to Ann, which read:

Dearest Ann: Here is the edited version. Your text has been mightily reduced, as you will see. Don't be too angry, but this is roughly the limit of space that the paper can go to. Even these extracts will take five or six weeks to publish, the longest run the paper has ever given to a serial.

Will you send to my private address (above) any suggestions, corrections, amendments, pleas, commands, demands, cajolings and the rest and I'll see what can be done?

If you feel like a trip to London, you could write to the Editor saying there are things you must discuss personally. I think he'd willingly underwrite your expenses.

Roth is in Rome at the moment. Once he's back in London, I'll let you know his reactions if he lives to tell the tale. I've a personal belief that he'll die of apoplexy half-way through.

This letter also continued for several pages, but those have little bearing on my story. Perhaps diarists are apt to prompt their correspondents into a competitive loquaciousness.

PART V

—I—

The rest of my story is part conjecture, part known fact.

The first known fact is that Roth returned early the following week from Rome. His lightning tour round the paper's correspondents in Paris, Bonn and Rome seemed to have mellowed him. Striding purposefully into my office on the following Tuesday afternoon he seemed a wholly different person from the tetchy, self-pitying creature I'd met in Washington a month before. He was expansive, almost complacent.

He talked about the things which had particularly interested him in Europe. Only at the end of half an hour's genial reminiscing and gossip did he mention our recent contretemps. 'The editor gave me your version of the Toynbee journals to read last night. . . .'

He plainly expected me to rush in, but I thought I'd let him go on solo. After a pause he did—in rather a disconcerted manner, I thought. But what he had to say was surprisingly conciliatory: 'I never had a chance to see the original material, of course, but I gather from Mason that you had a fantastic editing job to do. Cutting ninety per cent; is that right?'

I nodded.

'Quite a job. I think it reads remarkably well. Stirling comes out of it as almost human.'

Roth's carefully contrived conciliatory smile was worthy of a bishop at a high-class baptism.

'I always thought you saw him in that light.'

'I'm afraid I was always inclined to see him as something almost superhuman from which a human being was trying to escape. I think you've succeeded in the translation.'

'Give the credit to Miss Toynbee.'

I was puzzled by Roth's reaction, and prodded further: 'To my mind, he still emerges as a pretty cold fish in his political ambitions and a pretty predatory numero in his womanizing. Wouldn't you agree?'

'In your version, these sides of his character—and, God knows, they were there—become an understandable part of a complex yet somehow unusually complete man. You've captured his humanity and compassion. . . .'

'You mean Ann Toynbee has . . .' I said again. 'Believe me, Bernie, there's not a single word of mine in what you read. Whatever is there is there by grace and favour of Ann Toynbee.'

'Well, perhaps she's less of a cold-blooded little nympho than I though she was.'

'Almost human?' I queried, but he didn't rise. His thoughts were plainly elsewhere.

I was still puzzled. I needed to persist: 'You don't think he emerges as something a good deal less than your symbol for a new meaning in American politics?'

'Not necessarily. Not destructively so, anyway.'

'In view of what is, to me, your somewhat surprising reaction to the script, Bernie, how does that leave things as far as the threats in your letters are concerned?'

'Please, Paul. Take it easy. Not threats. I merely put down certain sincerely held views. I put forward what seemed to me a quite reasonable ultimatum. I said, quite simply, that if I thought Stirling's posthumous reputation was going to be smeared, I would resign and do my best to stop publication or discredit the whole story. Right?'

I felt the way Melanie Stirling must have felt when I rang her from the Turnpike Inn as I heard myself saying, 'That may seem like a genial ultimatum–between friends–to you, but it still seems like a steely threat to me.'

'A matter of semantics. Anyway, it doesn't arise. I think you've done a masterly job and I wish you well with it.'

'Do your good wishes extend to Ann Toynbee? I shall be writing to her later this week. Shall I give her the good news?'

'Do, by all means,' he said as if he'd disposed of the whole matter, and then: 'Any chance of lunching before I go back?'

'When's that?'

'Sunday morning. I'd like to hang around here on Saturday. I always enjoy seeing you all at work and it helps me in my own work to carry a mind's eye picture of the Saturday scene here.'

'Let's lunch on Friday, then?'

'Good. I'd like that.'

'Collect me here and we'll wander round to the Terrazza in Chancery Lane?'

He rattled on for another ten minutes or so about his recent travels. Once again he referred to the Toynbee journals, but, again, too casually. I had the odd feeling that he was seeking to let me know that Ann's record had taken its due place as a lowly item in a busy European round. To my mind he seemed to be overdoing his act of impressing on me the fact that although the journals had undoubtedly been the cause of his trip, they were no longer cause for alarm.

But I wasn't satisfied.

–2–

I still wasn't satisfied, even after Mason had wandered in the following morning with further soothing words. 'I gather Bernie talked to you about his new-found willingness to accept Stirling as a human being and not as the Second Coming.'

'Relief and something of a major surprise.'

'To me, too.'

'How d'you think he was able to square his conscience so flexibly?'

'I take some of the credit,' Mason said. 'Admittedly, Tom and Gerry share credit for the original idea of bringing him over, but once he got here I thought the idea of sending him off round Europe might help. Give him a fresh perspective on Stirling against the European background. In the event it seems to have worked.'

'He certainly seems more relaxed.'

'He is. When he arrived from the States–you were still in Ireland –he was breathing fire and brimstone like a Welsh valley preacher. I sent him off within twenty-four hours.'

'Are you sure you'll get the owners on your side now?'

'Who can say? I think so. Otherwise, I think they'd want to know the reason why I let the story go, especially if another paper hopped in and put on a hundred thousand extra copies as a result.'

'If you'd let 'em know you'd shot it down, that is.'

'They'd know soon enough. How many Fleet Street secrets are there? Name six.'

He almost snorted in his triumph at my inability to vouch for one. In cheerful mood he left the room.

–3–

I mentioned my general bewilderment later in the morning to Vaughan, who heard me out and then said, quite calmly, that he still thought Mason would rat.

'But why should he? With Roth on his side, almost certainly Ann Toynbee I'd say, and with only Mrs Stirling's OK to come, he'll have all the aces.'

'Three aces. What about the fourth? The trouble is there's several unknown fourth aces in this game, apart from as many jokers. The American and British political establishments for a pair. Very potent indeed. Wait till they get wind of things and start rumbling into action in their ponderous and appalling but quite effective ways. And I don't think Mason, ultimately, is bred for that kind of battle.

'What makes you think that?'

'He's always been a crusader for, battler against, *ideas*. He's never dealt with people. As far as I can gather, he's always stayed put in that editorial sanctum sanctimonious of his, scribbling away at his tablets. This would be a brand new kind of battle for him–and he'd be all on his own. He'd be bang up against real tough Establishment types. And basically he's on their side. In a cosy old liberal way, of course. He'd have to upset the genes of a lifetime to go ahead. This is the most explosive piece of dynamite to hit Fleet Street in years. It makes Keeler look like the poor mixed-up waif she was. Stirling was God for young America; Toynbee's a beautiful young intellectual. Well, isn't she?'

I nodded. 'Go on,' I said. 'Surely there's more to come.'

Vaughan smiled. 'We've been through it all before,' he said, resignedly. 'I've said my piece, made my predictions. Mason will rat.'

'Based on a hunch.'

'Based on character-reading, as I've said so often before–to a disbeliever. Mason's simply not up to that kind of warfare. He's a swivel-chair warrior.'

'You'll use that phrase again,' I said.

He grinned and left.

–4–

I didn't have my lunch with Roth. A note addressed from the Connaught awaited me the following morning:

Dear Paul: I had a late chat with the Editor this evening and he thinks I've been away from the Washington scene a bit too long. Somewhat regretfully I had to agree. So I'm catching the BOAC plane tomorrow morning and thus, alas, won't be able to make that Friday lunch. I'm very sorry. There were so many things we had to talk about. I'll write fully later. Bernie.

Nothing about Toynbee.

'Why should Mason have done it?' I queried Vaughan later that afternoon.

'Just to get him away from the rest of us. D'you realise that none of us, apart from Markham and yourself, briefly, saw Roth before he went off? They've made an arrangement, I'll bet.'

'But Mason and Markham are Roth's only logical contacts here at any time,' I pointed out.

'Why shouldn't he have met the rest of us for a little domestic teach-in about the state of the game in Washington? I gather from Logan that that's always been the usual Mason drill whenever a foreign correspondent dropped in.'

I agreed, adding slyly: 'One of the side benefits of the Toynbee story has been the way it's reconciled you and Logan.'

'A passing gentle zephyr,' Vaughan said casually. 'As soon as this Toynbee thing's over one way or another we'll be at each other's throats again. Just wait and watch.'

'But why such buddies on this venture and so few others.'

'Curiously enough, we both want it for exactly the same reasons,' Vaughan said surprisingly. 'First, it's a marvellous story. Second, it proves this paper isn't as genteel, liberal, unctuous, moribund and mealy-mouthed as it's often said to be. Third, it would put on sales. Fourth, it would bring in other offers.'

'No other reason all your very own?'

'As far as I'm concerned, it's a test-case for Mason.'

'Isn't that your main reason?'

'Maybe. I'll let you know.'

'And if Mason let's you down?'

'I'll have him out, sooner rather than later. I vow I will.'

'He's building up quite a lot of people he'll have to do battle with, if he lets it drop.'

'I don't think so. I think he could kill it off with very little opposition inside this place. Mine venomous; Logan's vociferous; yours mildly censorious. No more.'

'But somebody else would step in and grab it.'

'That, my dear Watson, is the unknown factor. My own belief is that Mason would like to kill it off for good—and probably could, but is scared of the aftermath if somebody else gets it. How's that for a real outsider-hunch?'

'If you're so sure of your character-reading what are you doing to combat the Mason gambits?'

'Nothing, dammit.'

'Why not?'

'Because, as you put it, with your usual unerring gift for denigration, I'm working on no more than a hunch based on intuition, experience and character study.'

'Well, keep me in touch with any developments in the three-pronged Vaughan intelligence division. Don't forget I'm involved too.'

'Too mildly,' he amended.

'Might it help your scheme or schemes, whatever it is or they are –in which I admit I'm deeply interested–if Ann Toynbee were to come over as Roth goes back?'

'That's quite an idea. Shall I raise it with Mason?'

'You can or I can.'

'I will.'

He seemed so eager that I made no demur.

'It might be a useful move in flushing Mason out into the open,' he said reflectively. 'We could probably get a chance to see how genuine he is once we start suggesting photographs of Toynbee herself. If things started to hot up like that he might begin to show he's as chicken as I suspect he is.'

'You're obsessed,' I said.

He laughed. 'It's true. I am. When can you lunch?'

'Friday,' I said without even looking at my book.

–5–

'Why did you send Roth back so suddenly?' I asked Mason later that afternoon.

'He was homesick for his Washington set-up; he was getting on my nerves; and he's been away too long.'

'Why didn't you give him a chance to tell the rest of us something about the Washington scene? He loves opining.'

'A teach-in here was too high a price for not getting a Washington piece in this week's paper.'

'He certainly made a quick getaway.'

'It was my idea. I thought he was drifting a bit. He didn't take much persuading.'

He changed the subject.

–6–

The following day I got a cable from Ann:

EDITING SUPERLATIVE SURGICAL ACHIEVEMENT STOP REGRETFULLY APPROVE THROUGH TEAR-MISTED CORNEAE STOP HOPEFULLY AWAIT LONDON COMMAND

LOVE ANN

–7–

Over lunch on Friday I returned to the subject of Vaughan's creeping obsession.

'Creepy, I'll admit, but not so creeping. More like a mountain stream in flood.'

'Why?'

Vaughan was now really out in the open. At least with me. 'Because Mason's such a damn stick-in-the-mud. Because he's in the way. Because he's an outsize bore.'

'Because he edits the paper you want to edit.'

'Of course.'

'Could you do it better?'

'How can one ever say? Who's to measure whether mine would be a better paper? The owners, the readers, the staff? Nobody but me. To me it would be better.'

'It might merely be different,' I pointed out.

'O K, then, different. Very different. In truth, I couldn't promise more than that. But I wouldn't sit on my technical, mental and imaginative backside, year in, year out. Let's face it, Mason *is* moribund. Has been half-mummified for thirty years.'

'He did a good job on the daily.'

'What good job? He kept it alive. How many new readers did he get?'

'Is that your main test?'

'It's high on my list. It's no good sitting back and saying our appeal is to the intelligent minority. That way lies sterility and complacency. I don't go for intelligent minorities, anyway. This country's packed out with a dozen intelligent majorities. Young people, hundreds of thousands of 'em. Far more than Mason reckons. They're dished up Sunday trash or Sunday trad, both dressed up to look like swinging newspapers. I want some real stuff.'

'Is that why you're so mad for this Toynbee thing?'

'Well, at least it's a real thing of our time. A girl who really does make sense about equality of the sexes means something. A girl who's given us a record that's every bit as important a slice of recent history as any of the man-made records of the post-war years. And it's too hot for Mason to handle. That's the long and short of it.'

And so we went on and on, with Vaughan doing most of the ding-dong talking.

At the end I said, 'Well, if your plan works, you'll be meeting Miss Ann Toynbee. You can then size her up for yourself.'

Despite the headstrong obsessive way he had run on about Mason, his fairly cool brain was still ticking over. 'That's fixed, by the way,' he said. 'I should've mentioned it earlier. I cornered Mason yesterday. You're to ask her over for a week as soon as you like.'

'Very cool work. How did you do it?'

'Mason's playing a deep game. And he's playing it well. I'll give him that. Needed no apparent persuasion from me. He's playing to the last ditch that's he's going ahead. He couldn't have a better ploy than getting her over, could he? In fact, in a way, he rather called my bluff. Anyway I look forward to meeting the girl. Wonder how many of us she'll think worth seducing–if that's the word.'

'Seduction's not the word or her line. She thinks it's a matter of exchanging.'

'I see. Willing buyer, willing seller, and all that.'

'No money crosses the counter. Basically, it's a barter system, I'm told. Didn't you gather that, too?'

'I did, indeed. Sounds ideal.'

–8–

A week after Roth had returned to Washington, Ann Toynbee arrived in London.

I dined her that evening, picking her up from the Cavendish where she was staying.

'I'm beginning to like this top brass transatlantic way of life,' she said as I took her arm to cross St James's Street.

'Perhaps you'd better write a journal a year.'

'That could easily be misinterpreted as a beastly remark.'

'Meant only as a challenge.'

'Worse still. Where are you taking me now?'

'The Coq d'Or, just the other side of Piccadilly.'

'I like that. You're very thoughtful for the well-being of your contributors.'

'You're sure you've no major criticism of the editing. You're not saving up some hand-made bomb to lob across the dining-table.'

'None, I promise. I wish you'd kept in a few more purple passages. I'd rather see more of that than the political stuff. That's what women are interested in. Not Greg's insatiable longing for power.'

'Just his insatiable longing for you?'

She laughed. 'Why not?'

'Both are there,' I said firmly. 'And the rest. My version aims at some kind of balance between about five different facets of the relationship. And, oddly enough, we have both sexes as readers.'

'It's the sexual side between the sexes which is still in a state or chaos and needs a little searchlight.'

'Write another book to elaborate your ideas.'

'You're very brutal, but I might do just that. Why have you let my arm go?'

'Because we're not crossing any main roads.'

'But I like having you hold my arm. Imagine you're crossing one long main road. I adore that firm yet gentle pressure on my humerus.'

'A term–like corneae–you no doubt picked up in Caracas.'

She laughed. 'I'm apt to forget you know all about my previous life.'

'Only as it appears in odd confessionals to Stirling. A curious way to learn about a woman's life. I think your Caracas doctor friend got under Stirling's skin a bit.'

'Greg was the most competitive man I ever met, although he disguised it pretty well. But it was always there. He had to excel in every damn department of life.'

'Well, if a man's that way inclined, it's pretty certain he'll want to be top boy at sex, too.'

'It's mad. Like most other worth-while things, sex takes time, the one commodity Greg never had enough of. Golly, I'm hungry. I hope I'm going to see a lot of Paul Mortimer while I'm here.'

'As much as you like.'

'Good. Now I can relax.'

–9–

The Thursday meeting in Mason's office between Ann and the rest of us–Vaughan, Markham, Spicer, Logan and myself–was the most odd and hilarious editorial discussions I'd ever attended in that room.

Mason set the meeting going by gallantly if somewhat unnecessarily introducing Ann. Obviously, as everyone had read her journals in the original, she was an object of extreme curiosity.

I admired the easy and amused assurance with which she took their surreptitious but searching examination of herself. She was seated in an elbow chair at Mason's side. He was at his desk. The rest of us faced the pair of them in our usual ragged crescent.

Fortunately, Mason, plainly enjoying his unusual role as master of ceremonies got the whole thing off to a good start. 'Well, here is

Miss Toynbee at last,' he said, turning towards her. 'I think it's reasonable to say that we're all so well acquainted with you by now, Miss Toynbee, that I need call you Miss Toynbee no longer. From now on we'll call you Ann, if you don't mind.'

She said she'd be delighted.

'Good. Well, then, as you well know, Paul has reduced your absorbing record to what we believe is now a publishable length. As I gather, you approve of Paul's handiwork and propose only to go through it to clarify odd points here and there. That means we can just discuss the whole thing off the cuff and, I need hardly add, off the record.'

Mason was at his best in such facilitating, felicitating circumstances.

The atmosphere in the room was immediately a good deal more relaxed.

He went on: 'Now I've got that over, I'm sure the best thing is for anyone who has any questions to ask you to fire ahead. Would you object?'

'Not at all,' Ann said. 'I'll do my best to answer to my satisfaction.'

We all laughed. A fleeting moment of silence was broken by Vaughan in his best television interviewing manner, Christian name and all: 'I hope I'm not touching on too tender a spot with this question, Ann, but one of the things which most fascinated me about your record, was trying to discover what exactly were *your* feelings for Stirling? Perhaps you haven't worked them out yourself, but you seemed so unusually detached that I couldn't help but wonder. If it's not too boorish of me. . . .'

He tailed off expertly. She said, 'Was I in love with him, you mean?'

'Basically, yes.'

'To use a very flexible and expressive English phrase, I was very fond of him. I was very very sad when he died as I hope my friends will be sad when I die. But life goes on. His death wasn't any kind of emotional death for me, if you see what I mean.'

'I do, but that suggests that you might possibly be a rather cold-blooded young woman, Yet I don't get that impression.'

'Hear! hear!' said Logan and although I daresay we all priggishly deprecated the interjection, I'm equally sure we all secretly agreed with his hearty words.

Ann smiled, and went on: 'I don't see how anyone with a grain of detachment could have become too emotionally involved with Greg,' she said quietly. 'He was so madly and emotionally involved with himself. When a man gets to those levels of public ambition he's beyond the reach of normal people. Anyone getting emotionally involved with such a person–I almost said institution–would be an outsize masochist. There were such women in his life, of course. There always are. In Greg's case there were many. But I wasn't one of them.'

'Were you hooked, hypnotized or whatever the word, by his larger-than-life-size persona–as I imagine it must have been?' Logan asked.

'I think these so-called larger-than-life-size personalities are, to a very great extent, a matter of media build-ups. I think men who run great commercial corporations, great financial houses, editors of great newspapers–no, I'm dead serious,' she said as we all, including Mason, smiled, 'could, if politically motivated, just as easily run large government departments, even the government itself. As I found out for myself, great public figures aren't necessarily larger-than-life when they start out or even as they go on. But gradually they get that way. Some of them are undoubtedly exceptional men, but no more than that. If they're honest with themselves they recognize that and don't take the ballyhoo too seriously, but it's a terribly difficult drug to resist–what I call headline-mania. By now I'm fairly sceptical, generally speaking, about so-called great men.'

'But surely you'd agree that Stirling deserved the label of great?' Markham asked.

'Not at all. I'd readily agree that he was an exceptional man but even then only on the *quid pro quo* that you'd agree that he had some very exceptional advantages as a springboard into politics.'

'I'd agree on that, but I don't see why his great wealth should be held against him when he also showed by his words and deeds that he was a remarkably able man.'

'I don't hold his wealth against him. It had always been with him like the mole on the back of his neck. Nevertheless, great wealth now gives any American who's politically minded a head start, the same way that wealth plus an Etonian education still gives a politically minded Englishman a head start in this country. I don't think one should discount the enormous advantages of these enormous actualities.'

'Would he have gone places without his wealth?' Spicer asked.

'I don't know. The only thing I do know is that as things supposedly become more democratic, so it becomes more and more difficult for a poor man to get into the White House?'

'Was there any quality in Stirling which you would have accounted great?' Vaughan asked.

'Great ambition,' Ann said swiftly.

We all laughed.

'Nothing else?' Vaughan persisted.

'Great energy.'

'Self-confidence?'

'I don't think men who need such prominent positions of supposed power in order to prove themselves are necessarily the most self-confident of men,' Ann said quietly. 'Rather the reverse. I think the most truly self-confident men I've known are masters of special techniques: my father as a surgeon; one or two doctors, I've known; one or two architects and engineers; a few musicians. They are confident of themselves within the limits of highly demanding techniques. When crises blow up they know they are on their own. That kind of self-knowledge is apt to give such men a great deal of confidence in other divisions of life. Outside their particular genius or technique they're apt to be quiet men, not especially given to displays of self-confidence. A politician is always dependent on other people, their expertise, their opinions, their belief in him. He is forced to put on a show of self-confidence even though he's always in search of reassurance himself. That doesn't seem, to me, a formula for basic inner self-confidence.'

'Would you say you were self-confident yourself?' Vaughan asked, smiling.

'I'm quite self-confident in front of a typewriter tackling my special subject, which is mass-housing. I'm not all that self-confident when dealing with my daily cleaning lady in New York. And the idea of dealing self-confidently with the lives, hopes, ambitions of millions of people would be, to me, utterly preposterous and soul-destroying or perhaps self-destroying. A nightmare.'

'Yet surely we need these political figures?' Mason said. 'We don't seem able to do without them.'

'We've never tried,' Ann said. 'As Lewis Mumford wrote in his book, *The City in History*, our earliest leaders started out as hunters and, to my mind, they're still a predatory cut-throat lot.'

Again we all laughed.

'Will you mind–if these journals of yours are published–your name being dragged through the mud, Miss Toynbee?' Spicer asked suddenly.

'Whose mud, Mr Spicer. Your mud?'

The question-answer was so coolly and swiftly uttered that I heard one subdued gasp–from Logan, I suspect. Spicer wholly disconcerted, thought for a long moment before replying. 'The world's mud,' he amended rather feebly, I thought.

'With which you seem to identify yourself, it seems to me. Frankly, I don't see it that way. If a woman sleeps with a man as part of an intimate friendship I think that's fairly unmuddy. If other people want to churn up the mud, that's strictly their affair. It's a free world, part muddy, part unmuddy. No, I don't think I'd mind unduly if you insist that mud is the only word–your word.'

'What about your parents–if they're still alive?' Spicer went on, rather sheepishly.

'They're both alive and flourishing. They'll be all right. My father says one has one's children until they're seventeen or eighteen. After that they're close friends, distant friends, acquaintances or enemies. Just like the rest of the people you happen to know. I think my parents are close friends. We seem to act on that assumption.'

'And they know about these journals?'

'Of course. I wrote them both long letters about them. Anyway, they both know I've been a psychotic diarist since I was a child. It's one of the family jokes.'

'A private letter's a far different matter from reading the same kind of thing in a national newspaper, wouldn't you say?'

'Undoubtedly, but as I shall never know, as friends, more than half a dozen of your readers, it doesn't really bother me. I think it's a record that will interest a lot of women. I don't ask much more than that.'

'And you still think your parents wouldn't mind? Spicer persisted. He was game, even if somewhat insensitive, I thought.

'You seem unduly concerned about my parents, Mr Spicer.' Spicer shrugged rather helplessly, out of his depth. 'They always thought I was a bit of a blue-stocking,' Ann went on. 'Even a nut case, building a lot of flat-roofed houses down in Caracas. They're rather impressed, even reassured, by my extra-mural activities, as you might call them. I saw my parents last evening, Mr Spicer. I brought them up-to-date–quite comprehensively. They didn't seem to have the vapours.'

Spicer, routed, retired. The rest of us laughed, fairly mercilessly it seemed to me.

'What about the likely fame or notoriety?' Vaughan asked. 'Will you mind that?'

'We all like to think we're going to escape from the anonymity of the womb one day, don't we, Mr Vaughan? Put it down to a normal healthy desire to be noticed, pointed out in a crowd. I shan't mind.'

'So you won't mind being photographed before you go back?' Logan asked.

'No, I think I'd like that.'

'What will you do after publication of your journals in book form–sometime next spring, I imagine?' Vaughan asked. 'Life will never be the same again for you?'

'Who can say? Life's obviously going to be a lot different. I'm rather looking forward to that. I like change, but, basically, I suppose, I shall go on being the kind of escapist-architect I've been for years, dealing with words and theories about building rather than bricks and mortar. I don't, of course, see myself getting a lot of dining-out invitations from ambitious politicians.'

'Frankly, no,' Vaughan said, chuckling.

We all laughed. Loudly.

'I want to return to what seems to me a fundamental point, Miss Toynbee,' Spicer said, fighting back, although he still plainly couldn't bring himself to Christian-name terms.

'How can someone like yourself–a delightful English girl, obviously well educated and cultivated–allow the secrets of her bedroom to be blazoned abroad?' His question was so ingenuously genuine and heartfelt that nobody blushed for him. Nobody even chuckled.

'I'm always amused by this secrets-of-the-bedroom appeal, Mr Spicer. To my mind, this appalling secrecy is the cause of half the sexual ailments of the world. There are no secrets of the kitchen or the living-room. Precious few, these days, of the bathroom. It's sex –in and out of bedrooms–that's so secret. A man or a woman can admit to being a vegetarian, a glutton, a somnambulist, a cold-bath fetishist or whatever, but he or she daren't admit to being a homosexual, a transvestite or a poor old solitary masturbator. This seems to me all wrong. Are these things crimes any more than gluttony or cowardice? I think we need less secrecy in the bedroom rather than more. If my book helps on that score, so much the better. My father agrees, and so does my greatest friend, a doctor in Caracas who is mentioned I believe'–here she smiled–'in the book.'

The meeting, which had started at ten-thirty, went on until almost one o'clock. By then I think everyone round the desk would have been willing for the questionnaire–which had become something of a 'teach-in' on a variety of rarely raised subjects–to have continued all day. Fortunately, Mason, Vaughan and Markham had lunch dates and Ann had a date with a one-time classmate from the AA. We broke up unwillingly.

'I hope we shall have another chance for a similar session, Ann,' Logan said.

'If it can be arranged, I'd be delighted.'

Logan beamed.

—10—

'I thought your protégée acquitted herself in rather notable fashion,' Mason said that afternoon, wandering into my office. In turn I congratulated him on the way he'd put everybody at ease in potentially tricky circumstances. He modestly accepted my words, plainly pleased with his part in the morning's proceedings.

'The avuncular touch,' he said.

Did he expect me to contradict? Reassure him that age didn't come into it? I let it go.

'Where do we go from here?' he asked.

'We just wait for Mrs Stirling's O K. If it comes we're ready to go. If it's thumbs down, we're way back past square one.'

'When would you expect to hear?'

'Pretty soon. She's had the script now for almost three weeks. She should have seen her lawyers by now–if she's going to see 'em. But my guess is that this is something that's going to be worked out strictly between herself and her boy friend.'

'But they mayn't see eye to eye.'

'They've been seeing eye to eye for the past ten years, and would have done for a lifetime if Stirling hadn't stepped in. I suggest we give her another week. If we haven't heard then I'll drop her a note.'

—11—

But I didn't have to give her another week. Two days later, the script was returned in a red-sealed package with a covering letter marked *Strictly Personal and Confidential.*

Dear Mr Mortimer: Thank you for sending me your adaptation of the journals of Ann Toynbee which you so kindly came here to discuss with me.

Basically, I find nothing objectionable in this record. Miss Toynbee seems to have made certain small but significant errors concerning my late husband's early life, mainly in dating, which have been incorporated in your own text. I have made marginal correction on these matters.

I have been carefully through this record with a close friend and personal advisor, who also finds little that could be considered objectionable. These few paragraphs have been pencilled through. It would be, I think, generally a good thing if these comments were deleted.

Apart from these amendments and corrections you are free, as far as I am concerned, to publish this version of the journals.

I think the portrait of Greg Stirling which emerges from this record is a reasonably faithful one. The depiction is obviously a personal view and not one that everyone would share, but we are all many-faceted creatures and Miss Toynbee seems to have found herself in a peculiarly advantageous position for preparing such a portrait.

My own view of the controversial issues which will doubtless arise after these records have been published is quite clear. Many of the matters which Miss Toynbee writes about cannot help but distress me, but I think it only right that as truthful a picture as possible of any public figure should be given to the world. Such a picture can only be given if more than one view is available.

I should add that I have had a copy of your script made which, with my suggested amendments, I propose to retain. I feel sure that you would agree that this is only reasonable. I should also like, in due course, to see advance proofs of the material which your Editor would propose to publish.

None of the foregoing, I must emphatically add, gives any kind of approval for publication of Miss Toynbee's journals in book form. That is a matter which will have to be separately discussed.

Yours sincerely, Melanie Claudine Stirling.

That final paragraph seemed to carry implications of a difficult time ahead for Ann. Our own publication it seemed, would do enough for Melanie Stirling, without any help from a more fulsome record. The letter certainly gave us the all-clear for our own project.

Mason was delighted, but Vaughan, curiously enough, was markedly less cheerful at a meeting between the three of us. 'In view of what she says about the book,' he said, 'd'you think we'd be wise to say our serialization was based on extracts from the book' or 'condensed from the forthcoming book,' or what? The book will never get off the ground to judge by that implied threat in her last paragraph.'

'We'll come to that nearer the day,' Mason said. 'The main thing is we've got our version cleared. Miss Toynbee and her advisors–or advisor,' he added pointedly, 'will have to fight their separate battles on that front. All I'm concerned with here and now is that we have ample enough approval to go ahead.'

'It's a shrewd letter,' Vaughan said.

'Sly, too,' Mason said. 'I like her remark about Miss Toynbee's peculiarly advantageous position. Horizontal, presumably. Quite a nice, bitchy touch, didn't you think?'

But Vaughan was in no mood for Mason's masculine jocularity.

–12–

'Are you still as dubious about the editor's enthusiasm now?' I asked Vaughan an hour or so later.

'Despite all evidence and appearances to the contrary, I still don't think he wants it in this paper. It's just not his kind of journalism. He basically sees himself as a latterday C. P. Scott. He should have been working on the *Guardian* half-a-century ago. In the Manchester Office, too, with all the rest of those liberal scribberals as I called 'em on a programme last year.'

'The phrase brought down the house, no doubt?'

'You're a bit of a snake in your own way, too,' he said cheerfully. 'You've got a well-developed technique for leading one on. Then comes one of those dreary pay-off lines you specialize in.'

I denied the accusation. Not very hotly.

–13–

I showed Ann the letter from Mrs Stirling that evening at dinner.

'Looks as though I may have problems,' she said, handing the letter back. 'Why d'you think she's holding back on the book idea? If she wants Greg demolished, surely the book would do a bigger and better job from her point of view?'

'Not necessarily. Once what I'll call the potted Toynbee version is published it will be splashed throughout the States. Every paper will lead on it. As she sees it, she'll get the maximum publicity in one hair-raising week. She'll probably be abroad. Stirling will never rise again except for the very young. For Establishment America he'll be finished. Our serial publication will have done her job for her. She'll be able to marry de Marais as soon as she likes. Even within a month. The whole of the South will approve. If her major objective is achieved by this simple means, why should she let your book go ahead? That might–indeed it certainly would–contain far too much to upset her pride, and it would revive controversy all over again in a year's time when she'd much rather the whole subject had died forever.'

'You seem to have got it all worked out as if you're the personal friend and advisor she writes about. Sure you aren't?'

'That's de Marais. I'd like to see your journals published, or about half of 'em.'

'Why only half?'

'Pepys, War and Peace, Pickwick Papers, Decline and Fall, Ann Toynbee–all the great books could do with a little pruning and streamlining.'

'I see your point. Are you suggesting that your Toynbee version is better than the original?'

'God forbid. Mine is an unforgivable but necessary précis. It should be at least five times longer, but I'm thinking of the book as a personal record rather than the historical archives you've produced.'

She smiled. 'You're wrapping it up very nicely. How much d'you really think I ought to publish?'

'Hand your publisher the lot. If he wants to publish the lot, I'd say fine.'

'If I ever get near a publisher after that letter I'll be lucky. You've certainly outlined quite a new lot of fresh obstacles. Damn, damn, damn. Just when I was feeling at one with Pepys, Rousseau, Evelyn, Creevey and the rest.'

'Bear up.'

'Why don't I skip publication in your paper and hold out for the book?'

'You could do that, but you'd have some real problems on your hands–as I think Melanie S makes clear.'

'So you think I ought to settle for the bird in hand.'

At least it gets it off the ground. No sooner will it appear in our rag than you'll have the world's book publishers on your doorstep.

'How will you announce your version? You won't be able to talk about extracts from a book that may never appear.'

'We'll probably say extracts from a journal kept by a young Englishwoman, Ann Toynbee. If that doesn't get every publisher from here to Tokyo after you, I'll eat my version.'

'But that won't help me much if Mrs S decides to shoot the whole thing down, having achieved her own objective.'

'Publishers can be very inventive and ingenious in not letting their Patagonian partners know what their Portuguese partners are up to.'

'I hope you're right. How depressing. But it doesn't seem to be putting me off my appetite, does it? How I do love English oysters.'

Within five minutes she was as animated as ever, the setback of Melanie Stirling's letter seemingly forgotten.

Vitality and the sheer range of her interests ousted defeatism, I decided, as we walked back towards Chelsea.

I saw a good deal of Ann during her remaining three days in London, neglecting familiar faces and duties. But I knew intuitively that this fleeting time would never be repeated and I was never one to cast away the rarer pleasures of life.

–14–

Roth's timing was impeccable.

Mason got the letter the following Tuesday, the day after Ann returned to New York, half-way through September.

Mason called me in, and handed me the letter, saying: 'I think you'd better see this before anyone else. It involves you almost as much as it does myself. I'll read it to the others at the meeting in half-an-hour.' I read:

Dear David: I should like to thank you for the opportunity you gave me to see around Europe. However speedy these trips are, they do help to give one's outlook a somewhat wider international perspective. Vast as this country is, it does sometimes seem over-poweringly claustrophobic and introverted to a European. After which, all that follows may seem to you somewhat churlish, to say the least.

Briefly, after long and deep reflection, I have decided that as it is clear that you now propose to publish Paul Mortimer's edited version of the Toynbee journals I am resigning forthwith from the paper. I shall file all relevant material this week-end and next, but I shall do this ex gratia and expect no thanks or payment. It is the least I can do in the circumstances, but I need to feel free immediately to do what my conscience tells me I have to do.

I am sorry to leave you in a bit of a fix but I do not see why my resignation need present too great or hurtful a problem. Daniels could take over here. He is knowledgeable and reliable. Or I could arrange for one of the BBC people here to fill in until you find my successor. But my recommendation would be to put Daniels here and to send out a replacement for the New York office.

Thank you for retaining me here after you took over the paper. I have enjoyed working with you. Bernie.

'He played us like a shoal of day-old carp,' I said.
'Seems like it.'
'So now he'll do his damndest to sink the Toynbee job.'
'I'd say so.'
'Damn him.'
'It's sad for Miss Toynbee, too,' Mason said. He sounded as if he meant his words.

– 15 –

Mason read the letter out at the meeting.

After a long pause, whilst everyone waited for somebody else's first comment, Spicer said: 'Aren't his activities likely to put paid to the Toynbee project? Roth's still got quite a lot of friends in quite high places, even though his best friend's gone. He's got a dozen fruitful contacts in the State Department alone.'

'Would the Republicans object to seeing a little dirty Democratic linen washed out in public?' Vaughan asked.

'When it came to the real crunch, I rather think they'd see it as dirty American linen,' Markham said. 'They've had enough self-flagellation over this assassination, piled on top of the others. They're very apt to close ranks if they think the Stars and Stripes is being trampled on around the globe.'

Mason agreed.

'What are you proposing to write and tell Roth?' Markham demanded. 'Obviously I'd like to know as Foreign Editor and so forth.'

'What can I say? I have to accept. It's a *fait accompli*, isn't it? You don't expect me to cave in and dump the Toynbee, story, do you?'

'That would be too much to hope for, I suppose,' Markham said unhopefully, 'but there is the question of replacement, and that's not so easy with a man of Roth's calibre.'

'I don't see why that's so difficult,' Mason countered. 'Roth recommends Daniels. So do Dick and Paul. We all seem agreed he's good and worth a trial.'

'Apart from Daniels there are several men extremely well-informed about American affairs who might do as well,' Vaughan said. 'The BBC have trained a dozen over the past five years. In any case, I've never seen Roth as the great interpreter of the American scene that others do around here.'

This was the most outspoken of Vaughan's personal opinions so far. I rather agreed with him.

Markham certainly didn't. 'Come, come, Tom, that's going a bit far. I regard Roth's as the most authoritative and detached view of the Washington scene that we get in this country.'

'That's your view,' Vaughan said evenly, 'and I accept it as a personal outlook. As mine was. Let's leave it at that.'

But would Mason leave it at that? I wondered. He said: 'Frankly, Tom, I think yours is rather an extreme view. Roth may not be the twentieth-century Bryce, but he's certainly the best foreign correspondent this paper has.'

I was amused to note that Logan, somewhat ironically, remained silent. He had never liked Roth, his works or his words, but he wasn't prepared to be seen as backing Vaughan in yet another direction.

If Vaughan does get the editorship, it'll be curtains for Roth and Logan, I thought, and wondered how many others would go.

'You and I had better talk it over later, Gerry,' Mason said, turning to Markham, and plainly letting Vaughan know who was editor. In common with most of Mason's apparent decisions, this was essentially another decision to postpone a decision. Some men have a talent for making instant action look like intuitive wisdom. Mason's talent was its polarity, making procrastination look like reflective wisdom.

The meeting drooled on in a lack-lustre mood.

–16–

The belief that officialdom is one hundred per cent bumbledom, works ponderously and slowly via its own jealously guarded official channels and finally grinds to a well docketed halt, is one of the great modern myths. In thousands upon thousands of cases this may well be so: in London, Paris, Rome, Madrid and any other capital. You name it, they'll sit on it. Yet when the higher reaches of officialdom are menaced, or seem to be, by outside assault, their collective speed in action can be positively atomic.

The day after Mason had received Roth's letter of resignation–on the Wednesday, that is–he wandered into my room. He looked rather lost and seemingly needed to talk to somebody. I was usually cast as confidant on such occasions.

He asked what was coming along for *Faces & Places*. I told him. He listened, fairly perfunctorily, I thought, and then said, too casually, 'Gerry Markham's been asked to go down to see the head of the Foreign Office, North American section. He's down there now. No particular reason given. No press conference. Just-a-general-chit-chat-haven't-seen-you-for-some-time kind of thing.'

'What did Markham say?'

'OK. He went off like a boy scout to a jamboree. He loves these jaunts. Makes him feel wanted and in touch.'

'You think it's the Toynbee job.'

'I'd say so; wouldn't you?'

'Could be. Obviously that would be one of Roth's first moves. He's got his contacts.'

'Well, Gerry's their man. He'll see eye to eye with 'em all the way if it is the Toynbee job.'

'That might leave us fighting a rearguard action,' I said.

'I don't see why. We've got the material and we've got permission to publish from the major party concerned. What else do we need?'

'Nothing, as far as I can see. But I can also guess how effectively they'll get to work on Gerry. Is your paper publishing this girl's story merely to cock a snook at the Establishment of another nation and so on? Has your paper got the skids under it that you have to publish this sort of thing?'

Despite Mason's bold and positive assertions, I still thought Vaughan's hunch was probably correct. Despite all contrary evidence I somehow believed that Mason was still hoping that some kind of *force majeure* might intercede to stop publication and save his face at the same time. And here, indeed, was the beginnings of a force unless I was very much mistaken.

'Well, let's hope it's something else they want to see Gerry for, but I doubt it,' Mason said heavily and wandered out again.

I watched him go. There, but for grace of some pagan gods, goes the last of Toynbee, I thought.

–17–

That was, indeed, precisely the purpose of the FO call to Markham, as he explained that afternoon on his return.

Mason called me on the inter-com.

Markham and Vaughan were also there.

'As I guessed, Paul,' the editor said as I entered the room, 'Bernie's moved fairly smartly and the FO have put it to Gerry that it wouldn't do Anglo-American relations any good at this moment–or any other foreseeable moment as far as they're concerned – to publish the Toynbee journals. Bernie has clearly indicated to somebody pretty high-placed that we have 'em and that they're dynamite.'

'But could the F O put a stop-order on publication?'

'They admit, quite candidly, that they can't and that even to try they'd have to go very high indeed,' Markham said, equally candidly.

'There's nobody that high if you decide to go ahead,' Vaughan said roughly. He then turned to Markham as if he'd taken over the meeting: 'What was your attitude?'

'I admitted we had the story, explained that the editor thought it a remarkable record of an unusual relationship and that as far as I could see, or judge, nothing would stop us going ahead.'

'Is that how you left it?'

'Almost my last words.'

'And the very last.'

'Well, Sir Michael said he doubted whether it would be left quite like that. He implied that the whole thing might escalate. He pulled out all the stops, of course. Flattery, blarney, courtesy, the lot. Had it been a different kind of paper involved they'd have treated it with contempt etcetera etcetera, but as they were dealing with a great British newspaper and so on. All in all, a straight plea for a deal on the old boy net.'

'D'you think he was bluffing?'

'Not for a moment. He made it quite clear that this was a preliminary meeting on which they'd placed high hopes, but that it could and would go higher if he drew a blank with me.'

'The editor next, in fact?'

'Editor versus Foreign Secretary, no less,' Markham said with a thin smile.

'And what effect does that have on the editor?' Vaughan asked, turning to Mason, as if to an elder statesman who'd just dropped in on his way to the almshouse.

'An interesting situation, I'd say,' Mason said, but his looks belied him. I had an impression that if only Vaughan and myself could have been spirited from the room by some cooperative genie, Mason would have fallen upon Markham in gratitude for seeking to extricate him from the untoward situation into which he had been manœvured by two or three underlings – against his better judgment, of course.

'Well, as it's essentially old-boy-net stuff and any journalist joins such Establishment networks at his peril, I vote we press on regardless,' Vaughan said.

'Come off it,' Tom,' Markham said quickly, 'You know as well as I do that journalists live by such networks.'

'Live by them, live with them, live off them,' Vaughan agreed genially, 'but there's no need to join 'em.'

'What about your own membership of Boodle's and White's?'

'Means to ends. No more. And they're peripheral stuff. As I see it, journalists are society's undercover men. We have to mix with some very dodgy numeros in much the same way CID types have to mix with quite a number of unsavoury underworld thugs, but once they join the villains they're finished. And once we're in the pockets of the PM's press staff, FO spokesmen, military advisors, PROs and the rest of the professional purveyors of leaked and loaded so-called news we're cooked, too.' He turned to Mason. 'Sorry to digress into a lecture, David. Put it down to the curse of the television panel game.'

'I was very impressed' Mason said warily. 'As a definition of *detached* journalism I thought it excellent. But there's also such a thing as *involved* journalism and I think the Toynbee story comes under that heading. Ann Toynbee was highly involved. Then we come to our very different kind of involvement. We can make or break the Stirling image which means a lot to millions of men and women.'

'We've been through all that before. If the image was phoney, why not bust it?'

'But the image, as it exists, may work for the ultimate betterment of American politics and possibly all Western politics,' Markham said, sounding pretty episcopal.

'A Goebbels in reverse, so to speak?' Vaughan scoffed.

'Not at all,' Mason said defiantly.

'On that basis, half the stories of graft and general chicanery that get published in quite reputable local papers wouldn't see the light of day,' Vaughan said, giving no quarter, and, as far as I could judge, asking for none.

In full cry he went on: 'Is the story of a dentist who screws girls under anaesthetic to be spiked because he's terrific with teenage teeth and very successful slow-to-medium offbreak bowler in the local side?'

By now he was thoroughly and rhetorically enjoying himself: 'Is the story of a local housing officer who slips a young widow a length for finding her a top-floor council flat to be spiked because he's a choirmaster, youth club leader and won last year's prize for the hollyhock of the year at the local flower show? Come off it.'

'Up the local press,' I said and laughed.

Mason and Markham didn't even smile. All Markham could say was: 'There are shades and subtleties in every story. Not every tale is solid black and white.'

'Fortunately, most of the grey ones finally get published. Even this augustan sheet goes out on a limb occasionally on a scandal story,' Vaughan said.

'We do because I've always been an involved journalist,' Mason suddenly said as if he thought the chief editorial voice were needed to stabilize the discussion. 'It's one of the reasons I'm here.'

'But now, in this story, you seem prepared to make it a suppressive –or, as I suppose you'd call it, selective kind of involvement,' Vaughan said. 'Is suppression of these aspects of Stirling's general promiscuity and amorality justified because he happens to have a great posthumous potential for mass-hope? Is that your idea of involvement? If so, leave me out of it.'

Mason flushed. 'All journalism is ultimately selective,' he said fiercely as if he'd decided that the moment had come to snuff out Vaughan's would-be crusading spark. 'What else is Paul's editing of the journals but selection?'

'Hair-splitting! You know as well as I do that Paul's précis omits none of the essential story.'

I found the sight and sound of Vaughan becoming quite open in his clashes, first with Logan and Markham and now with Mason, wholly absorbing. There were moments when Mason, like an old man of the sea with a lively tricky marling on the end of his line, seemed to be reeling and unreeling his line with uncommon skill. One moment he seemed to be putting his foot down: the next moment relaxing as if to see how far Vaughan would go. Was he infinitely more subtle than we'd ever given him credit for?

Now, once again, he seemed to step in to stop Vaughan from going too far *vis-à-vis* either Markham or himself. He said gently, looking in my direction: 'Paul's is what I call truly creative selectivity.'

Vaughan gave up. For the moment, at least. The discussion continued on more urbane lines.

Once again, Mason decided that we would continue to prepare the Toynbee journals for publication as if no Foreign Office plea and/or pressure had even been mentioned. 'After all,' he said, 'Paul has still some finishing touches to put to his selective editing, if you'll forgive the expression, Paul. And we haven't got the exact date for the first publicity drive or even the first instalment settled yet. Roth will have used his big guns straightaway. If we stay quiet, they may well think their mailed-fist-velvet-glove line has put us out of action. We'll see how things stand a week from now.'

All of which reasoning had the touch I'd come to know only too well by now. Inwardly I saluted what I had come to recognize as his personal reaction to problems and crises. Baldwin, thou shouldst be living at this hour, I thought.

–18–

On Tuesday morning of the following week, during the early stages of what I came to term the phoney war between Mason and the Foreign Office, I got an unexpected letter from Ann, addressed to Swan Court.

After some warming references to the way I'd looked after her in London, and on visits to Oxford and the Cotswolds, during her time in England, she got to the main purpose of her letter. . . .

. . . You'll remember that Irish-Spanish doctor in Caracas I told you about–Bartolomé O'Connor, the one devoted to the poor and so forth, the one with whom I had the only long affair I've ever had. Well, he was in New York last week for lectures and meetings and so on. We took up where we left off. Before he'd been here three days he'd suggested that we ought to marry. I laughed and said Why? I was always available when he got to New York. He said he wanted me for keeps. To my continuing astonishment I found the idea rather tempting. In fact I've been rather knocked over by the idea. He's always seemed to me the most coolly self-sufficient of men, the only natural solitary I've ever encountered in sophisticated society. That kind of masculine self-sufficiency is always challenging to a woman–my kind, anyway. Apart from that I admire the work he does.

I pointed all this out to him. To which he made the surprising reply that I was the congenital complement to a solitary introvert–a gregarious extrovert.

But at least we had certain intellectual interests in common, I said.

Not at all, he said. 'Intellectual' was a label used by the intellectually insecure to cover fears and doubts concerning their IQs or emotional inadequacy and to make sure their acquaintances were left in no doubt about how they regarded themselves. Nobody reasonably aware of his or her intelligence or emotional worth would bother with such a preposterously complacent label.

Duly abashed, I stayed silent, but he wasn't done. In any case, he went on, neither architecture nor medicine was a pursuit of the intellect, but merely a technical means of indulging certain egotistical fantasies. The architect thinks he's building for posterity and improving on the past. The doctor thinks he's correcting the mistakes of God and/or nature. Both are invariably wrong. And so on and so on.

We went at it for hours. Well, I said at last, we did have a mutual interest in sex. I was really on the defensive by then. But at last I'd said something with which he agreed and we thereupon settled for our mutuality so to speak.

He's now back in Caracas. I think I love him, Paul.

Although he decries my intellect and so on, he always responds, listens, and the rest. I admire him intensely for the work he does. He always says that no other hospital wanted him, but I know that is a cover-up for an unparalleled crusader-type. I also like Caracas, which is important. I'd be dead scared, of course, but that's normal, healthy and reasonable in the circumstances, don't you think?

All of which brings me, at last, to the question of the journal.

I've told Bartolomé about it, of course. The contents. Where it is. What the proposition is. All the rest of it. He said if we married I could do whatever I wished. If I wanted to see myself famous or infamous that was my affair (no pun!). He quite saw my viewpoint. It was the kind of identity-reassurance an extrovert might well need from time to time, he said. He'd expect a Caracas journal in due course if we were to marry.

In his experience, he said, all autobiographers were generally rather dubious exhibitionists masquerading as honest journeymen. All this was said with a wide grin, I hasten to add. In a way he is infuriating, as you can see, but marvellous for me.

In short, as far as he was concerned, I could go ahead. Above everything else in the world, he wanted to marry me and if the journal and its publication were as important to me as it seemed, then why not publish? It was part of me. His own circle of acquaintances was so limited and so easy-going that the journal would be merely a matter for a few days' interested and amused discussion, ruthless analysis and easy-going ribaldry.

No worries there.

But wouldn't the local Spanish community be outraged, point fingers at him and say he's married a whore and all that? I said.

He said that like a true autobiographer I was already over-dramatizing a situation unlikely to arise. For one thing, the so-called

Spanish community he moved amongst was diseased, illiterate and regarded whoring as a necessary job for some less fortunate, some occasionally more fortunate women. For another, his immediate community, his friends are–as I ought to know, having lived with them for six months–are as thorough-going an international lot as one could find–Swedes, Irish, Germans and Scotsmen and very few English and those scarcely worshippers of the normal English social values and so-called verities. Finally, thanks to centuries of papal brain-washing, he said, every Spaniard and every Irishman (and he's both, he emphasized) longs to marry a whore, so that he can do a real good job of reforming and then lie back and enjoy the fruits of her erstwhile expertise. So you'd better take your self-dramatizing exercises somewhere else if you've got a really big self-dramatizing part lined up for yourself, he added for good measure. Caracas will swallow 'em up, unnoticed.

So you see, Paul, how good he is for me.

So there's the dilemma. And in a truly feminine way I'm going to hand the journal problem over to you.

I think I shall marry Bartolomé. Probably pretty soon, too, now I've thrown this at you in this bitchy fashion. Let me know what your decision is. Or preferably what your decision was after it's been made and is utterly irrevocable. It's the only way. Once it's done one way or the other, I shan't have any arrière pensée *worth a damn. I promise.*

But it's a once-and-for-all decision I need. That's for sure. If I don't publish now I shan't want to publish later. That's also for sure. So, over to you, dearest Paul. I'm sorry to land you with it, but it's my only way. Love Ann.

–19–

'Damn you, Ann. Damn you for a woman,' I said aloud, putting down the letter.

I couldn't help but have a momentary pang linked with the dashing of some far-off dreams of my own. No man likes losing a new-found rare kind of intimate friend, so to speak. No man likes reading so lengthy an extolling of another man's virtues.

After a drawn-out breakfast of toast and honey and a lot more coffee, I sat for an hour or more brooding over this new turn in the tangled story.

After that I shaved and dressed. By that time it was well after eleven o'clock. I rang Pat Gow and said I wouldn't be in until after lunch: I was on to a story, which was, indeed, the truth. Then I went out into the King's Road and walked along to Sloane Square to get a midday *Standard*, which I took into Kenco to read over a coffee and a cigarette. But I couldn't read. I was too engaged elsewhere: in some limbo or never-never land poised somewhere between New York and London.

I thought in circles: of Ann, her dilemma, of her Bartolomé, of our brief friendship and finally of her story, now all mine to play around with like an international make-or-break publisher.

I put a few questions to myself.

Did I want the story published?

I thought I did: it was a riveting story and I'd done a great deal of work on it.

Did Ann want the story published?

I thought so, but difficult to make out.

Did she want a decision made for her so that she could accept it or fight it?

Possibly. She was a wayward numero.

Did Mason want the journals published?

No.

If the story weren't published, should Ann be paid?

Not necessarily–if it were her decision to call it off.

What if it were Mason's?

Quite a different matter.

Why?

Circumstances alter cases, I told myself, and thus conveniently ended the questionnaire. By then it was half-past eleven and I made my way back to Swan Court. There I put a call through to Ann's number in New York. Within a quarter-of-an-hour the call came through and I said 'Hello, Ann' to her very great surprise, and went on to apologize for so early a start: '. . . but I had your letter and thought I'd better call you.'

'You're very thoughtful–and understanding.'

'So understanding that I'm mildly surprised to find you still in New York. I thought you might be in Caracas by now.'

'It was a possibility.'

'What's the situation at this moment?'

'I think I shall go, Paul.'

'I think you will, too.'

'But not just yet.'

'How long?'

'A month or so.'

'I think not.'

'We'll see. What about the journal?'

'I'm brooding on that.'

'I still think I'd like to go ahead. It's too much part of me. I'd like to see it published.'

'Then we'll go ahead.'

'And then sometimes I wonder: would it be fair to Bartolomé if I married him.'

'Not in my old-fashioned terms, it wouldn't.'

'That's what I think. I'm appalled to find I've got old-fashioned notions too, Paul.'

'They can be sensibly corrective, provide a kind of balance to new notions and all that. Meantime, promise me one strange thing.'

'If it's within my scope or whatever.'

'If you do marry your Bartolomé, keep quiet about it. Don't ask your father to put it in *The Times*.'

'It's the kind of thing he would do. All right, I won't. It's quite unnecessary, anyway.'

'Have you told your parents you might?'

'I rang them last night.'

'Well, if you do, leave the news of the *fait accompli* for a week or so before telling 'em.'

'Why?'

'It's a thought I want to brood and to work on.'

'You'll tell me later?'

'Of course.'

'Oh, Paul, I wish you were here,' she said suddenly.

'Just for someone to talk to?'

'Amongst other things. I need a little friendly advice.'

'Advice is what we seek to confirm what we intend to do.'

'Not always, Paul. Anyway, it was sweet and kind of you to ring. The main thing is you want me to keep you up-to-date if I go off to Caracas.'

'In a ghastly kind of way, I'll need to know the worst or best as soon as possible.'

'I will. I will. I suppose you'll have to go now. Are you calling from that dear little Chelsea flat?'

'A charitable way of describing it.'

'I don't want you to hang up.'

'Well, carry on.'

She didn't sound the same girl who'd kept five or six probing journalists quite easily at bay a couple of weeks before.

We talked for a few moments longer, exchanged further tendernesses and further goodbyes and then, finally, I was back once again in London, in the same flat.

But it was a somewhat bleak return. I damned Dr O'Connor, Mason, Vaughan, and partly Ann herself.

—20—

That was Tuesday. Early on Saturday morning, an overnight cable from Caracas was telephoned through to Swan Court.

YOU WERE RIGHT DARLING MORTIMER GREETINGS AND LOVE FROM MRS SPECIAL LICENCE O'CONNOR ADDRESS TEN CALLE CRISTOBAL COLON CARACAS COLOMBIA STOP MILLIONS THANKS FOR CALLING STOP JOURNALS SITUATION STILL AS THEN STOP AFRAID BALL CONTINUES BOUNCING MORTIMER COURT STOP ANN.

Well, she was certainly a girl for action, I thought, as I telephoned a cable of congratulations and, went back to finish my breakfast with an acute sense of apprehension as I faced the fact that Ann was dead accurate. The play was certainly in my court and the ball bouncing very awkwardly indeed.

Wasn't this the moment to call the whole thing off? But somehow I was too obstinately involved. The thing couldn't be as simple as all that. After due reflection I decided to imitate Mason's own delaying tactics and let things move along a little under their own ponderous momentum for a day or so. Not so deep down I believed I still wanted to see those journals in print. Or did I want to see what would happen?

—21—

'The grapevine says Mason's been invited to one of these Number Ten luncheons,' Vaughan said later that week.

'He's been before. Prime Ministers and Fleet Street editors believe they need these exchanges. Why disillusion them? When?'

'Next week. Tuesday, I think. I suppose the Toynbee tale's got something to do with the sudden invitation.'

'Probably. The Establishment closing its ranks, and all that. More of Roth's work working itself out.'

'You're undoubtedly dead right,' Vaughan agreed gloomily.

I offered him crumbs of comfort I could sweep his way. 'They may find Mason more resistant than you think. Isn't the Toynbee tale his one big chance to show how trendy he's become?'

'The fact that he's been offered the story is enough to build up the trendy touch for him. He hopes something really big will ditch it for him. Want to bet on it?'

I shook my head and said. 'No go. Six weeks from now, with the first instalment of the Toynbee tale hitting the headlines, you'll look like an out-of-work soothsayer.'

Vaughan repeated his challenge. 'Want to bet on it?'

'I don't think so.'

'A very sensible decision. Six weeks from now the Toynbee tale will be a dead dead duck—at least as far as we're concerned. You'll have to pass it on elsewhere.'

—22—

Mason arrived back very late indeed from his luncheon at No 10.

'A long lunch,' he said later, coming into my office, very pleased with himself. Pat Gow was out. I was typing. He took the armchair. 'A hell of a lot of hard-hitting. And afterwards I was asked to stay on. Any chance of your being able to lunch tomorrow or Thursday, Paul? Preferably tomorrow.'

'Of course.'

He looked suitably grateful and, if possible, even more serious than normal. He then switched to *Faces & Places*. 'I met a curious fellow today who might interest you, Paul. I must say these lunches do give one a chance to see how the other half lives—and works. This chap is a trimaran designer and builder. Quite fantastic-sized craft. He contends they're the craft of the future. Not just for sailing, but powered. Not just racing craft but freighters and tankers. Hundred thousand tons and over. Dotty if you like, but he's got one or two of the Greek people really interested, I gather. Odd name of Ricardo Greensleeve.'

'Made up?'

'Assured me it wasn't. Spanish mother, English father. An old Somerset name, he says. Might be worth following up. I made a note of his address down at Gosport. Here it is.'

We chatted on for ten minutes or so. I had the feeling that he would willingly have stayed in the armchair to talk for another hour or more. I knew the signs.

–23–

The signs were there again at Rules the next day. After we'd ordered he said, 'As we may get involved in a fairly long discussion, I'll come to the point straightaway. I need hardly tell you the PM's had news of the Toynbee story and doesn't like it. Nobody likes it. Our special relationship with the US and all that. The heat's really on for us not to publish.'

'Stirling didn't hold any official position.'

'I pointed that out, of course, I also made it quite clear that this was the most compelling reading I'd come across in twenty years of editing newspapers.'

'I suppose Roth tipped 'em off.'

'Seems like it. Shows how one's estimates of people can go awry.'

'He did give his copy back to you, by the way?' I asked.

Mason nodded and then added, rather sheepishly, 'Unfortunately, he did keep it overnight. Said he had to. Nobody could read thirty thousand words in a day in a Fleet Street office.'

'He probably had a copy made at one of these xerox places. There's one in Chancery Lane. Only one hundred and fifty pages. A couple of hour's work for an efficient operator.'

'I'm not so sure. I don't think Bernie would have risked having a copy with him,' Mason said defensively. 'He'd have been too scared. If he'd shown it to one of his contacts in the State Department and word had got round he'd have been in a tricky position. Journalists out there can be very enterprising in an offbeat way. A journal like that could disappear and turn up in a newspaper. They could have quoted extracts from your extracts, named no sources and so on.'

Mason sipped and approved the Piesporter as the smoked salmon was brought to the table.

'So what kind of promise have you given?' I asked.

'I've promised nothing.'

'Not even to consider the request?'

'I said I'd consider and put it to my board.'

'Surely it's essentially an editorial decision. OK'd by Mrs Stirling. OK'd by Ann Toynbee. Legalled by our own lawyer. What other approval do you need?'

'There may be reasons overriding all those OKs Paul. I need time to think. I need you to help me to think. I want to know what to do for the best.'

For whose best? I wondered, watching him. I said 'Ultimately, it depends only on you, on how keen you are to publish.'

'I admit I'm not as mad keen as Vaughan and yourself–and Logan, of course,' he added as an after-thought. 'But I'm a good deal keener than Spicer or Markham.'

'I should hope so. They'd burn it.'

'It's part of an editor's job to listen before acting.'

'Possibly.'

'It's also true to say I was keener a week ago than I am now with all these pressures building up.'

'But we all recognized from the beginning that pressures would build up.'

'Not quite of this order and consequence. I sometimes think I was over-convinced by the enthusiasm of yourself and Tom.'

'Have you put all this to Tom yet?'

'Not yet. I thought I owed it to you to tell you first. You've put a vast amount of work into the job,' he mumbled, putting down knife and fork.

'I enjoyed it. You sound as though you'd already made your decision.'

He shook his head. 'Not yet.' And then he added the crucial proviso, 'I might if I knew that no other paper would get hold of it and make a killing.'

'Isn't that rather a dog-in-the-manger touch?'

'Maybe, but it's what I don't want to happen. I've too much at stake, personally.'

Mason the laughing-stock of Fleet Street, I thought. That's the rub.

We waited for our steaks, each staring stonily at the prints on the opposite wall.

'I need time,' he said again, as if trying, without overmuch belief, to make me see his side of things.

'When are you going to tell the others?' I asked.

'Probably tomorrow or Friday. Or I may brood over things during the weekend. I said I'd let the PM know next week.'

'Who did Bernie go to first, d'you think?'

'You're jumping your guns a bit too soon, Paul. We don't know that it was Bernie. Vaughan, in his enthusiasm, may inadvertently have let one or two of his television people know. Logan might have let word slip. Or Gerry. He's never been keen on it. Or Dick. All that youthful naval and rectory brain-washing may have persuaded him that any means are justified if the end is morally right.'

'What about me? You haven't incriminated me yet.'

'Oh, come on, Paul.'

As if scornful of his own tactic he said limply, 'But I suppose you're right; it probably was Bernie.'

'He's the only man in the know who was neurotically fanatical about keeping the Stirling image untarnished.'

The waiter put down our steaks, began to serve vegetables.

We discussed various aspects of this new development as we went on with our meal, but the discussion was desultory.

'I think you ought to call a meeting today,' I said. 'A thing like this ought to be thrashed out as soon as possible.'

'Ultimately there's no need for any thrashing out, Paul,' Mason reminded me touchily. 'As editor I can say yea or nay to anything that's submitted for publication. I shall choose my own time and I expect you to keep my confidences to yourself for the time being.'

'Of course, David,' I said, fairly wearily.

When all else gives out pomposity comes in. If only Mason had been as decisive about being an editor as he was about acting like one.

'I'll call a meeting for Friday morning,' he said after a long silence. 'Would that satisfy you?'

'Nothing about this business satisfies me, but at least it's an advance on sometime next week.'

I didn't walk back to the office with him. I said I needed to check a point at the London Library. I left him in Golden Lane.

–24–

'I've called this meeting,' Mason began at the Friday morning meeting, 'because by some means or another–presumably Roth–the Prime Minister's office has learned of the Toynbee story and wants us to postpone it, or, better still, kill it. That, simply enough, is what we're here to discuss.'

He picked up an ivory paper-knife from the desk and began to consider the silver handle. He was pale, nervous, tense.

'What about a rival getting hold of it?' Vaughan asked.

'I think they'd run into the same kind of top-level trouble,' Mason replied. 'It's generally thought–I imagine by the FO–that publication of such memoirs at this time could do sizeable harm to Anglo-American relations.'

'Foreign Office phooey.' Logan said.

'It is certainly not phooey as you term it,' Markham said icily. 'From the FO point of view it could be a real headache. The mere fact that these matters could be published, anyway, would be a matter for regret. They'd harm Republicans as well as Democrats.

Politicians on both sides of the Atlantic are going through a pretty rough time *vis-à-vis* the public, as we all know only too well. I think this kind of thing brings Parliament as well as Congress into disrepute. Material of this kind is ready-made for agitators and embryonic dictators.'

'A cover-up for the politicians all round . . . is that what we're being asked for?' Logan asked.

'Not a cover-up,' Markham said as if dealing with a particularly ungifted child. 'These confessions by this over-sexed girl can't but distort and exacerbate the relationship between politicians and the public. Dangerously, to my mind. The affair was a side-line for Stirling and she's turned it into a life-story. Are we to chisel away at a system of government that works reasonably well because of a remarkable man's peccadilloes and a young woman's passion for the limelight.'

'So we're to do anything to preserve the Stirling mystique?' Vaughan said.

'To do our bit to preserve democracy if that doesn't sound too high-flown for you,' Markham barked.

'I'm afraid it does,' Vaughan said curtly. 'In fact it sounds like a lot of pseudo-democratic balls to me.'

Markham flushed but stayed silent.

Mason came back again: 'I agree with Gerry, Tom. I, for one, am far less concerned with the preservation of Stirling's mystique as you term it, than I am with the preservation of the democratic system as we know it.'

'Even to the suppression of views that run contrary to your own.'

'As you know, my word is selection not suppression. We have to select all the time–news, features, letters.'

'Absolutely,' Markham said.

'According to the editor's view last week, that's exactly what Paul's been doing,' Vaughan said smoothly, 'selecting forty thousand words out of a quarter-of-a-million. And now you don't want a single one of 'em.'

Markham, rattled, said, 'Fine, you've scored a good debating point. Take a bow?'

Vaughan, imperturbable, said: 'Selection on your terms now seems to mean complete suppression. Right?'

'Unhesitatingly–in this case,' Markham said.

'So that Stirling keeps his legend as a paragon of all the virtues, domestic, political and the rest.'

'I don't care a damn about Stirling or his legend,' Markham

snapped. 'But I do care about Anglo-American relations, and, oddly enough, about the renown of this paper. I can't think that our authority would be enhanced, for instance, by that paragraph early on–which Paul has retained, I notice–"Greg told me he'd had scores of one-night stands and three-week liaisons". Then she says: "Couldn't we make ours unique by making it a month?" '

'An entertainingly laconic remark in the circumstances. Well worth going on the record,' Vaughan said.

'Now be fair, Gerry,' Mason interjected. 'Our net sales would take an almighty jump if we published the Toynbee journals, and I see nothing wrong in what you've just quoted. Don't let's discuss everything in terms of prejudice. Personally, I rather enjoyed all her little remarks along those lines. She has an engaging throwaway touch about such matters. Fair's fair!'

'Frankly, I don't see why we're here,' Vaughan said. He turned to Mason: 'Have you decided for or against publishing? It all boils down to that. No old chewed-over regurgitated arguments in this room will change the present line-up: Steve, Paul and myself for: Gerry and Dick–and, I imagine, yourself–against.'

'You take too much for granted,' Mason said, still on his fence. 'I haven't made my decision.'

He seemed determined to parade to the full the great responsibilities of an editor, the decisions that kept him awake, the wish to see all points of view, the need to balance the paper's own position against the national need and all that. We started all over again. But by half-past twelve we all knew, as we had known at ten-thirty, that the Toynbee journals were finito as far as we were concerned.

'Doing anything for lunch?' Vaughan asked as we left.

I said I'd cancel anything to re-discuss that morning's meeting. He smiled, but not in mirth.

–25–

I had no date to cancel and we wander round to the Terrazza in Chancery Lane.

'You show no particular signs of elation in the accuracy of your forecasting,' I said after we'd ordered our pasta. 'Even though the editor still reserves his decision.'

'My character-reading was better than my character-manipulation. I went adrift in what I thought Mason would do, given certain circumstances.'

'And he didn't. Poor Tom's acold. Explain.'

'From the word go, I thought Mason's major objective in his new editorial chair–and with the rest of us anywhere between ten and twenty-five years his junior–would be to show us–and the rest of Fleet Street–that he was as young and nimble as anybody in the game. Awareness, anti-Establishment and the rest of the trendy repertoire. Right?'

'You're the theorizer. Press on.'

'Well, it was on the cards that sooner or later we'd get something comparable with the Toynbee story–although I'd never hoped for anything half so good.'

The wine waiter came. 'What shall we drink?' Vaughan asked. As we invariably went dutch at these lunches we could ask these fairly free-and-easy questions. I chose a Pimms. He wanted a large whisky. He went on: 'When that time came I thought Mason would have to go through with it. Just to show how agile and youthful he was–or is–despite the years, the paunch, the grey hairs and so on.'

'Leave him a skeleton to rattle,' I said.

Vaughan laughed.

'You hadn't reckoned on Ministers stepping in?' I went on.

'Certainly not that, but I did think that, given enough rope, Mason might get so damn swinging he might make a good tight inescapable noose for himself.'

'Hang himself or get kicked upstairs to some editorial advisory job whilst young Tom stepped in.'

'It was the vaguest of plans,' Vaughan said airily.

'It wasn't a bad plan, all the same.'

'I made one or two mistakes,' he admitted, almost handsomely. 'I pushed the Toynbee thing too hard, and, in the process, pushed Mason too hard. He had to react the way he did. The old-fashioned pendulum swing. I see that now.'

'Did you push it so hard *merely* to spring a trap-door for Mason.'

'Not a chance. I still think it's a terrific story. So terrific I thought Mason would have to publish.'

'And then find himself with the biggest hullabaloo Fleet Street's known for years about his ears?'

'That's what I more or less banked on.'

'With Vaughan giving the hullabaloo a little extra TV aid from time to time.'

'Something like that.'

'What went wrong?'

'First, as I say, I pushed Mason too hard. Then I hadn't reckoned on Dick Spicer being quite such a stick-in-the-mud.'

'Come! Come! Royal Navy and his old man a canon. You couldn't get better Establishment material than that if you worked it out by computer.'

Vaughan bowed his head in mock shame. 'Too true, my friend,' he said, skilfully manipulating his lasagne. 'I misjudged that salty, bawdy humour. I thought it went all the way through like Brighton rock.'

'Spicer's RN all the way through. I did National Service in the Navy. I recognise the species.'

Vaughan sighed. 'It's not a type I've come across. We don't get many Senior Service types on the goggle-box. I shan't make the same mistake again. I also misjudged Logan. I thought he'd be agin me, whatever the reason. In a way, Logan limping along with Mason would have made things easier.'

'How did you enjoy having him as ally?'

'It had its ironic as well as nauseating moments. Steve's all right as philistines go. We may get along better after this.'

'I doubt it.'

'You're too depressing.'

'I've got my character-reading aids, too.'

He smiled. 'They're overweighted on the negative side.'

'Will you try upsetting Mason's apple-cart again?' I asked.

'But of course,' Vaughan said, wiping tomato sauce from his mouth with gusto. 'I want his job. Badly,' he added simply.

–26–

Late that afternoon Mason rang through and asked whether I'd go across to his room.

As I went in he got up from his desk crossed to the door into his secretary's room, put his head round the door and said, 'Meg, I want no interruption of any kind. Not even if the monarch is struck by lightning or thrown from her horse, God preserve her regal self.'

He came back to his desk, sat down, got up.

'It's not really a time for desks,' he said, as if to himself, and crossed to the leather chesterfield at the far end of the long room. 'Take a pew, Paul.'

His manner was so nervous yet so portentous that even whilst taking an armchair, I wondered whether this was to be my pay-off or Mason's confession of his.

Instead he said: 'Paul, I'm in the biggest fix of my life and you're the only person, as far as I can see, who can even begin to help me out of it.'

'Big words.'

'I mean 'em. I lunched with the Foreign Secretary today. . . .'

'You're certainly moving in stratospheric circles these days. But isn't even he a bit of a come-down after the PM?'

'That was a softening-up job. This was the real broadside. Apparently it *was* Roth who blew the gaff. I gather he's provided a pretty thorough rundown on the Toynbee text. He must have made some copious notes or have total recall in the great Macaulay manner.'

'Or taken a copy,' I amended.

'He does have a prodigious memory,' Mason added as if his own memory had just been rejogged. 'I should have borne that in mind.'

He still couldn't take my canard that Roth had xeroxed the lot.

'We shouldn't have let him see it,' I said.

'I had to. It was the only course open to me.' Anyway, that's water under the bridge. The main thing now is that the Foreign Secretary's a very bothered man indeed. Went over all that the PM said last week plus some more. Spades were spades, I can tell you.'

'And he's more or less begged you to drop it?'

'I'm afraid so. As simple as that.'

'Another newspaper will get it,' I said, probing. I wanted to know how far Mason had capitulated to the ministerial plea. Not that he would have proved very obdurate material.

'I'm coming to that,' he said. 'Obviously if one of the pops had got hold of it and set it up as a great sex-in-high-places sensation thing–it would be upsetting, but nowhere near as disturbing in its ramifications as if a serious newspaper were to do it. We've been through all that.'

He paused. I waited. 'But the Foreign Secretary doesn't want to take that chance. Briefly, he wants us to use what persuasive powers we can use to stop Miss Toynbee publishing her story anywhere, at any time.'

'That's a pretty tall order, even an insulting one.'

'I know, I know,' Mason limply agreed.

'We could only effectively do that by not letting her have the typescript back.'

'By buying and not publishing, you mean?'

'It's been known.'

'We've never actually discussed a figure, have we?'

'Not so far. She rather left that side of things to me. She hasn't got an agent. How much would we have paid her?'

'Not less than five thousand, I imagine. Probably six or seven. She'd have got three or four times that anywhere else.'

'That's true,' I said. 'But even after we'd paid her, I believe she's legally entitled to call on us to publish within a certain specified time or return her manuscript, isn't she?'

'And we'd be delaying her book chances which would be another twenty or thirty grand,' Mason said mournfully.

'At least, with world rights,' I said.

'That's true. But the longer we delayed publishing, the more her story would become legitimate history, less newspaper headline material.'

I smiled inwardly at the spectacle of Mason so swiftly becoming so self-persuasive.

'I doubt whether she'd let us keep it for ten or twenty years before wanting it back.'

Mason grinned gamely at the would-be joke. I went on: 'We could, of course, pay her, destroy all the original material, blame it all on some poor innocent librarian or archivist and everybody would be happy–except Miss Toynbee.'

'Now take it easy, Paul,' Mason said hastily. 'Don't joke about this. Especially sick jokes like that. It means a hell of a lot to all of us.'

Especially to you, I thought.

'Particularly to me,' he added as if thought-reading. 'I'm in a tricky situation with Vaughan breathing down my neck all the time. I never know what kind of hot-line he's got to his Lordship.'

I was amused to get, in these curious circumstances, Mason's first admission that Vaughan might be on intimate terms with the owners. I said: 'I'm not joking. At least I don't think so. If you paid Ann Toynbee handsomely, then lost the manuscript, you'd probably be squaring your conscience, doing your duty by the Foreign Office, the Democratic Party of the United States, Uncle Tom Cobley and all.'

'When you're in one of these extravaganza moods of yours, I can never work out whether you're being dead serious or trying to be funny, Paul. But it's no laughing matter for me. If I could shoot this whole thing down I'd be the white-haired boy of the FO, that's certain. But I might also have the owners paying me off pronto for turning down the biggest circulation-builder of all time–especially if a rival were to get hold of it. Vaughan would let everybody know it was available for offer quickly enough.'

Now we're at the crux of the matter, I thought.

'Things being what they are and always were in Fleet Street,'

I said. 'But once again I have to point out that destroying Ann Toynbee's original version–plus all the copies of my edited version –would get rid of all your problems at one–and I use the phrase carefully–fell swoop.'

Mason was in no mood for banter. He frowned, 'Are you being serious Paul?'

'Absolutely.'

'Advising me to do that?' he said, part in query, part in sheer astonishment. 'After all your advocacy on behalf of Ann Toynbee and her story?'

'I'm not advising. You presented me with *your* problem. I'm in a subjunctival mood, let's say.'

I enjoyed emphasizing the personal aspect, and added: 'My problem is different. Mine would be how to deal with Miss Toynbee.'

'You're not being very helpful, Paul.'

'I think I'm being extremely helpful.'

'You merely substitute one complication for another. Presumably indulging your usual twisted sense of humour.'

He smiled a twisted kind of smile. 'I can't make you out. Paul. A week ago you were Ann Toynbee's passionate admirer and advocate. Today you're suggesting a course of action I couldn't even begin to condone.'

'You're wrong on every count. I'm more than ever her passionate admirer. I still think her journal would prove the most compulsive reading any newspaper's put before the public in years. And I'm not suggesting anything. I'm merely outlining a proposal that would deal with *your* problem. So far I've no problem other than to try to get you to go ahead and publish a story I've put a lot of work into and now begin to see it's caput.'

'I know, I know,' he said, so wearily that I almost felt sorry for him.

'Why not sleep on it?' I said.

The recommendation that he should follow his own unwavering formula was unappreciated for once.

'What the hell is there to sleep on?' he snapped. 'Nettles piled on nettles.'

'Only made by your own irresolution,' I heard myself saying to my own surprise.

I was even more surprised to hear his agreement. 'It must seem like that, but, unfortunately, I'm caught in too many cross-currents and I want to make a decision that copes with all of 'em, and I'm beginning to realise it needs a man with a far more ruthless or far more devious turn of mind than I have.'

'You underrate yourself,' I said soothingly.

'In that respect, no,' he said firmly. 'I like simpler, clearer-cut problems.'

'Like the difference between good and bad?'

He laughed. 'I see I'm unlikely to get any more sense out of you today. What you've outlined–as you term it–would make sense if I were the ruthless man of action I see myself in my more Walter Mitty moments. I wish I had the nerve, that's all.' He sat staring out of the window then said suddenly, 'Would you do it–in my position?' he asked suddenly.

'The hypothetical solution I outlined just now, you mean?' I asked, enjoying the moment.

'Yes, yes. You know damn well I mean that.'

'If I had as much at stake as you seem to think you have, I might –probably– would.'

'Too many provisos, Paul.'

'Provisos are inevitable when dealing with other people's problems. One's only got one's own genes to work with.'

He laughed. 'I deserve that. I'll also remember it when anybody next asks me for advice. Thanks a lot, Paul. In your own sardonic fashion you've been a help. I can't think I'll match your melodramatic suggestions for action, but it's a thought.'

So I left him with the thought.

–27–

Yet I had no intention that he might, on the spur of a fanciful moment, take up my suggestion and destroy the original Toynbee material. I had my edited copy, but that was the palest shadow of the original.

'I think I'll have a final look at the Toynbee stuff this evening,' I told Pat Gow. 'Tell the library I'm coming down to collect in ten minutes. I've got the car here. I'll take it away.'

I dictated a request for withdrawal from the safe and took it down on my way out. I felt better with the box-files in my possession. I didn't want Mason taking my light-hearted advice too literally.

At Swan Court I cleared the deep bottom drawer of my own desk and there deposited the files. Scarcely equal to the security offered by the office library safe, but, perhaps, I reflected, rather more secure now that Mason had his problem to work out with my fanciful yet logical suggestion buzzing around in his head.

I thought so even more emphatically the following morning when Mason, coming into my room, said: 'I gather you took the Toynbee papers away last night, Paul.'

Pat Gow diplomatically–almost invisibly–left the room. She had an unerring instinct for such moments.

'After our talk I thought I'd have yet another look at the material to see how much of it was real dynamite.'

'I had much the same idea, but found the bird had flown.'

'You weren't thinking of putting a match to the lot?'

He laughed. 'I lack the necessary fire-bug instinct–or resolve.'

I wasn't convinced. I thought I'd go on prodding and returned to my theme; 'Supposing somebody else did the dirty work.'

'What? Destroyed it? Never.'

'Well, at least caused the whole thing to be called off?'

'As far as we're concerned, you mean?'

'As far as *you're* concerned,' I again amended mercilessly. He ignored that, saying instead: 'It's not possible.'

'It might be worth a shot.'

Mason's eyes narrowed. 'How?'

'I don't know, but it might be. It could be an entertaining exercise for somebody. Somebody more devious than you. Vaughan, for instance.'

'God forbid. Let's go across to my room,' he said, quietly but decisively.

Once there, he closed the door, once again told Meg no interruptions, and then made the most direct statement he'd ever made to me in five years: 'If this can be done, Paul, it'll have to be done as a one-man show. I can't come into it. I don't know what influence–if any–you have with Ann Toynbee, but if you can somehow persuade her, bribe her, browbeat her into a lifetime's all-round silence, it'll mean a lot to me.'

'As a journalist, a man, a liberal or what?' I asked, genuinely interested.

'As David Mason, whatever he may be.'

'Give me a cheque and I'll have a go.'

'But it's got to be a complete and final job, Paul. I can't afford any bosh shot with the whole story going elsewhere. My dilemma is quite simple. I don't want to publish. If I'm honest, I suppose I never did. But neither do I want anyone else to publish. I wish I'd never touched the damn thing. I know I may seem an old fuddy-duddy to people like yourself and Vaughan, but there it is. I got persuaded into it against a lifetime's instinct, taste, judgment, call it what you like. Above all, I still don't think it was ever the right kind of material for us. I should have said so at the beginning, I know, but I didn't. Now I'm paying for my weakness.'

'Not necessarily weakness.'

'Yes, it was,' he insisted.

I let him have his weakness without further protest.

He went on: 'I was over-persuaded by the arguments put forward by Vaughan and yourself: that because this was an intellectual's account of an affair with a politician of high ideals it made the story a publishing proposition for a newspaper of our standing. In the event the background we would have provided would merely have heightened the story's sensationalism. That kind of thing always does. The pleasures of paradox, I daresay.'

'But we've been through all this before, a score of times,' I said as patiently as I could. But he had to flay himself with a few more strokes.

'I know. I know. But if another Sunday were to get hold of it and put on a hundred thousand–or double that, it's possible–I'd look a proper Charlie at the inevitable post-mortem. You know the kind of whisper. Mason's really lost his touch. Make way for Vaughan, the wonder boy.'

Now the truth was really out. 'So you want the story sunk without trace and without the remotest chance of its surfacing elsewhere?'

'That's about the measure of it. That, impossible as it may sound to you, is what I'd like. After all, it's your own solution. I sometimes wake these nights and curse the day you ever brought the bloody journal into the office.'

'And you think I ought to do the sinking?'

'I didn't say that.'

He stood up suddenly and began to pace the long room. 'I didn't say that,' he repeated.

'Who else is there? What else is there?'

'Nobody and nothing,' he said flatly.

'But it's what you'd like to happen?'

'Of course I would. Wouldn't any editor in my position? I wouldn't be human if I wasn't plagued by the nightmare that if another paper gets hold of it, everyone in Fleet Street would think I'd been plain crazy to have let the damn thing go. I'd be finished.'

'Are you sure you're not being over-impressed by the Foreign Office bogey men?'

'I may be, but basically I'm on their side. At rock-bottom, my standards are pretty conventional–and unfashionable nowadays, I suppose. Dealing fairly with the Royals; putting each side of a case; decent oblivion for the dead. That kind of thing. I share the Foreign Secretary's viewpoint one hundred per cent.'

'The great face-saving Establishment formulas.'

He stopped, laughed briefly and said: 'And why not? In any case, you don't mean that.'

'But I do. We're the North and South Poles, David.'

'Frankly I don't believe it.'

He didn't want to believe it.

'Yet I'd publish. Where does that put us?'

'You'd publish because you loathe politicians and I won't because I believe, fallible as they are, that they're the best substitute we have for–and protection against–anarchy or dictatorship.'

'If the story never sees the light of day anywhere here, in Russia or the States, you'd be the FO's golden boy,' I said, musing aloud. 'And the State Department's, of course.'

'They'd all probably think I was this week's miracle man,' he said candidly. 'Quite unjustifiably, of course.'

So I asked the question I'd been waiting to ask, the question which, for me, was the heart of the matter: 'So you'd be prepared to shell out the money if you knew that we'd never publish the story and that nobody else would? Would you, in fact, pay eight or ten thousand to suppress it utterly and completely? It's as simple as that–cold cash.'

In common with most other liberal-minded men, Mason never normally liked unambiguous questions. He liked things wrapped up in a certain amount of cotton wool. He liked at least two sides to an answer to any question. But that morning wasn't a normal occassion. After scarcely a moment's pause, he said, 'Yes, I would, but I've also been given to understand–off the record, of course–that the FO's contingency funds might help out. As you can gather, these were very frank exchanges.'

'As you can also gather, too, if I can get Ann Toynbee to lay off, it's equivalent to asking her to forego a minimum of a hundred grand by the time she's sold book rights, world syndication rights and the rest.'

'D'you think I haven't faced that side of the affair a hundred times in the past two or three days? Nobody knows better than I do what she'd be asked to give up.'

I almost laughed aloud at the preposterous absurdity of the areas in which I now found myself operating, and, to my own great surprise, my rising enjoyment of the situation. As if watching and listening to a smooth character in a movie, I heard myself say, 'So I can go to ten thousand?'

Mason hesitated as any man would probably have hesitated in such circumstances. But there was too much at stake for dilly-dallying. He said: 'On condition she turns in the whole project. Forever and a day. After all, those are the only terms which make sense to the nation, the paper and to me, finally. I don't see how or why she should or would, but there it is.'

'Sense for everyone except Ann Toynbee, in fact.'

He nodded. 'She's young enough to get over it–if it comes off. And you're forgetting your own part. Trying to do this–even if you do try–can't be a very pleasant exercise for you.'

'I'm in the kind of go-between situation the uninvolved are always apt to find themselves involved in.'

'Then why do it?' he asked.

I could see he wasn't keen on the question lest it provoked self-questioning on my part. But he had to voice the query. To have glossed over this side of things, to have evaded asking the sixty-four dollar question, wouldn't have been fair or honest by his standards. So I gave him the answer he wanted above all others.

'If pressed, I'd probably say I was doing this out of a bogus sense of loyalty to you rather than to a dead man's memory or for the nation or anyone or anything along those lines.'

'You're very kind, Paul.'

'Wait until it's in the bag.'

'Even if it doesn't come off, I shall still think of your effort as being something well beyond anything you need have done or even attempted.'

'Hrumpf,' I said.

He smiled wanly. 'It's true,' he said. He didn't seem very optimistic, even when I said: 'Let me have that cheque for the first five thousand, then. I'll see what I can do.'

'Why not try the whole amount? Mightn't that be more persuasive?'

'Probably.'

'Will this mean your going to the States.'

'It might.'

'Do whatever you think best.'

'What will you do about Vaughan if the story gets killed off?' I asked.

'I'm stuck with Vaughan,' he said. 'You were right at that lunch six months ago – before you came back. I damned you for your hunch then.'

'Why not "insight" rather than "hunch"?'

'Insight's too flattering a word for a congenital talent,' he said, smiling. 'Your estimates of humanity have always been dyspeptic. You must have been a horribly worldly-wise schoolboy.'

I let that pass. 'You've been very fair with him.'

'In a way I had to be. I knew the set-up. And he's played very fair with me. At least, until these past two weeks. It's also true that he's been a tonic for me and the paper. Basically, I like him, although I know well enough he's after my job and wants it within two years.'

'Or less.'

'Probably. I never did get to know the exact time-table he had in mind,' Mason said with a rare touch of grim humour.

'D'you think he'll get it?'

'Not if I can help it.'

'If he lets his lordship know this thing got away your stock might take a dip.'

'I doubt it. Certainly not after his lordship had heard my side of the tale and possibly seen the Foreign Secretary. I've got that up my sleeve if things get really tough. But I'll have to meet that little problem if I come to it. When will you try your luck, Paul?'

'After I get the cheque.'

'I'll get it to you this afternoon.'

'I hope you'll get the Foreign Secretary's memoirs as part of the pay-off.'

'I daresay they'd be more our line,' he said, almost apologetically.

– 29 –

I was dining with Lord Scranton that evening at his flat.

There were just the two of us. Over our brandies I outlined the Toynbee story to him: Mason's dilemma and my own situation possessed of knowledge of Ann's wedding and her appointment of myself as decision-maker.

What would he do in my circumstances? I asked at the end. He could say exactly what he liked, no holds barred, for I'd already made my decision.

'Rather than engage in high-flown flights of fancy about what I would do in an utterly different profession and in circumstances in which I have never, fortunately, found myself, I'd rather hazard a guess–certainly nothing so pretentious as a surmise–concerning the course you will adopt, Paul. I will then give my reasons for my guesses,' he said as if summing-up in a murder trial.

'Go ahead,' I said, amused.

'I think you will suppress the story completely because you are rather less of a rebel in these matters than you may like to think you are.'

I laughed aloud. 'You're probably right. You've seen through the sham.'

He smiled and went on: 'I also think you will see that Mrs O'Connor gets the money because you are–or perhaps were–more intrigued or even moved by the young woman than you would care to admit. And, oddly enough, I think you have a somewhat old-fashioned protective instinct towards women.'

'I doubt whether my ex-wife would agree with you, but press on.'

'It is precisely your somewhat unconventional attitude towards your ex-wife that confirms my belief.'

'An old-fashioned sense of responsibility. What about Mason?'

'I think you would like to help Mason because you invariably seem sympathetic towards him whenever you speak of him. And now that you know of Mason's fears *vis-à-vis* Vaughan you will seek to help him that much more.'

'A succinct summing-up of the situation with a disturbing awareness of the defendant's sentimental weaknesses,' I said.

He smiled. 'They are the corollary of your affectation of cynicism.'

'But what shall I do with the journals themselves?'

'You could leave them to the British Museum with the wish that they should be opened fifty years after your death, or Mrs O'Connor's, or you could leave them to her children if any, or to your own daughter. Let me see, your present expectation of life would be about thirty-five years or so. Perhaps nearer forty as you seem to have few self-destructive vices. Even the ebullient Mrs O'Connor would scarcely be likely to live to one hundred or so.'

I laughed. 'You've got it pat.'

'I even have an even more pat and parochial suggestion to make,' he said, smiling.

'Go ahead,' I said. I was quite enjoying the judge's views.

'It is merely that the papers should be left to the librarian of our mutual college with the proviso that profits should be devoted to adding works to the college library divided equally between the subjects of jurisprudence and journalism.'

'The literature of journalism is very limited,' I pointed out. Journalists are notoriously incapable of putting words between hard covers. You'd better make it jurisprudence and literature. That would be fairer to any librarian.'

'Agreed,' he said.

'And about the money side? D'you see many moral scruples I've side-stepped in that part of the exercise?'

'My experience in the law has persuaded me that money is apt to make its own morals and scruples. The movement of a few thousand pounds from a millionaire's pocket to a young lady's reticule seems scarcely a moral issue. No undue force or threat has been used, I take it.' He smiled.

'It was almost forced on me,' I said unctuously.

'Quite,' he said in sympathy.

We had another brandy on the sheer logic and felicity of our agreement.

I walked home along the King's Road in a haze of goodwill towards most men and two or three women.

–30–

With some relish I wrote my letter to Ann:

Dearest Ann: First, of course, more elaborate congratulations on your marriage than international cablese allows. I hope you'll be very very happy. I know Dr O'Connor is an extremely lucky man and I hope you'll be a lucky woman.

Second, about your journals and the problem you so untimely threw at me. Briefly, I have now made arrangements whereby you get ten thousand pounds (cheque enclosed) in payment for all rights in your journals relating to your association with Greg van Beinum Stirling. I'm assuming you still have an account in this country, but if you haven't you can return the cheque to me and I'll arrange for a dollar draft to be sent to you. I'm sure the O'Connors will find the shekels useful in their new life together. But pray don't spend quite all *of it on cotton wool and ointment for poor Colombians. Do buy something from Jaeger and/or Fenwick's.*

There is one other point. Don't expect publication very soon – if ever. The difficulties surrounding the projected publication are considerable, but as you left everything to me, you must take my decision.

Meantime, I think of you often and frequently try to imagine what your new life is like. If you feel like telling me when acknowledging this note I'd be delighted.

There's one final point about your journals. If we don't publish and you let them rest, I'm arranging for them to be left in the care of an Oxford college so that sometime, half-way through the next century, they'll be opened and read. Let's hope your journals will bring you a similar fame to that which attended the journals of another notable diarist via another college. Meantime, they're in my care.

If you agree with what I've done on your behalf, I want you, sometime next week, to do the following—and trust me implicitly in the doing: Send this cable to the paper from New York.

MORTIMER PERSONAL REASONS COMPEL CANCELLATION PROJECTED PUBLICATION ANY PART MY JOURNALS YOU HOLD STOP MORTIMER TO RETAIN PERSONALLY MEANTIME STOP WILL ADVISE PLANS LATER BUT NO REPEAT NO PUBLICATION MY LIFETIME ANN TOYNBEE

Signing ANN TOYNBEE *is absolutely and vitally important.*

One day when you come to England again I'll tell you the full story and guarantee you half an hour's entertainment in the process. All love, Paul.

—31—

I posted the letter to Ann that Sunday afternoon and decided that this was the end of the affair. I would give her a week to reply, accepting or rejecting my suggestion, and the cheque.

But why had I done it, anyway? I asked myself a dozen times a day. Why the money? Why the involvement? Why anything? Why shouldn't I have let the journals die for a hundred years and then surface as a footnote to a history of our present contentious times.

Because, I told myself, I had enjoyed the out-of-character exercise. Because I'd found the involvement exhilarating rather than wearying. Because I'd enjoyed playing around, peripherally, perhaps and alas, with somebody else's cheque book. Because I'd enjoyed playing patron-by-proxy. Perhaps because I'd even enjoyed sailing near the wind, for once. And finally, perhaps, because I had become very fond indeed of Ann Toynbee.

Meanwhile I had to leave for Oxfordshire, that morning. I'd decided to do a piece on the out-of-season state of the Stately Homes. After the last of the tourists had gone, how did these great piles and their publicity-conscious owners subsist through the long autumn-winter lay-off? Did they enjoy their unpeopled acres and deserted State Rooms? I enjoyed my four-day excursion.

–32–

I got back on Thursday.

The following morning I had two cables from Ann. The first –from Caracas–telephoned through to Swan Court. The second –from New York–awaited me at the office.

The first read:

DEAREST BENEFICENT PAUL LOLLY GALORE AND REPUTATION VIRGO INTACTA STOP WHAT MORE COULD NEWWED WOULD-BE LITTERATEUR WANT STOP OTHER CABLE SENT OTHER PLACE YOUR LOVING TRUSTING ANN

That seemed promising. Mason seemed almost in the clear.

–33–

I took the other cable, phrased exactly as I'd suggested, through to Mason.

He read the helpful, hopeful words, took a deep deep breath of utmost relief, sat back in his chair and said, 'Thanks, Paul. I never thought I'd be grateful for being denied one of the best stories I've ever had a chance to publish, but that's the way it is. I won't ask how you did it. . . .'

'You'd better not.'

'One hopes your ways with women stop this side of blackmail, but they certainly seem to work. A very remarkable and persuasive performance. When Ann Toynbee was here–in this room–she seemed the very personification of resolution.'

'Don't ever ask me to do the same thing again. My luck mightn't hold.'

He looked years younger. 'We'd better tell the others,' he said, almost gleefully. 'I think it's a meeting I'm going to enjoy. Meg!' he called.

–34–

Mason explained the new situation briefly before passing the cable round, first to Markham.

'I'm very pleased and relieved,' Markham said. 'Do you know exactly what's happened? Probably had a better offer.'

'We shall look pretty foolish if she has and we've been sitting on it all these weeks–or is it months?' Vaughan said with some bitterness. 'If we'd started publication two weeks ago–as I suggested–we'd have beaten her to it. Damn her.'

'I'm jolly glad,' Spicer said. 'I don't care a damn what her personal reasons are. Any idea, Paul?'

I shook my head.

'But supposing somebody else gets it,' Logan persisted.

'You don't seem to have read the cable, Steve.' Mason said with heavy patience. 'She says clearly enough that there's to be no publication in her lifetime. And Paul has all the original material –the journal itself, all the cuttings, the whole shooting-match. He's also got his own edited copy.'

'Perhaps I ought to set up in business and flog 'em,' I said. 'Beneficent piracy should begin at home.'

'You'd get a lot more lolly than this place will ever pay you,' Logan said, and then, in the most bare-faced *volte face* I've ever listened to, added the immortal words: 'I'm not altogether desolate we're not publishing Miss Toynbee. I don't mind admitting that, now the battle's over. It might well have left a nasty taste in the mouth.'

I smiled at Vaughan in this swift and discreet desertion by his short-lived ally. Vaughan grinned back, accepting the message.

With his usual talent for never leaving well alone, Logan added: 'I imagine we might have had a lot of trouble with the Press Council.'

'Which we'd have lived down as usual,' Vaughan snapped.

I wondered what odds he would now offer on the chances of future co-existence between Vaughan and Logan.

'Where does this leave Roth?' Markham asked. 'Do we ask him to come back.'

'Oh, no!' Vaughan groaned. 'Having got rid of the old monster by his own hand can't we let him fade out? Give Daniels a chance. Everybody seems to think well of him.'

Markham was at his most pompous. 'Daniels is a good man. But his time will come. As of this moment Roth is the better man, better for us. More authoritative, more reliable, more contacts.

'And less readable,' Vaughan added, 'By the way, the phrase "as of this moment" presumably means "now"?'

Markham ignored the gibe, and went on: 'He may not be the ball of fire that other Washington correspondents set up to be, but neither is he the rumour-monger others sometimes turn out to be.' He turned pointedly to Mason: 'With your permission, David, I'd like to put a call through to him this morning and try to get him to reconsider his resignation.'

'Try! You won't have to try!' Vaughan scoffed. 'Two hours from now you'll have Roth back on the payroll. No struggle. Merely an expression of triumphant satisfaction at a good job well done. How he kept the reputation of his precious Greg Stirling untarnished.'

'Actually, he's taken a break in the Adirondacks,' Markham said. 'He also wrote to me to say he wouldn't be attempting to get another job for a month. So I think you've probably won your self-wager.'

'Hands down,' Vaughan agreed.

In a way I felt sorry for Vaughan. In ten minutes he'd found himself utterly alone. However sympathetic I might have felt towards his efforts to liven things up, to get the Toynbee journals published, I was, as recipient of the cable, inevitably ranged with the others.

The meeting concluded in what I can only describe as a modest state of euphoria. Mason and the others were as pleased as if they had just signed up one of the great stories of the decade instead of having shot one down. Only Vaughan and myself were missing from the circle of complacency.

Mason gave some pseudo-directives all round. Would I write to Ann Toynbee, offering our regrets, etc. etc.? Would I write to Mrs Stirling, explaining the situation? Would Markham contact Roth and return him to the fold? (Laughter). Would Logan redouble his efforts to replace the Toynbee story with something equally as good but a lot less controversial? (More laughter).

Poor Tom really is acold today, I thought, as we left the room.

–35–

Half an hour later Vaughan came into my room.

'The dug-ins won out, then,' he said taking an armchair as Pat left the room.

'They had no option. After all, it's Ann Toynbee's book and her decision. She's got the last word, surely.'

'It wan't that: it was the air of uncompounded masculine relief and unconfounded boyish glee in Mason's room that got me down.'

'A nice phrase.'

'I've used it before somewhere,' he said, smiling. 'Even as it bounced off the tongue, I had a certain feeling of staleness. This phrase has been here before, I thought. You probably know the sensation.'

I laughed. 'But of course. Yet what else could your colleagues have done?'

'Colleagues! Bah!' he barked, and went on: 'They would never have done it, anyway. This cable's a lifeline they'd never hoped for, but Mason would still have got out of it somehow at the last minute.'

'Even without Miss Toynbee's help?' I queried.

'But why did she do it? That's what I'd like to know. Just when she had the whole thing set up and going for her. Why? Why? Why?'

'Ladies are very unpredictable as the poet says somewhere.'

'Bah!' Vaughan snorted. He turned his attention to Roth. 'I still contend Mason gave Roth the go-ahead to spill the beans and then got him out of the country pronto. Everything has stemmed from that.'

'Wouldn't such a move make Mason a somewhat smarter operator than you've ever given him credit for?'

'God knows. I'll never know.'

'And wouldn't that have left the gates wide open for some other outfit to wander in and pick up the property?'

'Don't overdo the flagellation,' Vaughan said. 'I'm no masochist. In this case, Mason, the winner, really does take all. This place beats me.'

'Temporarily or permanently?'

'Ah, my friend, that is the question. I'll have to decide pretty soon. It would take a dozen bulldozers to move the monumental load of entrenched prejudice, prissiness, and pomposity of this place. I don't think I've got the time or strength for the job. I've been here six months and I haven't shifted it or them an inch.'

'You've made some very significant innovations.'

'Marginal, minimal, miniscule.' He spat out the words as if obscenities. 'Nothing fundamental. Nothing that would leave a scratch on the bloated surface of this place.'

'How close are you to his lordship?'

He looked at me for a long moment. 'Why should I be close at all? And even if I were, what difference would it make?'

'Owners fire editors.'

'He's a friend of my old man's,' Vaughan said. 'That's all. He thought this paper needed some fresh blood. He also thinks Mason has something. How he reconciles the two notions beats me. But he does. He asked me to join the paper to back up Mason, but how can I back up a man when half the time I want to see him off the premises? Scarcely an ideal working arrangement. For a couple of months I thought it might work. Now I know it won't. I can't stand his dithering ancient ways, his absolute genius for making procrastination look like prognostication.'

I laughed to hear my own views so well-expressed. 'Perhaps it's a kind of genius,' I said. 'A talent for instant decision-making hasn't always demonstrated proof of essential wisdom or even basic common sense.'

'You see!' he cried. 'You're infected!'

I laughed. I wasn't to be riled by Vaughan. I knew too much about him. I said: 'Your own middle names were Patient Griselda for a couple of months.'

'My Chaucerian affinities are a little more bawdy and robust than hers.'

Again I laughed. I found Vaughan, free of his self-imposed disciplines, an engaging performer.

'So what will you do?'

'If I stay here, it's a question of Mason or myself. I want his job. I think I'd make a better job of it. And that would make for difficulties.'

'I've told you before—you'd make a different job, not necessarily better.'

'Noted,' he said, riding on. 'A reasonable corrective which shows, basically, that you're Mason's man.'

I shook my head. 'Basically, I'm Mortimer's man,' I said.

'That's true, but in a very curious way,' he said. 'Which I'll analyse later. OK. So there it is. I'm not the deputy type. It's as simple as that.'

'You've done it quite well during recent months.'

'What! Counting up to a hundred every time Mason makes one of his guru pronouncements. Telling myself that sooner rather than later even the top brass upstairs would see what a clown the man is.'

'An order of clairvoyance given to few press lords. Mason's been around a long time. He's had much acclaim. And the daily did quite well under his editorship.'

'You sound like his PRO.'

I was finding Vaughan too entertaining to take offence. He could say what he liked.

'He gives me a free hand. Why should I want to chop him down?'

'But there's no drive, no impetus, no freshness in the paper.'

'Do readers rate drive above truth, impetus above integrity, freshness above reliability?'

'One lot needn't drive out the other.'

'So-called dynamic innovations can cause trouble in newspapers as well as car factories.'

'God, you're as bad as the rest! No, you're not. You're different. You're the only uncommitted man in this outfit. You've no central obsession to which everything else is geared. Mason's passion for the *status quo*. Logan's pathetic social climbing. Markham's foreign affairs punditry. My inordinate ambition.'

'I told you before: I'm very deeply committed to Mortimer.'

'In a very cool way indeed,' he said, getting up and crossing to the door. 'You don't even get caught up in undue enthusiasm for him or his works.'

'I was quite enthusiastic about the Toynbee story. Remember?'

'That's true. But that was a long time ago as these things go.'

I laughed.

'Be seeing you,' he said, going out.

I hoped he'd stay. Despite his wholesale denunciations I suspected we talked the same kind of language. Ultimately.

–36–

Dining with Helen at Milner Street that evening, I said: 'Those Toynbee journals you read – the ones I worked on in Ireland – won't be published after all.'

'Why not?'

'She got married.'

'And the new husband objected.'

'Actually, no. He left the decision to her and she left it to me.'

'Not very courageous of such a free-thinking operator, was it? Either the marriage or the decision-dodging. Why did she marry, anyway?'

'An old flame she couldn't get out of her system.'

'Wish I had one or two. Why did you decide not to publish 'em, anyway?'

'Mason didn't want to.'

'Did she get paid?'

'Quite handsomely.'

'What will happen to 'em now?'

'They'll probably be left to some Oxford college.'

'Yours, presumably.'

'Probably.'

'No undergraduate will ever get down to his set books once word gets around little hot pants is there on the shelves.'

I laughed. 'They won't be opened for ages ahead. Long after hot pants is dead, in fact.'

'Seems a pity. They were quite fun. Have the rest of the spag.'

I willingly accepted. Helen's touch with pasta was spectacular.

'I also think it's a pity the world won't hear about Stirling as a performer,' she said reflectively. 'Politicians are such damn dull dogs. Over here, at least. He did sound rather fun as well as a bit of a paranoid jerk.'

'Mason's rather relieved, I need hardly tell you.'

'Well, he's another damn dull dog.'

Conversation moved on to recollections of Ireland. Strange how so momentous a subject amongst men in Fetter Lane got put into perspective by a woman in Chelsea.

—37—

Vicky had her viewpoint too.

'Supposing you'd written your unblushing life-story, no holds barred, and somebody wanted to publish it. . . .'

'Give me another five years.'

'Too long.'

'Not really. I'm hoping you'd be in the story by then in a far bigger and more intimate way than you've been up to now,' she said meaningfully. I let it pass.

'Supposing on the eve of publication somebody got cold feet. . . .'

'You, for instance?'

'Not me. Somebody.'

'You're the only one likely to, although my ex might of course, especially if I told the truth about his selfish bloody ways.'

'Well, whoever it was, if he got cold feet and wanted to buy off the book, what would you say if he offered you cash to call the whole thing off?'

'How much?'

'Scads. But quite apart from the lolly, would you be upset not to see your handiwork published?'

'Depends how good I thought it was.'

'Supposing it was absolutely terrific.'

'I'd have to put in last year's flip with that Italian fashion photographer chap in Sardinia to guarantee that.'

'O K. Including that.'

'I'd take the lolly and try again, say, three years later. After all, I'd have a lot more to tell, wouldn't I?'

I said I didn't know, but hoped so.

She said I ought to know. I was certain to be a major part of the record.

I was glad to change the subject.

–38–

Penultimately, various letters:

That afternoon, I dictated this note:

Dear Mrs Stirling: The project I discussed with you in your home two months ago has, I fear, fallen through. Miss Toynbee has decided that, for personal reasons, she cannot go ahead with publication. I am sorry. I think the journals would have proved an unusually interesting contribution to the history of our times and to the reputation of a notable public figure.

Once again I would like to thank you for your hospitality and generosity in all things during my visit.

I trust, too, that your personal life is now set upon a more felicitous direction and that you are remaking your life along the lines you hoped for. Paul Mortimer.

From Swan Court I wrote:

Dearest Ann: Thank you for the cable: it was a necessary move in a localized but entertaining game. Your journals are in safe keeping and you can have them any time you like, although I prefer my notion of a collegiate resting-place for them. I have given my word, on your behalf, that they won't be published in any form–book, newspaper, magazine and so on–for many many years. After your letter I felt free to do that.

The whole exercise has been of enormous interest and one day I'll tell you all about it. Meantime, I await that long letter from Caracas. Paul.

A letter from Roth in Washington.

Dear Paul: Gerry Markham called me this morning to say the Toynbee business is off. I was very pleased and relieved to get the news.

I can't tell what part my own efforts, if any, played in this happy result. I suppose I shall never know, but I'm prepared to believe, for once at least, that the means justified the end.

Gerry tells me—as if I didn't know—that you had put a hell of a lot of work into the editing. It must be galling to have all the work you put into the job going unseen and all that. Part of the journalistic lot, I'm afraid. Perhaps one day. . . . But, then, I always thought her record was for history rather than journalism. If at all.

I hope to be in London next year and will hope to see you. Bernie.

—39—

Finally, three footnotes to my tale, not all of equal relevance, perhaps; indeed of no relevance at all perhaps. But who knows?

(*a*)

In the New Year's honours, Mason was made Sir David: 'For services to journalism,' of course.

Honi soit qui mal y pense, I thought as I scribbled a note of congratulation.

(*b*)

In the New Year, too, Vaughan went back to television. *Honi soit*, etc., etc. I thought again.

I missed him. The paper was duller without him. A lot duller.

(*c*)

Then, a couple of months ago, in a copy of *Time* magazine, under their weekly column MILESTONES, I read:

> *Married* in Athens, South Carolina, Melanie Louisa Stirling, 38, heiress, plantation owner, socialite, widow of Greg van Beinum Stirling, one-time front-runner for Democratic Presidential nomination, assassinated almost two years ago in Los Angeles, to Louis de Marais, 44, millionaire, plantation owner and real estate developer. She for the second time, he for the first.

I showed the paragraph to Helen that evening. 'It took her a little longer,' she said, 'but she made it. No fuss and probably even a blessing from the Pope.'

'And not even a single shadowy smear on the Stirling legend—thanks to Roth,' I added.

'Remember what a great world-shaking story it was going to be?' Helen said, amused.

'It would have been—at the time,' I said.

'A suitable epitaph for most so-called newspaper scoops.'

'I daresay Noah thought the flood was a bit of a personal scoop. Jesus walking on the waters probably made the local headlines, too.'

'Both tales still make fairly good reading.'

'So would–and will–Ann Toynbee's–in due course,' I said loyally.

'Like that Antony and Cleopatra pair, you mean,' she scoffed. 'Up the media. Anyway, it's time for bed.'